WASSTR

D0276482

A WASTELAND
OF STRANGERS

DOMINICK ABEL LITERARY AGENCY, INC.
146 West 82nd Street, Suite 1B
New York, New York 10024
(212) 877-0710

A WASTELAND OF STRANGERS

BILL PRONZINI

WALKER AND COMPANY
NEW YORK

For Michael Seidman, with thanks for giving
an old horse free rein on a fresh track

And for Marcia, for being there

First published in the United States of America in 1997
by Walker Publishing Company, Inc.

Published simultaneously in Canada by Thomas Allen & Son Canada, Limited,
Markham, Ontario

Library of Congress Cataloging-in-Publication Data
Pronzini, Bill.
A wasteland of strangers / Bill Pronzini.
p.   cm.
ISBN 0-8027-3301-8
I. Title.
PS3566.R67W3   1997
813'.54—dc21   96-50927
CIP

Printed in the United States of America
2 4 6 8 10 9 7 5 3 1

Author's Note

WHILE THE TOWN of Pomo, Lake Pomo, and Pomo County are loosely based on actual Northern California locales, they are nonetheless products of the author's imagination. Similarly, while the Pomo is a very real Native American tribe, and care has been taken to accurately describe its customs, legends, and historical and modern travails, the Pomo characters portrayed in these pages are fictitious. Also fictitious are all other characters, and the author's interpretations of social, economic, political, and racial issues concerning the general geographical region depicted herein; in no way are they intended to represent real people or actual, specific issues.

THANKS TO BETTE Golden Lamb and Melissa Ward for providing valuable research information and to Peter Crowther and Edward E. Kramer for including a much different, embryonic, novelette-length version of this novel, under the title "The Intruder," in their White Wolf anthology, *Heartlands*.

Which of us is not forever a stranger and alone?
—Thomas Wolfe,
Look Homeward, Angel

Part I

Thursday

Harry Richmond

I DIDN'T LIKE him the minute I laid eyes on him.

He made me nervous as hell, and I don't mind saying so. Big, mean-looking. Cords in his neck thick as ax blades, eyes like steel balls, pockmarks under his cheekbones, and a T-shaped scar on his chin. The way he talked and acted, too. Cold. Hard. Snotty. Like you were dirt and he was a new broom.

He drove up in front of the resort office about four o'clock. Sports car, one of those old Porsches, all dusty and dented in places. California license plates. I was glad to see the car at first because hadn't anybody checked in since Sunday night. Used to be around here that in late November we'd get a fair trickle of trade, even though fishing season was over. Overnight and weekend regulars, tourists passing through, route salesmen in hardware and other goods. Not anymore. Whole county's been on a decline the past twenty years, and not just in the tourist business. Agriculture, too; you don't see near as many pear and walnut orchards as you once did. Pomo, the county seat on the northwest shore, is still pretty much the same, on account of the large number of county employees and retired geezers who live there. But up here on the north shore, and all along the east shore down to Southport, things are bad. Restaurants, antique and junk stores, other kinds of shops— gone. Long-operating resorts like Nucooee Point Lodge, once the fanciest on this part of the lake, closed down and boarded up. For Sale signs and empty cottages and commercial buildings everywhere you look. Little hamlet of Brush Creek is practically a ghost town.

Me, now, I've got simple needs, and summers I still do enough business to keep the wolf from the door. But I can't do as much as I once did—man turns fifty, his joints don't want to let him, and that includes the joint hanging between his legs—and I can't afford to hire things done except when I can get one of the less shiftless Indians to do it cheap. If business doesn't improve I'll be forced to put the Lakeside Resort up for sale, too, and move down to San Carlos and live with Ella and my delinquent grandkids and the succession of losers Ella keeps letting into her bed. And if the resort never sells, which it might not, I'll be stuck down there until the day I die.

Blame what's happened on a lot of things. But the main one is, Pomo County's backwater—too far north of San Francisco and the Bay Area where most of our regulars and nonregulars came from in the old days. Lake Pomo and Clear Lake over in Lake County were fine for the lives most people led thirty years ago, but it all changed after Interstate 80 to Tahoe was finished in '64; these days, with superhighways everywhere and jet planes that can take folks to all sorts of exotic places in a few hours, they expect more for their money than a week or two in a rustic lakefront cabin. That doesn't necessarily apply to the enclave around Mt. Kahbel on the southwestern shore; quite a few rich people's summer homes clustered in the little bays and inlets there, fancy boats and a country club and resort that features big-name entertainers in the summer. Closed-off pocket is what Kahbel Shores is. Up here and on most of the rest of the lake, there just aren't enough attractions to lure visitors and keep 'em happy. Nevada-style casinos on the Indian rancherias have helped some, but not enough: Pomo County's as far from the Bay Area as Reno and Tahoe. Besides, most of the money the day-trip and weekend gamblers bring in stays in the casinos and goes into Indian pockets. It's not right or fair that whites should suffer while those buggers get theirs, but that's the way it is, no thanks to the goddamn government. Anyhow, if something doesn't happen to turn us around, and soon, this county's liable to turn into a wasteland full of the homeless and welfare squatters (plenty of those already in Southport) and rich Indians driving fancy cars and old people sitting around waiting to croak.

Well, none of that's got to do with this stranger drove up in his Porsche. He came into the office, and as soon as I had a good look at him I wasn't glad any longer that he'd picked my place to stop at. But what can you do? I had to rent him a cabin; I can't afford to turn down anybody's business. One thing I could do, though. I told him the rate was sixty-five a night instead of forty-five. Didn't faze him. He picked up the pen and filled out the card and then laid three twenties and a five down on top.

I turned the card around without touching the money so he wouldn't get the idea I was hungry for it. He wrote as hard as he looked, but I could read his scrawl plain enough. John C. Faith, Los Angeles. No street address, and you're supposed to list one, but I wasn't about to make an issue of it. Not with him.

I said, "How many nights, Mr. Faith?"

"Maybe one, maybe more. Depends."

"On what?"

He just looked at me with his cold eyes.

My mouth tasted dry; I licked some spit through it. "Business in the area? Or here on pleasure?"

"Could be."

"Could be . . . what?"

"Business or pleasure. Or neither one."

"Guess I don't quite get that."

"All right," he said.

See what I mean? Snotty.

"Going to do some gambling?" I asked.

"Gambling?"

"Brush Creek casino's a couple of miles down the east shore. You know about the Indian casinos here?"

"No."

"Oh, sure. Four of 'em in the county. Video slots, poker, keno. Cards, too. Blackjack. Or if you like high-stakes games, they've got tournaments—Texas Hold 'Em and Omaha Hi-Lo."

"That kind of gambling is for suckers."

"Well, some folks enjoy it—"

"They can have it, then."

I should've kept my mouth shut after that, but it's just not in my nature. Twenty-plus years in the resort business makes a man talkative. "Wouldn't be a fisherman, by any chance?"

"No, I wouldn't."

"Great sport, fishing. Just as well you're not, though."

"You think so? Why?"

"Fishing season ended last week. November fifteenth."

"That's a shame."

"Sure is. Lake's still full of bass. Bigmouths."

"Just the lake?"

". . . Say again?"

"Full of bigmouths."

That made me sore, but I didn't let on. I'm no fool. I said, "I was only making conversation. Trying to be friendly."

"All right."

"If you took it the wrong way—"

"What's a good place to eat around here?"

"You mean for dinner?"

"A good place to eat."

"Well, there's the Northlake Cafe. Or you might want to try Gunderson's, if you like lake bass or seafood. Gunderson's has a real nice cocktail lounge."

"Which one do you prefer?"

"Well . . . Gunderson's, I guess. Middle of town, block up from the county courthouse."

"How do I get to the other one?"

"Northlake's on the north end, just off the highway. Can't miss it. There's a big sign—"

"My key," he said.

"Key? Oh, sure. I'll put you in number six. That's one of the lake-front cabins. That okay?"

"Fine."

I handed him the key and he went out without saying anything else, and I don't mind admitting I was relieved to be rid of him. I don't like his kind, not one little bit. I wished I'd charged him seventy-five a night instead of sixty-five. Bet he'd have paid it, too. Must've had a thousand dollars or more stuffed into that pigskin wallet of his. Roll of bills fat enough to gag a sixty-pound Doberman.

I said out loud, "What's he want here, man like that?"

John C. Faith, Los Angeles. Phony name if I ever heard one.

What in hell *could* he want in a half-dead backwater like Pomo?

Zenna Wilson

HE SCARED ME half to death. And not just because he startled me, sneaking up as quiet as an Indian or a thief. My flesh went cold when I saw him looming there. He was a sight to give any decent soul the shudders even in broad daylight.

I was in the hardware store talking to Ken Treynor. I'd just bought a package of coffee filters, about the only thing I ever buy in the hardware store, really, because Howard gave me a Braun two Christmases ago and Braun coffeemakers take a special filter and Safeway doesn't stock them even though I've asked the manager half a dozen times to put them in so I can pick up a package when I do my regular shopping. It's frustrating and annoying, is what it is, when stores refuse to do simple things to accommodate good customers. Anyhow, I was telling Ken about Stephanie and her school project, the cute little animal faces she was making out of papier-mâché and how lifelike they were. My Stephanie is very talented that way, very artistic. I was describing the giraffe with its one eye closed, as if it were winking, when all of a sudden Ken's head jerked and his eyes opened wide and he wasn't looking at me any longer but at something behind me. So I turned around and there *he* was, the sneaky stranger.

I guess I uttered a sound and recoiled a bit, because he threw me a look of pure loathing. It made my scalp crawl. When I was a little girl about Stephanie's age, my older brother, Tom, used to terrify me with stories about a bogeyman who hid in dark places waiting for unsuspecting children to come along, and then he'd jump out and grab them and carry them off to his dark lair and bite their heads off. This man looked like he was capable of doing just that, biting someone's head off. Big and fearsome, with huge hands and a mouth full of sharp teeth. Bogey was the right word for the likes of him, all right.

Ken was also staring at him. He said, "Can I . . . was there something?"

"I can wait until you're finished with the lady." Voice to match his size, deep and rumbly, like thunder before a storm. And the way he said "lady" made it sound like a dirty word.

"Already finished," Ken told him.

"Battery for an Eveready utility lantern. Six-volt."

"Aisle three, halfway back."

I watched him walk into the aisle; I couldn't seem to take my eyes off him. Treynor's Hardware is in an old building, and he walked hard enough to make the wood floor shake. Above the items stacked on the top shelves I could see the crown of his head moving—that's how tall he was. His hair was long and dirty brown, and in the lights it looked greasy, like matted animal fur.

It didn't take him long to find what he wanted. He came back to the counter and paid Ken in cash—a fifty-dollar bill. Then, "There a bank in town that stays open this late?"

"First Northern, three blocks down Main."

"Thanks." He picked up his purchase and walked out, one side of his mouth bent upward in a ghastly sort of smile that wasn't a smile at all.

I blew out my breath and said to Ken, "My God! Did you ever see such a wicked-looking man?"

"No, and I hope I never see him again."

"Amen to that. You don't suppose he'll be here long?"

"Probably just passing through."

"Lord, I hope so."

I stayed there with Ken for another five minutes or so. I wanted to be certain the bogey was gone before I went out to the car. In my mind's eye I could still see him, that scarred face and those awful eyes and enormous hands. Animal paws that could crush the life out of a person, that may well have blood on them already for all I know.

Up to the devil's work, I thought, whoever he is and wherever he goes. If he stays in Pomo long enough, something terrible will happen.

I wished Howard wasn't away traveling for his job until tomorrow night. With a man like that one in town, a woman and her little girl weren't safe alone in their own home.

Richard Novak

I MIGHT NOT'VE even noticed the old red Porsche being illegally parked on the southeast corner of Main and Fifth if it hadn't been for the fact that Storm's silver-gray BMW was curbed in the legal space just behind. The BMW, like Storm herself, would have stood out in a crowd of a thousand and, like her, it had a magnetic attraction for my eye. Still carrying the torch after all these months. Not as large and hot a torch as the one for Eva, but still a long ways from burning itself out.

Ninety-nine times out of a hundred I would've let the violation go unchallenged. For one thing, it was minor, and the way things were, the Porsche's driver wasn't really at fault. For another, the car was unfamiliar and the city council has a general go-easy policy where visitors are concerned. And for a third, this sort of routine parking matter wasn't part of the police chief's duties, particularly when he happened to be tired and on his way home for the day. But I didn't let it slide, and I'm not sure why. To get Storm off my mind, maybe. Or maybe because this hadn't been much of a day and on off days I'm more inclined to enforce the strict letter of the law.

In any case, I swung the cruiser around onto Fifth and got out. The Porsche's driver was coming up onto the sidewalk when he saw me approaching; he stopped and stood waiting. I'm not small at six feet and two hundred pounds, but I felt dwarfed in this one's massive shadow. Rough-looking, too, with a hammered-down face and hard, bunched features. But there was nothing furtive or suspicious about him, nothing to put me on my guard.

He said in a flat, neutral voice, "Something wrong, Officer?"

"You can't park there."

"No? Why is that?"

"No-parking zone. Trucks have to swing too wide to get around the corner with another vehicle at the curb."

"Curb's not marked. No sign, either."

"The curb is marked, you just have to look closely to spot it this time of day. White paint and lettering are mostly worn off—long overdue for remarking. There was a sign, too, up until a couple of weeks ago when a drunk driver knocked it down; we're still waiting for a replacement. You can see what's left of the pole there."

"Uh-huh."

"Things don't get done as fast as they should sometimes." Rule of thumb in Pomo County nowadays, it seemed, no matter what needed doing or what had been requisitioned or how much prodding and cajoling public servants like myself were forced to indulge in. "You know how it is."

"Oh yeah, I know how it is. Do I get a ticket?"

"Not if you move your car to a legal space."

One corner of his mouth lifted. If it was a smile, it had little humor and a bitter edge. He could tell from my uniform and badge what my rank was, and he thought he was being hassled. A man used to hassles, I thought. The official kind and probably the personal kind, too.

"You don't have a problem with that, do you?" I asked him.

"No problem at all."

"Good. We appreciate cooperation."

He went around the Porsche and opened the driver's door. "You have a nice evening now, Officer," he said, not quite snottily, and folded himself inside before I could answer. I stayed put until he'd pulled out onto Main, driving neither fast nor slow. He was maneuvering into a legal space halfway into the next block when I returned to the cruiser.

Ordinarily I'd have forgotten the incident then and there, as trivial and easily resolved as it'd been. But the stranger stayed on my mind all the way home. Something about him, an indefinable quality, made me uneasy. I couldn't put my finger on it and so it kept bothering me, a nagging little irritation like a splinter under a fingernail.

George Petrie

HE CAME INTO the bank fifteen minutes before closing. There aren't many individuals who can take my attention away from Storm Carey for more than a few seconds, but he was one. At first it was his size and ugliness that held my gaze; then it was his actions. Instead of going directly to one of the tellers' windows, he walked around looking at things—walls, ceiling, floor, the arrangement of desks and tellers' cages, the location of the vault. And at Fred and Arlene in the cages, and me behind my desk, and Storm seated across from me with her long beautiful legs crossed and part of one stockinged thigh showing. But no more than a brief glance at each of us; his eyes didn't even linger on Storm. First Northern is an old bank as well as a small one, built in the twenties: rococo styling, black-veined marble columns and floors, dark, polished wood. That may have been what interested him. But the one thing he seemed to focus on longest was the open vault.

My God, what if he's planning to rob us?

The thought prickled the hairs on my neck. I tried to dismiss it. There hadn't been a holdup at First Northern in the sixteen years I'd been manager; as far as I knew, the bank had been held up only once in its seventy-two years of continuous operation—in 1936, by a hay grower who had lost his farm on a foreclosure. Armed robberies of any kind seldom happen in Pomo; we're too far off a major highway to attract roaming urban criminals, and the local ones have so far confined themselves to drug-dealing, car theft, and burglary. Still, I was sure I hadn't mistaken the stranger's interest in the open vault. Plus, there was the fact that he projected an aura of restrained violence. It was in his eyes, in the set of his shoulders and the bunching of his hands, in the way he moved. A violent and dangerous man . . .

He went at last to Fred's window. I tensed when he reached for his pocket, but the only thing he took out was his wallet. He was so wide he filled the window and I couldn't tell what he was doing or saying to Fred. Nothing sinister, though, because the transaction took less than a minute and when he turned away Fred wore his usual weary, dull expression.

As he passed my desk the stranger glanced again at Storm. She smiled slightly at him, the wet, tongue-tip-showing smile she reserves for too many males over the age of twenty. He didn't smile back. A few seconds later he was gone.

I realized my forehead was damp. I used my handkerchief to dry it. Storm had swung around to face me; she still wore the wet smile, but it was crooked now, faintly mocking in that infuriating way of hers.

"He make you nervous, George?"

"Of course not. It's warm in here."

She laughed. "I wonder who he is."

"I have no idea. I've never seen him before."

"So big," she said. Speculatively. "And so ugly."

"Don't tell me he attracted you."

"As a matter of fact, yes."

"For God's sake, Storm."

"Ugliness can be very appealing. The right kind of ugliness."

"Whatever that means."

"You're not a woman. You wouldn't understand."

"He looked dangerous," I said. "Violent."

"Did he?"

"To me he did."

"Maybe that's part of his appeal." She ran her hands through her hair—thick and rich brown like milk chocolate, soft as cat fur. Characteristic gesture, full of animal sexuality; it exposed the long, smooth lines of her neck, lifted her breasts high. But her brown eyes and red mouth spoiled the effect: mocking me again. "You're not jealous, are you, George?"

I didn't answer that. She knew how much I wanted her—how much of a fool I was willing to be to have her just once more. One night with Storm was better than a thousand nights of tepid passion with my darling, half-frigid wife; it put her in your blood forever. And it didn't matter that she'd slept with half the men in Pomo County since her husband dropped dead of a massive coronary six years ago. Perfect wife to Neal

Carey the whole time he was buying and selling county real estate,
building up his fortune, building the finest house on the north shore on
prime lakefront property; never a hint of infidelity. But once he was
dead . . . it was as though she'd been transformed somehow into an
entirely different person. One lover after another, sometimes two and
three at once, parading them in and out of the big white Carey house at
all hours. Married men as well as single—she didn't care. Couldn't get
enough. Couldn't give enough. I hadn't been able to touch Ramona for
weeks after the night Storm and I spent together, not that Ramona
minded very much, of course. All her juices, what there'd been of them,
had dried up before she turned forty. Her whispers in the dark were like
slaps: "Don't touch me there, George. You're hurting me, George. Can't
you hurry up, George?" Storm's bed sounds were shrieks, moans, four-
letter words wrapped in silk and velvet. Storm . . . God, how I wanted
her! But for some perverse reason she wouldn't let me near her again.
Presents, promises, pleadings, phone calls, furtive visits . . . none of it
did any good. Did she treat her other lovers that way, too? Probably.
There were times, like today, like now, when I was sure she came to the
bank two or three times a month not to talk over her accounts and
investments but to devil me. Wanton temptress, tease, slut—she'd been
called all of those things and she *was* all of those things . . .

". . . about me, George?"

"What did you say?"

"I asked if you were thinking about me."

"No. Just woolgathering."

The mocking smile again. "Is there anything else we need to discuss?"

"Not about financial matters, no."

"What else, then?"

"You know what else. Storm—"

"I've got to run. I'm meeting Doug Kent at Gunderson's for cock-
tails."

"Kent? Don't tell me you're sleeping with him now . . ."

"Green's not a good color on you, George. Really."

"Goddamn it—"

"Don't curse at me. You know I don't like it."

"I'm sorry. But can't you have a little pity?"

"Is that what you'll settle for?"

"Yes, if I have to."

"I don't give pity fucks," she said.

"Jesus! Not so loud . . ."

"Good night, George. Give my best to Ramona."

I was angry and bitter and frustrated after she left, the way I always seemed to be when I saw her. Wanting her and hating her at the same time. Hating Ramona, too. Hating myself most of all. Almost a year since that one night in Storm's bed, and it was as if it had happened twenty-four hours ago. I couldn't go on like this much longer. And yet what else could I do, where else could I go? I had no options, not anymore. Not since Harvey Patterson's real-estate scheme blew up in both our faces.

To take my mind off Storm I got up and crossed to Fred's window. He was just finishing up his accounting; he always had it done by closing unless he had customers. I asked him about the stranger's transaction. Change for a hundred-dollar bill: five twenties. That was all. Businesses in Pomo cater to tourists even in the off-season, and with the two Indian-owned casinos operating on the north and south shores, hundred-dollar bills were common enough. He could have spent a portion of his to get change or changed it outright in a dozen places without raising an eyebrow. Why come into the bank for his five twenties?

I returned to my desk, and now what was bothering me was the stranger. What if he came back? What if he really was planning to rob us?

Audrey Sixkiller

HE WAS STANDING alone on the pier when I brought the Chris-Craft into the downtown marina. At a distance, from his size, I thought he was Dick; I couldn't see him clearly because he was in shadow between two of the pale pier lamps. Pleasure stirred in me. Dick waiting for me like that would've been an omen—a good omen, for a change. He was mostly what I'd been thinking about the past two hours, cruising from Barrelhouse Slough on the north shore down past Nucooee Point and the Bluffs to Indian Head Bay near Southport. Late afternoon, twilight, nightfall are the best times on the lake, especially at this time of year when you can have all eighty-eight square miles of it to yourself; the water softens and changes color as the light fades, the surrounding hills blur gently and lose definition, the lights wink on all around the twisting shorelines. You're alone but not lonely. It's the best place and the best time for hoping.

I cut the throttle again as I came in past the marker buoys. Now that darkness had fallen, the wind was up and making the water choppy; I had to do some maneuvering and reversing to swing in next to the long board float that paralleled the pier. When I looked up again the man had moved, was walking toward the ramp through the fan of light from one of the lamps. I saw then that he wasn't Dick and some of the good feeling went away. He came down the ramp as I cut the power and the boat's port side brushed against the rubber float bumper; he caught hold of the bow cleat and steadied her. I shut off the engine and the running lights, took the stern line, and climbed up and made it fast. He tied off the bowline before I could do it.

"Thanks," I said. "Not necessary, but thanks."

He nodded. He was quite a bit bigger than Dick, I saw now—massive, like a professional football lineman. A stranger. And not dressed for the weather: light windbreaker and no hat or hand coverings. I could feel the cold even though I was bundled up in sweater, pea jacket, gloves, and William Sixkiller's old wool cap.

"Nice boat," he said. "When was it built?"

"My father bought it in fifty-two."

"He keeps it in good shape."

"He died seven years ago."

"Sorry. *You* keep it in good shape."

"He taught me well."

"I've been watching your lights," he said. "Only boat out tonight as far as I could see."

"I had the lake to myself. Mostly do, this time of year."

"You go out often by yourself at night?"

"Not often. Sometimes."

"Kind of lonesome, isn't it?"

"No. Peaceful."

He was silent for a little time. The wind gusted and I heard it whispering and rattling in the sycamores and incense cedars that grew in nearby Municipal Park. The ducks and loons were making a racket over there, too; there are always flocks of them foraging around the bandstand and along the shore walk in late fall and winter.

"I've always wanted a boat," the big man said, and there was an odd, wistful note in his voice. "Maybe I'll buy one someday."

"You won't regret it. Even if you don't live on a lake like Ka-ba-tin."

"I thought this was Lake Pomo."

"Ka-ba-tin is its Pomo Indian name."

"Oh."

"Visiting here, Mr.—?"

"Faith. John Faith. Yeah, visiting."

"John Faith. That sounds as if it could be Native American."

"It's not. Lot of Indians live around here, I understand."

"Several colonies, yes. Rancherias, we call them. Mainly Pomos— big surprise, right? Some Lake Miwok and Lileek Wappo. At one time, a hundred years ago, there were fifteen thousand Native Americans in Pomo County. Now . . . less than a thousand."

"You seem to know a lot about them."

I smiled. "I'm one myself."

"Is that right?"

"Southeastern Pomo—Elem. Not quite pureblood. One of my ancestors got seduced by a white man, but they still let me sit on the tribal council. My name is Audrey Sixkiller, by the way."

He didn't react to the name, as some whites do. Or make any attempt to come forward and shake hands; his were tucked into the pockets of his windbreaker. He just nodded.

"Aren't you cold, dressed like that?" I asked him.

"Forgot to bring my coat. It's back at the resort."

"Which one are you staying at?"

"Lakeside."

"Oh. Harry Richmond's place."

"Sounds like you don't much care for it. Or him."

Harry Richmond was neither a friend to Indians nor completely honest. But I don't believe in carrying tales, to people I know much less to strangers. "It's as comfortable as any on this end of the lake," I said. "Too bad fishing season is over. Barrelhouse Slough up that way is full of catfish. If you like catfish."

"Cooked on a plate by somebody else," he said. "I'm not a fisherman."

The wind gusted again. "Well, I'd better get my shopping done. The later it gets, the colder it'll be on the lake."

"Back out on the water tonight?"

"Unless I want to walk two miles home and another two miles back again tomorrow morning." I smiled again. "My ancestors had it a lot rougher. They used to go night fishing in balsa boats made of tules, dressed in not much more than animal hides."

"Hardy people, huh?"

"Very."

"So you're going to just leave your boat here?"

"Nobody will bother it. I've left it overnight before."

"Nice boat like this? Must not be much crime in Pomo."

"No serious crime, no. We have an aggressive chief of police." *Where crime is concerned, anyway.*

"What about kids? Vandalism?"

"We don't have much of that, either. And all the teenagers know this is my boat. Besides, I don't know if you noticed or not, but that lighted building across Park Street over there is the city police station."

"I noticed," he said. "You a teacher?"

"Yes. How did you guess that?"

He shrugged. "The way you said teenagers, I guess."

"History and social studies." I pulled the cap down tighter around my ears. "I do have to go. I've enjoyed talking to you, Mr. Faith."

"Same here. I didn't mean to hold you up."

"You haven't."

He hesitated. "Grocery store close by?"

"Safeway in the next block."

"If you'd like some company . . ."

"No, thanks." I smiled again to take the sting out of the rejection. "Enjoy your stay in Pomo."

He had no answering smile. All he said was "Sure." But he didn't sound put off or disappointed; his voice was without inflection, without even a ghost of the wistfulness that had been there earlier. He'd expected me to say no, as if he'd asked without any real hope.

I walked up the ramp to the pier and a ways along it before I glanced back. He was still standing on the float, not watching me but looking again at the Chris-Craft. The thought occurred to me that he might still be there when I returned with the groceries. Well, what if he was? Despite his size, he hadn't given me any cause to be wary of him. And as I'd pointed out to him, the police station was two hundred yards away across Park Street.

You're too trusting, Audrey.

Dick had said that more than once, and he wasn't the only one. It's true, I suppose; I've always believed that people are inherently good, even if some try hard enough to disprove it, and I have never been a fearful person. There's too much fear in the world. Too much blind judgment.

You know, sometimes I think you're a white-man Indian. You love everybody. One of these days some damn white eyes ain't gonna love you back.

Jimmy. My brother, Jimmy, who'd been just the opposite of me, who hadn't trusted anyone and judged blindly and didn't love enough. Dead at twenty-three, and with no one to blame but himself. Drunk and driving too fast on a country road near Petaluma, where he'd been working on a dairy ranch; took a turn too fast and rolled his pickup down an embankment into a ditch. Short, sad, empty life. I didn't want to die that way, with hate in my heart and nothing to show for my years on this earth, not even a legacy of smiles.

Still, he'd been right about one thing. There was a white eyes who didn't love me back. Prejudice had nothing to do with it; no one could ever fault Dick Novak for racial bias of any kind. It was his ex-wife. And Storm Carey. And me—something about me that I couldn't change, couldn't make right, because I didn't understand what it was and perhaps he didn't either.

Just as I reached the end of the pier I looked back again, and John Faith was still standing, motionless, next to the boat. Solitary figure, bent slightly against the wind. Alone in the dark.

Like you, Audrey Sixkiller, I thought. Pining away for a white eyes and spending too many nights alone in the dark.

Lori Banner

I NOTICED HIM right away when he walked into the Northlake Cafe. We were pretty busy for a Thursday night, but you don't miss seeing a guy like that—not even if you wanted to. I mean, he was *big*. And he had one of those craggy, scarred faces that turn a lot of people off but that I'd always kind of liked. Pretty men of any size turn *me* off and I don't like skimpy types with so-called normal looks. That was what first attracted me to Earle. I thought that man I married had character, but all it was was hard-rock meanness covered with a layer of bullshit.

I wasn't the only one who stared when the big stranger came in. Everybody did. It got kind of quiet for as long as it took him to glance around and then settle himself into the last available booth, which happened to be on the side of the room I was working. Customers kept giving him looks, mostly out of the corners of their eyes, but he didn't pay any attention. He sat there with his scoop-shovel hands on the table, waiting.

I had an order to pick up but instead I grabbed a menu and took it over to him. "Hi there," I said, and I showed him my best smile. I have a nice smile, if I do say so myself. My best feature. Third-best feature, Earle says. Mr. Crude. "Welcome to the number-one restaurant in Pomo."

He didn't smile back, at least not much, but there wasn't anything cold about the way he looked at me. Whoo, those eyes of his. They'd scare the pants off you if he was in a temper—scare most people just sitting here the way he was. Not me, though. Not once I looked straight into them. They weren't as hard as they seemed on the surface, all shiny and bright like polished silver. There was a gentleness in them, way back deep. Just the opposite of Earle's eyes, which look gentle on the surface but aren't. Earle doesn't even know what the word means.

"What's good tonight?" he asked without picking up the menu. I liked his voice, too. Real deep, like it came from the bottom of his chest.

"Well, everybody seems to like the special. Meat loaf, mashed potatoes, cream gravy."

"That what you had for dinner?"

"I haven't eaten yet. When I do . . . the venison stew, probably. But not everybody likes venison."

"I like it fine. That's what I'll have."

"Good choice. Something from the bar first?"

"Bud Light."

I went and put in his order and picked up the one that was waiting. Even as busy as I was the next few minutes, I couldn't keep from glancing over at him three or four times. He really interested me. Not that I wanted to do anything about it. Well, maybe I *wanted* to, a little, but I wasn't going to.

When I brought him his beer and a basket of French bread and butter I said, "You're from a big city, I'll bet. San Francisco?"

"L.A., recently. How'd you know?"

"You have kind of a big-city look about you."

"Is that good or bad?"

"I don't know. Only big city I've ever been in is San Francisco. You on vacation?"

"No."

"Just passing through?"

He shrugged. "I might stay for a while."

"Well," I said. Then I said, "This is the best place on the lake to eat, no kidding. Lunch or dinner."

"I'll keep that in mind."

Darlene came over as I was pouring coffee to take to the couple in booth nine. She tucked up a piece of her red hair and said, "That's some hunk over there. He looks like a refugee from a slasher movie."

"Looks can be deceiving."

"Yeah? You can't help liking 'em big and nasty, I guess."

"What's that mean?"

"You know what I mean, Lori. New bruise on your chin there, isn't it?"

"No."

"Makeup doesn't quite hide it. It wasn't there yesterday."

"Mind your own business, Darlene, okay?"

"I just hate the way that man treats you."

"Earle's got a temper. He can't help it."

"He doesn't have to take it out on you."

"He's getting better. He's trying."

"Sure he is."

"He is. He promised me he'll stop drinking."

"For what, the hundredth time?"

"I mean it, that's enough."

She said, "It's your life," and went back into the kitchen.

Well? It is, isn't it? My life?

The venison stew came out and I brought it to the big guy. I leaned low when I set the plate on the table and those silvery eyes went right where I knew they would. I let him look a few seconds before I straightened up. I've got nice boobs, firmer than most women in their midthirties; I don't mind men looking at them. There's no harm in looking, or being looked at. I think it's a compliment.

"Anything else you'd like?"

"Not right now," he said.

"Just wave if there is. My name's Lori."

He nodded.

"What's yours, if you don't mind my asking?"

I thought he wasn't going to tell me. Then he said, "John."

"John what?"

"Faith. John Faith."

"No kidding? You don't look like somebody with a name like that. No offense."

"None taken."

"What do you do? I mean, for a living."

"Does it matter?"

"I'm just curious."

"I work with my hands."

"I'll bet you do."

"I'm not married, if that's your next question."

"Huh?" It wasn't going to be.

"But you are," he said.

His eyes were on the gold band on my left hand. I glanced at it, too, before I said, "Yep, I sure am." But right then I wished I weren't.

"I don't play around with married women."

"Well, that puts you in the minority, John. Most men don't care who they play around with." Some women, too. Like Storm Carey, for instance.

"I'm not most men."

Lord, no. "Truth is, I don't play around either."

"Come on like you might."

"But I don't. See, I'm a friendly person," I said, because I didn't want him to keep thinking what he was thinking about me. "Naturally friendly. I like men and I guess I can't help flirting, but that's as far as it goes. Really, I mean it."

He stared at me like he was trying to see inside my skin. Then he smiled, slow—a genuine smile this time. "Okay," he said.

"You know, John, you ought to use that smile more often. It's a real nice one."

It was, too. He didn't seem as ugly when he smiled, and it made those silver eyes look a lot softer. He likes me, I thought, and I felt good that he'd changed his opinion. I want people to like me, the ones I like in particular.

"I'll keep that in mind, too," he said. He finished what was left of his beer. "How about getting me a refill and letting me eat my dinner before it gets cold?"

He said it like a joke, and I laughed. "Sure thing." I touched his arm, you know the way you do, just being friendly, and picked up his empty and turned away. But I hadn't taken more than about three steps when I happened to look over at the entrance, and all at once I lost my smile and the good feeling I had. If I'd eaten anything before coming on shift, I might've lost that, too.

Earle was standing inside the door.

Standing there with his hands on his hips, glaring at me and past me at big John Faith.

Trisha Marx

WE WERE AT Northlake Chevron, where Anthony's brother, Mateo, works, when the guy in the Porsche drove in. Just hanging, that's all, Anthony and Mateo talking cars cars cars the way they usually did when they were together. Major boring on a good night, and this one wasn't good. The whole week hadn't been good. Maybe the last couple of months—maybe my whole *life*. I was afraid it was gonna turn into total crap and I didn't know what to do to keep that from happening.

Talk to Anthony, sure. Pretty soon I'd have to. And he'd probably go ballistic, same as Daddy would when he found out. All Anthony cared about was cars, fast cars, and going down to Sears Point to watch the Formula One races and getting high and getting into my pants whenever I'd let him. It was his fault as much as mine, but would that matter to him? Would he want to marry me? And if he didn't, what was I gonna do then?

Total crap at seventeen. *If* I was really pregnant.

Two missed periods now, and throwing-up sick two mornings this week. *Sure* I was pregnant.

That's what I was thinking when the Porsche pulled in and this huge guy got out of it. I mean, really huge. Pretty old, around forty, with pocks and a scar on his chin and a head like a carved rock. Anthony and Mateo were staring at him, too, and it was plain they didn't like what they saw. As if he was there to give them a hassle or something, when all he wanted was to buy some gas. He wasn't paying any attention to any of us as he unhooked the hose and stuck the nozzle into the tank.

Anthony said, "Man, will you look at him."

"Ugly fucker," Mateo said. "Wonder if he's tough as he looks."

"Why don't you go find out, man?"

"Yeah."

"So why don't you?"

"Shit, man, I can't just go pop the dude, can I?"

"Think you could take him?"

"If I had to. Yeah, sure, I'm big enough. Look at that face, man. Makes you want to bust it up some more, don't it?"

"Yeah."

"Face like that . . . man, you just want to smash it. You know what I'm saying?"

"Like that Cisneros dude down in Southport."

"Yeah, like him. Ugly *puto* like that . . . what's he doing around here?"

"Go ask him, man."

"Freak him. I don't care what he's doing here, man."

I quit listening to them. Stupid talk. I don't know what's the matter with guys sometimes. Wanting to beat up somebody just because of the way they look. A person can't help it if they're ugly or deformed or something, can they? And don't they have the right not to be hassled, same as everybody else?

Anthony isn't always such a macho jerk. Only when he's with his buddies, and worst of all when he's with Mateo. His brother's three years older and a total asshole. Always strutting around and starting trouble. Once, when a bunch of us were partying at Nucooee Point, he put his hand up my skirt and tried to tear my panties off—he was drunk on Green Death, that ale from up in Washington, and he's even more of a pig when he's ripped—and I practically had to scream rape before he let me alone. I told Anthony about it and he just laughed. As far as he's concerned, Mateo never does anything wrong. Mateo could blow up the courthouse and Anthony would probably think it was a cool thing to do.

So the huge guy finished pumping his gas and came over to pay

Mateo for it. Mateo gave his badass sneer and said something I didn't hear and Anthony laughed. The huge guy looked at them, one and then the other, not saying a word. Anthony stopped laughing and Mateo stopped sneering, just like that. So then the huge guy reached out and tucked a ten-dollar bill into Mateo's shirt pocket, hard and with a sneer of his own, and Mateo didn't move or say a word. Not then and not until the Porsche's engine roared and its tires laid rubber as it went zooming out of the station.

Then Macho Man gave the finger, jabbing it into the air half a dozen times, and yelled, *"¡Carajo! Vete al carajo! Tu madre!"* at the top of his voice.

"You should've popped him, man," Anthony said.

"Yeah. Next time I see him I'll break his ugly fuckin' head with a fuckin' tire iron."

I said, "Only if you sneak up behind him in a dark alley."

He raked me with his eyes. "What'd *you* say?"

"He didn't do anything to you."

"Came in here with a chip on. Tough guy."

"No, he didn't."

Anthony said, "You saw the way the dude looked at us. Mean, man, like he wanted to break our heads."

"Why don't you grow up, Anthony."

"What?"

"You heard me."

"Say that again, Trish, I'll bust your lip."

"Now who's being mean?"

"I'm telling you, man. Go bitch on me and I'll pop you."

I'm pregnant! I'm gonna have your kid!

I felt like screaming the words at him. But I didn't, because then maybe he really would smack me. He'd never laid a hand on me before, but there's always a first time. His eyes were hot and squinty, his face all scrunched up like a little boy getting ready to throw a tantrum. I've always thought Anthony's the handsomest hunk in Pomo and that I was, like, beyond lucky when he first asked me out; I practically wet my pants the first time he kissed me. But he didn't look handsome now. He looked mean, like he'd accused the Porsche guy of being. And a lot uglier, somehow.

Funny, but all of a sudden I wasn't so sure I wanted him to marry me. I wasn't even sure I wanted to keep on being with him, whether or not I had his damn baby.

Douglas Kent

STORM'S EYES WERE all over the strange beast as soon as it lumbered into Gunderson's Lounge. When it settled its hairy bulk at the other end of the bar, she shifted slightly on her stool so she could keep watching it without turning her head. Large, the way she liked 'em. Large and unsightly and endowed, no doubt, with no more than two active brain cells. What did she talk to them about afterward? Or were her postcoital conversations limited to contented sighs on her part, satisfied animal grunts and purrs on theirs?

You'll never know, Kent.

No Stormy nights for you, bucko—past, present, or future.

I lit a weed and studied my glass through the smoke. One more swallow to savor and on to the next. Dry martinis, the universal salve. The good folks at AA tell you that if you can't imagine a world without booze, you're a major-league alcoholic. I couldn't imagine a *universe* without booze. So what did that make me?

I knew what it made me, yes indeedy. My own brain cells pickled and expiring in daily droves. Ah, but there were still plenty left—too many, as a matter of fact. And the too many too active.

"How about another?" I asked Storm.

"No, I don't think so." Still staring at the Incredible Hulk who had wandered in out of the cold. "You go ahead, Doug."

"Don't mind if I do."

I took the last swallow and signaled to Mike for a refill. He brought it dutifully and quickly; Mike and I have an understanding based on mutual need. His, of course, being filthy lucre.

When I had it cozily in hand and a third of the salve working its warm way into the Kent depths I said, "Bigfoot lives."

"What?"

"Him. Humongous, isn't he?"

"Mmm. He came into the bank today while I was there."

"Did he now."

"I wonder who he is."

"Why don't you go ask him?"

Out came the tongue to slick her lips. The tip of it stayed out at one corner. I knew that gesture and the sultry expression that went with it; I'd seen them aimed at a dozen different men in the past three years. Never at me, however. The gesture and expression I knew well, but the moist lips and tongue themselves I didn't know at all and never would. Kent the deprived.

"I'll bet he's hung like a horse," I said.

"Don't be vulgar."

I applied more salve. "Sure you won't have another, pal?"

"I'm sure." Then, delayed reaction: "Why did you say that?"

"Say what?"

"Call me pal."

"Why not? We're drinking buddies, aren't we?"

"I suppose we are." Eyes on the fresh meat again.

"Aloof drinking buddies," I said. "Martinis and chaste good-night handshakes."

No answer this time. She wasn't even listening.

I gave my glass closer scrutiny, holding it up so the back-bar lights reflected in tiny distorted glints off the salve's oily surface. Time once again to ponder the oft-pondered question: Was I in love with Storm Carey, or was she just another whip-hard unit in the Kent bag of sticks? Tonight I felt more philosophical than usual. Tonight I decided it was a mixture of the two. Long ago I'd come to the conclusion that I was incapable of real love, the selfless, giving kind; but I was capable of a pallid, selfish version and within its boundaries, yes, I loved her. Ah, but was it Storm the woman that I loved pallidly and selfishly, or was it the insoluble mystery of her, her hidden eye that I couldn't reach or ever possess? A little of both, I decided again. Which was what made the stick that was Storm whip hard, the pain more exquisite when it was applied to the tender portions of the Kent psyche.

Not a new insight, but a sharper one than usual. Very good. I rewarded myself with more salve.

How long has it been that I've been gathering sticks for the old bag? Long time. Long, long time. The first few had been picked up in the bosom of Pa Kent's dysfunctional family. One or two more in Philly, fresh out of Penn State's redoubtable journalism school, suffering through graveyard shifts on the AP rewrite desk. None in Pasadena that

I could recall; my first job on a real newspaper, brash and eager and confident and still harboring a few of what I laughably considered ideals. Santa Monica? Yep, I'd gathered quite a few in good old Santa Monica after the promise of a freehand daily think piece became instead a restricted twice-weekly Pap smear and then, after four months, evolved into a reason to quit when the bastard city editor arbitrarily determined that I wasn't columnist material after all and kicked me back onto the City Hall beat.

They came fast and often after that, all the sticks on the twenty-year ride to the bottom. One more large-city daily (never a big-city daily where Kent could strut his stuff) and on to a couple of small-city dailies, a succession of small-town dailies, and small-town twice weeklies, and finally all the way down, *plunk*, to the tiny-town, once-a-week sheets. How many papers and towns altogether in twenty years? A score? Two dozen? They were all pasted together in my memory, a gray blur like the booze-soaked remnants of a cheap montage. The only things from each stop along the route that I remembered clearly were the sticks: missed deadlines, broken promises, bitter firings, random rants and clashes. But those weren't the only mementos of the past two decades; there were plenty of other sticks, too, courtesy of one ex-wife (I wonder who's laying her now?), a gaggle of ex-girlfriends, more than one episode involving the nonperformance of a once dependable pecker, a clutch of drunk-driving charges, two or three sodden fistfights. Kent used them all, one by one (often, with certain favorites like the Storm stick), in the grand sport of Kent-bashing. And still the bag wasn't full nor the psyche fully flayed, nor would they ever be even if my liver and lungs held out for another ten years or more. Which was about as likely as a black lesbian with AIDS being elected to the White House.

Spend the rest of my short unhappy life in Pomo? Nope. Definitely not. The tiniest town yet, true, but there were tinier ones; tinier weeklies, too, than the Pomo *Advocate*, whose owners could be persuaded to tolerate the fine, ink-stained hand of Douglas Kent, crusading editor. The truth was, Pomo was wearing thin on me after three years. I wasn't used to holding a job that long, staying in one place that long. I should have been fired long ago. Instead, I was still enjoying undeserved freedom, the largesse of a large-assed absentee owner whose only interest in the *Advocate* was a modest annual profit gleaned from its advertisers. He cared not a whit for the contents of the paper. Neither, for that matter, did its subscribers; *their* primary interest lay in a weekly search for the correct wording and spacing of their ads, the mention and correct spelling of their names and those of friends and relatives, *ad nauseam*.

Perfect case in point: the long Kent-generated article last spring on alcoholism and its root causes in Pomo County. Isolation, alienation, high poverty level on and off the Indian rancherias, high jobless rate, high density of the homeless and elderly retirees and welfare recipients, lack of adequate social services—all the usual crap, reshat and recycled. A temperance tract, in content and tone, on the insidious, long-range effects of John Barleycorn and his various spirited cousins.

I wrote it drunk, of course.

Blind drunk.

Kent was amazed when he read the piece in print. About a quarter of it was borderline brilliant, some of the best writing I'd done in years, drunk or sober. The other three quarters was mostly incoherent. Sentences that made no sense, paragraphs that had little or no continuity, logic that was illogical, misquotes, even a couple of dangling participles. A shameful mess, in sum, from the first word to the final period.

And the magnificent irony was, nobody noticed.

We received not a single phone call or letter of protest. One of the city councilmen, by God, stopped me on the street the day it ran and actually congratulated me on a "hard-hitting and thought-provoking article." If I'd been drunk at the time I would have laughed in his face. Riotously.

The humor struck me again now, and a sound burst from my larynx that had a tonal quality similar to the famous baying outside Baskerville Hall. Storm swiveled her head toward me. Others, too, including Mike and the Hulk, but I had eyes only for Storm.

"What's so funny?" she asked.

"Nothing," I said. "Nothing's funny."

"Poor Doug," she said, and immediately resumed her optical foreplay with the brute.

I swallowed the dregs from my glass, ate the olive, fired up another cancer stick, and got quietly off the stool and wove my way to the can. Where I took a leak and, of course, managed to dribble on myself before I got the shriveled-up, uncooperative old soldier safely tucked away again inside his Fruit of the Loom bunker. When I turned on the sink tap, water splashed up out of the bowl and wet my shirtfront. Naturally.

"You're pathetic, Kent," somebody said.

I looked up. In the mirror a bleary-eyed, smoke-haloed gent was giving me the eye. Looked just like me, poor bugger, poor Doug. I winked at him; he winked right back.

"A cliché," he said, "that's what you are. The cynical, drunken newspaperman. A bloody cliché."

"Right," I said. "Absolutely right."

"You were born a cliché," the face said. "From the moment you popped out of the old lady with the umbilical cord wrapped around your scrawny neck and your wizened little puss blue from cyanosis, you were doomed to lead the kind of miserable life you've led. A cliché using a series of clichés to grow into an even bigger cliché, and never once rising above the sum of your parts. You're a self-fulfilled prophecy, Kent, that's what you are."

"You bet," I said. "Fucking A."

"That's why you ended up here—in Pomo, in Gunderson's, in this smelly crapper talking to your fuzzy, clichéd image in the mirror. You couldn't have ended up anywhere else. You'll sink lower, too, and when you finally die it will be in the most clichéd way possible. You pathetic schmuck, you."

Squinting, I saluted the son of a bitch. Squinting, the son of a bitch saluted me.

I wove back out to the bar. Storm, as expected, had moved in on the strange beast; she was sitting on the stool next to him, her head close to his, her hand already on his thigh. Kent, I thought, you ought to be a weather forecaster. You can predict a Storm with the best of 'em.

I kept on weaving to the door. Nobody noticed, of course. Nobody paid the slightest attention as the crusading editor, the self-pitying gutter philosopher, the cliché supreme stumbled out into the night in search of more salve and another stick for his heavy, heavy bag.

Storm Carey

THE HUNGER WANTED so badly to fuck him, this new one in town. He'd been on the edge of my mind since the bank, and when he walked into the lounge I thought it must be fated for the Hunger to get its wish. It thought so, too. Its demands were immediate. As I watched the stranger hunched over the bar sipping his beer, the demands grew feverish. Never satisfied, wanting more, wanting new, wanting . . . what? What else besides what I kept feeding it?

Almost from my first awareness of the Hunger, two months after Neal's fatal coronary, I thought of it as a mouth, a thick-lipped, nibbling mouth deep within my body. Shrunken at first, the nibbles tiny, then expanding as its need grew, opening wider, nibbling more insistently, probing with something like a tongue as it moved down through my chest, hardening my nipples, down, tightening my stomach and groin, down, fiery breath making me wet, fiery tongue licking . . .

Cunnilingus from within. That was the sensation and that was how I described it to the shrink I visited for a while in San Francisco. She was very interested in the concept; what woman wouldn't be? Her interpretation was that the Hunger was grief-born, grief-sustained. Neal and I had been deeply, passionately in love, had enjoyed fabulous sex together throughout our marriage; his sudden death not only left an enormous gap in my life, but in my sex life as well, and so psychologically I had created the Hunger in an effort to fill the emptiness for brief periods. All the men were substitutes, surrogates: Through them I was trying to resurrect both Neal and the powerful physical intimacy we'd shared. But, of course, that was impossible, which was why the sex with them was never satisfying (and why it left me feeling cheap and disgusted with myself), why the Hunger renewed its hot, nibbling demands again so soon afterward.

All well and good—a reasonable analysis as far as it went. But the Hunger was more than just sexual need, more than a yearning for Neal and what we'd had for nine years, more than a gap filler and a psychological desire for love and intense human connection. The Hunger was something dark, too, hidden behind the mouth's thick lips and searching tongue. Something I couldn't reach or understand, and until I did, something I couldn't hope to satisfy. The Hunger's purely sexual demands frightened me, but not half so much as its unknown dark part. I tried to explain this to the shrink, and she seemed sympathetic, but her opinion was that it was, in fact, sexual: the so-called dark side of sex, childhood fears, religious and societal taboos, all that. When she kept trying to convince me of this, I ended our sessions. She was wrong; whatever the dark element was, it was not sexually related. And not she nor anyone else could help me find out what it really was. I was the only one who could do that, and someday I would.

But not tonight. Tonight the Hunger was all sex, raging sex, with no hint of anything else.

I couldn't sit still any longer. When Doug Kent got up and lurched away to the men's room, it was like a release. I slid off the stool, smoothed the tight skirt down over my hips. It was an effort not to seem too eager as I walked over and sat next to the Hunger's new target.

He knew I was there—he couldn't help knowing—but he neither moved nor looked at me until I said, "Don't you like my scent?" His sideways glance then was without apparent interest, and there was no change in his expression even after he'd examined my face and the hollow between my breasts. Not even the faintest spark of lust that usually flares in men's eyes. His were so pale in the dim light that the irises blended into the whites, to the point of invisibility; it was like meeting the gaze of a blind man. They gave me a small frisson.

"It's very expensive," I said.

"What is?"

"My perfume. It's called Paris Nights."

"Your husband give it to you?"

"I don't have a husband."

"Boyfriend, then."

"I don't have a boyfriend."

"Guy you're with's a relative, is that it?"

"No. A casual acquaintance. You didn't answer my question."

"I don't remember what it was."

"I asked if you liked my scent."

"Perfume's okay. It's the other one I don't like."

"Other one?"

"Gin. Smell of gin on a woman's breath turns me off."

"I have a bottle of Listerine in my bathroom."

"I'd still smell the gin."

"There are other ways to keep that from happening."

"Direct as hell, aren't you?"

"Yes. When I see something I want."

"Something. Uh-huh."

"I meant someone."

"Sure you did. Do I look like a necrophiliac?"

". . . Now, what is that supposed to mean?"

"I like my women active, not passed out."

"I won't pass out. I haven't had that much to drink."

"Your eyes and your voice say different."

I put my hand on his thigh, stroked it gently. "I promise to be alert and *very* active."

"Give it up, lady." He pushed my hand away.

"Oh, now. You're not even a little interested?"

"Not even a little."

"Why not? Don't you find me attractive?"

"Too attractive."

"Another cryptic statement. This one meaning?"

"Why me? I'm no prize."

"I find big men exciting."

"Big men with run-over faces. Yeah."

"I like your face." I didn't, though; it was ugly. But the Hunger didn't care. His ugliness, the animal power he projected, only made the Hunger want him more.

He tilted the bottle to his mouth. It seemed dwarfed in the circle of his thick-furred fingers. "Slumming," he said then.

"Excuse me?"

"You heard me. Rich bitch out slumming."

"If you're trying to insult me . . ."

"Trying? I've been doing it ever since you sat down."

"I'm not slumming," I said. "And I'm not exactly rich."

"What about the bitch part?"

"Have it your way."

"Paris Nights perfume, expensive clothes, expensive hairdo . . . . you've got money, all right. I know your type."

"Not as well as you think you do."

"Don't bet on it."

"My name is Storm. What's yours?"

"Storm. Yeah, right."

"I was born during one, and my parents had a fanciful streak. Would you like to see my driver's license?"

"No. I don't want to see anything of yours."

"Now who's being direct? You didn't tell me your name."

"No, and I'm not going to." This time, when he tilted the bottle, he took a long, deep swallow. His throat and the line of his neck and jaw were massive; they made me think of a grizzly bear I once saw at the San Francisco zoo. "I've had about enough of this game."

"I'm not playing a game," I said. "Would you like to leave now?"

"Not with you."

"You won't be sorry if you do."

"Sure I would. So would you. You wouldn't like it with me and I wouldn't like it with you and we'd both hate ourselves afterward."

"You're wrong. I'd enjoy it with you very much. And I guarantee you'd enjoy it with me. It won't take long to find out. My house is only about three miles from here."

"Your house. Uh-huh. You live alone?"

"Yes."

"And you're willing to take me there, a complete stranger—just like that. No worries I might tie you up and steal the silverware? Or cut you up into little pieces, maybe?"

I felt another frisson. "I don't believe you're that kind of man."

"But you don't know that I'm not, do you?"

"Are you trying to frighten me?"

"No, lady," he said slowly and distinctly, as if he were attempting to reason with a child, "I'm trying to get rid of you." He put the bottle down and swung away from me, onto his feet. "Good night and happy hunting."

"Wait . . ."

He didn't wait. He went away into the dark.

I nearly chased after him. But it wouldn't have done any good and I didn't care to make a public scene; I have very little pride left, but there is just enough to dictate a certain decorum. Neal taught me so many things; a sense of propriety was one of them.

I took a moment to compose myself and then returned to my original seat. Mike Gunderson smirked at me dourly as I sat down. He'd been watching the stranger and me, but at a discreet distance; eavesdropping wasn't one of his faults. He had been a friend of Neal's and he neither liked the widow nor approved of her behavior. One of many Storm-haters in Pomo, not that I or the Hunger cared. If he hadn't had an inordinate fondness for the almighty dollar he would have declared me persona non grata long ago.

"No luck tonight, Mrs. Carey?" he said. He refused any longer to call me by my first name. "Too bad."

"I'll have another martini, please."

"Yes, ma'am. I guess you need it."

For the first time I noticed that Doug was still absent, his place at the bar cleared away. "Did Mr. Kent leave?"

"While you were having your . . . conversation."

"Did he say where he was going?"

"No. He just left."

Poor Doug. I liked him, I truly did, and I felt sorry for him. Not a day or night goes by now that I don't despise myself, but my self-loathing is nothing compared to his. His is long-nurtured and has to do with weakness and failure—part of the reason he wants me so desperately, because he knows he can't have me and the knowledge fuels his destructive impulses. If it were up to me I'd take him to bed, but it's not up to me. The Hunger doesn't want him. Many men, yes, some men, no, and I'm not involved in the selection process. No mercy fucks for the Hunger. It knows exactly what it craves, and what it craved tonight was the hulking animal presence that had rejected it, me, both of us.

The demands of the mouth, lips, tongue, fire breath were still intense. *Feed me, feed me . . .* like the plant creature in *Little Shop of Horrors.* And I would have to feed it, and soon, or it would give me no peace through the long, long night. In my mind we opened the file of men the Hunger had chosen in the past; one of them would have to do. We flipped through the names, looking for one the Hunger considered suitable, one who could be induced to come to us on short notice. No. No. No. No. No. No.

Yes.

Mike set the fresh martini in front of me, turned away without speaking. One sip, another, a third. Then, with the Hunger prodding me, I went to the public telephone near the rest rooms and made my siren's call.

Richard Novak

I COULDN'T SEEM to sit still tonight. No particular reason, unless it was a residue of the uneasiness the stranger in the Porsche had built in me. A combination of things piling up over a period of time. Tonight wasn't the first that I'd felt restless, dissatisfied; too often lately my life seemed empty on the one hand, overburdened and loaded with frustrations on the other. It needed something, some kind of shift or change or sense of purpose. But I couldn't seem to make up my mind what it could or should be.

Part of the problem was the daily grind of my job. There was little enough felony crime in Pomo, but as if to make up for that we had more than our fair share of the other kinds, particularly those that plague economically depressed rural towns with a population in the ten-thousand range—domestic violence and abuse, belligerent drunks and drunk driving, kids on drugs, adults on drugs, automobile theft, and vandalism. All of this on a continuing basis, and just me and ten full-time and four part-time male and female officers to handle it. The county sheriff's office is supposed to provide assistance and backup, but they have their hands full elsewhere; the Southport area, which is loaded with welfare cases and homeless people, has the highest crime rate in the county. Besides, Sheriff Leo Thayer is a political hack who doesn't know his ass from a tree stump, and more often than not we ended up at loggerheads on even petty law-enforcement issues. There was no money in the city or county treasuries for more manpower or modern equipment or new patrol cars; we had to make do with what we had, and with underpaid civilians in dispatcher and clerk and other positions that should've been filed by professionals. Even absolute necessities such as weapons and shortwave-radio repairs couldn't be gotten or gotten done without a hassle. I spent too much time playing politics—Pomo's mayor, Burton Seeley, is also top dog in the machine that runs the county—and begging favors. And on top of that I had to indulge Seeley and the city council by attending civic functions at an average of one a week in order to "maintain a high standard of community relations," one of the top dog's pet policies. Half the time I was in uniform I felt harried, bullied, short-tempered, and hamstrung—and wishing I'd stayed in law enforcement in Monterey County and worked my way up through the ranks toward a captaincy, instead of jumping at the first police chief's job that was offered to me seven years ago. If I had, maybe Eva and I—

No. Moving to Pomo hadn't finished us. The miscarriage had done that. The miscarriage and the part of Eva I'd never been able to reach.

The women in and out of my life—that was another reason for the restlessness, the dissatisfaction. Eva. And Storm after Eva was gone. And the hollow series of brief flings and one-night stands after it ended with Storm. And now Audrey and the uncertain feelings I had for her. Once I'd been so sure of what I wanted from a woman and a relationship. Not anymore. I wasn't sure of much of anything anymore.

Midlife crisis? Call it that, or whatever. At thirty-seven I was starting to drift, to go through the motions. If I didn't do something about it, get down inside myself and find some direction again, I'd wind up a non-alcoholic version of Douglas Kent—a scooped-out, burned-out mass filling up time and space while he waited for the hearse to come and haul him away.

After supper I tried reading and I tried watching TV. Mack whining to go out gave me something else to do for a while. I put the leash on him and walked him down by the lake, a good, long, brisk walk even though the temperature had dropped into the forties. Mack liked the cold; it made him frisky. Big old black Lab with a sweet disposition—a better friend than any human I knew in Pomo, with the possible exception of Audrey. I'd bought him for Eva after the miscarriage, a misguided attempt to fill some of the emptiness. Instead, she'd resented him—he was alive and her baby wasn't—and had refused to have anything to do with him. Tried to get me to give him away, and when I wouldn't do it, because I needed Mack even if she didn't, she withdrew even more.

Withdrawal was her way of coping. From me, from the life we'd had, from the fact that she couldn't have any more children. When her body was healed she wouldn't let me touch her. Couldn't stand to have me touch her anymore, she said. She'd always been religious; she withdrew into religion. Hours spent reading the Bible, praying aloud. Two, three, four days a week away from home doing church work. Six months of this, and then one day she was gone—moved out, moved back to Monterey to live with her mother. Saved herself and left me alone to find some other way to save myself. It hurt then and it still hurt now, after four years—a dull ache that came and went, came and went. The last I'd heard, five months ago through an old family friend, she was in a religious retreat somewhere near San Luis Obispo. One of us, at least, had found an answer.

The long walk tired me but did nothing for the restlessness. I called the station to see how things were. Verne Erickson, the night man in charge—actually, he's a lieutenant and second in command; he works nights by choice—said things were relatively quiet. One D&D arrest, one minor traffic accident out on the Northlake Cutoff, nothing else so far. So I didn't even have an excuse to go back to work.

I made a cup of cocoa, sprinkled nutmeg on top the way Eva had in the early days of our marriage. One of our little rituals: a cup of cocoa before bed every night that I managed to make it home by bedtime. It'd been good with us in those days . . . hadn't it? Good, yes, but even then there'd been a distance between us. Less passion, sexual and otherwise, than I would've liked. Less connection on important issues. She wanted children, and her job at a day-care center in Carmel Valley only made her want them more. I was ambivalent, and at some level I think she blamed me for the fact that she wasn't able to conceive. She didn't like my work; it kept me away from home too much and there was too much danger, too much violence involved in it. She believed in thou shalt not kill, turn the other cheek, the meek shall inherit. In her mind it would've been almost as bad if I'd shot someone in the line of duty as if someone had shot me. Friction there, friction over the inability to conceive, little frictions on other fronts, too. Then she'd gotten pregnant, and she was so happy she glowed. Things really had been good until the sixth month, the sudden pains and bleeding, the miscarriage . . .

Christ, Novak, I thought, what's the point of living it all again? Why beat yourself up like this?

I sat in the living room of my nice, comfortable, two-bedroom, rent-free home—one of the perks that had induced me to accept the otherwise low-paying chief's job seven years ago—and drank my cocoa and stared at the blank TV screen. Mack came in and laid his head on my knee, looked up at me with his dark, liquid eyes. He knew how I was feeling tonight. Dogs are sensitive that way. I patted him, switched on the tube, switched it off again.

Get out of here, go do something, I told myself, before the walls start closing in.

Go get laid. It's been a while—maybe that's what you need.

Storm?

No, no way. Over and done with, and except for the sex, not so good while it lasted. Too many frictions there, too; too many angry words. And don't forget the flap it caused. The chief of police and the once respected, now vilified Mrs. Carey—tongues had really wagged and there'd been no mistaking the serious warning behind Burt Seeley's private lecture about public image and civic responsibility. Take up with Storm again and I'd be even more strung out, and out of a job to boot. And then what would I do?

God, though, she was amazing in bed. The best ever.

Yeah, well, she'd had plenty of practice, hadn't she? A hundred, two hundred others before and since. A wonder she hadn't contracted AIDS or some other sexually transmitted disease—one of the things we'd argued about when she'd admitted to sleeping with others while she was sleeping with me. Hell, for all I knew maybe she did have a disease by now.

Stay away from her. No ifs, ands, or buts.

Out to the kitchen again, Mack padding along behind. I started to make another cup of cocoa, but I didn't want any more goddamn cocoa. What did I want?

Audrey?

She wanted me; she'd made that plain enough. Smart, attractive, caring, funny, undemanding—everything a man could want in a woman. Casual, our relationship so far; a few dates, a couple of passionate clinches, nothing else, but I could sleep with her if I wanted to. She'd made that plain, too. Only if I did, then it wouldn't be casual any longer because the one thing she wasn't was a casual lay. It'd be a commitment, at least on her part, and then if I couldn't follow through she'd be hurt badly. And I didn't think I would be able to follow through. And I didn't want to hurt her.

One strike against us: She was twenty-seven, ten years younger than me. Another: I liked her, more than a little, but I didn't love her. No feelings of almost desperate yearning, the way it'd been when I first met Eva. No hammering lust, the way it'd been with Storm. Another: Audrey loved kids, wanted children of her own; she was quiet domesticity, traditional family values. I'd had all that, or a taste of it, with Eva, and it hadn't led to anything but pain; I couldn't stand to live that kind of life again even if the person and the outcome were different. I was better off unmarried. I functioned better when the only responsibility I had was to myself.

Right. And how about the other two strikes you don't want to admit to: Audrey's heritage and your job security. Seeley and the city council and the rest of the town didn't like you making it with Storm and they wouldn't like it any better if you took a Native American wife, now would they? Ask Burt Seeley if there was prejudice against Pomos in Pomo and he'd look appalled and vehemently deny it. But it was there, all right, in him and plenty of others, crawling like worms beneath the surface, so goddamn subtle sometimes you could barely see it or smell it for what it was. The Pomos and Lake Miwoks and Lileek Wappos were here a century or more before white settlers, the town and lake and county and a dozen other places and businesses were named for them, but the whites ran things and had ever since they'd shown up. Their word was law, and their laws were meant to protect their own. The natives were tolerated as long as they kept their place, stayed for the most part on their handout reservation lands, and didn't try to change the status quo. It was all right for an Indian woman to teach at a mainly white high school, as long as it was subjects that didn't matter too much in their way of thinking, like American history; and it was all right for a white man to date an Indian woman, and lay her if he felt like it, but when it came to taking one for his wife, particularly if he happened to be an appointed member of the white power structure and she happened to be the daughter of an uppity free spirit who'd had the gall to buy a piece of nonreservation land and build a home on it in their midst, well, that just wasn't acceptable. No sir, not acceptable at all.

Screw them, I thought. I don't care that much about the frigging job, and Audrey being Pomo has nothing one way or another to do with my feelings toward her. Do *I* think Native Americans or any other nonwhite race is inferior? Hell, no. I treat everybody as an individual, some good, some bad, whites or blacks or reds or browns. If I wanted to marry Audrey I'd damned well marry her. I'm—

What?

What the hell am I?

What *do* I want?

Mack whined and nuzzled my leg. My head was pounding, the ache sharp behind my eyes as I reached down to pat him.

And that was when the telephone rang.

Audrey Sixkiller

SOMEONE WAS TRYING to break into my house.

I knew it as soon as I came awake. I'm a light sleeper, but I don't wake up to normal night sounds, even loud ones. I lay very still, listening. The wind, the flutter of a loose shingle on the roof, and then the sound that wasn't normal—a slow scraping, faint and stealthy. Where? Somewhere in back. It came again, followed by a different noise that might have been metal slipping on metal and digging into wood. The back porch, either the window there or the rear door: some kind of tool being used to force the lock on one or the other.

It made me angry, not afraid. In the heavy darkness I lifted my legs out from under the covers, sat up, slid open the nightstand drawer. Whoever was out there must be white; Indians know how to function in complete silence even in the dead of night. Just as I'd kept William Sixkiller's house and boat, I'd kept his hunting rifle and shotgun and handgun. I lifted the .32 Ruger automatic out of the drawer, eased off the safety with my thumb. Its clip was always kept fully loaded; he'd taught me that when he'd taught me how to shoot.

Scrape. Scrape.

Up from the bed with the gun cold in my fingers. The sleep was out of my eyes now; I could make out the familiar bedroom shapes as I crept across it and into the hall.

Snap!

I knew that sound: the push-button lock on the back door releasing. I'd been foolish not to listen to Dick and have a dead-bolt lock installed instead.

Down the hall to the kitchen. Into the kitchen. I keep the swing door that leads to the enclosed porch propped open; it's easier that way to carry in groceries, laundry back and forth to the washer and dryer. Through the opening I could tell that the prowler had the back door pulled all the way open, but I couldn't see him clearly; he was behind the screen door and the cloudy night at his back was only a shade or two lighter than he was. Big, that much I could make out: He filled the doorway. Otherwise he was a shapeless mass of black.

He was pushing on the screen door; I heard it and the eye hook creak. Not trying to break the hook loose from the wood—that would've made too much noise—but creating a slit at the jamb so he could wedge something through to lift the hook free. More scraping, metal on metal, as I detoured around the dinette table, past the stove to the open swing door. My bare feet made the softest of whispers on the cold linoleum. But he wouldn't have heard me in any case because of the sounds he was making.

It would have been easy to reach through the doorway, around to the porch light switch. But if I did that, with my eyes dilated as they were, the sudden flare would half blind me for two or three seconds; and if the light triggered him to break through instead of run away, he might have enough time to overpower me before I could get off a shot to stop him. I would shoot him only as a last resort. So I braced my left shoulder against the door edge, spread my feet, extended the automatic in a two-handed grip. It was steadied and aimed when the hook popped free, making a thin, jangling sound as it dropped. The screen door started to creak inward.

"Don't come any farther. I have a gun and I'll use it."

My voice rising so suddenly out of the darkness froze him. Four or five seconds passed; then the door creaked again, louder, and the lumpy shapes of his head and shoulders appeared around its edge.

"One more step, I'll shoot."

Creak.

He didn't believe I was armed, so I made him believe it. I raised the Ruger slightly and to the left and squeezed the trigger.

The report, magnified by the closed space and low ceiling, was a heavy pressure against my eardrums. The bullet went into the wall alongside the jamb, and in the muzzle flash I saw him duck his head below an upraised arm. That brief glimpse caused me to suck in my breath. I saw his eyes, bulging, wild, but that was all I saw.

He was wearing a ski mask.

In the darkness the screen door banged shut as he let go of it and backed off on the landing. Then he was thumping down the steps, off onto the brick path that angles down to the dock. It was a few seconds before my legs would work; then I was at the screen, yanking it open and rushing outside. By then he was off the path, running toward the low fence that separates my property from the closed-up cottage on the north that belongs to summer people. The absence of any nearby lights and the low, thick cloud cover made him little more than a moving shadow; his clothing was dark, too, so I couldn't even tell what he was wearing. He vaulted the fence, stumbled, righted himself, and disappeared behind the junipers that grew at the rear of the cottage.

The wind off the lake was icy; I was aware of it all of a sudden, stabbing through the thin cotton of my pajamas, prickling my bare feet and arms. Back inside, quickly. I put the porch light on, and when my eyes adjusted I peered at the door lock. Scratched, the wood around the plate gouged; but it still worked all right. I set the button, closed the door, then rehooked the screen door. The splintered hole in the wall was about twelve inches from the jamb, at head height—exactly where I'd intended the bullet to go.

I switched on the kitchen light, entered the front room, and turned on a lamp in there. The clock over the fireplace said that it was one-thirty. The gunshot had seemed explosively loud, but the house on the south side of me was also empty—up for sale—and the noise hadn't carried far enough to arouse any neighbors farther away on this side or across the street. When I drew back an edge of the front-window curtain, Lakeshore Road was deserted and all the houses I could see were dark. Everything looked normal, peaceful, as if the entire incident might have been a dream.

Goose bumps still covered my arms; there was a crawly sensation up and down my back. In the bedroom I put on my woolly slippers, the terry-cloth robe that was the heaviest I owned. The chill didn't go away. I turned the furnace up over seventy and stood in front of the heat register until warm and then hot air began to pulse out.

I kept seeing his image in the muzzle flash, the upflung arm, the wild eyes bulging in the holes of the ski mask. Burglar? There hadn't been a nighttime break-in of an occupied house—what Dick calls a "hot prowl"—in Pomo in as long as I could remember. The penalties were much more severe for that kind of crime than they were for daylight burglaries. Besides, thieves weren't likely to wear ski masks.

Rapists wore ski masks.

Rape wasn't uncommon in Pomo County. The home invasion kind was, but still, it happened elsewhere—it could happen here, too. Young woman living alone, a man with a sick sexual bent decides to take advantage—

If you'd like some company . . .

My God. The stranger on the pier tonight?

Big, and a little odd. And I'd told him we didn't have much serious crime in Pomo. I hadn't told him I lived alone, but when I'd said I had to take the boat home or walk two miles and another two back in the morning, the inference had been there. He'd been gone when I returned from Safeway with my groceries, but he could've been lurking somewhere, watching; he could've followed the running lights on the Chris-

Craft—Lakeshore Road does what its name implies, follows the water-line all along the northwest shore—and seen where I docked and that the house was dark; he could've watched the house and when no one else came he'd have known for sure I was alone . . .

But I was jumping to conclusions. It didn't have to be the stranger; it could be anyone, a resident as well as an outsider. And what if I hadn't scared him off permanently? What if he came back, tonight or some other night?

I was still angry, angrier than before, because whoever he was, he'd made me afraid. That was the one thing William Sixkiller had never let me be, that I hated being more than anything else. Afraid.

In the front room I peeked out again through the drapes. Lakeshore Road was as deserted as before. I sat on the couch and picked up the phone. If I called the police station to report what had happened, it would mean patrol cars, questions, neighbors being woken up . . . people knowing I was afraid. But I had to tell someone, and that meant Dick. He was the only one I could talk to right now.

I tapped out his number. And it rang and rang and rang without answer.

Where was he, for heaven's sake? Why wasn't Dick home at 1:40 in the morning?

Part II

Friday

George Petrie

RAMONA SAID, "I asked you a question, George. Where were you last night?"

I heard her that time, but the words didn't register right away. I had so damn many things on my mind. My head felt stuffed, the way it does when you have a bad cold. I couldn't concentrate on any one thing. It was all churned together, pieces here and there breaking off like swirls of color in a kaleidoscope; hang on to one, focus on it for a few seconds, and then it would slide back into the vortex and there'd be another and the same thing would happen.

"Well?"

"Well what, for Chrissake?"

"You don't listen to me anymore," she said. "You act as if you're alone half the time we're in the same room."

"Ramona, don't start—"

" 'Ramona, don't start.' " Like a goddamn parrot. Hair all frizzy after her shower, nose like a beak jutting at me, mouth flapping open and shut, open and shut. And that dressing gown of hers, green and red, white feathery wisps at the neck and on the sleeves. Wings, feathers, bright little bird eyes . . . a scrawny, scruffy, middle-aged, chattering parrot. What did I ever see in her?

"What did I ever see in you?" I muttered aloud.

"What? What did you say?"

"Nothing." Sip of coffee. Bite of toast. Glance at my watch even though I know what time it is. "I'd better get to the bank."

"It's only eight-twenty," Ramona said. "I want an answer first."

"Answer to what?"

"God, you can be an exasperating man. Where you were until after two o'clock in the morning. On a weeknight."

The squawking and screeching echoed inside my head, making it ache. My eyeballs actually hurt from the pressure.

"George. Where were you?"

"At the Elks Lodge, playing cards."

"Until two A.M.?"

"Yes, until two A.M. Pinochle. I lost nine dollars and had four drinks and then I drove home. Does that satisfy you? Or do you want to know who else was in the game and who won and how much and how many drinks each of them had?"

"You don't have to yell—"

"And you don't have to interrogate me as if I were a fucking criminal."

Her mouth pinched until it wasn't a mouth any longer, just a bunch of hard ridges and vertical creases. Kissing that mouth was like kissing two strips of granite. Was it ever soft, even on our honeymoon? I couldn't remember her lips ever being soft.

"At the breakfast table, George?" Hard and tight like her mouth. "That kind of language at eight-twenty in the morning?"

For a few seconds I lost it. Couldn't stop myself from saying, "That's right, you don't like fucking, do you? In any way, shape, or form, verbal or physical."

She reacted as though I'd slapped her. Good! Up on my feet, in such a spasm I jostled the table and spilled the coffee, to hell with the coffee and her, too.

"How can you say things like that to me? I won't stand for it, I won't be abused. You'll be sorry if you think—"

I went out and slammed the door on the rest of the squawking and screeching.

In the Buick I lit a cigarette. I don't smoke much anymore, but I needed something to try to calm down. My head . . . how was I going to get through the day? And the weekend coming up? And next week, and the week after, and the week after that?

Ramona, Storm, Harvey Patterson, that stranger yesterday . . . them and the rest in this town, all the people with their small minds and small ways. And me stuck here in a dead-end job and a lousy marriage, wanting a woman I couldn't have, a hundred other things I couldn't have. Facing a future that could be even worse, a genuine hell on earth. It could happen.

If that stranger robbed the bank, it *would* happen.

I told myself for the twentieth time it was a damn-fool notion. The stranger didn't have to be what he looked like; he was probably gone by now and I'd never see him again. But I kept right on imagining the worst.

I couldn't stop him if he walked in and showed a gun. I'm not brave, I don't own a gun myself or even know how to fire one. Fred and Arlene would do what they were told and so would I. We'd hand over the money in the cash drawers, the money in the vault, and chances were he'd get away with it.

And then there'd have to be an accounting.

Bank examiners, within hours.

It wouldn't take them long to find the shortage. A day, two at the most.

Covered it as best I could, but no one can doctor bank records cleverly enough to fool an examiner. It was just a little more than seven thousand dollars, only I didn't have the cash to replace it and no certain way of getting that much on short notice. The house was mortgaged to the hilt, the Indian Head Bay property Ramona had inherited wasn't worth enough to support a loan, Burt Seeley poor-mouthing when he turned me down, Storm laughing in my face, and there was nobody else except maybe Charley Horne. Yearly audit was still three months away; the Indian Head Bay property had to have sold by then, priced rock-bottom the way it was. It had to. But I couldn't cover the shortage *now* without going begging to Charley Horne, and he doesn't like me any more than I like him after that zoning flap four years ago when he tried to expand his Ford dealership. He might loan me the money at an exorbitant rate, but more likely he'd tell me to go to hell. I've been afraid to find out because he's my absolute last resort. If he turned me down—

Prison.

I'd go to prison for borrowing a measly seven thousand, for believing in that son of a bitch Harvey Patterson and his big talk about a sure-thing real-estate killing.

I couldn't stand being locked up. The idea of spending years in the company of brutal men like that stranger terrifies me so much I can't think about it without starting to shake and sweat.

Options? Sorry, Petrie, you're fresh out. All you can do is wait and pray the hold-up notion really is a crazy fantasy and the economy picks up and somebody buys the Indian Head Bay property and you don't get caught.

Except that I was already caught. That was what was tearing me up inside, making me wriggle and jump and lose my temper and think wild thoughts. More than one kind of prison for a man to be locked up in. Even if I managed to cover the shortage without being found out— caught, trapped, locked up in Pomo until the day I died.

Harry Richmond

MARIA LORENZO COULDN'T get it through her thick Indian head that I didn't want her to do any maid service in cabin six. She kept saying, "But if he stays another night he'll need clean towels. And the bed—who will make up the bed?"

"He can make up his own bed," I said.

"No clean towels?"

"I told you, no. Don't even go near it."

"How come you don't want to give this man service?"

"That's my business. You mind your own."

"Okay, you're the boss." But it still bothered her; she kept frowning and shaking her head. "You want me to clean the office and your rooms?"

"It's your day, isn't it?"

"Change the sheets, put out fresh towels?"

Indians! Skulls thick as granite. "Everything, Maria, same as you always do on Fridays."

"What about tomorrow?"

"Well? What about it?"

"Should I come and clean six then?"

"If Faith checks out. I'll let you know."

"But not if he stays? Still no service?"

"That's right. Nothing. *Nada.*"

She shook her head again, muttered something in Pomo, and went around the counter into my living quarters. Stupid cow. But she had a nice ass, round and plump. Like Dottie's when we were first married, before she got hog-fat after Ella was born. I couldn't get near Dottie the last few years. All that lard . . . it made me want to puke when I saw her naked. Her own damn fault when she dropped dead of a heart attack. Two hundred and eighty-seven pounds . . .

I shut Dottie out of my mind and watched Maria wiggle around, bend over to straighten the papers and magazines on the coffee table. Dried my throat to see that ass of hers stuck up in the air, all round and inviting. She was in her late thirties and starting to wrinkle and lose her shape like a lot of Indian women at that age, but she was still attractive enough and her ass was just right. I craved a piece of that every time I saw her. But she wouldn't have any of me. Some other white man, maybe, but not Harry Richmond. One time I made a pass she shot me down cold. Didn't get offended or angry, just gave me a reproachful look and said, "I have a husband and three children, Mr. Richmond, and I believe with all my heart in the teachings of our savior, Jesus Christ." Sure. But what if I'd been thirty instead of fifty and had all my hair and a flat belly? Bet she'd have sung a different tune then. Most Indian women are sluts, and the pious ones are the worst.

Indian women. Maria Lorenzo, that snooty little Audrey Sixkiller... what was it about the attractive ones that made me want it so much?

No use standing around here getting myself worked up for nothing. I went outside to the shed and fetched my tool kit. One of the downspouts on cabin three was loose, and this was as good a time as any to fix it. Maria knew enough to answer the phone if it rang.

Cold this morning. No sun, mist rising in the marshes, a high wind pushing thick clouds inland, with more scudding in behind. Couldn't tell yet if we'd get rain on the weekend. Probably would, my luck being what it was. If it did rain, I wouldn't get half a dozen rentals through Sunday night. I ought to be grateful to any guest deciding to stay another night, but not when that guest was John Faith. I'd take his money as long as he wanted to give it to me, but that didn't mean I had to like it or anything about him. No telling what he was up to around here. Whatever it was, I wished he'd tend to it and go back where he came from. I'd sleep better when he was gone, that was for sure.

I was hammering a new clamp on the drain spout when the police cruiser drove in off the highway. Gave me a jolt to see Chief Novak at the wheel. Lakeside Resort is within Pomo township's jurisdiction, just barely, but the town cops don't patrol much out this way. No reason they should, really. I hadn't had to call in the law in over three years, since the couple from Walnut Creek got into a drunken fight in cabin four and the man busted his wife's arm for her. She had it coming, if you ask me, the way she kept running him down all the time, but that hadn't kept me from calling the police. I can't afford trouble.

Novak spotted me and pulled up. Instead of climbing out he rolled down his window. I pasted on a smile as I walked over.

"Morning, Chief. What brings you up here?"

"You have a guest named John Faith?"

No surprise there. I said, "That's what he calls himself."

"Check out already? I don't see his car."

"No, he paid me for another night."

"When did he pay you?"

"About an hour ago. Little after eight."

"Just one more night?"

"Just one. How come you're asking about him? He get himself into some trouble already?"

"I just want to talk to him." Novak's face, now I looked at it close, was tight-skinned and hard around the mouth and jaw. His eyes were bloodshot and bagged, as if he hadn't had much sleep last night. "What time'd he leave?"

"Right after he paid me."

"Tell you where he was going?"

"Didn't say a thing."

"You know if he was here between midnight and two A.M.?"

"Midnight and two? Why? Something happen then?"

"*Was* he here, Harry?"

"Well . . . not when I went to bed around eleven-thirty. He's in six and the windows were dark and no sign of that Porsche of his. I was awake another thirty, forty minutes and I didn't hear him come in." The wind had chapped my lips; I took out my tube of Blistex. "Tell you this, Chief. Whatever he's done, it won't surprise me."

"Why do you say that?"

"You had a good look at him, up close?"

"Yesterday."

"Then you know what I mean. Makes me nervous as hell having him here, but I can't afford to turn down anybody's business."

"How'd he pay you? Cash or credit card?"

"Cash. Both times. Wad of bills in his wallet big enough to gag a Doberman."

"What address did he put on his registration card?"

"Los Angeles, that's all."

"No street or box number?"

"Nope. I should've asked, I guess, but he's not somebody you want to prod. Touchy. Mean and touchy. I can tell you his car license number, if you want that."

"I already know it."

"Well, how about the cabin he's in?"

"What about it?"

"You want to take a look inside?"

Novak shook his head. "Not enough cause."

"I could just unlock the door with my passkey and then go on about my business. Never know it if you happened to step inside for a minute or two—"

"No."

"But if he's guilty of something—"

"I don't know that he is. Don't you go invading his privacy either, Harry."

"Not me. No, sir," I said. "Sure you can't give me an idea of what it's all about? A man can't help being curious—"

"I'm sure," Novak said. He slid his window up, swung around, and drove back out to the highway.

Well, I thought. Didn't I see it coming? Didn't I know Faith was trouble the minute I laid eyes on him?

I waited a couple of minutes to make sure Novak didn't decide to come back. Then I took out my passkey and headed for cabin six.

Storm Carey

WHEN NEAL WAS alive we almost always ate breakfast on the sun porch, no matter what the weather. The upper halves of the three outer walls are glass, with panels that slide open to let in air and garden fragrance, and you can look down the sloping rear lawn to the lakefront and the white finger of our dock, north to the sloughs, east all along the sharp, shadowed folds of the hills, brown now with their dark-green spottings of oak and madrone, south down the lake's thirty-mile length as far as Kahbel Shores at the foot of Mt. Kahbel. A lordly view, Neal called it. Lord and lady of the manor, surveying their domain.

But the lord is dead and the lady is a tramp, and I seldom eat on the porch anymore, or even go out there. This morning, however, I felt drawn to it. I sat at the rosewood table and drank my coffee and ate my two pieces of toast and surveyed what was left of the domain and thought about Neal. He'd been warm in my thoughts when I'd awakened, almost as if he were still alive, as if he'd gotten up before me and was waiting on the porch for me to join him. Some mornings it's like that, the feeling that he's still here with me so acute I actually believe it for a minute or two. But, of course, the illusion soon fades and again becomes unbearable loss—a cramping deep inside like severe menstrual cramps, or what I imagine childbirth would have been if we'd ever managed to conceive. Then that, too, fades and I'm able to get up, shower, dress, do all the things that begin another day, that lead to another night.

The bed was a mess this morning, the sheets stained and even torn in one place, smelling rankly of the Hunger. Him, too, last night's fodder for the voracious mouth. Here for two or three hours, and then gone again in the early-morning darkness. Night phantom, incubus. Strange, but when I closed my eyes I couldn't picture his face or remember his name, even though I know him as well as I know anyone in Pomo, even though he's been in my bed before. Instead, it was Neal's face I saw, Neal's lips and hands and body I remembered.

Before I showered I wadded up the sheets and pillowcases and the bathroom towel he'd used and took them out to the garbage. The girl would be in to clean today and she would remake the bed, but I didn't want her to have to handle the Hunger's dirty leavings. Some more residue of propriety, I supposed. And a pathetic residue at that: I seem to care more about a cleaning woman's feelings than I do about my own.

So I sat alone on the porch and watched the clouds race across the sky, creating patterns of light and shadow on the lake's surface, on the brown and dark-green hills, and drank more coffee to ease the dull hangover pain behind my eyes, and thought about Neal. The first night we'd met, at the party to celebrate the opening of a new winery in the Alexander Valley: the shy daughter of a Ukiah farmer and the handsome real-estate developer with hair that was already starting to silver even though he was only a dozen years older than my twenty-three. The first time we went to bed, and how patient he was with me . . . the evening at the Top of the Mark in San Francisco when he asked me to marry him . . . the month-long honeymoon cruise in the Caribbean . . . the day this house he'd built for us was finished and the way we'd celebrated, naked in bed, drinking Mumm's, pouring it on each other's body and then licking it off . . .

Those, and so many more memories. But I wasn't allowed to be alone with them this morning. Other thoughts intruded, another face appeared in my mind's eye—not the face of last night's incubus but the ugly visage of John Faith. An effort to block it out did no good; instead it was Neal's image that blurred and turned to shadow and faded away.

The Hunger wasn't satisfied. I'd known it in the shower earlier, when the mouth began to stir again inside me. For some reason it still wanted John Faith. Another surrogate like all the others, another incubus . . . or was he? The Hunger seemed to sense a difference, something to do with the part that remained hidden from me. It wanted Faith—that was enough for me to know now.

It wanted him and so I would have to find a way to feed it what it craved.

I left the porch, the lordly view, the warm memories of Neal, everything that had once meant something, and went to do the Hunger's bidding.

Audrey Sixkiller

I KEPT BLANKING out on my class notes, on what the kids were saying and doing. Usually I have no problem maintaining order in my classes; today I couldn't even maintain order in my own mind. The prowler last night had shaken me more than I cared to admit. That, and not being able to reach Dick until after three, and then not being able to sleep again after he left. Zombie woman. I probably shouldn't have come to school at all, but at dawn it had seemed more important not to give in to the anxiety, to plunge right back into my normal routine. Now I wasn't so sure.

Well, I could still take the afternoon off. Hang on until noon, then go home and regroup in private.

I wondered if Dick had found out anything. Chances were he hadn't. He'd said he would have a talk with John Faith, but if the man was guilty he would hardly admit it; all Dick could do, really, was to try to scare him into leaving Pomo County and not coming back. And if he was innocent, there was nothing to point to anyone else. Dick had come back this morning, a while before I left for school, and searched my yard and the neighboring yard and hadn't found even a scrap of evidence. He'd tried to convince me that the shot I fired would keep the intruder, whoever he was, from trying it again, but we both knew that wasn't necessarily true. Being shot at could just as well make a would-be rapist even more determined to finish what he'd started.

Dick worried me, too. His concern had been genuine but he'd seemed remote, as if other things were weighing heavily on his mind. All he'd say when I asked where he'd been so late was that he couldn't sleep and had gone for a long drive around the lake. He suffered from insomnia—Verne Erickson once told me it started after his wife left him—and quite a few insomniacs are night riders, but he'd never admitted before to being one of those. There was so much about him I knew little or nothing about.

Yes, and a few things I did know and wished I didn't. I couldn't help wondering if he was seeing Storm Carey again, if that was where he'd really been last night . . .

Giggle. Giggle, giggle.

The sounds penetrated, and all at once I realized the entire class—my ten o'clock, California History II—was staring at me. I'd been sitting there God knew how long, lost inside myself. The expressions on their faces told me what they'd be saying to their friends later on. "Wow, Ms. Sixkiller went brain-dead for a little while this morning." Or "It was, like, you know, she lapsed into some kind of Indian trance thing."

I cleared my throat. "Okay. Where were we?"

"We were right here," Anthony Munoz said. "Where were you?"

That broke them up. I laughed with them; you don't get anywhere with kids nowadays by being either authoritarian or humorless, a lesson a couple of Pomo High's other teachers have yet to learn. And Anthony was the class clown, a leader the others followed. A poor student, barely passing, and a sometime troublemaker, particularly when he was around his older brother. Mateo was a bad influence—drugs, antiauthority behavior, Attitude with a capital A. He'd been expelled two years ago when another teacher and I caught him using cocaine inside the school. Anthony looked up to him; it troubled me that he might be led in the same direction, drop out or get himself expelled, too, one of these days. Underneath, Anthony wasn't a bad kid. All he needed was to use common sense and develop a purpose in his life, one that would settle him down. Meanwhile, you had to walk a very careful line with him.

I glanced at my notes. "Upper California under Spanish rule, right? Established as a province of the newly established Mexican republic. What year was that, Anthony?"

"What year was what?"

"That California became a province of Mexico."

"Who knows, man?"

"And who cares, right?"

A little more laughter.

"Well, I do," I said. "And you should too, *un poco*. Come on, Anthony. What year did California become a Mexican province?"

"I dunno."

Better, not quite as smart-ass. "I'll give you a hint. It was twenty years after it became a province of Spain."

"Yeah? What year was that?"

"1804. You can add twenty and four, can't you?"

He scowled at me. But then his girlfriend, Trisha Marx, leaned over and poked his arm and said, "Yeah, Anthony, twenty plus four equals fifty-three, right?" Everybody laughed again. Anthony decided to laugh with them. He said, "No, fifty-seven, you dumb Angla," and there was more laughter and then they settled down.

I treated them to a five-minute monologue on the period 1824 to 1844, the political turbulence that sprang up then and its root causes: anticlericalism, separatist sentiment, dissatisfaction with Mexican rule, demands for secularization of the missions. I was defining secularization for them—the smarter ones were taking notes, those like Anthony looking bored and getting ready to bolt—when the bell rang.

I reminded them of the reading assignment for next week and let them go. The room emptied in the usual jostling, noisy rush. I was arranging my notes for my next class when a tentative voice spoke my name.

Trisha Marx, alone and looking nervous. A bright girl, Trisha; if she applied herself, her grades would be much better and she'd have a more promising future than most kids in Pomo. But she'd fallen under Anthony Munoz's spell, begun hanging out with him and his brother and their crowd, skirting the edges of real trouble. She needed the same thing Anthony did: a settling purpose in her life. I liked her and I hoped for her. In some ways she reminded me of myself at her age.

"Yes, Trisha?"

"You suppose I could . . . well . . ."

"Yes?"

". . . Like, talk to you about something?"

"Class work?"

"No. It's, you know, personal."

"Important?"

"Kind of, yeah."

"Of course we can talk. But I have another class . . ."

"I don't mean now. Later. I've got something to do first."

"Well, I'm thinking of playing hooky this afternoon. And you know where I live. Why don't you come by my house and we can talk there?"

"Um, when?"

"After school. Say around four?"

"I don't know," she said, "maybe it'd be better if I do what I have to tonight, instead of . . . um, yeah, it would be." She nibbled dark-red lipstick off her lower lip. "Would it be okay . . . tomorrow morning? Could I come by then?"

"If it's early, by nine. I have a tribal council meeting at the Elem rancheria at eleven."

"I'll be there before nine. I . . . thanks, Ms. Sixkiller." And she hurried out, clutching her books.

Now, what was that all about?

But even as other kids began to drift in for my next class, my mind shifted back to Dick's absence last night. I wanted to believe he wouldn't be foolish enough to take up with Storm Carey again, but I knew men well enough to understand that once bitten, twice shy was an axiom that didn't always apply. If she crooked her finger in the right way, waggled her tail on a night when he was feeling lonesome . . . yes, it was very possible he'd go running to her. If he *was* seeing her again, how could I hope to compete? I could be just as good in bed, but a man couldn't tell it by looking at me. One sideways glance at Storm Carey and he'd know it instantly.

I thought wryly of the old Pomo stories about the bear people, men and women who had the power to transform themselves and to go prowling at night in their hides and cloaks of feathers. They were fierce defenders of their territory; when they encountered interlopers, others like them or spooks such as the *walépu*, tremendous battles were fought using magic powers, great leaps into the air, bellows so loud they caused landslides, eardrum-shattering shrieks and whistles—whatever it took to intimidate and then to vanquish or destroy their rivals.

Too bad I couldn't be one of the bear people and have their powers for just one night . . .

Zenna Wilson

NO MORE THAN a minute after Stephanie and Kitty Waylon left for school I happened to walk out onto the front porch, to trim the hanging fern as I'd been meaning to do for days. If I hadn't gone out there . . . well, I don't dare let myself think about *that*. Thank the Lord I did go out.

He was there on the street, the bogey who'd scared me half to death in Treynor's Hardware. Driving by our house in a disreputable old sports car, the window rolled down, inching along with his ugly face turned my way, staring first at the house, and then, as he passed it, staring at the girls skipping along the sidewalk, Steffie bundled in her cute fur-trimmed parka and Kitty wearing that tattered old brown thing her mother lets her out in public in. And the smile on his dirty mouth was nothing short of lewd.

I nearly had a seizure. By the time I raced down the steps and across the lawn I was gasping for breath and all I could manage was a weak shout that not even the girls heard. I don't know if he saw me or not. He probably did, because he kept on going into the next block, though he didn't bother to speed up so much as a hair. And he was still watching Stephanie and Kitty in his mirror—I swear I could see the tilt of his head through the back window.

The girls didn't know what was going on, poor things, when I ran up all excited and out of breath and hugged them both. I didn't want to scare them, so I made myself calm down before I asked, "Did that man say anything to you? Anything at all?"

They both said, "*What* man?" They hadn't even noticed him!

I made them come back to the house with me and get in the car, and I drove them to school. It would've been sheer madness to let them walk with that intruder still around somewhere. He may not have said anything, but the way he'd been looking, and that lewd smile on his wicked face . . . well. I warned Stephanie again to beware of strangers, to never, ever, under any circumstances, let any strange man come near her and especially not a big ugly one driving an old red sports car. I warned Kitty, too, no doubt the first time the child had ever had such good sense put into her head, Linda Waylon being the kind of woman *she* is, off in a fog half the time and forever chattering nonsense the whole time she does my hair.

Well, I was still in a state when I got back from the school. There was no sign of *him*, but I didn't let that stop me, not after what I'd seen, what might've happened if I hadn't gone out on the porch when I did. I called the police right away. Chief Novak wasn't in, so I had to talk to a female officer, Della Feldman, and I didn't mince words with her. The police weren't the only ones I called, either. People have a right to know when there's a threat in their midst. I'd be a sorry soldier in God's Christian army if I kept silent, wouldn't I?

Richard Novak

I FINALLY TRACKED down John Faith a little after ten o'clock. At the one place in Pomo I least expected to find him—Cypress Hill Cemetery.

I'd been all through town, half around the lake, and just missed him twice—once at the Northlake Cafe, where he'd had a late breakfast while I was out talking to Harry Richmond, and once on Redbud Street. Della Feldman, the day sergeant in charge, had had a frantic call from Zenna Wilson, who claimed Faith had been stalking her daughter and a playmate on their way to school. The Wilson woman was a nuisance and a wolf-crier, and the claim was likely another of her hysterical fantasies; still, after the prowler at Audrey's home last night, I wasn't about to treat any report of suspicious activity lightly.

But there was no sign of Faith or his Porsche in the Redbud neighborhood, and that frustrated me even more. I had no real reason to suspect the man of any wrongdoing, just the vague uneasiness he'd stirred in me yesterday, but there was a slippery, secretive quality to the way he kept moving around town, one place to another with no apparent motive. I should've gone out to Lakeside Resort as soon as I left Audrey's the first time, rousted him out of bed, and to hell with protocol and a natural reluctance to hassle a man without provocation. But instead I'd gone to the station, given Verne Erickson the Porsche's license number, and had him start a computer background check on Faith—find out if he was wanted for anything, if he had a criminal record of any kind.

I'd told Verne about the attempted break-in at Audrey's and asked him to keep quiet about it for the time being. There was no sense in inciting fear of night prowlers and masked rapists. Zenna Wilson was a perfect example of why things like this needed to be kept under wraps until, if, and when it presented a public threat. Then, as tired as I was, I'd managed a couple of hours' sleep on my office couch. Long, bad night. Half a pot of coffee and some breakfast at Nelson's Diner, after which I wasted another half hour looking around Audrey's yard and the cottage next door. And after that, Faith kept eluding me—until, as I was passing by on my way back from Redbud, I spotted his Porsche in the parking area just inside the cemetery gates.

I turned around and drove in and parked next to the Porsche. Faith wasn't inside, or anywhere in the vicinity, and I didn't see him on the narrow roads that led up into the older sections of Cypress Hill. But with all the trees and hillside hollows you can't see much more than half the grounds from below.

The Porsche wasn't locked. I opened the door, bent for a look inside. An old army blanket on the backseat, a plastic bag full of trash on the floor in front of the passenger bucket—that was all. I leaned across to depress the button on the glove compartment. Owner's manual, a packet of maps bound with a rubber band, two unopened packages of licorice drops. And under the maps, the car's registration slip. John Faith, street address in L.A. proper; the registration was current and had been issued eighteen months ago. I made a mental note of the street address, put the slip back where I'd found it, closed the box, and leaned back out.

"Finding everything all right, Officer?"

He was propped against one of the cypress trees about thirty feet away, in a patch of the pale sunlight that had come out a while ago. One corner of his mouth was curved upward—a smile that wasn't a smile, just a sardonic twisting of the lips.

"More or less," I said. "You mind, Mr. Faith?"

"Would it matter if I did?"

"It might."

"Sure. Release lever's on the left there, if you want to check inside the trunk, too. Nothing in there except a spare tire, some tools, and an emergency flashlight, but don't take my word for it. Go ahead and look for yourself."

"I think I will."

I yanked the release, went up front, and peered into the shallow trunk compartment. Spare tire, some tools, an emergency lantern. Nothing else.

He came over to stand next to me as I shut the lid. "Mind telling me what you're looking for?"

"What would you say if I told you a ski mask?"

"A ski mask. Uh-huh. I guess I'd tell you I don't ski. Couldn't if I wanted to in country like this, since there aren't any mountains and not even a flake of snow on the ground."

"Where were you between midnight and two A.M.?"

"In bed, asleep."

"Not according to the owner of the Lakeside Resort. He says he was awake at twelve-thirty and you weren't in your cabin."

"Is that right?"

"But you say you were."

"I was. He's either blind or a damn liar."

"Why would he lie?"

"Why would I lie? Somebody wearing a ski mask do something between midnight and two A.M.?"

"Somebody tried to do something. Attempted break-in, possibly with intent to commit rape."

"Yeah? Well, it wasn't me."

"I hope not."

"You have any reason to think it was me?"

"No particular reason."

"Just figured you'd hassle the biggest, ugliest stranger you could find."

"I'm not hassling you. Asking questions, that's all."

He showed me the non-smile again. "Anything else, Chief?"

"Your car registration says you live in Los Angeles," I said. "Pomo is a long way from L.A."

"Pomo's a long way from anywhere."

"Then why'd you come here?"

"Why not? Everybody got to be somewhere."

"Answer the question."

"Yes, sir, Chief. L.A.'s where I used to live. Got to be a town I didn't like anymore, so I pulled up stakes a couple of weeks ago. You might say I'm scouting a new location."

"Pomo?"

He shrugged. "I doubt it."

"What'd you do down in L.A.? For a living, I mean."

"Construction work."

"You won't find much new construction around here. This is a depressed county, in case you haven't noticed."

"I noticed. I'm not interested in a job right now."

"No? Why is that?"

"I made good money down south and I saved enough to treat myself to some time off. I've got about five hundred in my wallet, if you want to see it."

"Why would I want to see your money?"

"Come on, Chief. We both know the difference between transient and vagrant."

"I don't think you're a vagrant."

"Just a prowler and would-be rapist."

That jabbed my temper. "Don't get smart with me."

"Smart?" He spread his hands. "I'm cooperating the best way I know how."

"You do that and we'll get along," I said. "I'm not accusing you of anything, I'm just doing my job the best way *I* know how. You may not believe it, but I try to take people at face value—until I have cause to take them otherwise."

He laughed, a quick, barking sound. "Me too, Chief. Me too."

"A few more questions and you can go on about your business. What were you doing on Redbud Street earlier?"

"Redbud Street?"

"Residential neighborhood not far from here."

"The one with all the trees and older houses? Looking, that's all."

"Why?"

"Seemed like it'd be a nice street to live on."

"It is. Nice and quiet—a family street. Why were you driving so slowly?"

"Can't see much when you drive fast," Faith said. "Somebody call in to complain, Chief? Afraid I might be casing the neighborhood, looking for another house to break into?"

I let it go. He wasn't going to tell me anything more than he already had. "What is it you're after, Mr. Faith? What're you looking for in a new location?"

"Not much. A little peace and quiet."

I waved a hand at the plots and markers uphill. "This kind?"

"I like cemeteries," he said. "Nobody bothers you in one—usually. And you can tell a lot about a place by the kind of graveyard it has."

"What does Cypress Hill tell you about Pomo?"

"That it could've been what I want but isn't."

"Meaning?"

"Just that."

"So you'll be moving on soon."

"Pretty soon."

"Tomorrow? I understand you've paid for another night at the Lakeside."

"That's right. Unless you're going to invite me to leave by sundown tonight."

"I'm not going to invite you to do anything except obey the law. Are you leaving tomorrow?"

"Yes, sir. Tomorrow for sure."

"What're you planning for the rest of today?"

"Nothing different than what I've been doing." Another replay of the non-smile, so brief this time it was like a dim light flicked on and off. "And none of it involves ski masks or forcible entry—houses or women."

"I'm glad to hear it. One piece of advice."

"I'm all ears."

"As long as you're here, keep in mind that citizens in small towns tend to be leery of a stranger who looks too close at them and their surroundings—as if he might have more on his mind than a friendly visit. As if he might actually be a threat. You understand?"

"Oh, I understand, Chief. I hear you loud and clear. I'll do my best not to alarm the good citizens of Pomo while I'm enjoying your fine hospitality."

The sarcasm was just mild enough not to provoke me. I said, "Then we won't need to have another talk, will we?"

"I sure hope not."

I got into the cruiser, still feeling frustrated; the conversation hadn't satisfied me on any level. As I drove out through the gates, Faith was on his way uphill into the older part of the cemetery. And he wasn't looking back.

Douglas Kent

I DIDN'T BELIEVE the Wilson woman's story for a minute, of course. She'd called the *Advocate* before, with complaints about this and that or to offer a juicy hunk of speculative gossip that invariably turned out to be both slanderous and imaginary. Viper-tongued busybody and self-appointed guardian of public morals. Or, in the eloquent phrasing of old Pa Kent, "a fookin' shit-disturber." (Mine papa: bargeman, boozer, brawler, and barroom bard. He'd fallen into the Monongahela half a dozen times, dead drunk; the last time they fished him out, when I was a freshman at Penn State, he was just plain dead. If he'd had time for a final coherent thought before he sank into the depths, I knew exactly what it'd been—the same as mine would be under similar circumstances: "Fook it." Ah, the sins of the father.)

I assured the biddy that I would personally investigate the matter and that the *Advocate* would do whatever it could to keep the citizens and streets of Pomo safe, and hung up before she could fill my ear with any more bullshit. After which I fired a fresh gasper and administered a little more hangover medicine to the Kent insides. Shakier than usual, this A.M. I'd applied so much salve to the old wounds last night that I hadn't even the haziest memory of where I'd gone after staggering out of Gunderson's. Last clear image: Storm with her hand on Bigfoot's thigh, crooning her old black magic into his hairy ear. Woke up this morning on the couch in my living room, my head bulging with the percussive beat of a Pomo Indian ceremonial drum. A hell of a toot, all right. But I'd had provocation. Yes, indeed. Didn't I always?

When the salve began to work its restorative powers, I tucked the bottle into the desk-drawer cranny and leaned back in my chair and closed my eyes. The poisonous Mrs. Wilson's voice echoed faintly in my mind. Her alleged child molester was, of course, Storm's last conquest, the beast who'd wandered in out of the cold. On the hunt for nine-year-old brats after a glorious night of fooking with the Whore of Pomo? Not too bloody likely.

An interesting theory, though. The lumbering hulk with the Frankenstein phiz, an actual monster in monster's disguise? Nice irony there. And what would dear Storm say if she learned that the hands that had groped her fair body were, in fact, bloody claws? Would she be horrified? Sickened enough to change her profligate ways? Kent should live so long. Still, it'd be a cunning little joke on her, would it not? Give her a twinge or two—let her feel what she made me feel. A joy to see her face when she received a different kind of prick than she was used to . . .

An idea began to form in the aching cells and ganglia behind my eyes. I'd promised the biddy the *Advocate* would take up cudgels on behalf of Pomo public safety; well, then, why not do just that? An article written in the usual hard-hitting Kent style: yellow journalism at its most inflammatory. Nothing slanderous; no direct mention of the horse-hung beast, no specific allusion to child molestation or other such nefarious acts. But just enough neatly and thinly veiled references to "strangers in our midst," "drifters of frightening mien and presence," "possible influx into our fair town of the more base criminal element," etc., so that Storm would know exactly who had inspired the piece. Know, and wonder. And then along would come Kent with his little prick: "I hate to tell you this, Storm, but there's a possibility your latest bed partner is, in fact, the worst sort of vicious pervert . . ."

Well, Kent? Do you really want to sink that low?

Does a Sasquatch crap in the woods? Did the old man sink into the depths of the Monongahela?

Ah, but timing was the key. The piece had to run in today's issue in order for it to have the desired impact. Could it still be done?

I took a squint at the wall clock. Ten past ten. The main-section deadline was eight A.M., and the press run usually begins at ten sharp. Today, however, the schedule was off; the *Advocate*'s presses are old and cranky, in spirit not unlike the rag's crusading editor, and they'd been down when Kent staggered into the building a little over an hour ago. Joe Peterson, the pressroom foreman, thought he'd have them ready and rolling by ten, but that estimate obviously had been off by at least ten minutes. The entire building rumbles and rattles when the big Goss press begins its iron-throated roar, and the place had been mercifully quiet unto the present moment.

I got on the horn to the pressroom. Joe was still working on the bugger; his assistant said he thought he'd have it ready to do by tenthirty. I told him to tell Joe to hold the press run, that new photographic plates would have to be made of page one and page eight. Hot editorial to be substituted for one of the existing news stories, I said; I was working on it now. He grumbled some but he didn't argue. Kent's word is law in the bowels of the Pomo *Advocate*, if nowhere else. Besides, did anyone in this godforsaken county really give a flying fook if Friday's No-Star Final was a couple of hours late being printed and delivered?

On one corner of my desk were placement dummies for each of the pages in the main news section. I hauled over page one for a quick scan. The usual boring crap; I could dump the entire lot, with the possible exception of the news item on a three-car pileup that had put a local walnut grower out of his misery. I settled on the longest piece, a dull rehash of facts on the upcoming sewer bond issue and its various pros and cons, poorly concocted by Jay Dietrich, the *Advocate*'s young Jimmy Olsen. Twenty column inches, twelve on the front page and the rest on page eight. Kent, a chip off the old cliché of fast-copy newspaper hacks, could knock off twenty column inches in half an hour without breaking a sweat. Twenty-five minutes or less if the immediate reward was another slug of old Doc Beefeater.

All systems go. 'Twas ordained that Pa Kent's boy have his fun with Storm and the Incredible Hulk, else circumstances wouldn't have conspired to make it possible. *No es verdad?*

I fired up the trusty Compaq and set to work. Words flowed from the first sentence; Kent hadn't been this sharp and persuasive, this coherent, in many a moon. Did I feel even a moment's guilt or reluctance? I did not. Hell, I might actually *be* performing a public service here. For all I knew, Storm's latest conquest really was a monster in monster's guise.

Madeline Pearce

I SAW JORDAN today.

Well, no, that's not true. It wasn't Jordan. But he does look like Jordan, the resemblance is quite striking—

No. Stop it now. He doesn't look anything like Jordan. He's a large man, that's all, in the same way Jordan was large. And he startled me, appearing so suddenly from behind the marble obelisk that marks our family plot. The sun was in my eyes—

Yes, and for just a second I thought he was Jordan. I truly did. But only for a moment. Only long enough to say, "Oh! Jordan!"

He stopped and looked at me, and, of course, I realized then that he wasn't really anyone I'd ever known. A large, homely stranger with pale eyes—no, nothing at all like Jordan. Jordan was so handsome, the handsomest man I've ever seen, especially when he was wearing his uniform. Is it any wonder I fell in love with him that summer?

"My name isn't Jordan," he said.

"Oh, I know," I said. "But when you stepped out so suddenly, why, for a moment I thought you were."

"I didn't mean to startle you."

"You didn't, really. That's ours, you know."

"Yours?"

"The Pearce family plot. My father and mother are buried there. And my brother, Tom, and my sister Pauline, and both their spouses. Alice's husband, too. Alice is my older sister. She and I are the only Pearces left now." I smiled at him. "My name is Madeline, but everyone calls me Maddie."

"How are you, Maddie?"

"Oh, I'm fine. I don't believe I've ever seen you before. Are you visiting relatives here, too?"

"In Pomo, you mean?"

"No, *here*. Does your family have a plot in Cypress Hill?"

"I don't have a family," he said. He sounded sad, and I felt sorry for him. Everyone should have a family.

"Visiting a friend, then?" I asked.

"No. I like cemeteries, is all."

"So do I. So lovely and peaceful with all the shade trees and flowers."

"It was more peaceful when I first got here."

"It was? How is that possible?"

"Nobody around. Not that I mind your company."

"That's nice of you, young man. I don't mind yours, either."

He laughed. His laugh was a bit like Jordan's, too, deep-chested and robust. "This part's pretty old," he said. "Can't read the names on some of the stones and markers."

"I find that sad, don't you?"

"Yeah. I do."

"Cypress Hill is more than a century old, you know." I found myself smiling at him again. Such a nice young man. "Even older than me."

"You're not so old, Maddie."

"Seventy-nine."

"Is that right? I'd have said nine or ten years younger."

"Well. You're very gallant."

"Me?" His laugh, this time, had a different pitch. "You're the first person who ever called me that."

"Well, I hope I'm not the last."

"I hope so, too. But I'll bet you are. First and last."

"I come here every week to visit my family," I told him. "Usually Alice drives me, but she had a doctor's appointment today. A neighbor brought me; she's waiting in the car. She wants me to come and live with her."

"Your neighbor?"

"No, my sister. Alice. She thinks I'd be better off, because I'm getting on, but I'm not sure I would be. I can't make up my mind. I've lived alone such a long time."

"Widow?"

"Oh, no. I've never been married. Once I nearly was, but . . . God has His reasons."

"Was it Jordan you almost married?"

"Yes, it was. How did you know?"

"What kept it from happening?"

"He went away. He was a soldier, and he went away to Korea. He promised he'd come back and we'd be married, but he never did."

"Killed over there?"

"I don't believe so, no. Someone would have sent word if he'd been killed. For years I was certain he'd come and things would be the same as they were before he went away. But he didn't." I sighed and looked past him at the sky. Most of the clouds were gone; it was going to be a lovely day. "It was all such a long time ago, Jordan."

"I'm not Jordan. My name is John."

"John. You know, John, you don't look anything like him. Except for a moment, when I first saw you."

He didn't speak for quite some time, and then when he did he said the oddest thing.

"I'll tell you something, Maddie," he said. "If this were fifty years ago and I were Jordan, I'd have kept the promise he made. I'd've come back and married you. Then you wouldn't have had to live alone all those years."

We parted after that, but on the way home I thought about him and the odd thing he'd said. He *isn't* Jordan, he's nothing at all like Jordan except for his robust laugh, but I don't know how I could have thought he was homely and that his eyes were strange. Actually, he was rather good-looking. Not nearly as handsome as Jordan, of course, but in his own way quite an attractive young man.

I told all of this to Alice when she called after her doctor's appointment. "Oh, Maddie," she said, "I think it's time you came to live with me. Honestly, it's time."

I've made up my mind. I think so, too.

Earle Banner

I CAME HOME from Stan's Auto Body fifteen minutes early, and Lori wasn't there. No sign of her, no note, nothing fixed in the kitchen even though I'd told her I might be home for lunch. Testing her, and she'd flunked again. How stupid does she think I am?

Wouldn't be surprised if she was out screwing that big bastard she was pawing in the Northlake last night. Two of 'em laughing together like they were old pals, her with her hand on his arm, and everybody in the place looking and whispering. Her and him whispering before that . . . making plans for today? Son of a bitch wanders into town and she's all over him like a bad rash. She likes 'em big, big all over. Big horse with a cock to match. Just right for a cheating little mare in heat.

Sometimes, Christ, I think I oughta just shoot her. Let her have one in the head with my .38, put her out of her misery. That movie I seen once, the one about the dance contest back in the thirties, guy who wrote that had it right. They shoot horses, don't they?

Lying to me, all the time lying. Wasn't what it looked like, Earle. Nothing between me and him or anybody else, Earle. Why won't you believe me, Earle. Lies. Lies and horseshit. Why do I keep letting her do it to me? I don't love her no more. Good lay, but the world's full of good lays. Why don't I walk? I oughta walk. Oughta've smashed her lying mouth again last night and then walked, but no, I let her whine and plead me right out of it. Don't hit me, Earle, you promised you wouldn't hit me anymore. Like it's *my* fault. Like I'm the one playing around all the time. Once in a while, sure, a man don't let a chance for some strange tail pass him by when it wiggles right up and begs for it. Storm Carey—oh, yeah! Gave that high-and-mighty bitch what she was begging for. Somebody oughta give her what else she's begging for, smash *her* high-and-mighty mouth for her. Women. Lousy, lying bitches. Better not hit me anymore, Earle, I won't stand for you hitting me anymore. Yeah? But I'm supposed to stand for her spreading her legs for every big bastard comes along. Well, I had enough, too. Man can only take so much—

Here she comes. Damn little Jap car of hers sounds like a washing machine, hear it coming half a mile away. I hate that crappy Jap car. Why the hell wouldn't she listen to me and buy American like I told her? Push that friggin' car off a cliff someday. Yeah, and maybe with her in it.

I went into the living room and stood there so she'd see me soon as she walked in. She almost dropped the grocery sack she was carrying. Her eyes got wide and scared. Good. I liked that. I liked it just fine.

"Earle," she said.

"Didn't expect to see me, did you?"

"Well, you said you might be home for lunch—"

"But you took a chance I wouldn't be."

"A chance? I don't know what—"

"You know what, all right. You know what."

"Earle, please don't be mad."

"How was it, baby? Huh?"

"How was what? Safeway? That's where I've been, I had to pick up a few things—"

"I know what you picked up. That big, ugly bastard and his horse cock, that's what you went out and picked up."

"Oh God! I swear I was at *Safeway*. Go down and ask Sally Smith, she was my checker, she'll tell you—"

"Lie to me, you mean. All you bitches lie for each other. You think I don't know how it is?"

"I've never cheated on you, Earle. Never, not even once. Listen to me, honey, please—"

"I'm through listening, you damn cheap little whore."

"Stop it! Stop it!"

I stopped it, all right. I stopped it with my fist smack in her lying mouth.

George Petrie

THE WAY OUT occurred to me right after lunch. At least that was when I was first conscious of it. It may have been there all along, planted days ago or even longer, hidden and growing under all the pressures piling up and rotting inside my head like a compost heap. Taking seed and finally poking up like a little green shoot into the light.

When I saw it I was thinking again about the stranger, John Faith. I hadn't thought about much else all day, hadn't done much work. Every time the doors opened I expected it to be him. He hadn't showed yet, but he didn't have to walk in waving a gun during business hours. He could be cleverer than that. Usually I arrive each morning half an hour before Fred and Arlene, enter through the rear door from the parking lot; it wouldn't be difficult for Faith to find that out, lie in wait for me some morning. Or worse, come right to the house and take me hostage there. Either way, he could force me to let him into the bank, empty the vault when the time lock released, shut me inside, and be long gone by the time anyone found me.

Did he have any idea how much cash we keep on hand for a small-town bank? Quite a lot. Must be around $200,000 in the vault right now. Some of the bills are marked, and we keep a record of the serial numbers; we also have one of those indelible red-dye packets. But if Faith is a professional thief, he'll know ways to avoid traps like that. All that money, $200,000 in cash—his to spend, free and clear.

Unless somebody else took it first.

And there it was, the way out: Unless *I* took it first.

The idea is absolutely terrifying. But it also excites me. Danger-ous . . . yet not any more so than taking the seven thousand. And not any more frightening than the prison sentence I'm already facing. It's my one and only chance at escape, freedom, the brass ring. No more Ramona, no more Pomo, no more worries. And $200,000 in tax-free, spendable cash!

But if I did dare to take it, where would I go? You can travel any-where in the world on that much money, to someplace that doesn't have an extradition treaty with the U.S. All you need is a passport. And I don't have one. Forever dreaming of far-off, exotic places, but I'd never been to any of them, couldn't afford it on my salary. I've never been anywhere. Forty-seven years old, lived my entire life in this town, never been any farther from it than Las Vegas.

I can't take the chance on waiting anywhere near the three or four weeks it takes for a passport application to be processed. And even if I could, even if I was able to leave the country myself, how would I get the money out? Airport security at both ends, no matter what the destination; carry-on and checked baggage inspection on international flights because of the terrorism threat. And I couldn't risk entrusting that much cash to the mails or one of the air-freight companies. If I had enough time I could convert it to bearer bonds or arrange for a wire transfer . . . Christ, what's the use in thinking about what can't be done? If I'm going to take the money, it has to be right away, before something happens or I lose what little nerve I have. Tonight, Friday night. Before I close the vault and set the time lock for nine-thirty Monday morning. Give me two and a half days to get far away from Pomo—

To where, damnit? Where can I go in this country that the FBI wouldn't be able to track me down, sooner or later?

Forget it. Demented idea. You'd never get away with it.

Maybe I could. If I were very careful about where I went, how and when and where I spent the money . . . maybe I *could* beat the odds.

I couldn't get it out of my mind. Prison is death, but so is Pomo, and all that cash is life. My last chance to live, really live. It was almost as if I were entitled to the money, as if it were mine already by right of custodianship. Mine, nobody else's.

I wanted that $200,000 so badly, the hunger for it gave me an erection. Sitting there at my desk with a hard-on, wondering if I really did have the balls that went with it . . .

Richard Novak

THE BACKGROUND CHECK on John Faith didn't satisfy me any more than my talk with him at the cemetery had. On the one hand, there were enough facts to provide a clearer picture of him. On the other hand, the details were sketchy and superficial and open to all sorts of interpretation.

Faith was his real name—John Charles Faith. Born in Indianapolis thirty-eight years ago, orphaned at an early age, no family other than his deceased parents. Grew up in a series of foster homes, ran away from the last one at age sixteen. Married once, for six months, a dozen years ago in Dallas; no children. No military service. Spotty employment record, mostly construction work, in a dozen midwestern, southwestern, and western states; the longest he'd held any job was sixteen months. No credit history: He'd never applied for credit cards or a home or automobile loan. Arrested seven times in seven different cities and towns for brawling, public drunkenness, public nuisance, the last more than five years ago; two convictions, thirty days' sentence on each. Arrested once in Mesa, Arizona, on a charge of aggravated assault that was later dropped. No known criminal activities, associates, or links. No outstanding warrants of any kind.

Some citizens—Zenna Wilson, for instance—would look at that background and find plenty of fuel for ominous speculation. I looked at it and saw little to indicate he was much of a threat to the community at large. Unless he'd come here for a specific purpose, some sort of strong-arm action, maybe . . . but that was city stuff, L.A. stuff. What was there in Pomo to attract a ham-fisted urban tough? *Who* was there in Pomo to attract one? Then there was the fact that he was smarter than your average street thug. No formal education, streetwise enough, but there was a sharp intelligence behind that scarred face and bitter smile. Cunning, too? Some kind of wise-guy agenda?

Looking for peace and quiet, he'd said. He hadn't had much of that the past two days, yet he was still here and planning to stay another night. Why?

What did he really want in or from Pomo?

Storm Carey

HARRY RICHMOND TELEPHONED, finally, at two-fifteen. "He just pulled in, Mrs. Carey."

"I'll be right over."

"You want me to tell him you're on the way?"

"No. Not unless he tries to leave again before I arrive."

"Anything you say, Mrs. Carey."

Anything for twenty dollars; that was what I'd paid him earlier to keep an eye out and make the call. I hung up without saying good-bye and hurried out to the BMW.

The distance from my house across the Northlake Cutoff to Harry Richmond's resort is a little better than five miles; I drove too fast and was there in under ten minutes. Richmond was on the office stoop, waiting. He came down the steps to meet me as I stepped out of the car.

"Still here," he said.

"Which cabin?"

He didn't answer immediately. Leer on his fat lips and his eyes fondling my breasts. His tongue appeared like a pink slug wiggling out of a hole, flicking from side to side as if he were imagining my nipples and how they would taste. Imagine was all he would ever do. A sleaze-ball, Mr. Richmond. Soft-bellied, dirty-minded, and money-grubbing. The Hunger wanted nothing to do with men like him, thank God.

"I asked you which cabin, please."

"Six. His car's parked in front. Have fun, now."

I took my eyes off him. The only way to deal with the Harry Richmonds of the world is to deny their existence whenever possible—and let them know you're doing it. I detoured around him and along the side of the office building into the central courtyard. I could feel him watching me, the crawl of his gaze on my buttocks; the Hunger and I pretended his eyes were hands and that the hands belonged to John Faith.

Faith's mode of transportation suited him perfectly: battered and scarred, powerful, a ride that would be fast and exciting and not a little dangerous. The comparison put a smile on my face as I stepped onto the tiny porch. But I wiped it off before I knocked; I wanted him to see a different Storm Carey this afternoon, serious and sober and just a touch contrite.

He was surprised when he opened the door, but it lasted for only a second or two. Then his expression reshaped into a faint upturning of his lips, lopsided and sardonic. "Well, well," he said. "Storm, isn't it?"

He seemed even bigger in the daylight. Bigger and uglier, with those pale eyes and facial scars. His shirt was off; hair grew in thick tufts on his chest, black flecked with gray, and underneath it muscles and sinews rippled, flowed, like a deadly undertow beneath a calm surface. Frightening and compelling at the same time. Touch him and you might be hurt, but that only made you want to touch him more.

The mouth, the nibbling lips began to move again inside me. "Yes. Storm Carey."

"What do you want, Mrs. Carey?"

"I told you last night, I'm not married."

"So you did."

"Do you mind if I come in?"

"Pretty small, these cabins. Not much inside except a bed, and I don't feel much like lying down."

"That isn't why I'm here," I said.

"No?"

"No. I came to apologize. I shouldn't have come on to you the way I did. I'm not usually so brazen."

"Only when you drink too much, is that it?"

"I had too many martinis, yes. There are reasons, but I won't bore you with them. The point is, I'm sober today. No gin on my breath, no Paris Nights perfume. Just me."

"Just you. So why're you here?"

"I came to apologize, as I said."

"Why bother? Two strangers in a bar, that's all."

"I didn't want to leave you with the wrong impression."

"That matters to you? What I think?"

"Yes. I really wasn't slumming last night. And I wasn't after a quick lay with the first man who came along."

"Right. But you find big men exciting."

"Not all big men. The other thing I told you is true, too: I like your face."

"That's what booze does to you. Gives you hallucinations."

"I still like it. Cold sober and in broad daylight."

"Sure you do." The words were skeptical, but the pale eyes had softened: He was looking at me in a new way. The way most men look at me, the way the Hunger wanted the chosen ones to look. Not quite convinced yet, holding back, but seeing me as a desirable woman for the first time. The Hunger and I can always tell when a man's testosterone level is on the rise.

"I'm sincere," I lied. "Why else would I be here?"

"All right, you're sincere. I'm flattered."

"Apology accepted, then?"

"Sure, why not. Accepted."

"Well, that's a relief." I smiled. And hesitated just the right length of time before I said, "Suppose we start over in a more civilized fashion. Have dinner together tonight, get acquainted."

"Dinner. You and me."

"Yes."

"Where?"

"Anywhere you like. Gunderson's. Or there's a good Italian restaurant on the south end of town."

"You wouldn't mind being seen in public with me?"

"Why should I mind? Is it really so hard for you to believe that I find you attractive?"

"Not if I stay away from mirrors."

"Oh, come now. You've had your share of women, I'm sure."

"My share. Too many I wish had been somebody else's share."

"I could say the same thing, since my husband died."

"How long ago was that?"

"Six years. I still miss him."

"Yeah."

"I mean it, I do. Were you ever married?"

A long pause before he said, "Once."

"Did you lose her, too?"

"She lost me. She liked gin and one-night stands better than she liked having a husband."

"And that's why you don't care for the smell of gin on a woman's breath. Or casual pickups in cocktail lounges."

"That's why."

"About dinner tonight," I said. "I promise not to drink gin. Or anything else except in moderation."

His eyes moved over my face, a harsh, visual caress that made the Hunger tremble. Then he said, "I don't think I'm up to being stared at in any more public places. Pomo's not the friendliest town I've been in."

"No, it isn't. But you do have a certain . . . presence."

He laughed. "Presence. That's one of the things I've got, all right."

"I could fix us something," I said.

"At your house?"

"At my house. I'm a very good cook."

"Uh-huh."

"If you're reluctant because of last night . . ."

He shrugged; the currents under his mat of chest fur quickened. And the mouth and tongue moved again inside me, nibbling and licking downward.

"You don't have any other plans for this evening?"

"No."

"Nothing better to do?"

"No."

"Come for dinner, then. Or at least for drinks—wine, beer. Or something nonalcoholic, if you prefer."

A few moments while he considered. And then a heightening of the suspense when he said, "Tell you what. Give me your phone number and I'll call you later, let you know if I can make it."

"How much later?"

"By six, if I'm coming. Okay?"

"Yes, fine." I touched his arm, gently. The feel of his skin sent the Hunger into a momentary frenzy. "Please call and please come, John. You don't mind if I call you John?"

"It's my name."

"I really would enjoy your company."

"All right, Storm."

The use of my first name was a good sign, very good. I wrote my address and telephone number on a slip of paper from my purse. He put it into his wallet rather than his pants pocket—another good sign. "Until later," I said, and left him quickly. I could feel his eyes on my buttocks as I walked away—the third and best sign of all.

Out front, as I was opening the BMW's door, Harry Richmond reappeared from under his rock. "That was sure quick, Mrs. Carey." Smarmy, with the leer to underscore the words.

I denied his existence again. I started the car and drove away, the Hunger and I thinking that John Faith would surely call, both of us looking ahead to the evening—but not too far ahead, savoring the suspense and the various possibilities.

It was in my mind to bathe, a long, hot, scented soak in the tub, as soon as I arrived home. But I was forced to delay it because I had a visitor. Doug Kent was sitting on the front porch when I drove up, a martini in one hand, a cigarette burning in the other. Another glass and a half-full pitcher were on the wrought-iron table beside him.

"I took the liberty of making us a batch of Doc Beefeater's favorite home remedy," he said when I came up the stairs. He winked; he was already more than a little drunk, and in one of his crafty moods. "I know where you keep your spare key."

"I'll have to find a new place for it. What do you want, Doug?"

"Want? The pleasure of your company, of course. My good drinking buddy, Storm."

"Not today."

He pretended astonishment. "You don't want a martini?"

"No. I'm off gin for a while."

"I didn't hear that. Sit down and have at least one to be sociable." He patted a folded newspaper on the table next to the pitcher. "I brought you the latest *Advocate*, hot off the press."

"Really, Doug, no. I have things to do."

"Such as?"

"Private things."

"Wouldn't happen to involve Bigfoot, would they?"

"Bigfoot?"

"The strange beast in Gunderson's last night."

"His name is John Faith."

"John Faith. My God."

"Just leave everything on the table when you go. My spare key, too, if you haven't already put it back where you found it." I started past him to the front door.

He put out a restraining hand and said in a voice that was half irritated, half sly, "Better read my editorial, dear heart. Front page. Very edifying—one of my more provocative pieces, if I do say so myself."

I might have gone on inside without responding; he can be exasperating at times. But he was holding the paper out toward me now and I didn't like the expectant shine in his eyes. I took the paper and shook it open.

The editorial was at the top of the front page, under the headline STRANGERS IN OUR MIDST. "It has come to the attention of the *Advocate* that a new breed of visitor is on the prowl on the quiet streets and byways of Pomo. Not the benign vacationer and fisherman who are the lifeblood of our community, but a less wholesome variety of outsider—denizens of the urban jungle whose motives are at best shadowy and whose continued presence invites concern for public safety . . ." The rest of it was in the same inflammatory vein. And there was no mistaking the personal references toward the end, or the malicious intent behind them.

Doug was grinning at me when I finished reading. I threw the paper at him; it hit his arm and spilled some of his drink.

"You son of a bitch," I said.

"Now, now, don't be nasty—"

"Nasty! What's the idea of writing crap like this?"

"To make the public aware of potential—"

"Bullshit. You did it to get back at me."

"Why would I want to get back at you?"

"Because I won't sleep with you. Because you think I slept with John Faith last night and you're jealous. My God, you did everything but name him outright and brand him a homicidal maniac."

"Well, he may be one."

". . . What are you talking about?"

"Seen following two little girls this morning. Stalking them. A pervert and a predator—"

"I don't believe it. Who saw him? Who told you that?"

"I have my sources," he said, but his grin had faded and so had his self-satisfied slyness. "Don't know anything about the man, do you? Except how much of a beast he is in bed—"

"I didn't sleep with him."

"What?"

"I didn't sleep with him, damn you. I tried to pick him up, but he turned me down and walked out. So you've played your vicious little game for nothing."

He drained his glass, reached out to the pitcher, and slopped it full again. His hands weren't steady.

"You're disgusting, Doug," I said. "A disgusting, mean-spirited, irresponsible drunk."

My anger kindled anger in him. "You can't talk to me that way—"

"I'll talk to you any way I choose. That editorial gives me the right. You hate yourself and the whole world, but that's not enough so you take it out on everybody else. Some pretty insufferable bastards live in this town, but I thought you were better than most. Kinder, at least. But you're one of the worst. I don't want anything more to do with you."

"You don't mean that, Storm." Whining now.

"Don't I? Get off my porch and off my property. And don't come back, not for any reason. If you do, I'll call the police and have you arrested for trespassing."

For a few seconds he stared at me without moving. The hate in his eyes was for me now, as well as for himself. Then he guzzled his drink, lurched to his feet, and deliberately smashed the glass on the floor before brushing past me to the stairs, muttering, "Slut. Whore of Pomo."

"That's what it all comes down to, isn't it?" I shut my ears to whatever else he had to say, and went inside to soak away my anger and wait for John Faith's call.

Howard Wilson

ZENNA STARTED IN as soon as I walked in the door. Didn't ask how the Redding trip had gone, didn't give me even a minute of peace. Mouth like a snake's, that woman: Half the time when she opens it, venom comes spewing out. There's an old proverb, or maybe a curse—Buddhist or something—that says gossips and troublemakers and hatemongers are doomed to spend eternity hanging by their tongues. If it's true, a force somewhere already has a noose ready with Zenna's name on it.

She wasn't like that when we first started going together. Or if she was, I didn't see it. Too much in love in those days, or maybe too blinded by testosterone. Good-looking woman and I wanted her badly, but she wouldn't give in, made a lot of whispered promises about how it would be after we were married, and finally I was the one who gave in. And it wasn't worth waiting for. I may've thought so back then, but not anymore. Except for Stephanie . . . but she'd come along too quick, and when the doctor told Zenna she couldn't have any more, that was when she changed or got worse. Poking her nose in everybody's business, yakking about people behind their backs, hunting dirt every place she went and with everybody she dealt with. Self-righteous, holier-than-thou. The worst kind of hypocrite.

More than ten years I've put up with it, mostly for Stephanie's sake. But I work hard, too hard sometimes, and I don't ask for much or want much out of life, and when I can't even get the little I do ask . . . well, every man has his limits. Is it any wonder I've been driven past mine?

No, it isn't. The wonder is that it didn't happen sooner.

". . . tell you, Howard," she was prattling on now, "that man is one of Satan's own. Something terrible will happen if he's allowed to run loose on our streets. You mark my words." Shrill, that voice of hers, like a razor slicing into my eardrums.

"What makes you so sure?" I asked wearily.

"If you'd seen him you wouldn't have to ask that question. He has an evil face. Pure evil."

"Man can't help how he looks."

"Howard, he's been in Pomo two days now. And all he does is drive around in that old car of his, hardly saying a word to anybody. Just *looking*."

"Looking at what?"

"Everything. Our house, this morning. Driving by so slowly he was hardly moving and staring right at our house."

"So? Maybe he likes this kind of old-fashioned style—"

"Oh, for heaven's sake, Howard! That's not it at all. I *know* why he was staring. It gives me chills just thinking about it."

"You figure he's a rapist, I suppose? Hot after housewives?"

"You're not funny, not one little bit. Rape is serious enough, but there are worse crimes."

"Such as?"

"Kidnapping. Child molesting."

"Jesus, Zenna!"

"Blaspheme all you like, but you weren't here and I was. Our house wasn't all he was staring at—he was staring at Stephanie and Kitty Waylon, too. Watching them on their way to school."

She'd been saving that, easing into it for maximum effect; I could tell by the way she said it, with a kind of triumph mixed in with the fearful condemnation. Still, the words gave *me* a chill. I'd lost all love and respect for my wife, but Stephanie . . . I loved that kid more than anything else in the world.

"Are you sure? You weren't just imagining the worst?"

"I was there, wasn't I? I know what I saw. If I hadn't stepped out on the porch just then, the Lord knows what might've happened."

"What did you do?"

"Ran out and got the girls and drove them to school."

"Did he say anything to them? Try to get them into his car?"

"No. They didn't even know he was there."

"What'd he do when you ran out?"

"Drove away. He saw me, that's why."

"Has he been back?"

"No, thank the good Lord. But the police haven't seen fit to do their duty; he's still in town, up to the devil knows what. Claire Bishop saw him less than an hour ago—"

"You called the police?"

"Well, of course I called the police."

"And they said what?"

"What they always say. They'll look into it. But I told you, they haven't done anything—he's still roaming around free."

The edge was off my concern now. I'd been through this kind of thing too often with her—too damn often. Another false alarm, another pot of trouble stirred and boiled for little or no reason. The only danger Stephanie was likely in was from too much exposure to her mother.

I snapped open a beer, drank half before I lowered the can. It didn't take away the sour taste in my mouth. "Made a bunch of other calls, too, I'll bet. All your cronies."

"Cronies? What kind of word is that to use?"

"The mayor? You call him, too?"

"No, I didn't call Mayor Seeley."

"The newspaper?"

That produced one of her tight little smiles. "Yes, I called the *Advocate*. I spoke to Douglas Kent himself. He listened to what I had to say. And *he* did something, at least."

"What did he do?"

"Wrote an editorial," she said, and the triumph was in her voice again—sharper this time, almost savage in its self-satisfaction. She pushed today's issue under my nose. "Right there on the front page. Read it, Howard, then you'll see. Go ahead and read it."

I read it. When I was done, I didn't say a word. Zenna was waiting for me to make some comment, but if I'd opened my mouth I'd have said what I was thinking, and I wasn't ready to do that yet. Soon, but not yet.

I'd have said, "This is why, Zenna, exactly why I've been driven way past my limits." And then, with the same savage triumph in my voice, I'd have told her where I really was and what I was really doing last night when she thought I was sitting alone in a Redding motel room.

Audrey Sixkiller

DICK SAID, "I'M worried about you, Audrey. You sure you're all right?"

It was what I wanted to hear. But I couldn't help thinking: If you're so worried, why didn't you stop by instead of calling? Or at least call earlier?

"Don't I sound all right?" I said. "I'm fine, really."

"Maybe you'd better not stay there alone tonight."

"Where would I go?" *Your house?*

"Stay with a friend."

"I won't be driven out of my home, not even for one night."

"Then ask someone to come and stay with you."

How about you? I almost said it. And at that, what came out was a variation: "Why don't you come over after you're off duty? I'll make something to eat, and we can talk."

". . . I don't know, Audrey. I'd like to, but I'm pretty tired and likely to be here late as it is. You know how Friday nights can be. I don't want to make any promises I can't keep."

Oh, I knew how Friday nights could be. Lonely. And I knew excuses when I heard them, too. I had an impulse to ask him if he was too tired to accept an invitation from Storm Carey, but that would have been senseless and catty. I didn't *know* he was seeing her again. Didn't want to know if he was, not right now.

"Try to make it if you can," I said. "For supper or . . . anytime."

"All right. In any case, I'll have one of the patrols keep an eye on your house."

"Please, Dick, I really do want to see you . . . I need you tonight." Shameless. How much plainer did I have to make it? Four-letter words? Storm Carey plain?

All he said was, "I'll try."

I went into the kitchen and brewed a pot of tea. The old, bitter Elem variety made from pepperwood leaves. William Sixkiller's favorite cure-all for colds, fevers, sores, boils, and general malaise. When it was ready I carried a cup back into the living room. But instead of sitting down, I stood, sipping the tea in front of my memory cabinet.

After William Sixkiller died I gave most of the native artifacts he'd collected—woven sedge baskets, beadwork, bows and arrows, spear points—to the Pomo County museum. But I'd kept a few special items, favorites of mine and his. Looking at them, touching them, made me feel close to him. I slid the glass door open, ran fingers over the blackened bowl of the long pipe he'd carved from wild mahogany and smoked for forty years. He had helped to make the baby basket, too, that had been mine when I was an infant; the beads and bird feathers and other sleep-inducing charms attached to the hoop above the head were still bright after nearly three decades. The elderberry-shoot flute he'd played so sweetly had belonged to his grandfather. Even older was the musical bow made of a willow branch two feet long, with its twin sinew strings and the small stick you struck against the strings while you blew into the hollowed end of the bow; it dated to the days before the white man came, when, according to legend, the People were giants and the blood of the young warrior Kah-bel, slain in a battle over his beloved Lupi-yoma, daughter of powerful Chief Konocti, painted the hills red and Lupiyoma's tears of grief formed the mineral spring called Oma-racharbe.

Wise Father, I thought, what am I going to do?

Well, I knew what he would say if he were beside me now. "Stop this foolish mooning over a white man," he'd say. "Stop your white-acting ways. An Indian woman belongs with her own kind. If you wish to marry, choose a Pomo for your husband, or at least a man from another tribe."

A man like Hector Toms, Father? Handsome young Hector, my first lover. Simple, gentle, one of the finest woodworkers in Pomo County until prejudice cost him three good jobs, one after the other, and bitter-ness and weakness made him turn—as brother Jimmy and so many others had—to alcohol and drugs. When I went away to school at UC Berkeley, Hector had left too, drifted to Sonoma County to pick fruit and then to San Francisco, Los Angeles, Dallas. A string of small and large cities, the new Trail of Tears. By then Native Americans were no longer being relocated to large urban centers by the Bureau of Indian Affairs—a well-intentioned (or was it?) program sponsored by the Eisenhower administration that was supposed to "mainstream" the Indian, end his reliance on Federal aid and benefits by providing employment training and housing in a more "acculturated" environment. Instead it suc-ceeded only in uprooting 200,000 men, women, and children from their cultural and spiritual homes, dropping them into uncaring, alien cities and ultimately forcing some into menial jobs, the unintegrated majority into even more dependence on the government. The new Trail of Tears remained after the mainstreaming program was finally ruled a failure in the mid-seventies; it still remained today. And Hector had drifted onto it and was lost. The last I heard of him, years ago, he was said to be homeless in Chicago, a simple, gentle Elem woodworker with an alcohol and drug dependency living and dying alone on the cold, acculturated streets of a white man's city.

Better off with my own kind? None of us is any better off with our own kind than we are with the white man's kind, it seems. None of us.

And to that William Sixkiller might say, "Then don't marry and bear children of any blood. Spend more time educating the white man's children. Spend more time helping the cause of our people." Yes, Father, except that I want a husband, children, and I already spend so much time teaching and in volunteer work I have little enough left for myself. Five days a week at the high school, adult education courses two evenings, graduate studies toward my master's at Berkeley in the summer; the tribal council, aid and counseling service on the rancheria, one Saturday a month at the Indian Health Center in Santa Rosa. What more can I do?

My tea had cooled. I finished it, put the cup into the kitchen sink, and wandered into the back bedroom that had once belonged to Jimmy, that I had turned into my study. There were themes on the California missions to be corrected; I'd been doing that, with half my mind, when Dick called. I sat down and looked at the top one on the stack. The computer-generated type seemed blurred even after I rubbed at my eyes with a tissue.

Dick Novak isn't the answer, I thought, more teaching and volunteer services aren't the answers. What's the answer?

Maybe there is none, at least not in this life. Live today, live tomorrow when it comes and not before. Events will happen, certain things will change—that's inevitable. Some will be good; some will make you happy, if only for a while. Live for those.

William Sixkiller would approve of that philosophy. His daughter approved of it, too. But William Sixkiller was one of the spirits now and his daughter was still among the living, and the simple truth was, she wanted the white eyes so badly he was an ache in her heart and a fever in her soul . . .

I made an effort to concentrate on the themes. It took an hour to grade them all. Only three were worth more than a generous C, and half a dozen deserved F's and received D's instead. F grades were discouraged by Pomo's civic-minded school board.

Time, then, to take the boat out. I'd been cooped up too long; alone on open water was much better than alone in a box. I was shrugging into my pea jacket when something smacked against the front door. I tensed until I remembered that this was Friday. Paper delivery, later than usual. I went and got it.

Front-page editorial: STRANGERS IN OUR MIDST.

What in God's name is the matter with Douglas Kent? I thought angrily when I finished reading it. He might as well have headed this crap AN INVITATION TO VIOLENCE.

George Petrie

I DID IT.

Oh God, I did it, I took the money!

All afternoon I worried that I wouldn't have enough nerve when the time came, the anxiety building as the bank clock crept toward six. Wasn't until I said good night to Fred and Arlene and locked the rear door behind them that I knew for sure I was going through with it. And then, even while I was doing it, it all seemed to be some kind of waking dream—everything happening in slow motion, real and yet not real. Half of me watching the other half: Empty the vault of every bill except one-dollar notes. Carry the bags to the rear door. Set the time lock and close the vault. Tear up the printed list of serial numbers and flush the scraps down the toilet. Falsify some of the set of numbers on the computer and consign the rest to cyberspace limbo. Unlock the back door, make sure the lot was clear. Carry the bags out two at a time. Relock the door and get into the car. Seemed to take hours; my watch said forty-five minutes. Three quarters of an hour, 2,700 seconds, to steal $200,000.

I'm still sitting here behind the wheel, another three or four minutes gone, waiting for my hands to stop shaking. I need a drink desperately, but I don't dare stop anywhere before I get home. I feel numb, awed. All that money stuffed into six plastic garbage bags, the kind we use in the paper-towel hampers in the bathroom. Garbage bags! I want to laugh, but I'm afraid if I do I won't be able to stop.

Calm, everything depends on remaining calm. Can't stay here much longer . . . suppose a patrol car comes in and the officers see me sitting alone in the dark? Mustn't do anything to call attention to myself, arouse suspicion. If only my hands will steady enough so I can drive. Once I'm home, with a stiff jolt of scotch inside me, I'll be all right. Even if Ramona notices how wired I am, it won't matter. Won't be there long, just long enough to pack. One thing worked out, the story I'll tell her: Have to drive down to Santa Rosa; Harvey Patterson called and the real-estate deal may be on again after all, could mean big money for us, lot of details to be worked out in a hurry so I'll probably be gone all weekend, might even stay over until Monday morning and then drive straight up to open the bank. Maybe she'll believe it and maybe she'll think I'm up to something, but she won't try to stop me. Questions, yes, Ramona the parrot with her bright little bird eyes, but I can handle her questions. She won't tell anybody I'm away for the weekend—I'll swear her to secrecy, claim the real-estate deal has to remain hush-hush for the time being. She'll sulk, but she'll do what I say. I don't have anything to worry about from Ramona.

On the road no later than eight-thirty, out of this damn prison for good. But I won't head south. East. Spend the night somewhere beyond Sacramento, up in the Sierras. Not sure yet where I'll go from there, but I'll have plenty of time to make up my mind. Have to make it as far away from Pomo as possible by Monday morning, that's definite. Means a lot of driving, careful driving with the precious cargo in the trunk, but that can't be helped. I'll manage. Have to get rid of the Buick at some point, but maybe that can wait until I get to wherever I'm going. Some place I can settle in unobtrusively for a long, quiet stay. Change my appearance before I get there, too—dye my hair, buy a pair of glasses. Then rent a house or cabin with no close neighbors, hole up for a month, two months, even longer just to be safe. The FBI investigation has to've been back-burnered by the first of the year. Then I can travel again, go somewhere warm, somewhere exciting, Florida Gold Coast maybe, where I can start spending some of the money. Start living again.

But that's all in the future. First things first. Start the car, drive away from here, drive home. Can't go anywhere without going home first.

Christ, why won't my hands stop shaking?

Trisha Marx

OUT THERE IN the dark, Anthony kept shouting my name. He'd sounded annoyed at first, then kind of exasperated; now he was just pissed. He had a flashlight from the car and he kept shining it here and there over the trees and bushes, trying to find me. But he didn't even come close to where I was hiding under a big pile of dead branches and oak leaves.

"Trish, goddamn it! You better come out, man. I'll leave you here, I mean it, I'll drive off and you can freakin' walk home. That ain't gonna make things any better. Trish? Shit, Trisha!"

The flashlight beam danced and stabbed. It was hard, white, like frozen light, and it kept cutting weird wedges and strips out of the dark—parts of tree trunks and limbs, ferns, rocks, like pieces in the magazine montage on the wall of my room. Don't like all those pieces . . . I'm still stoned. Three joints, *way* too many. Why'd I think it'd be easier to tell him if I smoked some dope first? Stupid. Weirded me out and made him horny. *Come on,* querida, *I'm getting lover's nuts.* Oh yeah? *Come on, Anthony, I'm already pregnant with your kid.* Wham. No more lover's nuts, huh, Anthony?

It ain't mine. I always used a rubber.

At least one time you didn't.

It ain't mine. You been screwing somebody else.

That's the lowest, Anthony. You know better.

I don't want no freakin' kid!

You think I do?

Get rid of it.

No.

You want me to marry you? No way, man.

What happened to "I love you, Trish"? Just bullshit to get into my pants, right?

I ain't getting married. Lose the kid or we're quits.

I knew it. I knew it'd be like this. I knew it!

Slapped him, hard, harder than I ever thought I could hit anybody. And then out of the car, into the woods. And here I am.

"One more minute, Trisha. That's all you got."

Jerking light, pieces of the night. But I couldn't see him at all. Good. I never wanted to see his crappy, lying face again.

"I mean it. One minute and I'm outta here, I'm history."

Fuck you, Anthony. You're already history.

I lay there shivering, waiting for him to go away, get the hell out of my life. The wind up here on the Bluffs was like ice, even down low to the ground where I was. The water in the lake must be like ice, too. Black ice. Deep, black ice.

"Okay! That's the way you want it, man, it's on your head. I'm gone."

The light blinked out. So dark again I couldn't see a thing through the leaves, not even the shapes of the oak branches swaying in the moany wind overhead. But I could hear him crunching around out there, heading back to his junky TransAm. Door slam, revving engine. Light again, spraying the trees, spraying the bare ground out toward the cliff edge as he swung away onto the road. Run, you asshole, go ahead and run. And the light faded away and he was gone and I was alone. Stoned and pregnant and all alone.

He wouldn't come back. If I knew him, he'd go find Mateo and the two of them'd buy some coke or crank and really get whacked. If I knew him . . . only I didn't. I thought I did and how he felt about me, but I was wrong. Wrong, wrong, wrong. My mistake. My kid. All alone.

"I don't care," I said out loud. "Doesn't matter. I don't give a shit about anything anymore."

Then I started to bawl. I couldn't help it. I lay there bawling my head off, with my knees pulled up against my chest, and I couldn't stop—for the longest time I couldn't stop. Couldn't suck in enough air and then I got too much and started to hiccup and then finally I stopped hiccuping and just lay there, tear-wet and cold and empty.

Empty, man.

After a while I crawled out from under the leaves and dead stuff and stood up, all shaky and feeling even more weirded out than before. That wind was really icy. Black ice up here, black ice down in the lake. The open part of the Bluffs was off to my left and I went in that direction, toward the road. Once I tripped over something and fell and skinned my knee, but I didn't care about that either. I wasn't thinking about anything anymore. I felt so empty and weird. When I came out of the trees I saw the road, empty like I was, leading down, but I didn't go that way. Instead I walked out toward the cliff edge. I still wasn't thinking about anything.

Then I was standing right on the edge, where the ground falls away sharp and straight down. Seventy or eighty feet straight down. The wind shoved at me like hands, so hard I could barely keep my balance. Over on the far shore the town lights and house lights winked and shimmered, reflecting off the black ice. Anthony was over there by now, maybe. And

Daddy . . . Oh, God, how could I tell him? He'd have a hemorrhage. I quit looking at the lights and looked straight down instead. Some rocks down there, in among the cottonwoods and willows . . . never mind that. Look at how shiny the black ice is, out away from the shore. Lean forward so you can see better. Heights don't bother me. Deep, black ice doesn't bother me either. I felt so weird. The dope . . . Anthony . . . the baby . . . my trashed life. But I wasn't afraid. Shiny, black ice. Lean out just a little farther—

Noises behind me, quick and close and louder than the wind. And somebody said, "You don't want to do that."

I almost lost my balance turning to look. My foot started to slip. But he was almost on top of me then, a big, black shape that caught my arm and yanked me back and swung me around before he let go. Then he was the one standing at the edge, with his back to it, like a wall that had sprung up there.

"Pretty close call," he said. "You ought to be more careful."

I couldn't see his face too clearly. All I could see was that he was big, real big. My arm hurt where he'd grabbed me.

"Who're you?" My voice sounded funny, like somebody pulling up a rusty nail. "Where'd you come from?"

"I've been up here awhile. Where'd *you* come from? The car that drove off a few minutes ago?"

"Doesn't matter." I was still thinking about black ice, but I didn't feel so spacey anymore. The weed high was starting to wear off. "Why'd you grab me like that?"

"I didn't want you to fall."

"Why should you care?"

"Why shouldn't I? What's your name?"

"Trisha."

"Trisha what?"

"Marx, okay? What's yours?"

"John Faith."

I rubbed my arm. "You're the guy in the Porsche. At the Chevron station yesterday."

"That's right."

"Stranger everybody's talking about." I guess I should've been afraid then, on account of the things people were saying about him, but I wasn't. Not even a little.

He didn't say anything, so I said, "What're you doing up on the Bluffs?"

"Watching the lights."

"What lights?"

"Around the lake."

"By yourself? What for?"

"Safer than spending the evening with an armful of potential trouble."

"Huh?"

"Never mind. You have a fight with your boyfriend?"

"More than a fight. He's not my boyfriend anymore. I hate his guts."

"That's the way you feel now. Tomorrow . . ."

"Tomorrow I'll hate him even more."

"Why? He do something to you?"

"He did something, all right. I wish I could do something to him."

Like cut off his lover's nuts.

"What'd he do, Trisha?"

"He got me pregnant."

I don't know why I told him. A guy I didn't know, a stranger everybody was saying was some kind of criminal. I don't think I could've told Selena straight out like that, and she's my best friend. But I wasn't sorry I told him. It was like spitting out something that was choking you.

"And he doesn't want to marry you, right? That's why he's gone and you're still here."

"Yeah."

"Your parents know yet?"

"No. My mother wouldn't care if she did—she's been gone three years and she didn't even send me a card on my last birthday. Daddy cares, but he'll have a hemorrhage when he finds out."

"Maybe he'll surprise you."

"Doesn't matter anyway," I said. "*I* don't care. About the kid or his asshole father or what happens to me. I just don't give a shit anymore."

"Sure you do. You care, Trisha."

"Oh, right, you know more about me than I do. What makes you so smart?"

"Hurt inside, don't you? Worst pain you've ever felt?"

"No. Yeah. So what if I do?"

"Then you care. People who don't care don't hurt. Think about it. The more you hurt, the more you care."

"I don't want to think about it. All I want is to stop hurting."

"That's what everybody wants. Bottom line. Everybody hurts, everybody wants to stop hurting. Trick is to find a way to do it without hurting anyone else. Or yourself."

"Isn't any way."

"Not for some. But you're young. You'll be all right if you don't let yourself stop caring."

I was shivering again, hard. That wind was really cold. And the high was all gone, and most of the weirdness, and some of the emptiness. I could still see the lake down below, the deep, black ice; then I shook my head and the shiny image went away. I hugged myself.

"How about if I give you a ride home?" John Faith said. "My car's off the road a ways and the heater works good."

Don't ever accept rides from strangers. How many times had *that* been drummed into my head? But I didn't hesitate. He didn't scare me; I wasn't scared of him at all.

I said, "All right," and went with him into the dark.

Zenna Wilson

THE LORD WORKS in mysterious ways, His wonders to perform. For the second time that day He put me in a position to bear witness to the evil in our midst and do something about it.

I had just finished checking the chain and dead-bolt locks on the front door, and was standing by the window, testing its catch, when I heard a car outside. It was noisy, noisy-familiar, and when I parted the drapes I saw the disreputable car of that stranger, John Faith, rattle by and swing to the curb a short distance up the street. The passenger door flew open almost immediately and a young girl jumped out and ran off. It gave me quite a shock. The more so when I recognized Trisha Marx as soon as she passed under the streetlamp over there.

Her house was where she ran to, three north of ours. I expected the bogey to leap out and chase after her, but he didn't. Took him by surprise, no doubt, and he knew he couldn't catch her. In any event, he sat inside with the headlights still on and the engine puffing out exhaust fumes until Trisha disappeared around back. Then he U-turned and drove off the way they'd come.

Another outrage, pure and simple. Had he put his huge, dirty hands on that poor child? Well, he must've tried; otherwise why would she jump out and run home the way she had? She's only seventeen. And poorly taught and plain foolish, I say, to let a man like that get her into his car in the first place.

I hurried into the kitchen. Stephanie was upstairs in her room, working on her papier-mâché animals, and Howard was already in bed even though it was only a little past nine; tired out from his trip and in a snippy mood because of it. A good thing he wasn't down here, or he'd have tried to stop me from calling Trisha's father, which is what I did that very minute. My Howard is a good man, a good provider, but he's too easygoing, too trusting, and he expects me to bury my head in the sand the way he does. But I was born with a mind of my own. Someone has to keep vigil and speak out when the need arises, and I don't see why it shouldn't be me.

Brian Marx was home for a change, not off throwing good money after bad at the Brush Creek Indian Casino like he does most Friday and Saturday nights. He has a gambling problem—gambling is a sin, no matter what the Indians would have us believe; our pastor has spoken out against it on more than one occasion—and that's one of the reasons Trisha is as wild as she is. That mother of hers is another, running off the way she did three years ago. And with a Jew, at that! Anyhow, I told Brian just what I'd seen, without mincing words, and of course he flew into a rage. He said he'd talk to Trisha and find out what happened. He said some other things, too, but I turned a deaf ear to them; Brian Marx has a foul mouth when he's upset or has had too much to drink. I asked him to let me know as soon as he knew the whole story, but he hung up without saying he would or wouldn't and without so much as a thank-you. Not that I blame him for being rude, under the circumstances.

If the bogey did try to attack Trisha, I wonder if Brian will go after him with a gun? He has two or three rifles and a pistol, and he's hot-headed. (A wonder he didn't go after Grace and her Jew when they ran off together.) Vengeance is mine, saith the Lord, but in a case like this, with the police not willing or able to do their job, well, Brian would have every right to do what ought to be done. Yes, and he'd be forgiven at the Judgment, unless I miss my guess.

Well, whatever happens, it's out of my hands now. I've done my duty and the Lord's work not once but twice today. If I don't hear from Brian by morning, I'll call him at home again or at Westside Lumber where he works. I'm entitled, if anyone is, to a full account of that poor girl's ordeal.

Lori Banner

IT WAS ABOUT ten-fifteen when John Faith walked into the North-lake. We weren't busy; eight or nine customers is all. But everybody stopped talking when they saw him, just like last night, only this time the stares were more hostile, and in one booth there was some angry muttering. I was the only one there who didn't wish he was somewhere else, like in jail or lost in the Sahara Desert—and for no good reason.

He walked back to the counter and sat on the last stool nearest the entrance. That was Darlene's station, but when I asked her if I could take him she gave me one of her looks and said, "Better you than me. I'd rather stay away from trouble." She was still miffed; she'd started ragging on me as soon as she saw the new cut and swelling on my lip, and I stood it as long as I could and then told her to shut her face and mind her own business. I didn't need any more lectures. Not tonight, I didn't.

I put on a big smile as I approached John, even though the stretch hurt my lip. Most of it was for him, but partly it was for the customers with the narrow eyes and narrower minds. I wanted them to know there was one person in Pomo who didn't believe all the crap she read in the newspaper.

"Hi there," I said. "Cold night, huh?"

"Not so warm in here, either."

"You shouldn't let 'em get to you."

He shrugged. "Coffee. Black."

"Nothing to eat?"

"I'm not hungry."

I poured a cup and set it in front of him. He took a couple of sips, and when I kept on standing there he said, "World'd be a hell of a lot better place if people quit hurting people and left each other alone."

"Is that a hint for me to go away?"

"No. I didn't mean it that way."

"Editorial's bothering you, huh?"

"Editorial?"

"I wouldn't take it too personally. Doug Kent's a drunk and a jerk and he likes to stir things up."

". . . What're we talking about here?"

"The editorial in this week's *Advocate*. Didn't you see it?"

"No. Something about me?"

"Well, he didn't mention you by name. I think there's a copy around somewhere if you want to read it."

"Pomo, the friendly town that just keeps on giving. No, I don't want to read it. I can imagine what it says."

"So if it wasn't the editorial, what'd you mean about—" I got it then, from the way he was looking at me, and without meaning to I lifted a finger to touch my sore lip. "Oh, this."

"Pretty swollen."

"Not so bad. It just needs some more ice on it."

"That kind of thing happen very often?"

"Why do you want to know?"

"Just asking."

"Well, it's none of your business, John. And anyway, maybe I walked into a door."

"Sure. And maybe you ought to see somebody about it."

"A doctor? For a fat lip?"

"I didn't mean a doctor."

"I know what you meant," I said. "I guess you think I'm pretty dumb, huh? Just another dumb coffee-shop waitress."

"I don't think you're dumb, Lori."

"Well, you're right, I'm not. I didn't have to take this kind of job, you know. I could've been a nurse. That's what I wanted to be—a registered nurse. I almost was, too, and I'd've been a good one. I had nearly all the training."

"What happened?"

"Nothing happened. I quit the program."

"Why?"

I met Earle, that's why. He didn't want me to be a nurse; he didn't like the hours, he said, or the smell of hospitals and medicine, or women in starched, white uniforms. I loved him so much in those days, before the hitting started. I'd have done anything for him in those days, anything he wanted.

"I just quit, that's all." A guy in one of my booths called my name; I pretended I didn't hear. I asked John, "You want a warm-up on your coffee?"

"No, thanks."

I went halfway down the counter and then turned around and came back. "You know something, John?"

"What's that?"

"You were right, what you said before. People ought to stop hurting each other and everybody leave everybody else alone."

"It'll never happen," he said.

"Some of us can make it happen."

"And some of us can't. Not in this lifetime."

I really saw him then, for the first time. How sad he was inside. Big overgrown hunk like him, and inside he was as sad and unhappy as a lost little boy.

Brian Marx

I SHOULDN'T'VE GONE after him the way I did, I guess. But Jesus, Trisha is just a kid. And she had her bedroom door locked and wouldn't open it, wouldn't tell me how she came to be in that bastard's car or where Anthony Munoz was or why *he* hadn't been the one to bring her home—none of it. Too upset; I could hear her bawling in there. I'm no good with girls, I never know how to handle them when they get emotional. Damn Grace for running out on me the way she did. To hell and gone in Kansas City now, married to that union jerk she met down at Kahbel Shores, living the good life, and me stuck here with all the responsibility.

All I knew was what Zenna Wilson told me on the phone, and that had me half nuts, imagining the worst. So finally I ran out and jumped in the pickup and started driving. Lucky for me I didn't think to take my pistol along. Shape I was in, I might've started waving it around when I found Faith and shot him or somebody else by accident, the way it can happen when a man's armed and mad as hell and not thinking straight. Then what'd've happened to Trisha?

It didn't take me long to run him down. I barreled up Main and out along the highway, no reason for going that way except I'd heard he was staying up at Lakeside Resort, and as I was passing the Northlake Cafe I spotted his car in the lot. Parked there big as life—you couldn't mistake a low-slung job like that, in such a beat-up condition. I slammed on the brakes, skidded into the lot, and bulled inside the cafe.

I saw him right off. Sitting alone at the counter, hunched over a cup of coffee. Lori Banner was hovering around near him, saying something as I rushed up, but she quit talking and backed off a step when she saw my face. I'd heard Faith was a big mother, and he was. Hard-looking. But I didn't care right then.

I caught his shoulder and pulled him around on the stool and got down in his face, so close I could've spit on the scar like a dead white worm across his chin. And I said, loud, "What's the idea messing with my daughter?"

It got real quiet in there after that. That sudden quiet like when you mute the volume on the TV. Faith didn't flinch or jerk away. He just scowled up at me. Man, he had eyes like the guy used to play for the Bears, Mike Singletary. Linebacker eyes.

We stayed like that, eye-wrestling, for maybe five seconds. Then he said, "Who the hell're *you*?"

"Brian Marx. I asked you a question, mister."

"Marx. Right. Trisha's father."

"Yeah. What were you doing with her tonight?"

"Bringing her home. She needed a ride, and I gave her one."

"Ride from where?"

"Across the lake. High ground over there."

"The Bluffs? You and her . . . that's a friggin' lover's lane! She's a kid, for Chrissake!"

Everybody in the place was gawking at us. Muttering now, too. A guy behind me said something that sounded like, "Kent was right . . . worse than anybody figured."

Lori said, "Don't make trouble in here, Brian," and I gave her a quick glance. She was one to talk about trouble. Her lower lip was puffed up; Earle had belted her again.

"She's right," Faith said. "Suppose we take this outside."

Before I could say anything he shoved off the stool and brushed past me and walked out. Ignoring me and walking fast, so I had to trail after him like a goddamn dog. That was what made me lose it. I wanted to hit him, bad, and as soon as we were in the parking lot and he turned around,

I went ahead and let him have it. Nailed him under the eye with my right and knocked him on his ass. Some of the others were out there, too, by then, and a guy I didn't know said, "Yeah! Serves the bastard right."

But Faith got up fast, and I set myself because I thought he was gonna bull-rush me. Wrong. All he did was flex his shoulders, then let his meat hooks hang down loose at his sides.

"I won't fight you, Marx."

"What's the matter? Afraid of it?"

"There's no reason to fight. The only thing I did was give your daughter a ride home."

"Says you."

"What does she say?"

"Never mind that. Answer what I asked you before. What were you doing with her on the Bluffs?"

"I wasn't with her. She was there with her boyfriend."

"Yeah? What were you there for?"

"No reason. Driving around, taking in the sights."

The mouthy guy in the bunch said, "Horseshit. Out hunting young girls—"

Faith glared his way and he shut up. Then he said to me, "She had an argument with the boyfriend and went and hid in the woods. He drove off and left her."

"And you found her, huh?"

"If you want to put it like that. I heard him yelling for her, saw her wandering around after he left. She was pretty shaken up. I talked to her, calmed her down, gave her a ride home. That's all."

"If that's all, why'd you stop down the street from my house? Why'd she jump out of your car and run away? You try to put your hands on her?"

"No. Who told you she ran away? Not Trisha."

"Don't matter who told me."

"It matters," he said, "because it's a lie. She didn't run, she walked fast. And I stopped where I did because that's where she told me to stop."

"She locked herself in her room, she was crying . . ."

"I told you, she had a blowup with her boyfriend. Ask her, why don't you? She'll tell you the same thing."

Some of the crazy anger was starting to seep out of me. He was an ugly bugger and I wanted to keep on hating his guts, but I couldn't seem to do it. Didn't sound like he was lying. That damn Zenna, twisting things, making them seem worse than they were . . . I should've known you can't believe half of what she says. And Anthony Munoz, no-good, smart-ass spic . . . driving off and leaving her was just the kind of thing he'd do. How many times had I warned her about him, that he'd get her in hot water someday if she didn't watch out?

Yeah, Faith was telling the truth. He wasn't any coward either. He could've taken me apart anytime he wanted to. I knew it then and everybody else that'd come out of the cafe knew it, too. They all kept their distance, and not even the mouthy guy had anything more to say.

I wasn't yelling anymore when I said, "All right, man. But Trisha better not tell me you did anything but what you said—talked to her and took her straight home. She better not tell me you put so much as a finger on her."

"She won't," Faith said, "because I didn't."

"All right, then. All right."

And that was the end of it. I didn't say I was sorry for popping him, and he didn't ask me to. We didn't say anything more to each other. He went to where Lori was and took a couple of bills out of his wallet and handed them to her. "For the coffee," he said. Then he said, "See? Not in this lifetime," and he walked away to his Porsche and fired it up to a roar and burned rubber all the way out into the street. Pissed. Holding it in check but mad as hell underneath. Yeah, he could've kicked the holy crap out of me if he'd wanted to.

So why hadn't he?

The mouthy guy came up next to me and breathed onions in my face. "Maybe that bastard didn't mess with your kid," he said, "but he's trouble anyway. Big trouble."

"How do you know so much?" Lori said to him. She sounded pissed, too. "He never bothered anybody. All he wants is to be left alone."

"Yeah? What you want to defend him for?"

"What you want to condemn him for?"

"You like his looks, Lori?"

"Better than yours," she said. "His personality, too." And she stormed back inside.

The guy said, "Women." He laid a hand on my arm. "You read the paper tonight? Kent's right. Stranger's up to no good, else what's he hanging around town for?'"

I shrugged his hand off and didn't answer. I was feeling crappy about the whole business, thinking that I shouldn't've chased after Faith the way I did, should've talked to Trisha first. It all left a bad taste in my mouth. Right then it did, anyway.

But as I was driving home I got to thinking that it wasn't *all* my fault. Faith had some blame coming, too. He shouldn't've been hanging around up on the Bluffs at night, not for any reason. He shouldn't be hanging around Pomo, either. Hell, he shouldn't've come here in the first place. Maybe Kent and the mouthy guy were right after all. Maybe this Faith was up to no good. Nasty-looking type like him, with his linebacker eyes . . . yeah.

What else except up to no damn good?

Storm Carey

ALL EVENING I'VE had the strangest feeling. I can't quite define it, except as a kind of . . . waiting. The kind you feel when you know someone is coming to see you, someone you've been expecting for a long time and the arrival is imminent. Anticipation. Not really intense, lacking eagerness, and yet . . . I don't know, I can't describe it. I can only feel it, sense the immediacy.

It isn't John Faith I'm waiting for. At least I don't believe it is. The feeling started after six, after the deadline for his call, and I've heard nothing from him since then. Not coming. Changed his mind. The Hunger and I were disappointed at first, but not as much as we would have been on another night. Now it seems not to matter at all.

Who is it we're waiting for?

One of the other surrogates, incubuses? But none of them have called; there were no casual meetings today, not a word or a smile in the past few days that could be mistaken for invitation or encouragement. And I'm almost always the one to take the initiative, make the arrangements. The Hunger doesn't permit unannounced drop-ins. Anticipation, enough time for the mouth and tongue to indulge their maddening foreplay, is an essential part of its need.

But the anticipation tonight is different. The mouth is closed, the tongue hidden, the lips still. Different and asexual, this waiting.

For what, then?

Soon. The word seems to sing in my mind. *Soon.*

I wander through the house, aimlessly. I haven't eaten since noon, but I have no appetite. Or any interest in alcohol. The house is quiet, almost breathlessly so, as if it, too, is waiting, yet I also have no interest in music or radio or television noise. I prefer the silence. I turn on lights and turn them off again; I prefer the shadows.

Such a strange feeling . . .

In Neal's study I gently run my fingers over the glass-smooth surface of his cherrywood desk, his leather "thinking" chair. I look at the Brueghel prints on the walls, the cabinets filled with his collection of antique snuffboxes and bottles. All just the same as it was when he was here. Carefully preserved: I could never bring myself to change or remove any of it. A kind of shrine—memories of his life. Memento mori— reminders of his death.

I go upstairs to the bedroom we shared, and standing in the darkness I look at the bed I've shared with so many others. Faceless, all of them; it's Neal I see lying there, arms outstretched, beckoning to me. I want to cry, but there are no tears left. I turn away.

Outside in the night, there is the sound of a car. Light flashes across the window curtains as it comes uphill fast.

I hurry to the window, peer out. The car stops in that moment, in the shadow of the big cedar that towers above the garage. Its headlights wink out. No moon tonight, and restless clouds hiding the stars: I can't tell whose car it is, or even if it's one I've seen before. Nor can I quite make out the person who slips quickly through the driver's door.

But I know who it is.

All at once my mind seems to open up like a night flower, and clearly, as if I've been gifted with second sight, I know who is out there and why I've felt so strange and what it is the Hunger and I have been waiting for, not just tonight but the two thousand previous nights. I know exactly what will happen in just a little while. I see the face close to mine, I hear the exchange of harsh words, I feel the outsurge of violent anger wash over me. An arm rises, something glints in soft light, the arm whips down—

Sharp knocking on the front door.

Inside me the mouth is active again, nibbling, licking downward in what quickly grows into a frenzy. More urgent than ever before, with a need so great it is unbearable. But the need is not for sex. The Hunger has never really been sexual at all; I understand that, too, now. From the first it was searching for another kind of release, another kind of fulfillment—*I've* been searching for them, yearning for them ever since Neal left me. Everything I've done in the past six years has been motivated by a single desire that I could neither admit to nor consummate on my own.

I yearn to go where Neal has gone. I ache to join him in the darkness or the light.

The knocking grows louder, more insistent. But I am not afraid; a feeling of peace seems to be settling into me. I smile as I move away from the window. Face the truth, embrace it, and it will set you free.

I make my way downstairs, not quite hurrying, and unlock the door. And I face Death standing there on the other side. And I say, smiling, "Come in."

Richard Novak

I WAS HALFWAY up the drive when John Faith came running out through the front door of Storm's house.

The cruiser's headlights picked out his car first, parked under the tree near the garage, and then him as he tore across the porch and off the stairs in one leap. The lights pinned him as he hit the path. His stride broke and he threw up an arm against the glare, took another couple of faltering steps. I jabbed the switch for the bar flashers, and when they came on, smearing the darkness with swirls of clotted red, he froze in a crouch with one leg bent and his eyes wide and shining, like a trapped animal's.

I put the cruiser into a sliding half turn, jammed on the brakes; the rear end stopped a few inches from the Porsche's, blocking it. My service revolver was in my hand as I got out. He stayed put; the only move he made was to lower the one arm to his side. Past him I could see the front door of the house flung wide open, light spilling out from inside. My stomach kicked over; I could taste bile in the back of my throat.

Storm.

I halted a few paces from Faith, the revolver on him belt high. "What's going on? What're you doing up here?"

"This isn't what it looks like." Eyes flicking from the weapon to my face and back to the weapon. "I've only been here a couple of minutes—"

"Not what I asked you. Why were you running?"

"On my way to call for help. I didn't want to touch anything in there."

"Where's Mrs. Carey?"

"Inside. Better look for yourself."

"Show me. And don't make any funny moves on the way."

The hallway lights were on; so were the lights in the front parlor. Faith went in there and off to one side, and when I saw her lying sprawled across the arm of the couch, broken and limp, the silky fan of her hair matted and dark red with blood, the sickness rose hot into my throat; I had to swallow three or four times to keep it down. *Storm!* Her name, this time, was like a scream in my mind.

"I didn't do it," Faith said. "I found her just the way you see her."

Just the way I saw her. The deep wounds in the back of her skull . . . white and gray and red, bone and brain tissue and blood. And the thing beside her, flung down and half-hidden by the flare of her skirt, the goddamn thing that had done it . . . round and heavy, the glass surface all smeared with gore, like an organ that had been torn from inside her body and then cast aside. I tried to make myself go to her, check for a pulse, but it would be futile and I couldn't bear to touch her like that. I dragged my gaze away, kept it tight on Faith.

He said, "It's the truth—I found her like that. Not two minutes before you showed up."

"What're you doing here?" My voice had a wounded sound, hard and scraped raw.

"I was invited."

"She invited you?"

"This afternoon. She came out to the place where I'm staying."

"Just showed up at the Lakeside Resort and invited you to her home."

"I met her at Gunderson's last night. She was drunk and she tried to pick me up."

"Tried?"

"I turned her down."

"Woman like Storm Carey? Why?"

"I like my bed partners sober. The bartender there can vouch for the way it was." No expression on his battered face as he spoke. Blood-scabbed cut on his cheek, I noticed then, and it hadn't been there long. "She came out to the resort to apologize. Her initiative, not mine."

"And then she invited you to her home."

"That's right."

"At ten-thirty at night."

"No, she wanted me to come earlier. For dinner, she said."

"Why would she invite a stranger to dinner?"

"Why do you think? I told you she tried to pick me up last night. You must know the kind of woman she was—"

"Shut up about that. You didn't know her, you don't have any idea what kind of woman she was."

His eyes kept flicking between my face and the revolver. He didn't like guns pointed at him, that was plain. Afraid of me, the law? "All right," he said.

"You didn't come for dinner—why not?"

"Figured she was trouble and I'd be smart not to get involved with her." His mouth quirked in that non-smile of his. "Looks like I figured right."

"Why'd you change your mind?"

"I had it changed for me."

"Yeah? How'd you get that cut on your cheek?"

"Part of what changed my mind. Hassle at the Northlake Cafe a little while ago, not my fault."

"What kind of hassle?"

"The misunderstanding kind. I did somebody a favor and it got taken the wrong way and I got jumped for it. So I said the hell with it, I might as well get laid before I quit this lousy town. I drove here to see if she was still interested."

"And?"

"Found her dead just like I said. I passed a car on the road, not far from her driveway. It could've come from up here."

"What kind of car?"

"No idea. I didn't pay much attention."

"What color? New or old?"

"I told you—"

"Yeah, you told me," I said. "I don't think there was any car. I think you're trying to throw up a smoke screen, divert suspicion. She was alive when you got here."

"The hell she was."

"What'd she do, Faith? Turn you down this time? Tell you she changed *her* mind, go away and leave her alone?"

"No. She was dead when I—"

"You got mad, you saw red, you picked up the big glass paperweight off the end table there—"

"No."

"—and hit her with it. Hit her again, crushed her skull, and then threw the paperweight down and ran out in a panic—"

"Look at her, man, she's been dead longer than a couple of minutes—"

"—and if I hadn't shown up when I did, you'd've been halfway to the Oregon border by now. Isn't that the way it really went down, Faith?"

"No! You're not railroading me for this."

"Nobody's railroading anybody. All right, let's go."

"Go where?"

"Out to the cruiser."

"You're arresting me, is that it?"

"Move."

"You've had it in for me ever since I got to this paradise of yours. You and two thirds of the people I've run into. I've taken as much as I can stand, Novak. I won't be your fall guy for this."

"You'll do as I say, or I swear I'll put a bullet in your leg and add resisting arrest to the charges. Move!"

His eyes flashed at me a couple of seconds longer, flicked again to my revolver, and then he moved—jerkily, his arms flat against his sides. I backed around to keep a distance between us as he passed through the doorway into the hall. I made myself glance once more at Storm; the image of her was like a burning thing in my mind as I followed Faith outside. I felt sick and torn up inside and half crazy. I loved her, I knew that now. Not the way I loved Eva, but still a fire-in-the-blood kind of love. And now her blood was all over the room in there . . .

The bar flashers on the cruiser were still going, painting the night and the dark lake water with streaks and glints of red, as if the night were also bleeding. I watched Faith's back and the palm of my hand began to sweat around the revolver's handle. *No! Not that way!* My head ached and there was a grittiness in my eyes; the lids felt stuck down at the corners.

"Stand there in the headlights," I said to him.

When he obeyed I circled around behind him, transferring the revolver to my left hand, and leaned in through the driver's window to unhook the radio handset. Verne Erickson had arrived early to relieve Della Feldman; I said when he came on, "I'm at Storm Carey's house. She's dead, murdered. Skull crushed, two blows with a glass paperweight. Suspect in custody—John Faith." My voice still had that wounded sound; it cracked a little once or twice.

Verne said he'd have a backup unit and an ambulance there in a hurry. Calm, professional—and why shouldn't he be? Nothing personal in it for him.

I replaced the handset and said to Faith, "Come around here, lean against the hood. Weight on your hands, legs back and spread."

He did what he was told. I patted him down with my free hand. No weapon of any kind.

"All right. Left hand behind your back."

He did that, too, without hesitation or argument. The revolver was still in my left hand; I reached around with my right to take the handcuffs off my belt.

That was when he made his move.

He shouldn't have gotten away with it; I knew all the tricks and how to counteract them. But I wasn't as alert as I should have been—too badly shaken, the image of Storm's crushed and bloody head still searing my brain. So when he kicked back with his foot he managed to hook my ankle, even though I hopped and sidestepped the way you're supposed to. Before I could fire he jerked the foot, spinning off the cruiser, and I spun and staggered the other way, off balance but not getting my feet tangled, staying upright.

He came after me, clawing for the gun. I squeezed off a wild shot close to his face, the report like a blow to the eardrums, and then we were in tight together and grappling. He had size and weight and strength advantages, but I wouldn't let him pry the weapon loose. *Never give up your piece.* Drummed into our heads at the academy. *If a perp gets control of it you're dead meat.* Even when he clubbed me in the face with a rocklike fist, smashed my nose, sent me reeling backward and down and skidding on my ass, I kept possession of the revolver.

I scrambled around, up onto one knee. Blood spurted from my nose, warm and slick and salty on my mouth; some of it got in my eyes, so I couldn't see him except as a looming figure backlit against the red-swirled sky. I managed to shift the weapon into my right hand, raked my left over my face to clear off some of the blood; still couldn't see him clearly. I leveled the gun and fired anyway.

Missed.

He was running by then. In a low, stumbling crouch, past the cars and into the tree shadows.

I heaved to my feet, ducking my head against my uniform jacket, blinking furiously. By the time I could see well enough to give chase, he was out of sight. Heading for the lake, I thought, on the lawn toward the lake. I ran that way, sucking in air, and when I got to where the lawn began its gradual downward slope, he was visible again, at an angle to the right of the pier. Nothing in that direction but the black water, a section of rushes, a series of low rock shelves that rose to fifty yards of high ground and then fell away again to the waterline. He'd trapped himself.

I pulled up and steadied my arm and fired another round.

Hit him with that one. He reared up, staggered—but he didn't go down.

I triggered a third shot. That one was a clear miss: He kept right on running. But he had nowhere to go except up onto the shelves, and when he did that he'd be silhouetted against the sky. I'm a good shot; I wouldn't miss that kind of target at fifty yards.

Down the lawn, taking the same angle he was. The grass was night-damp and I slipped once, almost fell. When I had my balance I saw him start onto the first shelf . . . and then at the last second he changed his mind. His only other option was the lake, frigid at night this time of year, too cold for any kind of distance swimming, but either he didn't realize that or he was consumed by panic. He went straight off the rocky sliver of beach and into the lake in a flat, running dive.

It took me less than a minute to get to where he'd gone in, but as dark as it was I couldn't make out any sign of him from the water's edge. I climbed onto the first shelf, then the next, and the next, and I still couldn't spot him anywhere. Sank to the bottom, dragged down by the weight of his shoes and clothing? Drowned? I climbed higher; as far as I could see the lake's surface remained unbroken except for wind-made wavelets. With the bullet I'd put into him he couldn't have made it all the way around the rocks yet, be hidden among the cattails farther down, not unless he was an Olympic-caliber swimmer. He *had* to've gone down.

But I didn't believe it. I couldn't make myself believe it.

Sirens had begun to wail in the distance. Or maybe they'd been wailing for some time and I hadn't been hearing them. The backup unit and the ambulance, close now. *Go up and meet them.* But I didn't do it. I stayed put on the rocks, the blood still pouring out of my busted nose, barely even aware of the pain. Thinking of her up there in the house with her skull crushed in, scanning the black water and the muddy shore and not seeing any sign of Faith and still not believing the son of a bitch was as dead as Storm, Storm, Storm, Storm . . .

Part III

Saturday

Verne Erickson

IT'S BEEN A zoo around here all night. Just a damn zoo, ever since the Chief radioed in with the news about Mrs. Carey and John Faith. My wife and I have lived in Pomo eleven years and I can't remember another time that even comes close to the past few hours. But then, there's never been a homicide in Pomo County like this one—prominent citizen bludgeoned to death, chief of police beaten up in a fight with the alleged perpetrator, the suspect an outsider with a cloud over him anyway, shot trying to escape and either drowned or dead of hypothermia. Or maybe not dead, if Dick Novak's right in what he thinks. Anyhow, no sign of Faith or his body has turned up so far, and it's been more than six hours since he disappeared into the lake.

The whole town's caught up in it, seems like. Word spread like wildfire, and for a couple of hours after midnight the streets were jammed with cars and people. Young punks in groups, swilling beer, and some no doubt using controlled substances; drunks emptying out of the bars; cars cruising, horns honking; a lot of yelling and wild talk and trespassing on private property. For a while there things got pretty dicey. Looked as though we might have rat-pack vandalizing and maybe some looting. But with the help of Sheriff Thayer and several of his deputies, we managed to defuse the situation, get the crowds dispersed and the traffic thinned away and a handful of toughs arrested or cited without any real trouble starting up.

The media made matters that much worse. Reporters from Ukiah and Santa Rosa and two or three other towns in Lake and other nearby counties, TV camera trucks, even a helicopter from one of the TV stations down in San Francisco that flew over Pomo and the lake and took live pictures and made too much noise and stirred things up again just as they were starting to settle down. We've had reporters and cameramen and photographers traipsing in and out of the station off and on all night, getting in the way and sticking microphones or flashing bulbs in everybody's face. Mayor Seeley and Joe Proctor, the county D.A., talked to them; so did Thayer, who's a blowhard and likes to be the center of attention. Around three or so the Chief came out briefly for a conference interview, not because he wanted to but because the media kept clamoring for him and the mayor figured he'd better oblige. Seeley's big on maintaining friendly relations with the press and civic responsibility and all that. But Novak didn't stick with it very long. Once the reporters got a look at the condition of his face, it was like a feeding frenzy: volleys of questions, Minicams and regular cameras grinding and popping as close as they could get. He cut off the interview after three or four minutes and shut himself inside his office and hasn't done much talking to anybody since.

Fact is, the Chief's in a bad way, physically and mentally both. It's personal with him, and not just because Faith busted his nose. (Busted it bad. Paramedics couldn't stop the bleeding out at the Carey house, but it was an hour before anybody could drag him off to Pomo General's ER. Doctor there packed it and bandaged it and tried to convince him to spend the night or at least go straight home to bed, but he said no way; wouldn't take anything for the pain, either, except some aspirin. Just went right back out on the job. A smashed nose causes swelling and discoloration around the eyes and across the cheekbones; that was what excited the reporters when he came out. By then he was already starting to look like a victim of Eastwood's wrath in a Dirty Harry movie.) No, it's not just the broken nose. Novak and Storm Carey had an affair a while back, and it's plain enough he's been carrying the torch. You can't blame him, I guess. She was quite a looker. There's no more happily married man in this county than me, but even I'd've been tempted under the right, or wrong circumstances. Promiscuous as hell, Mrs. Carey was—the media got wind of that in a hurry, and that's another reason they're so hot on the story—but she had class and she was always polite and friendly, even with the bluenoses who snubbed her on the street. She sure as hell didn't deserve to die the way she did. Nobody deserves that kind of death, and when it's a person you know well, maybe even loved . . . well, it's no wonder the Chief's in the state he's in right now.

He won't go home and he won't let up, on himself or on the rest of us. He's been back out to the Carey house twice to supervise the hunt for Faith's body. And earlier, he had a shouting argument with Thayer that might've come to blows if Seeley hadn't gotten between them. Novak wanted to put up roadblocks at both ends of town, in case Faith managed to survive the lake and elude the patrols and steal a car, and the sheriff kept insisting it wasn't necessary because Faith was sure as hell dead and, besides, city and county combined didn't have the manpower for it. That was while the young punks were congregating and it still looked as though we might have a near riot on our hands. It's not often I agree with Leo Thayer, but in this case I did. It was more important to keep the peace than anything else right then, and roadblocks would only have complicated matters and provoked hostility. But even though Thayer wouldn't provide even one deputy and we're shorthanded, Novak wouldn't back down on stationing a car at each of the three exits from town. The officers are still out there waiting and watching and not seeing a damn thing.

The Chief's also got a search team continuing to work the shoreline north and south of the Carey property. Half an hour ago I took a short break to get some fresh air and have a smoke, and when I went across into Municipal Park I could see the searchlights on the curve of land up there, in the sloughs and tule marshes on the north shore. They made the lake seem even darker under the cloud-packed sky, thicker somehow, more like a vast sink of oil or tar. Made *me* cold, looking at it and thinking what it would be like to die under all that heavy black out there.

I agree with Thayer on that issue, too. John Faith's dead. The Chief said to me when he first came into the station after his visit to the ER, "The son of bitch is still alive, Verne. I won't feel any different until I see his corpse stretched out on a slab." Obsession talking, not good sense. I understand how he feels, but I've always believed that obsession and police work don't mix. You have to keep an open mind, be objective, or lose perspective and then you not only don't get the job done, you wind up causing friction and making enemies.

Bottom line is that Lake Pomo is fed by volcanic springs and it's butt-freezing cold at night this time of year. The odds of a man with a bullet in him and an open wound, even a big, strong type like Faith, surviving a lengthy swim in waterlogged clothing are pretty near zero. If he didn't drown, hypothermia would've got him quick enough. And if he'd managed to crawl out somewhere, the search teams would've found him by now. There aren't that many possible hiding places along that stretch of shoreline.

They hadn't found his body yet because the lake is deep and the currents plenty strong and unpredictable. Floaters have been fished out a long way from where they went in, as far as ten miles, and more than one has drifted into the sloughs and gotten hung up in reeds or submerged obstructions—in the case of one bass fisherman, on a tangle of broken line and sinkers and hooks in Barrelhouse Slough. Chances are, though, Faith's body is somewhere fairly close to shore near the Carey property, even up on the surface and hidden by the darkness. If so, it'll be spotted as soon as it's light enough. If not, well, it'll turn up eventually. The lake has claimed eight victims in my time here, and it's given every one of them up sooner or later. Fish-eaten and bloated and decomposing, maybe, but with still enough left for a positive ID.

Douglas Kent

SOMETIME IN THE night, in old F. Scott's dark night of the soul, Kent dreamed he was driving on a pitch-black road without headlights. I couldn't see a thing but I seemed to know where I was going, that there was something I had to do when I got there. Once, when I glanced over at the passenger seat, Pa Kent was squatting there and swigging from a bottle of Jack Daniel's, his favorite tipple. He winked at me and said, "You're a fool, boy, just like your old man." A little while later, when I looked again, he was gone and Storm was sitting stiffly in his place. She didn't wink. She hated me with her humid brown eyes. "You're disgusting, Doug," she said. "A disgusting, mean-spirited, irresponsible drunk, and I don't want anything more to do with you." Then she laughed, and I hated her, too, almost as much as I hated myself, and then I wasn't in the car any longer, the car was gone and Storm was gone and I was walking somewhere in the dark and calling her name, only she didn't answer. And a long time after that I heard a loud banging noise that went on and on, and somebody calling *my* name, saying, "Mr. Kent! Are you in there, Mr. Kent?" But I didn't get up. I was too drunk and too tired to get up. My eyes wouldn't open, or if they did open I couldn't see anything except black, night, black. Where am I? I thought. Where am I going? And from somewhere Pa Kent, the old fook, said, "Straight to the bottom, boy, just like me. Straight to the bottom of the Pit." I said, "No, no." And he said, "Yes, yes. You're already there, Dougie, right there at the gates. Go ahead, take a little peek at where you'll be spending eternity." But I kept my eyes tight shut and curled into a tiny ball and pulled the blackness close around me, cuddling it as if it were a woman.

An even longer time later, the blackness was gone and there was murky light and I was no longer in Fitzgerald country—I was awake, dream fragments clinging to my mind like cobwebs, but more or less lucid. Lucid enough to wish I wasn't.

Morning. The light came through a crack in the Levolor blinds, falling across my eyes and hurting them when I pried the lids open. Another hangover, a ripsnorter this time. But the pain I felt wasn't only booze-induced; I'd managed to bang up the Kent corpus somehow. I tried to remember. Too soon: The cobwebs clung stickily. Fah down, go boom? Oh yes, yes indeed. And not only that, I'd gone pukey-pukey all over somebody's carpet before passing out. Mine? I rolled over, gingerly, and with an almost superhuman effort Kent sat up and focused on his surroundings. Mine, all right. My carpet, my apartment. Home sweet home. That was one thing about the Kents, *pere et fils*: No matter how wasted they got of a long, dark night, they generally managed to lurch homeward and somehow arrive more or less in one piece.

My left knee throbbed. Pants leg ripped, blood on the cloth and blood scabbed on the skin underneath. I hunted for other tears, other wounds, and found two—left elbow, right shin. Fah down, go boom all over the place. Hell of a night, eh, Dougie? The old bag of sticks was heavier than usual this A.M., and all thanks to dear Storm.

Where had I gone after she threw me out of her life? Gunderson's, for a while, until the usually reliable Mike refused to serve me anymore. Then off to Mom and Pop's Saloon down by the boatyard. Loud voices, shitkicker music (wail it, Waylon, you old sumbitch), watered-down gin served with a Spanish olive. Abomination! A frigging *Spanish* olive! Harsh words, a few choice obscenities, and somebody's hands on my back and arse, hustling me out the door. And then . . . blank. The dream about driving somewhere? Alcoholic delusion. I seldom drove nowadays, and never when I was out gathering sticks and applying salve in preparation for another visit to Nightmareland.

This is your life, Douglas Kent. And a low one it is. Ten feet lower than a mole's ass and still digging, as the pater used to say.

I needed a drink.

Bad.

I managed to stand up, stay up, and waddle into the kitchen without falling on my face again. Gin? No gin. The only hooch I had left in the place was vodka. Two long, bitter swallows—gurgle, gurgle. The salve stayed down as unsteadily as I stayed up. I leaned on the counter and waited for the shakes to abate. Took three minutes or so for the medicine to straighten me up, literally. I treated myself to another swallow and then floated into the bathroom and peed lustily, always a good sign. After which I shed my torn, reeking, and bloody rags and climbed under the shower and stood it icy for as long as I could, then lukewarm, then hot. By the time I'd toweled off I decided I would probably live through another day.

I doctored my battle scars, brushed my teeth, scraped off stubble (nicking myself only twice, I noted with some pride), donned clean clothes, and had another squint at myself in the mirror. I looked like shit. Ah, but no bigger a pile than usual. And that, in the Kent household on any Saturday morning, let alone one after being Storm-lashed and cast away, was a major achievement.

Maybe not, though, I thought as I returned to the kitchen to drink the rest of my breakfast. Maybe shit, like water, simply seeks its own level. Interesting theory. I'd have to pursue it sometime when my head wasn't quite so stuffed with spider silk.

I was in the living room, puffing on my first weed of the day and making a halfhearted attempt to clean my barf off the rug, when somebody clumped up onto the front stoop and pounded on the door and began calling my name, both much louder than was tolerable. The pounding and yelling were the same as in my dream, which I deduced meant I hadn't dreamed them after all. I recognized the voice too: Jay Dietrich, the *Advocate*'s talentless cub and wanna-be.

I went and opened the door, reluctantly. Dietrich, with his horse face and walnut-sized Adam's apple and Pollyannaish exuberance, is never a pleasant sight. On a morning when Kent was suffering more than usual, Jaydee was positively repellent.

"What's the idea?" I demanded. "Don't tell me you've taken to moonlighting as a town crier?"

"What? Oh. I'm sorry, Mr. Kent, but I didn't know if you were here or not. Or if you were maybe . . . well, you know, sleeping. I didn't get any answer when I was here before, and then I couldn't find you anywhere else and things got so hectic—"

"Stop babbling. My head hurts enough as it is. When were you here before?"

"Around midnight. I came over as soon as I—"

"Midnight? Why in sweet Christ's name were you banging on my door and crying my name at midnight?"

"I'd just heard the news and I didn't know if you were—"

"News? What're you talking about?"

"Mrs. Carey. Storm Carey."

A sudden coldness formed in a knot under my sternum. A darkness, too, like an incipient black hole. "What about Mrs. Carey?"

"You don't know, then," Dietrich said, and his big Adam's apple bobbed and bobbed again. "She's dead. Murdered last night at her house. Bludgeoned with a paperweight, compound skull fracture."

The black hole grew and spread; I could feel the chill pull of it, like a vortex. But that was all I felt. Numb. *She's dead. Murdered last night at her house.* Just words—no reality to it yet. Cold and black and numb.

"That stranger," Dietrich said, "the one you wrote the editorial about, he did it. Faith. Chief Novak caught him up there right afterward. He broke the Chief's nose and then Mr. Novak shot him when he tried to escape and he jumped into the lake. Faith did. They think he's dead, drowned, but they still haven't found the body—"

"Where is she? Where'd they take her?"

"Mrs. Carey? Pomo General. I talked to Dr. Johanssen—"

"Take me there. Right now."

"Sure, Mr. Kent. But like I said, I already talked—"

"Now, damn you. *Now!*"

Audrey Sixkiller

WHEN I FIRST heard about it, from Joan Garcia, an Elem nurse at the hospital, I didn't know what to do or think. My first impulse was to rush down there, but I didn't give in to it. Dick wouldn't want or need me, and there was nothing I could do for him anyway. Later, when feelings weren't running quite so high and things were more settled—that was the time to make myself available to him.

I lay in bed with the lights on, prepared to endure another long, sleepless night. Instead, exhaustion dragged me under almost immediately. My dreams were unsettling. I dreamed of blood, which the old-time Indians believed was a sign of the devil: Blood spilled in a place poisoned it forever after. And I dreamed that I was one of the bear people, rushing through the night in my hides and feathers, and that I came upon Storm Carey and there was a terrible battle—two witches in a clash of magical powers that left her dead and me weeping as if my heart would break. Guilt, of course. I'd yearned for her to be gone from Dick's life, but I had never once wished her dead.

In the morning I was still tired, and achy, as though I might be coming down with something. I put a kettle on the stove, and while the water was boiling I called the police station. Dick was there but not accepting personal calls. I spoke with Verne Erickson, and he said Dick had been holed up in his office most of the night. Hadn't gone home, and as far as Verne knew, hadn't eaten or slept either. He blamed himself for John Faith getting away from him. The fact that neither Faith nor his body had been found yet only made him feel worse.

But that wasn't the only reason Dick was in such a state. I knew it, and I'm sure Verne did, too, even though neither of us mentioned it. Dick's feelings for Storm. Whether or not he'd been seeing her again, she'd meant more to him once than just sexual gratification. It was painful to think that even he might not have realized how much he cared for her until she was dead.

Before we rang off I said, "I'll stop by his house in an hour or so and take care of Mack. You might tell him when you get the chance."

"I will. Thanks, Audrey. He's probably forgotten all about the dog."

And me, I thought. Mack and me both.

Tea and a Pop-Tart for breakfast. Ten minutes in the shower and another twenty to dress and put on my face. I was shrugging into my pea jacket when the telephone rang. I hurried to answer it, thinking that Verne had relayed my message and Dick had thought to call me after all.

"Hello? Dick?"

"Dick's what you want, huh?" Thick, muffled man's voice. "Well, dick's what you're gonna get, and plenty more besides. Gun of yours won't stop me next time. You're dead, bitch. Dead as Storm Carey—and soon, real soon."

Trisha Marx

SATURDAY STARTED OUT just as shitty as Friday ended. I didn't get much sleep; at first I was too depressed and cried a lot, and then later there was all this noise, people driving around and yelling, a helicopter or something flying overhead in the middle of the night. I felt so down I didn't even care what was going on. Then this morning I was sick to my stomach and spent five minutes in the john trying to hurl as quietly as I could so Daddy wouldn't hear. Morning sickness again. Just freaking great. Then, after I got dressed and went downstairs, Daddy wanted to talk about Anthony. I told him we'd had a fight and it was all over between us, but I couldn't tell him about the baby yet. No way. He asked me how I'd gotten home last night, and the way he asked it I knew he already knew and that somebody must've seen John Faith dropping me off and snitched about it. So I told him what'd happened, everything except that Anthony and I'd been smoking dope and how close I'd come—so close it scared me when I thought about it—to falling off the Bluffs into the lake.

And he said, real dark and grim, "You're lucky, Trisha. You don't know how lucky. After that Faith character brought you home, he went out to Mrs. Carey's house and killed her. Bashed her head in."

"What!" I stared at him with my mouth open. He wasn't kidding. "John? It couldn't be. He wouldn't do anything like that . . ."

"Well, he did. Chief Novak caught him out there, and there was a fight and the Chief shot him."

"Oh, God, he's dead, too?"

"Looks like it. He went into the lake, probably drowned. They haven't found the body yet."

"All the noise last night—that's what it was?"

"Yeah. Whole town was in an uproar. I stayed here—didn't want to leave you alone again." Daddy rubbed his right hand; the knuckles looked scratched, as if he'd been in a fight himself. "He got what was coming to him, by God. Just not soon enough. Started causing trouble the minute he showed up in Pomo."

"He didn't cause me any trouble," I said.

"You're lucky, like I told you. If it hadn't been Storm Carey, it'd've been somebody else. Could've been you."

I felt sick again, and this time it had nothing to do with being knocked up. Mrs. Carey killed—that was awful. I didn't know her very well and people were always saying what a slut she was, the same people, I'll bet, who were saying John Faith had killed her and who wanted him to be dead. I remembered last night on the Bluffs, how he'd dragged me away from the cliff edge and the stuff he'd said to me there and on the drive home, and I couldn't believe he'd gone and bashed Mrs. Carey's head in right afterward. No matter what Daddy said, what anybody said, I didn't believe it.

Daddy tried to get me to eat some breakfast, but I couldn't. I would've hurled again if I'd tried to swallow so much as a glass of milk. He had to work half a day at the lumberyard, he said, but he'd be home around one and he wanted to find me here when he got back. I said okay. The last thing he asked before he left was did I intend to see Anthony anymore. I didn't lie to him. I said no way, José, and I meant it. Whatever I decided to do about the baby, Anthony wouldn't be any part of it. Anthony was a big pile of dog crap I'd avoid from now on.

Selena called after Daddy left and wanted to talk about all the excitement last night; she sounded positively thrilled. I told her I couldn't talk now, I'd call her later, but I knew I wouldn't. The only person I could talk to today was Ms. Sixkiller.

Upstairs I put my makeup on, fixed my hair, and was ready to go at twenty of nine. Twenty minutes was about how long it'd take me to walk to Ms. Sixkiller's house. I wished Daddy hadn't had to work this morning, because then he might've let me have his pickup for a couple of hours. Man, how I'd love to have a car of my own. Selena's folks bought *her* an old Volks bug for her seventeenth birthday, but Daddy says we can't afford a second car, even a junker, thanks to the Bitch. That's what he calls Mom; he won't even say her name anymore, not that I blame him. Probably be years before I can afford to buy myself a car, even longer if I have the kid—

Shit! Cars, babies . . . I don't know *what* I want or what I'm gonna do. I'm so screwed up. How'd I ever get this screwed up?

It was as cold this morning as last night. Sky all gray and twitchy, the way I felt inside. I walked fast over to Lakeshore Road. A car went by and honked, but I didn't bother to look and see who it was. What was the word for when you felt this way? Apathy? Right, apathy. If apathy was gold, I'd be as rich as Mrs. Carey was—

But I didn't want to think about Mrs. Carey.

When I got to where I could see along the north shore, there were a couple of big boats out and one of them looked to be the sheriff's launch from down in Southlake. Still hunting for John Faith's body. *Everybody hurts, everybody wants to stop hurting.* Well, he'd stopped hurting, all right. Poor John Faith.

Poor Trisha. When am I gonna stop hurting?

The more you hurt, the more you care. You'll be all right if you don't let yourself stop caring . . .

Ms. Sixkiller's house was like a cottage, a real retro type with a tall brick chimney and shingles and stuff. Her father built it a long time ago, when Indians didn't mix much with whites. He made some money hauling freight in wagons and boats and bought the land and built the house and pissed off all his white neighbors, but he wouldn't move or sell and they couldn't drive him out. Good for him. He must've been oneG141 tough old dude. His daughter's pretty tough, too. Best teacher at Pomo High, and that's not just my opinion. She'd listen, help me if she could. She *had* to help me because there just wasn't anybody else.

I went in through her gate and rang the bell, but Ms. Sixkiller didn't come to the door. Nothing but echoes inside when I rang again. I looked at my watch, and it was exactly nine o'clock. Oh, man, what if she forgot I was coming to see her and left early for her tribal council meeting? I went over to the garage and looked in through the side window. Her car wasn't there.

Now what was I gonna do?

But maybe she hadn't forgotten. Maybe she'd gone to the store or something and she'd be back any minute. I could sit on the porch and wait. Only I didn't feel like sitting, so I went between the house and the garage and across the back lawn to her dock. It's a long one, and about halfway out there's a security gate, and beyond that, underneath, a board float and a shedlike thing open at both ends where she keeps her boat. She must really love that old boat; you're always seeing her out in it, even in the winter. Once I saw her bouncing along when it was raining. Really raining, not, like, just a drizzle.

I walked out on the dock as far as the gate. When I pushed on the door set into the gate, not for any reason, just because it's the kind of thing you do sometimes, it popped right open. Some security gate. I went on through, over to the edge of the dock where a ladder led down to the float. From there I could see into the shed. Ms. Sixkiller has one of those electronic hoists, and her boat was up out of the water on it, a tarpaulin roped across the stern half to keep out moisture.

It was sure a nice one, even if it was retro like her house. A boat's something else I'd like to have someday, one of those sleek fiberglass jobs with gold glitter mixed into the paint. We owned a powerboat once, a fourteen-foot inboard, when the Bitch was still living with us. But we couldn't afford to keep it after she ran off with that jerk from Kansas City. Daddy used to let me drive it sometimes. Driving a boat's easier than driving a car. All you have to do is steer. Docking's the hard part, especially when the water's choppy like this morning—

What was that?

I was still standing by the ladder, looking now toward where the sheriff's launch was making loops offshore near the Carey house. I cocked my head and listened. Lots of sounds—the boat engines, loons crying somewhere, a kind of creaking from the dock pilings or the hoist under the Chris-Craft's weight—but not the one I thought I'd heard. I turned away and started back toward the gate. And then I heard it again. A funny kind of sound. I couldn't quite identify it or tell where it was coming from.

For about a minute I stood quiet, listening. Then I went back to where the ladder was and climbed down to the float. I heard the sound again then, but I still couldn't tell what was making it, and like a magnet or something, it drew me right in next to the boat. Pretty soon it came again, and this time it gave me goose bumps all over because I realized where it was coming from and what it was.

When I tugged at the heavy canvas, a flap of it lifted right up; it wasn't really tied on the float side. And when I looked underneath, there was John Faith, lying in the bottom of the boat, on his back behind the driver's seat. Clothes wet and all bloody on one side, his face twisted and his eyes shut tight, the sounds I'd heard—a kind of low moaning— coming from way down deep inside.

George Petrie

AT FIRST I didn't know where I was. I opened my eyes to an unfamiliar room full of shadows and dark shapes, and panic surged and drove me out of bed, halfway across rough carpeting. I stood, trembling and disoriented, my heart raging against my ribs. It wasn't until sounds penetrated from outside—traffic noise, distant voices, the slam of a car door—that the fog cleared away and I remembered.

Motel. Best Western just off Highway 80, outside Truckee.

On the run with a small fortune in stolen bank funds.

Sweet Christ, I really did do it, didn't I?

I groped back to the bed, sank down on the rock-hard mattress. The sheets were sweat-sodden; so were my pajamas. How long had I slept? Digital clock on the TV, red numerals shining blurrily in the gloom. I rubbed grit out of my eyes. Nine-twenty. I'd pulled in here at what . . . close to midnight? Bed an hour and a half later. Nearly eight hours—

The money!

I lunged to my feet again, fumbled the nightstand light on. Breath hissed out between my teeth: The garbage bags, all six, were on the far side of the bed, where I'd put them last night. This was a ground-floor unit and I'd backed the car in close, unloaded the bags two at a time. Nobody saw me, I made sure of that. Triple-locked the door, tested the lock on the window, and then pulled the drapes tightly closed. Nobody *could* have gotten in. But I went around the bed anyway, felt each bag, opened each to make certain the packets of bills were still there.

$209,840.

I'd counted it before I'd crawled into bed. Every packet and loose bill, not once, but twice. $209,840. More than I'd expected—a small fortune even in this inflated economy. So many things it can buy me. Women . . . better-looking women than Storm, younger and kinder and even better in bed. Not that it's possible for anybody to be much better in bed than Storm—

No, the hell with her. I won't think about her anymore. She's part of the past, the Pomo prison. Free of her, too, now. The money is the future, and the future is all that matters.

In the bathroom I splashed cold water on my face. My pulse rate was back to normal, but I was still twitchy. I kept thinking about the money, only instead of soothing me, it produced a worm of anxiety. Six garbage bags full of cash. And every mile I drove, every time I stopped somewhere to eat or fill the gas tank or use a rest room, I ran the risk of something going wrong. Accident, car-jacking, traffic violation, other possibilities I couldn't even imagine right now . . .

Cut it out, Petrie. Get a grip on yourself. Two more full days on the road, at least fifteen hundred miles between me and Pomo when the vault lock releases Monday morning, and I can't do it wired the whole time, worrying about everything, feeling and probably looking like a fugitive. That's how you make mistakes. Fatal mistakes. Tight control from now on. I'm finished otherwise. Remember that. Don't forget it for a second.

I felt better after a long, hot shower. Clearheaded. One thing I could do about the money was to get it out of those garbage bags and into a couple of suitcases. Large, lightweight suitcases. Nobody at a motel would think twice about a man carrying luggage from and to his car. Just another anonymous business traveler. Buy the cases in Reno or Sparks, make the transfer out in the desert somewhere or maybe wait until I reached Ely tonight.

When I came out of the bathroom, the digital clock read five past ten. Overdue getting back on the highway. But hunger gnawed at me—I hadn't eaten anything since noon yesterday, couldn't have choked down food last night if my life depended on it. There was a Denny's adjacent to the motel; I recalled seeing it when I drove in. Quick breakfast . . . no, better make it a large one, stoke up so I wouldn't have to stop again for food this side of Ely. Okay. I zippered my overnight bag, unlocked the door, and started out.

A scowling gray-haired man was standing in front of my car, peering down at the license plate.

Surprise made me suck in my breath, loud enough for him to hear. His head came up. I jumped back inside, shut and locked the door, leaned hard against it. Sweat dribbled on my face and neck; for a few seconds I couldn't seem to get enough air. I made myself breathe in shallow little pants, until the blood-pound in my ears diminished and the feeling of suffocation went away. Then I moved unsteadily to the window, eased aside a corner of the drape.

The gray-haired man was gone.

I fumbled the door open again, still clutching the overnight case, and stuck my head out. The parking lot seemed deserted. I ran to the Buick, dropped my keys twice before I got the trunk open. I threw the case inside, ran back into the room, caught up three of the garbage bags and hauled them out, stuffed them into the trunk, and then ran back for the others. Dripping sweat when I finished. Legs aching as if I'd run ten miles. I slammed the trunk lid, started around to the driver's door.

Christ, there he was again, hurrying toward me from the motel office. Still scowling. Gesturing. Calling out, "Hey! You, Mr. Smith. You just wait a minute—"

I lunged in under the wheel, locked the door. It took three tries to slot the key into the ignition.

He was close now. I saw his mouth move again, but I couldn't hear him over the roar of the engine. I jammed the gearshift lever into Drive, bore down too hard on the gas pedal, and almost lost control as the car surged ahead. At the exit then, out onto the business road paralleling Highway 80. The freeway entrance ramp was a short ways ahead; a red stoplight at the intersection turned green just in time. And I was on the ramp, on the highway, and in the mirror I could no longer see the motel lot or any sign of pursuit.

The words the gray-haired man had mouthed back there . . . something about signs, backing in? *Can't you read a sign? You're not supposed to back in.* Was that all it was about? Motel employee or self-righteous guest annoyed because of the way I'd parked my car?

I laughed. But it had a wild sound and I cut it off. I wasn't certain that was what he'd been saying; I couldn't be positive. It might've been something else. *He* might have been something else.

Suppose his car had been close by and he'd gotten to it in time to keep me in sight? Suppose he was back there right now, following me?

Eyes on the mirror again. Heavy traffic clogged all three lanes; too many other cars traveling at the same speed I was and none of them familiar. I goosed it up to seventy, seventy-five. Still couldn't tell. Too dangerous to drive so fast; highway patrol kept a close watch for speeders along 80. I slowed down to the legal limit and held it there.

All the way into Nevada I kept watching the mirror. Watching and wondering and struggling to regain the feeling of tight control.

Richard Novak

THAYER WADDLED INTO my office trailing smoke from one of his fifty-cent panatelas. He didn't stand or sit; instead he leaned his fat rump against the table under the window. "You look like hell, Novak," he said. "Why don't you go home, get some rest, before you fall apart?"

I knew how I looked. And I felt worse, but I wasn't about to admit that to Thayer. "You find Faith yet?"

"No."

"Then what're you doing here?"

"Came to tell you I called off the boat search. Sent Abrams and the launch back to Southlake."

"What!" Without thinking I jerked forward, slapped the desk with the flat of my hand. The sudden movement stoked the pain in my broken nose; it felt as though the middle of my face was on fire. "What'd you do that for?"

"Wasted effort, fuel, and manpower, that's why. Abrams was up and down the shoreline half a dozen times, a mile in both directions. If the body was on the surface anywhere, he'd have spotted it."

"What about Barrelhouse and the other sloughs?"

"What about them? Body couldn't have drifted that far."

"I'm not thinking about a dead body."

"Faith couldn't have swum that far either. Why the hell would he, even if he'd been able to?"

"You forget the Cutoff bridge?"

"No, I didn't forget the bridge. Deputies up there all night, you know that. Deputies in boats in the sloughs at dawn, too. Nothing. He's not in the marshes, dead or alive. Body's snagged somewhere along the shore, or on the bottom, farther out, weighted down by what he was wearing. Either way it'll come up sooner or later. There's nothing more any of us can do right now. And that's not just my opinion, it's Burt Seeley's, too."

"Goddamn it, why do you and Seeley and everybody else automatically assume Faith's dead?"

"You know better, huh?"

"I've got a feeling he's still alive."

"A feeling. That and a quarter'll buy you a pack of gum."

I had nothing to say to that.

"Where's this feeling tell you he is?" Thayer said. "No reports of stolen vehicles, so he'd have to be somewhere in the area."

"Holed up."

"Yeah, only there haven't been any reports of sightings or break-ins either. And the shore search teams checked every possible hiding place."

"You think so? There's always one or two that get overlooked, no matter how fine an area is combed."

Thayer made a derisive sound. "You say you put a bullet in him before he went into the lake. You sure about that?"

"I'm sure." I'd replayed the fight and chase a dozen times in my memory; every time, I saw Faith stagger after I fired the second round. No mistake: That slug hadn't missed. "Somewhere in the upper body. Too dark to tell just where."

"Okay. So you add shock, an open wound, and loss of blood to the temperature of the water. Man, I'd be surprised if he lasted more than ten minutes out there. The odds of him getting far enough to find an overlooked hidey-hole must be, what, a few thousand to one?"

"I don't care about the odds."

"Right. You got a feeling." Thayer sucked in smoke, blew it out in thin little spurts. He wasn't quite smiling, but I could tell he was enjoying himself—almost as much as he had with the media earlier. He didn't like me any more than I liked him. "Seasoned cop has a hunch biting his ass, he's right and everybody else is wrong. Hunches never lie."

"Up yours, Leo."

That almost made him mad. He settled for nasty instead. "What's the bottom line here, Novak? You want Faith to be alive so you can get your paws on him, pay him back personally for the busted nose and what he did to your bimbo?"

I pushed up out of my chair. The pain rush brought tears to my eyes. "Back off," I said.

"Hell, everybody in the county knows you were screwing her—"

"I said, back off!"

"Or else what? You're in no shape to get tough with me."

"Keep baiting me and we'll find out."

He started to say something more, thought better of it, and fixed me with a glare that looked hot on the surface but was lukewarm underneath. He didn't want any trouble with me, even as banged up as I was. There was no sand or steel in the man; just lard, bluster, and hot air. He was a piss-poor sheriff and a piss-poor excuse for a human being.

Say the same about yourself, Novak, after last night.

"You through talking, Leo? If so, get the hell out of my office."

He said, "Faith's dead. Rest of it is just bullshit," and stomped out and slammed the door behind him.

My nose was bleeding again; I could feel the dribbles through the packing. I sat down, tilted my chair and my head back. Focused on the pain, wrapped myself in it. As bad as it was, it was more tolerable than the hurt I felt inside. Storm, John Faith, Dick Novak . . . all of us bound together in one poisonous sack of blame and guilt. But Faith, damn him, was the magnet of my hate. A malignant force, like a plague carrier, ever since his arrival in Pomo; if he hadn't come here, none of it would have happened. And he was still out there somewhere, still alive, still malignant. I didn't just feel it, I *knew* it, the way you know that if you survive the dark of night you'll see daylight again. Until he was found there'd be no daylight for me—no ending, no closure, no new beginning. Faith dead or in custody wouldn't bring Storm back or make last night any easier to live with, but at least then I could go on.

Another knock on the door. This time it was Della Feldman who stepped inside.

"Somebody else to see you, Chief."

"If it's the mayor again—"

"Audrey Sixkiller."

"Audrey? Tell her I'm busy. I don't need my hand held."

"That's not why she came. Something important to tell you, she says."

"What is it?"

"Tell you, nobody else," Della said.

". . . All right. Send her in."

I was back on my feet when Audrey entered. She winced when she saw the bandage, the swelling and discoloration, but all she said was, "Dick, I'm so sorry."

"Me too. But the damage isn't permanent." Not on the outside, anyway.

She took a step toward me, as if she had it in her mind to touch or embrace me. It must've been my expression that stopped her, caused her to bite down on her lower lip. Poor Audrey. She was twice the woman Storm had been, probably twice the woman Eva was; but I didn't want her close to me, not now. Empty inside, scooped out. Nothing left for her or anybody else.

I asked her if she wanted to sit down and she said no. Then she said, "Dick, how certain are you John Faith is guilty of Storm's murder?"

"What kind of question is that?"

"Something happened a while ago that makes me wonder. *Is* there any chance he's innocent?"

"Not as far as I'm concerned. What happened?"

"A phone call. As I was leaving to feed Mack."

"From?"

"The man who tried to break into my house."

"The man who—!"

"He as much as said so."

". . . What else did he say?"

She took a breath. "That I'd be dead soon. That he'd make me as dead as Storm Carey. It didn't sound like an idle threat."

My face throbbed and burned. This, now, on top of everything else. "His voice . . . familiar?"

"No. Muffled, disguised."

"Faith," I said. "It could've been Faith."

"But he's dead, drowned . . ."

"Is he? I'm not so sure of that."

"Even so, it couldn't be him. Where would he go to make a phone call? *Why* would he?"

I shook my head. I wanted it to be Faith; simplify things, give me another reason to hate him. "Okay, maybe not. But it still could've been Faith in that ski mask the other night."

"How could it be? The caller—"

"Sicko taking advantage of the situation, playing games to scare you."

"No, Dick. The only people who know about the prowler are you and me and Verne. It's the same man in both cases—I'm sure of it. On the phone . . . he said my gun wouldn't stop him the next time. He couldn't know I shot at the prowler unless—"

"All right," I said. "Same man, and he's not Faith."

"His threat to make me as dead as Storm . . . couldn't that mean *he's* the one who killed her?"

"No. Her house wasn't broken into and she wasn't raped. She knew the man who did it. She let him in."

"She knew John Faith?"

"Yeah. She invited him there last night."

"Then . . . why would he kill her?"

"An argument, he lost his head and picked up that paperweight . . . Christ, Audrey, stop questioning me on this! Faith did it, nobody else. And the bastard who's stalking you—I'll find out who he is and I'll get him, too. I promise you that. I won't let anything happen to you."

"I know you won't."

"I mean it. One woman dead—"

I couldn't make myself say the rest of it. But Audrey understood. More than I'd thought she did. She said, "I'm sorry about Storm, Dick. I want you to know that. I really am sorry."

The words, the sympathy and compassion in her eyes, built a sudden sharp impulse to pull her close after all, let her comfort me, find some strength in her strength. But I couldn't do it. It was like there was a wall of glass between us. I kept my distance, hurting inside and out, feeding on the hurt. And all I could think to say was, "I'll put an end to it, one way or another. I'll get them—I'll get them both."

Trisha Marx

MS. SIXKILLER'S HOUSE was locked up tight. I hunted around in the backyard and found a rock and took it to the bathroom window on the north side. I kept thinking that this was crazy, that I was gonna get myself in some serious trouble here. But I couldn't just leave John Faith lying there in the boat, cold and wet and wounded, after what he'd done for me on the Bluffs. Nobody'd help him if I didn't. And suppose the wrong person found him next time, a cop or somebody who wanted to play Rambo?

The window breaking made a lot of noise, but there wasn't anybody around to hear it; the houses on both sides were empty. I reached inside and flipped the catch and then shoved the sash up far enough so I could wiggle through. A sliver of glass pricked my finger as I swung down off the toilet, but I hardly even felt it. My heart was pounding worse than the first night the bunch of us broke into Nucooee Point Lodge to party.

First thing I did was open the medicine cabinet. There was a bottle of hydrogen peroxide, some adhesive tape, and gauze pads. I grabbed all of those and took them with me.

In our house there's a linen closet that opens off the upstairs hall, but the hall here didn't have one. So I had to look around for a couple of minutes before I found Ms. Sixkiller's extra sheets and blankets in the closet in her bedroom. One blanket was heavy, made of wool; another was the all-weather thermal kind that keeps in heat and keeps out cold. I tucked both under my arm and then hurried through the kitchen to the back porch. I figured it'd be easier to go out that way, instead of back through the bathroom window, and it was. The screen door wasn't hooked, and the lock on the outer door was the push-button kind.

The police launch was still way up shore; I made sure of that before I ran out onto the dock. I climbed down the ladder one-handed—lifted the tarp again and pushed the blankets and stuff inside the boat, then climbed the hoist frame and dropped down next to where John Faith was lying. The way he'd been shaking when I left him, I was afraid I'd find him dead. But he was still breathing, hard and raspy. I touched the side of his face. His skin was cold and hot at the same time, and all puckered and sort of gray. Was that how you looked and felt when you had pneumonia?

Fumble-fingered, I unfolded the wool blanket and shook it out. But then I thought: It won't do him any good with those wet clothes plastered to his body. He wasn't wearing much, just a shirt and a pair of Levi's and socks, no shoes. The shirt had two bloody holes in it under the left shoulder, a small one in back and a bigger one in front. Two wounds. Shot twice, or maybe only once with the bullet going in one side and coming out the other.

The thing to do was to get everything off. Well? It wasn't like I'd never undressed a guy before. I managed to unbutton the shirt, but parts of it were stuck to the wounds and I was afraid to pull the fabric loose. Instead, I undid his belt and the top button of his Levi's. Unzipping the fly took longer on account of it stuck partway down. Then I took hold of the belt loops on either side, started to work the soaked pants down around his hips—

His eyes popped open.

I mean they just flew open, *boing!*, and all at once he was staring right at me—a wild and crazy stare, like Freddy Krueger before one of his slice-and-dice rampages.

It scared me so much I recoiled back against the gunwale and cracked my elbow. "Shit!" The boat wobbled a little, kept wobbling as he twisted over onto one hip and tried to sit up. He didn't have enough strength; he made the groaning sound in his throat and sank back, supporting himself with one hand flat on the deck. When he looked at me again, the craziness was gone. His eyes were still glazed, but in a hurt and confused way.

He said "Trisha?" as if he didn't believe it was me. His voice sounded like one of the frogs in the Budweiser commercials.

"Yeah." I wasn't afraid anymore. He wouldn't hurt me. I don't know how I could be so totally sure of that, but I was. I straightened up on my knees, rubbing my elbow. "I was trying to get those wet clothes off, you know? You were shivering so hard . . ."

"Cold," he said. He blinked a few times, ran his other hand over the dark stubble on his cheeks. "Where are we?"

"Boat shed."

"Whose?"

"Ms. Sixkiller's. This is her boat."

"Sixkiller . . . Audrey?"

"Yeah. You know her?"

"Met her. How'd you find me?"

"I was up on the dock and I heard you moaning."

"Just you? Alone?"

"Just me."

He tried to sit up again, but something hurt him this time; he grimaced and sucked in his breath. I could see part of the wound in front where the open shirt pulled away. Black and red-brown and scabby. It was bleeding again, too—little pimples of bright red.

I said, "I never saw bullet wounds before," because it was what I was thinking.

"Better hope they're the last you ever see."

"That one looks . . . man!"

"Feels that way, too." He was probing at it with two fingers, unsticking the rest of his shirt and wincing when it tore away a scab of blood. "Could've been worse. Bullet went straight through, didn't hit bone or bust me up inside."

"Lucky."

"Oh yeah. Mr. Lucky."

"I brought some peroxide," I said. I leaned over for the bottle and showed it to him. "I got it from Ms. Sixkiller's bathroom. It'll help, won't it?"

"Help a lot. Thanks."

"I also got some blankets."

"Help me sit up. Don't think I can manage by myself."

I scooted over, got behind him on my knees, and lifted on his good side until he was sitting up. Then between us we were able to drag the shirt back down over his arms and all the way off. He poured peroxide on and it, like, actually *hissed* on the open wounds, bubbled up white and frothy in a way that nearly made me gag. The pain must've been terrific; he jerked and twisted and tears leaked out of his eyes and he half-strangled on a yell to keep it from coming out loud.

I took some of the gauze pads out of their wrappings and he used half to clean the wounds and then we taped on the rest. He had a little trouble breathing when we were done, so I helped him lie back flat. Then, with him raising his butt and pushing with his hands and me tugging, we managed to get the Levi's off. He said, "You can leave my shorts on," but I said, "They're wet, and I've seen guys naked before," and I worked those off, too. I couldn't help sneaking a look at him down there. Oh, boy. Even shriveled up from the cold, his dick made Anthony's look like an Oscar Mayer reject.

When he was wrapped in the blankets, the thermal one underneath against his bare skin, he asked me what time it was. I looked at my watch and told him, "Quarter to ten."

"That late? A wonder I lasted long enough for you to find me."

"How long've you been here?"

"Most of the night."

"It must be more than a mile from here to Mrs. Carey's. You couldn't have swum all that way."

"No. I wasn't in the lake more than ten minutes the first time, maybe twenty altogether. Walked and crawled, mostly."

"How'd you keep them from seeing you?"

"Dark took care of that. Dark and blind luck. Couple of them got close enough to touch me, but I was hiding under a dock on a crosspiece where their lights didn't reach."

"Everybody thinks you drowned. Or else the cold got you."

"They were almost right. I couldn't've gotten any farther than here. Passed out as soon as I climbed in under the tarp." He looked at me for a few seconds, and then he said, "I didn't kill her, Trisha. Mrs. Carey."

"I know it. I wouldn't've helped you if I thought you did."

"I hope you don't regret it. If they find you here with me—"

"They won't. They're not looking down this far."

"But they are still looking."

"For your body, not for *you*."

"Audrey Sixkiller . . . where's she?"

"Probably down at the Elem rancheria by now. She has a tribal council meeting at eleven. I was supposed to meet her here at nine, but she must've forgot."

"Better beat it while you can."

"Don't worry, she won't be back until after one—"

I stopped because the wind slackened just then and I heard rumbling noises out on the lake. John heard them, too. He said, "What's that?"

"Boat engine. Sounds like the sheriff's launch."

"Coming this way?"

"Yeah, but they can't see us if we stay down."

I stretched out flat alongside him. The engine sounds got louder, closer. John was breathing fast and raspy again; I could feel him all tense inside the blankets. I felt bad for him. And mad, too, on account of what'd happened to him and how wrong everybody was about him. Why couldn't they see him the way I did—a good guy, not a bad one?

The launch glided past at least a hundred yards offshore without slowing any. I waited a couple of minutes more, until the engine sounds began to fade, then rose up and looked and couldn't see anything except gray water. I climbed out and went to the end of the float for a quick look. When I came back I said to John, "They're gone. On their way back to Southlake, looks like. That might mean they've called off the search."

"Might." But he didn't sound convinced.

"You want to sit up now?"

He said he did and I helped him. He huddled against the gunwale, not saying anything. He was still shaking but in little spasms, not hard like before. His skin color didn't seem as gray anymore.

"You look better," I said.

"Feel better. Warmer. I'll be okay."

"You sure?"

"I'm sure. You get going. The longer you hang around here, the more risk of you being caught with me."

"I don't care about that."

"I do. Go on, beat it."

"If I beat it, then what? What'll you do?"

"Sit here until I feel stronger."

"Then what?"

"You don't need to know that."

"Yes I do. Tell me, John."

"I don't know. See if I can hot-wire the ignition, maybe."

"That's good, getting away in the boat. But where to?"

"Somewhere on the other side of the lake. My problem, for Chrissake, not yours—"

"Big problem," I said, "if anybody sees you driving Ms. Sixkiller's boat. Everybody around here knows it's hers. And even if you do make it all the way across, what'll you do then? You're hurt too bad to do much except hide for a while, but you don't know the area well enough to find a safe place. And you'd have to leave the boat and they'd find it and then they'd know where you went. Right?"

He was quiet again, watching me.

"I do know a safe place," I said. "I can take you straight to it and get you inside."

". . . What place?"

"You'll see. It's safe, believe me. Nobody goes there. Nobody has any reason to anymore."

"Get there by boat?"

"Right to it. You won't need to try hot-wiring the ignition, either. I know where Ms. Sixkiller keeps the key." On a hook next to the fridge in her kitchen; I'd seen it and some others hanging there on my way out with the blankets and other stuff. "It'll only take me a couple of minutes to get it."

"You know how to drive a boat like this?"

"Sure. It's not hard. From a distance, with my scarf over my head, I'll pass for Ms. Sixkiller and you'll be hidden back here under the tarp. After you're safe, I'll bring the boat back and she'll never even know it was out."

"Unless she comes home meanwhile."

"It won't take more than an hour and a half, round trip. That's more than enough time."

"She could still come back early. What if she's here when you bring the boat in?"

"I'd tell her I went for a ride. She wouldn't turn me in to the cops or anything. Just yell at me a little. She's cool."

"The things you took from her house—she's bound to miss them."

"No, she won't." She *would*, once she saw the broken bathroom window, but I didn't care about that right now and I didn't want John to worry about it. I was so torqued up over helping him escape that nothing else seemed to matter, including the fetus growing inside me. It was dangerous, yeah, but it was also, like, major exciting. And I was doing it for all the right reasons, wasn't I? Besides, my life was so totally screwed up now, what difference did it make if it got even more screwed up later on?

John said, "I don't like it."

"But you know it's the only way. Neither of us wants you to go to prison or the gas chamber for something you didn't do."

"Yeah." He said it hard and angry, but it wasn't me he was pissed at. I knew that. "But you be careful. And you promise me something before we go. Promise me if we get caught together, you tell the law I forced you to help me. Threatened you, and you were too scared not to do what I told you."

"If you say so."

"I say so. Promise me, Trisha."

"I promise. So let's stop talking and just do it, okay?"

"Okay," he said in that same angry voice. "We'll do it."

Anthony Munoz

THE FIRST THING Mateo says when I walked into his pad was, "Where were you last night, little brother? You know what went down? You hear what a wild-ass scene it was?"

"I heard. The old man was yapping about it when I got up."

"Cracked her skull, man. Cracked it wide open."

"Yeah. Leaves a bad taste, man. That Mrs. Carey was a fox."

"*Lagarta*'s more like it. *Jode y una mamada*, that's all she was good for. Well, she picked the wrong dude this time."

"Yeah. But she didn't deserve no cracked skull."

"You don't think so? I think so."

"Why? Because she dissed you that time you tried to hit on her?"

"She was a bitch, man."

"I don't know, man. Dyin' like that . . ."

"Ain't no good way to die, is there?"

"Got that right. Old man says Faith drowned in the lake."

"Maybe the dude did, maybe he didn't."

"Or he iced out there. The old man says—"

"The old man don't know his dick from a paint scraper." Mateo laughed. "I'd love it if the dude's still alive, gets away with it. I'd love it, man."

"Why?"

"Told you, bro. She was a bitch and she had it comin'."

"I don't know, man."

"What *do* you know, man? Sometimes I wonder about you."

"Wonder what?"

"Just wonder. So where were you, Anthony? Man, we had a bigger street party than ten freakin' Fourth of Julys. Dudes cruisin', dudes doin' crank and blow and weed right in front of the heat, TV trucks, even a freakin' TV helicopter. A freakin' circus, man. And you missed the whole show."

"Yeah."

"Out balling Trisha, huh? Don't you ever get enough pussy?"

"Too much pussy, that's what I been getting."

"No such thing, man."

"She's knocked up."

"No shit? Trisha?"

"Who else."

"You go divin' without a wet suit?"

"One time. One freakin' time."

"That's all it takes, bro. Sure it's yours?"

"Yeah, it's mine. She don't lie, man."

"So what, then? She wants you to marry her?"

"What the hell else."

"What'd you tell her?"

"I told her no way, man."

"That's my man. Marriage sucks."

"Big time. Yeah."

"It's for jerks and squares, man."

"Yeah."

"Look at the old man and old lady. Him so wore out from paintin' houses all day, he can't do nothing at night except yell and swill down cheap wine. She ain't no better. Don't give a shit about me and you, each other, nothing but TV and Carlo Rossi."

"Yeah."

"Dudes like us, we got to be free. Free and easy, man. Go places, do things, see the fuckin' world, get ourselves a piece of the good life. No wives, no babies, no tied-down bullshit for Anthony and Mateo. Right?"

"Right."

"So how'd she take it? Trisha."

"Went ballistic, man. Jumped out of the car, ran off and hid in the freakin' trees. I couldn't find her."

"Where was this, man?"

"The Bluffs."

"So what'd you do?"

"Drove off and left her."

"Yeah, man." He put his hand out and I slapped it. "So then what'd you do?"

"I was pissed, you know? Wild. Drove around lookin' for you, Petey, somebody to hang with. Nobody around."

"We was partyin', man. Leon's homestead."

"Never thought to check Leon's. Shit."

"So then what'd you do?"

"Drove down to Southlake."

"Lookin' to score?"

"Yeah."

"What'd you get? Crank? Blow?"

"No man. Ecstasy."

"Cool. How was it?"

"Lame, man. I still don't feel right."

"How about some grass, pick you right up."

"Nah. I don't wanna get high."

"Half quarts of Green Death in the fridge."

"Not that neither. Too early, man."

"Never too early. Come on, let's pop one."

"Yeah, okay. What the hell."

Mateo went out to the kitchen to get the brews. I didn't want one, but I felt wrong for sure and I needed a lift. Wrong about leaving Trisha up there on the Bluffs even if she did go hag-crazy on me, all that *cagueta* about the baby and then running off and wouldn't come out of the freakin' trees. Wrong about that Mrs. Carey, too. Murder, man . . . it ain't right to kill somebody unless he's tryin' to ice you. It ain't right to hurt a chick that way, no matter who she is.

Mateo's pad is cool, man. Real dank. Old building down by the boatyard, second-floor pad with a little balcony so you can sit and check out the lake when the weather's right . . . suck down a brew or smoke a joint, whatever. Nobody lives here gives a Frenchman's fuck. He's got it fixed up with NASCAR posters, blowup color pix from Laguna Seca and Sears Point and Indy races. Not much furniture, none of the crap most people have. He's got the front seat out of a '52 Olds for a couch and buckets from a 'Vette and a TransAm for chairs. Can't get much more dank than that.

I got up from the tuck-and-roll 'Vette bucket and went to look at the biggest blowup. Real fiery Indy crash, one driver spinning out and hitting a wall, another car sliding into the flames. Cool. But I couldn't get my head into it. I kept flashing on Trisha and that goddamn baby, her going hag-crazy and me leaving her up there. Wasn't right, man. No matter what Mateo said, I shouldn't've done it.

Well, she'd got home okay. That was one thing I didn't have to sweat about. No answer when I buzzed her homestead this morning, so I took the wheels over there. Wasn't nobody home, but one of the neighbors says she seen Trisha walking off somewheres about a half hour before. So that was like a major relief, man. Didn't want nothing to do with me or she'd've tried to get in touch. Then why'd it keep bugging me like this? I didn't want a kid, and she wouldn't either when she thought it over hard enough. Her old man sure as hell wouldn't, not that dude. He'd tell her to lose it same as I did and she would and that'd be the end of it, right? She'd never have nothing more to do with me, but what the hell, I didn't love her or anything, right?

"What's the sad eye for?" Mateo was back with a couple of half quarts of Green Death. "Trisha?"

"Yeah." I popped the tab on my can and sucked down half the ale before I came up for air. "Trisha, that Mrs. Carey, the lame stuff I scored in Southlake . . . everything, man. Nothing feels right today."

"Most days, man."

"Yeah."

"It's this town, bro. Town, lake, county, the whole fuckin' sack."

I didn't say anything. I was thinking maybe I oughta go find Trisha, talk to her. Yeah. Talk some sense into her. I didn't want a kid, didn't love her, but that didn't mean I didn't have no feelings for her.

"Boneyard's what it is," Mateo says. "Keep on hangin' here, you end up hung dead and worm food. You know what I'm sayin'?"

"Loud and clear, man."

"So why don't we get out, man?"

"Get out?"

"Split for a place that's got life, action."

"Like where?"

"Like L.A. You know that's where I always wanted to be, man. I been thinkin' about it a lot lately."

"Yeah?"

"Yeah. Plenty happening down there, man. Couple of young dudes like us, hot with engines and wheels, we grab us a piece of the good life in no time." He winked. "Plenty of *almeja* down there, too, man."

"You mean just pick up and split?"

"We got nothing keepin' us here, right? Old man and old lady'd love it if you moved out, both of us outta their hair for good. And no more sweat about Trisha's kid. I mean, suppose she tries to stick you for support? Can't pry cash out of a dude if they can't find him, right?"

"Yeah. But when would we go?"

"Sooner the better. Tomorrow."

"Oh, man, that's too fast . . ."

"Listen, Anthony, either we put this hole behind us, change our freakin' lives, or we don't."

"I don't know, man. I got to think about it . . ."

"Yeah, sure," Mateo says. "Just don't think too long. I made up my mind—I'm outta here. With or without you, little brother, real soon."

Douglas Kent

THEY WOULDN'T LET me see her. I wasn't a relative by blood or marriage, friends of the victim were not allowed viewing privileges, members of the media weren't allowed viewing privileges, the autopsy had yet to be performed . . . a litany of official bullshit. The word "autopsy" funneled bile into my throat. Images of Storm with that beautiful head of hers shattered, lying cold and waxy and forever still on a metal table, was bad enough; images of her being drawn and quartered like a butchered heifer, her juices running in troughs or being sucked up through vacuum hoses, was intolerable.

I demanded an audience with the coroner, Johanssen. Pomo General's head nurse didn't want to let me see him, either. Head pounding, stomach churning, Kent pitched a small and voluble fit. When she saw I was perfectly willing to escalate into a large and disruptive fit, she went and fetched Johanssen.

Waste of time. Mine. He was harried and snippy and wouldn't tell me much of anything. Had instructions not to release specific details gleaned from his preliminary examination of the deceased, he said. That was what he called her, "the deceased," even though he'd known Storm well enough—they both belonged to the country club, attended the same charity fund-raisers.

No, Johanssen said, he couldn't tell me whether or not she'd been raped. No, he couldn't say if she had suffered any wounds or traumas other than the blows that had killed her. (But he insisted on providing me with a full medical description of the cause of death, as if he needed to prove his qualifications for the job of corpse handler. "Temporal skull fracture leading to subdural hematoma of mid brain. Death of brain due to necrosis or mass effect. Secondary edema causing herniation through foramen magnum, that is, the brain stem." Jesus!) Had I spoken to Chief Novak or Mayor Seeley yet? No? Well, why didn't I go and do that? Or perhaps I'd be better advised to go home and sleep it off.

"I'm not drunk," I said. Yet.

"Your breath and your appearance contradict that statement."

Kent stood in impotent rage as the pompous little prick walked off, his back straight and his bald pate gleaming in the hallway fluorescents.

A hand plucked at my sleeve. Dietrich, the overeager wanna-be; I'd forgotten he was there. "We'd better leave, Mr. Kent."

"I wish it'd been that bald head of his."

". . . Mr. Kent?"

"The temporal skull fracture, the subdural hematoma of mid brain," I said. "His head opened up like a melon, his glop that poured out. Him the corpse on the table instead of her."

"Oh, wow," Dietrich whispered.

"Yes. Exactly. All right, let's get out of here."

We went to the police station. Arrived just in time to catch Chief Novak exiting into the side parking lot, alone, hotfooting it for his cruiser as if he expected to be assailed by a mob of slavering Fourth Estaters at any second. The only Fourth Estaters in the vicinity, one slavering, the other wishing to Christ he had a drink, drew up alongside. He recognized us, but he went ahead and hopped into his cruiser anyway. No one wanted much to do with Kent today, it seemed. Including Dougie his own self.

I said, "Hold your horses, Chief. A few questions."

"Not now. I don't have time."

"At least tell me about Faith. Found yet?"

"No."

"Lakeshore still being searched?"

"Not the way I'd like it to be."

"Explain that."

"Talk to Sheriff Thayer. Or the mayor."

"Dissension in the ranks, Chief?"

He didn't answer that. His face, bruised, discolored, bandaged, resembled a Halloween fright mask; muscles wiggled under the skin surface like maggots on a chunk of spoiled meat. (Poor choice of simile, Kent. Summoned up fresh images of Storm on the autopsy table.) Novak's eyes burned hot: pain, hate, determination. I knew exactly how he felt. My lust had been unrequited, his hadn't; that was the only difference between us as torchbearers in the Storm Carey Olympics.

"Do you think he's dead?" That from Dietrich, butting in.

"Faith?" The Chief's mouth tightened; the muscle maggots seemed to scurry under his eyes and along his cheeks. "I can't answer that."

"Then there's a chance he's alive?"

"Without a body . . . yeah, there's a chance."

"What's your best guess?" I asked him. "Dead or alive?"

Headshake. He started the engine.

"If he is alive, there's no way he could escape, is there?" Dietrich again. "Find some way out of the area, evade capture altogether?"

"No," Novak said flatly, "there's no way."

He jammed the cruiser into gear, zoomed off toward Main.

"What now, Mr. Kent?"

"I don't suppose we can get onto the Carey property. Look around up there ourselves."

"No, they've got the entire area cordoned off. I drove by before I went to your place."

"All right, then it's back to the Kent digs." I needed salve. I needed to lie low for a while. So many sticks in the bag now, the combined weight was about to split me apart at the seams. Humpty-Dumpty Kent. "After you drop me off, come back here and hang around. If there are any new developments, I want to know about them right away."

"You'll be home all day?"

"No. At the office later on. One or the other."

"Are you planning to write the story about the murder, Mr. Kent? I mean, if you wouldn't mind, I'd like to take a shot at it myself."

"Go ahead." What did I care? I couldn't write it—not this one. "Just make sure you do it on your laptop at the station, and don't forget to let me know the minute there's any word on Faith."

"You can count on me," Dietrich said. "I sure hope they find him soon."

"They damn well better."

And he damn well better be dead when they do. The thought of Bigfoot alive, somehow managing to cheat capital punishment altogether, was even more intolerable than the thought of the corpse processor carving up the deceased with his trusty saw and scalpel.

Trisha Marx

WE DIDN'T HAVE any trouble crossing the lake and I found Nucooee Point okay, but getting us into the rickety old dock was kind of hairy. The water was covered with whitecaps, even though the wind wasn't strong over on the east shore, and Ms. Sixkiller's boat was bigger and had more power than the one we used to own. The first time I tried it, I shut down to idle in plenty of time but the current dragged us over faster than I expected and I didn't get the gear lever into reverse soon enough. The left side—port side—banged hard into the float edge and for a second after we bounced off I thought we might capsize. But I quick put the power on and the boat settled and then we were out away from the dock again, going backward. I slid into neutral and let us drift while I chilled enough to give it another try.

John had his head out from under the canvas. "Sorry about that," I said to him. "I'll do better next time."

"Still nobody in sight?"

"Uh-uh. You can come out now if you want."

He pushed the canvas all the way back and eased himself up against the port gunwale. He was still in a lot of pain, you could see that, but he'd gotten some of his strength back and he moved better than before. He took in the cottonwoods and willows that grew thick along the shoreline on down to the Bluffs half a mile away. The lodge buildings were scattered inland among oaks and pepperwood trees, all except for the old dance pavilion downshore, south of the dock.

He said, "Can't see the highway from here."

"No. It's on the other side of that big building straight ahead. Nobody out there can see us, either. Perfect, huh?"

"Yeah." He sat up a little more, onto one hip so he could lean out over the side. "Ready when you are."

I was more careful this time and I took us in with just a little bump and scrape against the float. John caught onto one of the rusty iron rings and held us close so I could clamber out and tie the bow line, then the stern line. I felt sort of spacey when I was done, like I was on this natural high. It made me tingle all over; I could feel it like a hand stroking down between my legs.

"Here," John said, "take my wallet." He must've got it out of his Levi's on the way over, before he tied up the rest of his stuff with some fishing line and a lead sinker from the storage locker and dropped the bundle overboard. "Give it back to me when we get where we're going."

I put the wallet into my pocket, along with what was left of the tape and gauze pads. The peroxide, and a quart of OJ and a couple of apples I'd lifted from Ms. Sixkiller's fridge when I went back for the key, I tied inside my jacket. It all made me bulge like a klepto on a spree. I kept the flashlight from the storage locker in my hand; we were gonna need it pretty soon. Then I helped John get out onto the float. Even with me to hang on to, his legs were so wobbly I was afraid he'd fall down. He said, "Let me rest a minute," and leaned against one of the pilings and sucked in a bunch of deep breaths, holding the blankets closed around him. We must've been some sight, me all bulgy and him like a monk or something in those blankets.

I said, "Think you can walk okay?"

"How far?"

"A ways. Maybe a couple of hundred yards?"

"I'll manage. We'll just have to take it slow."

We took it slow, my arm around his waist and his arm across my shoulders. There wasn't any ladder to climb; the float was hooked to a railed ramp and the ramp took us onto an overgrown path. When we got up there we stopped again to rest.

Real quiet here; the only sound was the wind swishing in the trees. Spooky place at night, but during the day it wasn't anything but a bunch of old redwood log buildings and what was left of a terrace and a couple of weedy tennis courts. The open-sided pavilion was in the worst shape;

its lakeside wall had cracks in it and pieces of concrete missing where the cracks were widest, and the roof sagged on one side like it was getting ready to collapse. The six boarded-up cabins, three on each side of the inlet, seemed to be sinking into the ground on account of all the weeds and tall grass and oleander shrubs that had grown up around them. The main lodge, two stories high, crowded by oaks on both sides, was in the best shape. At least it looked pretty solid from back here, even with all its windows and doors covered with shutters and sections of plywood. The terrace made you think of some kind of jungle ruins, with all the stuff growing up through the flagstones and hunks of the plaster statues that'd toppled over and big pieces of concrete busted off what'd once been a fancy waist-high wall.

John asked, "What is this place?"

"Nucooee Point Lodge. Nucooee's an Indian word for some kind of fish. Shiner fish, I think."

"Indian land?"

"Well, it was once, a long time ago." We were walking again, following what was left of the path leading to the terrace. "The lodge was built sixty or seventy years ago. Rich people's resort, you know?"

"Abandoned how long?"

"A year or so. Shut down for a long time in the eighties, then somebody bought it about five years ago and reopened it, but they couldn't get enough business. It's up for sale again. My daddy says if it sells, it'll just be for the land."

"Caretaker?"

"Uh-uh."

"Special patrols of any kind?"

"No. You don't have to worry, John. Nobody'll find you here."

"We going to the main lodge?"

"Yeah. There's a way inside."

"How do you know?"

"Been in there. Couple of times last summer, a bunch of us came over and snuck in and partied. And again on Halloween."

"Some place for a party."

"Pretty cool, actually. Except for the bats." I shuddered, remembering how one of the things had brushed past my face the first night. It made a sound like a leather belt being snapped close to your ear. Ugh. "Bats don't bother you, do they? Or rats or spiders?"

"Better company than most people. You don't bother them, they don't bother you."

We rested again at the crumbling terrace wall, then picked our way across to the south corner of the lodge. I kept glancing back at the lake, just to make sure no other boats came along. It looked wide and wind-blown from here; the homes and town buildings along the west shore were like miniatures about two inches high. I tried not to think about the long trip back across, alone, in Ms. Sixkiller's boat. Or of anything else that might happen later on. The major thing was getting John inside where it was safe.

The way in was on the south side—a service door that opened into a storeroom off the kitchen. The door was covered with plywood, but the first night, Anthony and Mateo had pried it off with a crowbar and then busted the door lock; afterward they'd put the plywood back up with the nails in their original holes, so unless you got up close and started messing around, you couldn't tell the section was loose.

I showed John, and together we stripped off the plywood. "I'll put it back up when I leave," I said, and he nodded and we went inside.

Dark, musty, and dusty. Muggy hot in the summer, cold on Hallow-een night and almost as chilly now. I switched on the flashlight. Empty shelves and cobwebs jumped out and jumped back as I swung the beam around and we moved ahead into the kitchen. There wasn't much left in there, just a couple of long metal tables and some old sinks and exposed piping. The door to the walk-in freezer was half open. Selena's boyfriend, Petey Dexter, had locked her in there for about ten minutes on Halloween and she'd been so pissed when he let her out she'd tried to kick him in the balls. We all thought it was pretty funny at the time. Somehow it didn't seem so funny now.

Across the kitchen was an archway that led into the dining room: more cobwebs and a bunch of stacked-up folding chairs. We'd taken some of the chairs into the big, wide lobby and arranged them in front of a fieldstone fireplace that must've been six feet across. The rest of the lobby was a mess. It was gloomy in there, but threads of daylight came through cracks in the plywood covering the tall front windows and let you see enough so you could move around without tripping over things. Candle stubs and beer cans and cigarette butts and bags from Mickey D's and other crap that we should've taken with us was thrown around on the moldy carpet. Rats and mice had been at the bags; they were all torn up. They'd been at the two old leather couches that'd been left behind, too, pulling out stuffing to make nests with or something. The front desk and the cubbyhole thing for mail and keys that'd been behind it were just a lot of splintered boards; Mateo, wasted on crank and Green Death, had broken them up with the crowbar the first night. Made so much noise we were all afraid somebody driving by on the highway would hear. Anthony and Mateo— the Loser Brothers.

John was wobbly again after the long walk, sweating and breathing hard. He nearly collapsed onto one of the couches, dust puffing up around him like smoke in the flash beam. Some little pelletlike things that were probably turds bounced off onto the floor. I said, "Might be mice nesting inside there," but he didn't seem to care. He laid his head back and sat there with the blankets all tangled around him.

"You okay, John?"

"Weak. Wound's bleeding again."

"Want some more of the peroxide?"

"Yeah."

He untangled himself, and I held the light so he could see to work off the bandages. Blood gleamed on them and on the wounds. He poured peroxide on and it frothed and hissed the way it had on the boat, only it didn't seem to hurt him so much this time. He taped on more of the gauze pads, and when he was done his face was white and dripping sweat.

"All you've done for me, Trisha," he said then, "I hate to ask for more. But it's either that or my chances aren't much better than they were before you found me."

"What d'you mean?"

"Peroxide and plain pads won't be enough to keep the wounds from infecting. I'll need other stuff."

"What kind of stuff?"

"Not sure. I've never been shot before."

"I'll get whatever you need. Maybe I can look it up in a book or something . . ."

"Might be a better way."

"Like what?"

"One that gets you out of it and puts somebody else at risk. I hate the idea, but I'd also hate sitting here and rotting."

"What're you talking about, John? What somebody else?"

"You know the blond waitress works nights at the Northlake Cafe? Lori?"

"Lori Banner? Sure, I know her. But—"

"She had some nurse's training. She'd know what you need to treat gunshot wounds and where to get it."

"What makes you think she'd help?"

"Just a feeling. If there's anybody else in Pomo besides you who thinks I'm innocent, it's Lori."

"You want me to talk to her?"

"If you're willing to take the chance."

"Like, just come right out and tell her you're alive and wounded and where you are?"

"No. Go slow, feel her out . . . no details until you're sure you can trust her. And don't say anything about helping me get over here. You happened to be snooping around and you found me by accident."

"Okay. If it's what you want."

"It's not what I want. It's what I've got to have to survive."

"More food, too, right? And some clothes?"

"Right. Lori can bring them if she agrees to come."

"Don't you want me to come back?"

"No. Not unless Lori refuses."

"Why not?"

"You know why not."

"Don't keep telling me how much trouble I can get into, all right? I'm already in trouble, man. Seventeen and knocked up, remember?"

Even in the poor light I could see he really hated all this, really did care about me not getting in trouble on account of him. It made me even more sure I was doing the right thing. Not many people cared what happened to me. Not Anthony, for instance. A stranger like John was a better friend than my own freaking boyfriend.

I gave him back his wallet. The flashlight, too; I didn't need it and he might. "You just rest easy, John," I said then. "Everything's gonna be okay. No kidding. It's gonna be okay."

He didn't say anything. He sat there staring at nothing, staring at shadows, while I made my way out.

Harry Richmond

ONE GOOD THING about Storm Carey getting herself killed—it's been a boon to business. I didn't even mind losing most of a night's sleep, what with cops and reporters and rubberneckers showing up in a steady stream until well past two A.M. and that TV helicopter making an ungodly racket and the police search teams with their bright lights along the northwest shore and in the sloughs above the Carey place. Why, I felt like a celebrity there for a while. First time in my life, and I don't mind saying I liked it just fine.

Novak and Sheriff Thayer came out first, asked questions, and then hunted through what Faith left behind in cabin six. I could've told them before I let them in with my passkey that they wouldn't find a thing, but of course I didn't. Nobody's business but mine that I'd been in there hunting myself on Friday, after Novak left. Pathetic, what that mean, snotty bastard carried in his only suitcase. Puzzling and annoying, too. Couple of shirts, one pair of slacks, one pair of jeans, some underwear and socks. Nothing else except for a tangle of dirty laundry. No personal items. No valuables. Yet he'd had that big wad of money in his wallet. What'd he spend it on, if not clothes or men's jewelry or electronic gadgets or a decent car? That's what I'd like to know.

It's what I asked the reporters that followed Novak and Thayer out, too. Asked the question on camera, in an interview with a Santa Rosa TV newswoman. Also told all about how Storm Carey came out yesterday afternoon and visited Faith in cabin six, and what a hot number she was and what a cold one he'd been. I came off pretty good—and that's not just me blowing my horn, it's what the newswoman told me afterward. Interview's supposed to be on sometime today. I watched the early news, but it wasn't on then. Noon, maybe. Or seven o'clock. They'd better use it sometime; it's sure to mean even more business, people showing up to get a look at the cabin where Storm Carey's murderer stayed and then likely staying on themselves, at least for one night.

Two of the reporters took cabins last night, one from the San Francisco *Chronicle*. He said he'd use my name and mention Lakeside Resort in his story—more free publicity. I had two other cabins rented before that, by weekenders up from the Bay Area to gamble at the Brush Creek casino, and the last two went after all the excitement died down to a couple from Ukiah who didn't want to drive back so late and to another couple, young and sure not married, that I figured were out for an all-night sex binge. I told the boy the rate was seventy-five and he paid it without an argument. None of my business what people do inside one of my cabins, long as they don't trash the place or steal sheets or towels or the TV.

I didn't have much time to myself this morning, either. Folks checking out, a few more rubberneckers, arguing on the phone with Maria Lorenzo because she wouldn't come in early like I asked her to. Had to go to a christening, she said. Her and her religion. One of the worst things the white man ever did, you ask me, was to convert the heathens to Christianity. She finally showed up at eleven-thirty, half an hour later than she'd promised, with a lame excuse about the start of the christening being delayed. I told her she'd better have all the cabins done by two and then went in to eat my lunch a little early. There's nothing like making money for a change to give a man an appetite.

Fixing lunch made me realize I was low on items like milk and bread and cold meat. I could've sent Maria out to buy my groceries when she was finished with her cleaning—I'd done it before—but then I'd have to pay her a couple of bucks extra. And it was a nice day, sunny, and I felt like getting out in the car for a while. I waited until the noon news came on the Santa Rosa channel, to see if they'd show my interview. They didn't. Long story about the murder, interviews with three other locals but not mine. A little miffed, I went out and yelled at Maria to keep an eye on the office. Then I got the car out and drove south to Brush Creek.

The grocery store there is the only shop in the village still open on Sundays. One of the few stores still open for business, period. The place looks like a ghost town with all the empty and boarded-up buildings. If Miller's Grocery dies, what's left of Brush Creek will die along with it and then it'll *be* a ghost town.

On the way back, on the stretch of road that runs close to the lake just north of the village, I noticed a boat heading shoreward on this side. It was well beyond the Bluffs, several hundred yards offshore. Looked like Audrey Sixkiller's old Chris-Craft. In fact, I was sure it was. There's no other like it on this part of the lake, and even at a distance you can't mistake those boxy lines and dark, burnished hull. Besides, this time of year she's about the only one you're likely to see out on the water. Crazy damn Indians'll do things a white man wouldn't if you paid him.

I drove on up and over the high ground, down past Nucooee Point, and it wasn't until I neared my resort that I had a wide view of the lake again. And there wasn't any sign of Audrey's boat anywhere. Not then and still not when I pulled into the Lakeside and took another look from there. Puzzled me. The shoreline above and below the Bluffs is too rocky and overgrown for even a fisherman's skiff to put in. There's only one spot you can dock along the two-mile wooded stretch where she'd been heading, and that had to be where she'd gone. The question was why.

Why in hell would Audrey Sixkiller want to put in at the ruins of Nucooee Point Lodge?

Zenna Wilson

HOWARD AND STEPHANIE came into the kitchen just as I hung up the phone. They both had their jackets on. And Steffie was wearing that dreadful Hootie and the Blowfish sweatshirt she's so fond of. Howard should never have bought it for her. That singing group may not be as bad as most nowadays, the ones with their filthy language and suggestive lyrics, but it's still not the proper music for an impressionable nine-year-old to be listening to and admiring.

"Well," I said, "where are you two off to?"

She said, "The park."

"Not Municipal, I hope. It's still a madhouse downtown, and the police station's right across the street. You know what I mean, Howard."

"Highland Park," Steffie said before he could answer.

"Oh, well, that's all right. But why don't you change first, sweetie? Put on a sweater and skirt."

She wrinkled her mouth in that pouty way she has lately. Lord knows which of her schoolmates she learned *that* little trick from. "We're gonna play Frisbee. You can't play Frisbee in a sweater and skirt."

"At least put on a different top."

"I like this one. Dad, what's wrong with this one?"

"Nothing, baby." Taking her side, naturally, the way he always does. "You look fine. Go on out to the car. I'll be along in a minute or two."

"Okay. 'Bye, Mom."

She skipped off and banged the door behind her. I swear she does it on purpose sometimes because she knows it annoys me.

Howard said, "I don't suppose you want to come with us."

"No, you go ahead. I have some things to do here."

"More phone calls?"

"Howard, please don't start. Lunch will be ready at twelve-thirty, so be sure you and Steffie—"

"You're glad Storm Carey's dead, aren't you? I mean, really happy about it."

". . . That's ridiculous. What on earth makes you say such a thing?"

"You sounded happy on the phone a minute ago."

"Don't be silly," I said. "A shocking murder not two miles from our home—that's hardly cause for rejoicing."

"I heard what you said to Helen Carter. 'The Jezebel got exactly what she deserved. We're all better off rid of the likes of her.'"

"Well? Aren't we better off?"

"No. She wasn't a whore, Zenna."

"Of course she was. How can you defend her?"

"I'm not defending her. I'm saying she wasn't a whore or an evil person just because she slept around. She had problems—"

"Problems!"

"Yes, problems. Losing her husband the way she did, for one. And she did plenty of good for this community."

"Fornicating with every man she could lay hands on, married as well as unmarried, flaunting her drunken ways in public . . . I don't see any good in any of that, Howard. You can't mock the Lord and His teachings without suffering the consequences."

"So you are glad she's dead. A woman who never did anything to you, never harmed anyone except herself—brutally murdered—and you're downright ecstatic."

"I am not ecstatic!" He was making me very angry.

"Yes, you are. Ecstatic she'd dead, ecstatic it was that stranger who killed her because it vindicates your judgment of him, too."

"My judgment? He was a degenerate, for heaven's sake! Anyone with half a mind could tell that."

"Cause for rejoicing, after all. Not one but two of Satan's minions destroyed in one night."

"All right! Yes, I'm glad they're dead, both of them, glad they're suffering in the Pit where they belong! Why shouldn't I be? Any good Christian should shout hallelujah and fall on his knees with joy when the Almighty cleanses away evil, and a good Christian woman is what I am and I won't apologize for it to you or anyone else."

The way he was staring at me stirred a coldness into my anger. "My God," he said in a tone I'd never heard from him before. And then again, before he went out, "My God."

I don't understand that man sometimes. I swear I don't. Even after more than ten years together under the same roof, there are moments when he's a complete stranger to me.

Audrey Sixkiller

W H E N I F O U N D the bathroom window broken, my first thought was that it must've been done by the stalker—that he might still be inside the house. Irrational, because I'd been home from the rancheria three or four minutes by then and nothing had happened, but that didn't prevent me from rushing to my purse and taking out the Ruger automatic. I'd put the gun in there this morning, after the phone call; it was illegal for me to carry it without a permit, but under the circumstances I didn't much care about technicalities and Dick hadn't either when I told him. With the Ruger in hand, I checked through the house room by room.

No one there but me.

But someone *had* been inside. I could feel it by then, the faint aura of intrusion, even though at first I didn't notice anything disturbed or missing. That came on closer inspection, on my second pass through.

A few items gone from the bathroom cabinet. Peroxide . . . gauze pads . . . adhesive tape. Anything missing from the bedroom? Yes. Empty space on the closet shelf where I'd kept my extra blankets. The living room? No. The kitchen? Yes. Orange juice and two apples from the fridge. My office? No. The back porch? No.

Medical supplies, blankets, food.

It didn't make sense. Or did it?

It could be the stalker, in an attempt to devil me—but I doubted he was that subtle. A man who tries to break into a woman's home in the dead of night wearing a ski mask, who makes the kind of phone threat he'd made to me, wouldn't break a window for any reason except to get in and at his victim. He wouldn't bother to steal a few inconsequential items, either.

Neither would a burglar; there were too many items of value, like my Apple PC, that hadn't been touched.

Neither would kids playing games. For the same reason, and because there was no sign of vandalism, nothing out of place.

It had to be someone who needed exactly what was stolen. Medical supplies, blankets, food. Someone hurt. And hungry. And cold and perhaps wet.

John Faith?

Not possible, I told myself. John Faith is dead, drowned in the lake. But of course it *was* possible. Dick believed the man was still alive, and his professional instincts were trustworthy. The prospect chilled me. John Faith in my house, a murderer in my home—

And then out of it again. Where would he go from here, with the things he'd taken?

The boat!

I threw my jacket on and ran out to the dock. The Chris-Craft was still there inside the shed, on the hoist and wearing its tarpaulin cover. But I went out on the dock anyway. The security door was unlatched, not that that meant anything because I wasn't always as careful as I should be about making sure it was closed tight. On an impulse I climbed down the ladder, went in along the float.

Even in the shadows I could see that the hoist frame was wet, and the long, fresh scrape on the port side of the hull above the waterline.

I stepped up on the frame, untied the tarp and folded it over, and climbed aboard. When I raised the engine housing, heat and the smell of warm oil radiated out at me. The deck had been washed down hastily, I thought, and not very carefully. On the rear of the pilot's seat was a stain of something crusty that looked like dried blood. Wool fibers, blanket fibers, were caught where the seat was bolted to the deck. I checked the storage locker. A spool of fishing line, a lead sinker, and my flashlight were gone.

Someone had had the boat out in my absence, and brought it back no more than an hour ago—someone who'd been careless docking it here or elsewhere. That much was clear. What wasn't clear was why the boat was here now. If it'd been John Faith, there was no earthly reason for him to bring it back . . .

I climbed out, and when I finished retying the tarp I had the answer. Not one person—two. John Faith and an accomplice who'd taken him to an unknown destination and then returned alone, hoping I wouldn't notice immediately that the boat had been used. That person was the one who'd broken into the house. Blood here but none inside.

It seemed fantastic, yet it was the only explanation that fit the facts. But who in Pomo would help a stranger like John Faith, a suspected murderer?

I was on my way back to the house when I remembered what I'd forgotten in all the chaotic events of last night and this morning. The appointment I'd made for nine o'clock, here, with Trisha Marx.

Lori Banner

I WAS PRETTY surprised when I opened the door and saw Trisha Marx standing on the porch. I knew her from the cafe; she'd been in dozens of times on my shift, usually with that good-looking Mexican boyfriend of hers and the rest of the semi-tough crowd she hangs out with. But she'd never been particularly friendly to me. And she'd sure never come to the house before, or even said two words to me anywhere outside the Northlake.

"Can I talk to you, Mrs. Banner?" Mrs. Banner, not Lori like in the cafe. "It's really important."

"Well . . ."

"*Really* important."

"If it's about the fight last night—"

"Fight? What fight?"

"Your dad didn't tell you about it?"

"No. He had a fight with somebody? Who?"

"John Faith." Saying his name brought back the down feeling I'd had when I first heard about him and Storm Carey. It was so hard to believe they were both dead. "At the Northlake, around ten-thirty."

"Oh, God. Was it about John giving me a ride home?"

"Yeah. Your dad accused him of trying to molest you and then took a sock at him. Knocked him down."

"What'd John do?"

"Nothing. Walked away."

She had an odd look on her face. "He never said a word. Not one word."

"Well, if that's not why you're here . . ."

"Can we talk in private? Just the two of us?"

"There's nobody home but me." Earle had gone out about ten. He hadn't said where and I didn't care anyway. I touched my mouth where he'd hit me yesterday; the upper lip was still sore, but the swelling was gone. One of my teeth was loose, too. He'd been all sorry and lovey-dovey last night, but that was because he wanted to get laid. I wouldn't let him. I'd had about all I was going to take of his abuse and I'd told him so. He said he'd never hit me again, swore up and down. Well, he'd better keep his promise this time. It's his last chance.

Trisha came in and we sat in the living room and the first thing she said was, "Isn't it awful, what happened to Mrs. Carey?"

"Worst thing in Pomo since I've lived here."

"You think he did it? John Faith?"

"Everybody says he did."

"But do you think so?"

I'd worried that around most of the morning. Sure, he'd looked capable of killing somebody, with his size and that craggy, scarred face and his silver eyes. But I kept remembering the deep-down gentleness in those eyes, and the little-boy-lost sadness in him, and what he'd said about the world being a better place if people quit hurting other people and left each other alone. His last words to me, too, after the trouble with Brian Marx, "See? Not in this lifetime." He could've taken Brian apart real easy, but he hadn't done anything except stand his ground. He may've looked violent, but inside, where it counts, he wasn't. Just the opposite of Earle. And we were supposed to believe he went out right afterward and beat Storm Carey's head in?

"No," I said.

"You mean that?"

"You bet I mean it."

"I don't think he did it either. I *know* he didn't."

"How could you know it?"

"I just do. He wouldn't hurt anybody unless they hurt him first. He's not what people say he is."

"No, not at all."

"I'd help him in a minute if I could," she said.

"Help him how?"

"You know, stay out of jail. Get away."

"Well, nobody can help him now."

"They could if he wasn't dead."

"You don't think he drowned in the lake?"

"Maybe not." She wet her lips. She looked intense, her blue eyes bright and shiny. "What if he's still alive? What if he's hurt and hiding somewhere?"

"Trisha, what're you trying to say?"

"Would *you* help him if you could? If you were the only person who could do what had to be done?"

A peculiar fluttery sensation had started under my breastbone. And all of a sudden my mouth was dry. I said, "How badly hurt?"

"Bad enough. Say, a couple of bullet wounds."

"In a vital spot?"

"No. Like under the shoulder."

"Bullet still inside?"

"Uh-uh. A *couple* of wounds."

"Entrance and exit. That's better, cleaner. Still, wounds like that can infect pretty easily."

"Yeah. He'd need antibiotics and other stuff, right? And somebody who'd had medical training to get it for him and then fix him up."

"Where is he, Trisha?"

"How should I know? At the bottom of the lake, maybe. We're just talking here."

"We're not just talking. You know where he is, don't you?"

"What if I do?"

"Is it someplace where he's safe?"

"Safe enough. You think I should tell the cops?"

"I didn't say that."

"They'd just put him in jail, maybe the gas chamber. For something he didn't do."

"I know."

"Should I just let him die?"

"No."

"So what would you do? If you knew for sure he was alive and wounded and where he was hiding."

"He asked you to talk to me, didn't he? Last night . . . I mentioned my nurse's training and he remembered."

"You didn't answer my question, Mrs. Banner."

"Lori," I said. Then I said, "I'd help him."

"No shit? Even though it'd be breaking the law?"

"Aiding and abetting a fugitive, it's called."

"Whatever. You wouldn't call the cops?"

"No, I wouldn't call the cops. I won't call them."

"Swear to God?"

"Swear to God. Where is he? How'd you find him?"

"I won't tell you that. Not yet."

"But you'd take me to him."

"If you had the stuff he needs."

"I can get it. All except a tetanus shot—there's no way I can manage that."

"Where'll you have to go?"

"Rexall Pharmacy."

"They won't get suspicious or anything?"

"No." I was breathing hard. Scared and hyped up both, the same as she was. Jeez-us!

"He'll have to have some food," Trisha said. "And clothes. All he's got to wear now are a couple of blankets."

"That's no problem. Plenty of food here. And Earle, my husband, is nearly the same size. Money, though . . . I don't have much."

"He doesn't need money. He's got his wallet."

"What about transportation? Do you have a car?"

"No. We'll have to go in yours."

"That's no problem. But I meant a way for him to travel when he's well enough . . . Oh, God, worry about that later. First things first. And we'd better hurry." Before I had time to think too much about what I was getting myself into. Before I could change my mind. And before Earle decided to come home. "Kitchen's through the doorway over there. You gather up some food—there're paper bags under the sink. I'll get the clothes."

We were both on our feet, and for about five seconds we stood with our eyes locked. Thinking the same thing, probably. When she'd arrived, less than twenty minutes ago, we'd been more or less strangers, a generation apart and barely civil to each other whenever we met. Now, thanks to John Faith, a kind of serious bonding thing had happened. Well, that was the sort he was, and I guess I knew it the first time I laid eyes on him in the Northlake. You were either for him or against him, no matter what he said or did. All the way, either way.

George Petrie

I *AM* BEING followed.

By a dark-green van, one of the small, newer ones with the slanted front end. I can't tell if the driver is the gray-haired man from the Truckee motel or somebody else; can't even be sure of how many people are inside. The van's windshield is tinted and splinters of sunlight off glass and metal make it even more difficult to see.

I first spotted the van outside Sparks, when I pulled back onto the highway after buying a pair of canvas suitcases to keep the money in. It stayed behind me when I took the Highway 50 cutoff, and it's been there ever since through Fallon and across the open desert past Sand Mountain. Every time I speed up or slow down or pass another car, it does the same.

It *has* to be the gray-haired man. No one from Pomo could've tracked me; no other stranger could possibly know about the garbage bags or suspect what's in them. I don't remember a dark-green van in the motel parking lot, but it could've been parked behind one of the units. Must've followed me all the way from Truckee. Too much traffic for me to pick it out until the flow thinned coming through Reno.

I don't know what to do.

Keep on going to Ely as planned? Another two hundred miles of empty desert and barren mountains, sun glare and heat shimmers off the highway, even at this time of year, that have my eyes burning, my head aching? No. Couldn't take the tension. And some of the country ahead is even more desolate. He could overtake me without much effort; this old Buick can't outrun a van like that. Force me off the road when there's no one around. He's bound to have a weapon, and there's nothing I can use to defend myself. Easy for him to kill me, bury my body where no one would ever find it—

Road sign. Junction with State Highway 361 six miles ahead.

There'll be a rest stop; usually is at a desert crossroads. Service station, convenience store, maybe a restaurant. People. If I pull in there he'll follow me and then . . . what? Confront him? He wouldn't dare try anything with people around. But confronting him won't accomplish anything. Let me get a good look at him, that's all. He'd deny following me. Brazen it out. Then sit back in his van and wait for me to drive out onto the highway again.

Three miles to the junction. And he's even closer behind me now, crowding up, the sun like fire on that tinted windshield.

Christ Jesus, what am I going to do!

Earle Banner

SATURDAY'S MY DAY off, but I went down to the shop anyway since I didn't have nothing else to do. Stan was there and we shot the bull for a while, mostly about what a piece Storm Carey was and how that bugger Faith got off too easy, sucking lake water. "Should've had his nuts put in a vise," Stan said, and I said, "Yeah, that's for sure," but I was thinking, Yeah, it's too bad about Storm, she was a sweet lay, some of the best I ever had, but that didn't change the fact she was a bitch and she'd been asking for what Faith give her for a long time. Same as Lori kept asking for it. Bet *she* didn't think Faith got off too easy. Bet she was sorry he was dead meat, even if she hadn't been letting him boink her and he'd had to go after Storm instead.

After a while a couple of the other guys showed up, and then somebody said why didn't we go over to Pandora's and get us a few cold ones? So we did that. Regulation pool table in Pandora's, better balanced than most you find in bars, and we started playing eight ball, loser buys a round. Before you knew it it was past noon and I'd had seven or eight Buds and was about half in the bag. Feeling good, yeah, and horny, too. Beer always does that to me, fires up the blood, puts lead in the old pencil. The guys wanted to shoot another game, but I said no, I was gonna go home and eat my old lady for lunch. They all laughed, and I walked out and headed for my Ford.

And who did I see across the street, leaving the Rexall Pharmacy with a big sack in her hot little hands? Yeah. Lori. My sweet, lying wife, supposed to be home, says to me this morning she was just gonna putter around the house all day.

She wasn't alone, neither. Had a passenger, somebody waiting for her in that little Jap car of hers. I couldn't see who it was, wrong angle and the windshield being dirty, but I figured it must be some lousy son of a bitch she'd picked up somewhere and I was about ready to charge over there and drag both their asses out into the street. But then she was inside and putting the car in gear and coming my way, so I ducked down behind a parked car. When I looked up again as they were passing I seen her passenger was a woman. No, not even that—a teenage kid. Brian Marx's kid, Trisha.

What the hell?

I ran around the corner to the Ford and made a fast U-turn and swung out onto Main. The Jap car was stopped at the light two blocks north. She could've been on her way to do more shopping, or going to Brian's house to drop the kid off, or going home—only she wasn't, none of those things. She stayed right on Main, and once she was clear of the business district she goosed it up to forty-five. Usually she don't drive no more than the speed limit, scared to death of getting a ticket. Heading for the Northlake Cutoff, on her way to someplace she had no business being, by God, her and that tight-assed little Trisha Marx.

Wherever she was going, she was gonna have company she didn't expect. Yeah, and if she was looking to let some other guy eat her for lunch, she'd be one sorry babe. I didn't feel horny no more. I felt mean as a snake with a gopher's balls stuck in its throat.

Trisha Marx

I DIDN'T TELL Lori where we were going until we were almost there. It wasn't a trust thing; I'd been pretty sure back there at her homestead and she hadn't done or said anything to make me change my mind: She wouldn't give John away to the cops. I guess what it was was that John and I had this secret together, a really special secret, the kind you'd be reluctant to let your best friend in on, and now I had to share it with somebody who was practically a stranger. You want to keep a secret like that all to yourself as long as you can, sort of savor it, because when you finally do share it it's never quite so special anymore.

When I finally told Lori it was Nucooee Point Lodge she said, "How'd he get all the way over here?"

"I took him."

"You took him? How?"

So I had to tell her about that, too. And afterward I felt kind of let down, not nearly so torqued as before. Right. Share a secret and it's never quite the same.

"A good thing you know how to drive a boat," she said. "If it'd been me, I don't think I could've done it."

That picked me up again, a little. "I didn't have any trouble."

"Must've been scary, though. All the way across the lake in a borrowed boat."

"No," I lied. "I wasn't scared a bit."

The turn for the lodge was just ahead. Once, the driveway was wide enough for a semi, but grass and oleanders had grown in on both sides and choked it down to one narrow lane. There was a chain across it, and a No Trespassing sign, but you could squeeze around the chain through high grass on the south side; that's how the bunch of us got in the three times we'd been over to party. I pointed out the way to Lori and we bounced over behind a screen of trees, onto what used to be a packed-dirt parking lot. The earth was all chewed up now, and tangled with blackberry bushes, and you had to go slow. But once you were at the back end, there was no way anybody could see in from the road.

We unloaded the food and clothes and medical stuff, took them around to the service door. As soon as we were inside I called out to John, so he'd know right away who was coming. When we got to the lobby he was sitting up on the couch, the blankets pulled around him to his chin.

"Any trouble?"

I said, "No. We've got all the stuff."

Lori said, "Let's have some light." I found the flashlight and switched it on. "Hold it steady, Trisha." I did that while she knelt beside the couch, laid her hand on his forehead. "How you doing?" she asked him.

"Holding my own."

"Well, you're not feverish. That's a good sign."

"Lori, I'm sorry to drag you into this . . ."

"Nobody dragged me here. I came because I wanted to. Are you in much pain?"

"Not as long as I stay still."

"Bleeding?"

"Doesn't feel like it."

She unwrapped the blankets and then took off the tape and pads. I saw the way she looked at the wounds and at him and I thought: She really cares about him. I felt this little pang of jealousy. Stupid, but I couldn't help it. I didn't like sharing John any more than I liked sharing his rescue.

"How bad?" he asked.

"Could be worse. Good thing Trisha found the peroxide. Holes look clean—no inflammation."

Well, okay. John probably wouldn't even be alive right now if I hadn't heard him moaning and did what I did to help him. That was something I'd *never* have to share.

"So I'll live."

"Chances are. When'd you last have a tetanus shot?"

". . . Can't remember."

"Within the past five years?"

"No, longer ago than that."

"Within the last ten?"

"Seven or eight, about."

"Should be okay, then. I wish I had a way to give you one, to be safe, but I don't." She was opening up one of the sacks, taking out stuff she'd bought at the pharmacy. Thin rubber gloves. Bottled water. A package of sponges. A thermometer. Lots of gauze and tape. Some tubes of Neosporin. A big bottle of aspirin. "I'll clean the wounds, put antibiotic ointment on, and pack them tight. That should do it for now. You'll have to change the dressing, put on more ointment, at least once a day. More often if there's any bleeding. Watch me and you'll know how to do it."

"Will I be okay to travel?"

"I'd say no if we were someplace else. You should rest a couple of days, minimum. But this place, all the dirt and dust and rodent crap . . . you'd be better off in a clean bed."

"A clean bed far away from Pomo County. Question is, how do I get there?"

Lori didn't answer. She had the gloves on and was sponging the wounds with bottled water. It was yucky to watch and I looked away. Nothing else to look at in the lobby except shapes and shadows. Something creaked upstairs. Back in the summer, some of the guys had climbed up there to explore; but not me, not after that bat flew so close to my head. Old hotels are weird places, all right. That one in the

Stephen King flick, where Jack Nicholson goes around grinning and waving an ax . . . wow.

It took Lori a long time to finish treating John's wounds. What seemed like a long time, anyway. I got tired standing up and holding the flashlight at arm's length, so I sat cross-legged on the grungy floor and propped my elbows on my knees and held it that way. Once I heard a skittering at the big open fireplace and swung the beam over there, and Lori said real sharp, "For God's sake, put that light back here." I didn't blame her for yelling. She couldn't see in the dark.

While she was taking John's temperature I went and picked up a couple of the candles that were on the fireplace hearth. I'd forgotten about them until I flashed the light over that way. I lit the wicks with some matches from my purse and set the candles on folding chairs, one at either end of the couch. The flames gave off plenty of light. Softer, too; the flash glare had started to hurt my eyes.

John's temperature was one degree above normal. Lori said that wasn't bad, after him being in the lake and in wet clothes all night. She gave him some aspirins and told him to take more every few hours. Then she unwrapped a nutrition bar she'd bought, made him eat it and drink more water. Then she laid out her husband's clothes and said, "You can get into these when we're gone. There's an extra shirt in case one gets bloody."

"I owe you," John said. "Both of you."

"You don't owe me a thing."

"Me neither," I said.

"Yeah I do, and I can't repay you. And I still have to ask one more favor, Lori."

"I know. Transportation."

"I can't walk away from here."

"You can't drive, either. I'm not about to steal a car for you. That leaves me and my Toyota."

"I wish it could be some other way."

"So do I. I'll do it, but not right away. For one thing, I have to take Trisha home—"

"I can get home on my own," I said.

"No, not from way over here. And if I don't go home myself pretty soon, he'll figure something's up. My husband, I mean. The last thing we need is for him to come looking."

John said, "If he lays a hand on you again—"

"Never mind that. Thing is, I won't be able to get back out again today without making him suspicious. Besides, you need to rest, build up strength. One night in this dump ought to be okay."

"How soon tomorrow?"

"Before noon sometime."

"You sure you can get out in the morning?"

"Pretty sure. I'll think up some kind of excuse."

I asked John, "Where'll you go that's safe?"

"As far from here as possible."

"And then what? After you're healed, I mean."

"You don't want to know. Neither of you."

"But—"

"No buts. Once I'm gone I'm out of your lives for good."

"We're supposed to just forget you?"

"That's right. Forget you ever met me."

"I'll never forget you, John. Never."

He was quiet while Lori and I got ready to leave. Then he said a funny thing, like we were already gone and he was talking to himself. He said, "The only ones who care . . . they're the ones you can hurt the most."

Earle Banner

NUCOOEE POINT LODGE.

Yeah. Oh yeah.

I was about three hundred yards back, just coming through a curve, when the little Jap car turned off. I braked and geared down, so when I rolled past the overgrown driveway I was doing less than twenty-five and I could see her plowing through grass and weeds to get around the chain barrier. I didn't see no other car, but you could've hidden a fuckin' house trailer back there behind the trees.

I drove on a ways until I found a spot where I could turn around. Then I come back and pulled off onto the verge just down from the driveway. Her and Brian's kid, nobody else? Couldn't get enough dick, so now she's after pussy too, teenage pussy? But I didn't think that was it. Not Lori, she was no AC-DC. Had to be they were meeting somebody at the lodge. One guy, maybe more—a goddamn orgy. Just thinking about it, the top of my head felt like it was gonna come off.

What I ached to do was go over there, catch them at it, beat the crap out of her and anybody else got in my way. If I'd had my .38 with me I might've done it. But I didn't have no idea how many guys was over there, who they were, how tough they were. Those two bitches might be taking on half a dozen, for all I knew. Without an equalizer, maybe I'd be the one to get stomped and wouldn't she love to see that?

Maybe I oughta go home, get the piece, and come back.

No. Take too long. And I still wouldn't know how many there was until I got in there and I didn't like the idea of using the gun unless I had to, not on anybody except Lori. Shit, it wasn't the guy's fault. Tail gets waved in a man's face, he grabs for it—you can't expect no different from a guy. Wasn't even the kid's fault. Teenager looking for kicks . . . all them teenage kids fuck like bunnies nowadays, the more the merrier. Lori'd set the whole thing up, most likely. Yeah. Set up an orgy, more the merrier for her, too. Kicks galore.

I'll give her kicks. Give her some kicks she'll never forget.

I sat there a while longer, steaming. A couple of cars whooshed by, and it come to me that one of 'em could've been a sheriff's deputy or highway patrolman. Better get out of here before a cop did come along and stop and ask what I was doing. I jammed her into gear, rolled out past the lodge entrance. Couldn't see nothing at all back there. Hid the Jap car and got inside somehow . . . humping in there on the floor with rats and spiders for an audience. Pictures that put in my head made me want to puke. I couldn't remember ever being this crazy mad before.

By the time I got back to Pomo I needed a shot real bad. I stopped at Luccetti's and a good thing wasn't nobody I knew in there, because I was in no mood for talk. I knocked back three straight shots of Bushmills, but they didn't do nothin' except sharpen the edge. Hell with sitting here paying tavern prices when I had a jug of the same at home. I slammed out of there, drove to the house, and put the Ford away inside the garage. If she saw I was home she might not come in right away, and I wanted her to walk right in. Oh, yeah, walk right in, baby, see what Earle's got waiting for you.

In the house I dragged the jug out and poured some into a glass and knocked it back. I started to pour another, then I thought, What the hell

I need a glass for? I threw it against a wall and took the next one straight from the neck. Like a man. Like a husband with a lying, cheating mare in heat for a wife.

I carried the bottle into the front room, sat in my chair, and worked on it. Lot of time passed and I got drunk, all right, but not too drunk because I didn't want to pass out.

Clock on the mantel bonged out four times. Four o'clock. Out there couple of hours now, fuck and suck and Christ knew what else. I got up and staggered over and grabbed the clock. Lori's clock, bought it at some garage sale, never liked that pissant clock. I threw it down and stomped on it. Stomped it flat. Felt good, real good, so I went back to the bedroom and stomped her clock radio, stomped her jewelry case, stomped her music box, stomped some other crap of hers, and all of it felt fine because the whole time it was *her* getting stomped, her face, her body, bust her up into little pieces scattered all over the floor.

Breathing hard when I was done. Yeah, and ready for another shot. Went out front again and picked up the bottle and knocked back a double. I was wiping my mouth when I heard the Jap car come whining into the driveway.

Well, well. Well, well.

Walk right in, baby, see what Earle's got for you.

And she walked in and there I was, waiting. She took one look at me and her face turned white as paper and she tried to go back out again. I cut her off. Didn't touch her, not yet, just cut her off and then grinned at her real big, like a junkyard dog grins at a piece of raw meat.

"Nucooee Point Lodge," I said.

She sucked in her breath. Look on her face made me happier and crazier than I'd been all afternoon.

Richard Novak

BY FOUR O'CLOCK I was dead on my ass, the pain in my broken nose so bad I couldn't see straight. And that made driving around the way I'd been—Storm's house, slough roads, possible hiding places along the shoreline that might've been overlooked, back and forth aimlessly and unproductively—made *me* a safety hazard to pedestrians and other drivers. I needed food, sleep. And I couldn't rest at the station;

too much activity, too much noise. Like it or not, I'd have to take myself out of action for a while.

I radioed Della Feldman and told her I was going home. She made approving noises. "Best thing for you, Chief," she said. Wrong. The best thing for me was finding Faith, dead or alive. It was the only way to close the books, all the books, on Storm's death, the only way for me to start putting my life back together again.

Mack was all over me when I let myself in the house. Jumping and wagging and nuzzling, as if I'd been away a week instead of twenty-four hours. "Hey, boy. Good old Mack." He needed to go out, but the shape I was in, I couldn't walk him half a block. I let him into the backyard instead.

In the kitchen I swallowed a couple of the codeine capsules they'd given me at the hospital. My stomach had been burning off and on all day: bile and emptiness. The burning started in again now. The thought of food was nauseating, but if I didn't eat something pretty quick I knew I'd puke up the painkillers. I made a sandwich, poured half a glass of milk. Let Mack back in and took the food into the living room and flopped on the couch.

It took ten minutes of little bites and sips to get the sandwich and milk down. It was like eating paste, but once it was into me it stayed there. I thought I ought to go in and lie on the bed, but I couldn't seem to move; my whole body felt heavy, as if all the bones and muscles and sinews were petrifying, turning me to stone. I couldn't even make myself lean over and untie my shoes. But that was all right. Better to keep all my clothes on, so I could respond immediately if any word came through on Faith.

I lay sprawled in the cold room, watching night close down outside the windows. The codeine started to work, easing some of the throbbing in my face. But whenever I closed my eyes, they wouldn't stay shut; I couldn't sleep yet. For a while my head was a vacuum, no thoughts of any kind, but then Storm was there again and pretty soon my skull seemed to swell with memories and images of her alive and dead. I must've made a sound, because Mack stirred at my feet, then jumped up beside me. I reached out to him, pulled him close, buried my face in the soft fur of his neck.

"Oh God, Mack. Oh God, Mack."

He whined and licked my hand, as if somehow he understood.

Audrey Sixkiller

I PROBABLY SHOULD have told Dick about my suspicions right away, but I didn't because suspicions is all they were. I had no proof John Faith was alive or that Trisha Marx had used my boat to help him get away. No proof, even, that either of them had been anywhere near my property this morning. Plus, there was the question of *why*. Why would she give aid and comfort to an accused murderer? Some sort of quixotic teenage impulse, perhaps; girls could be highly romantic and foolish at that age, as I had reason to remember. But even so, there must be something more to it than that and I had no idea what it might be. Rumors fly wildly in a small town; once a person comes under a cloud of suspicion, people are quick to convict and shun without benefit of evidence or trial. I didn't care to be responsible for branding anyone.

The thing to do before anything else, I decided, was to have a private talk with Trisha. I drove to her house on Redbud Street, and her father was home but she wasn't. He was angry because she was supposed to have been there when he returned from work at one o'clock. I asked him to let me know as soon as she came home. A school matter, I said, not serious but still rather important. Mr. Marx looked skeptical; I think he was afraid she might be in some kind of trouble. But he didn't question me further and he said he'd call when she showed up.

Back at my house, I taped a piece of cardboard across the broken bathroom window and cleaned up the glass shards. Then I microwaved a Stouffer's macaroni and cheese. Brian Marx hadn't called by the time I finished my belated lunch. I put the answering machine on and walked out to the dock for another look at the Chris-Craft.

Clouds, thick and dark-veined, had begun to gather to the north. There was the faint smell of ozone in the air. Rain sometime tonight, I thought. Gulls wheeled over the lake, more than a few of them—another sign of coming weather. Watching the gulls, I found myself thinking of the legend of the Huk, the mythical bird old-time Pomos believed had evil supernatural powers.

The Huk was said to be the size of a turkey buzzard, dark red in color, with long, fine feathers. A reddish liquid, like blood, filled the gills and would flow from end to end if the feathers were turned up and back down. The creature had hairy legs, an enormous head, a bill curved like that of a parrot. Its power lay in the fact that it brought death wherever it went. If it appeared and you heard its cry of "huk, huk," you or someone close to you was sure to die, immediately or within a few days.

I'm not superstitious; I believe in the old legends only as legends, campfire stories for adults and children. But I shivered just the same as I watched the gulls wheeling against the clouds, their wind-carried cries sounding more than a little like "huk, huk" in the quiet afternoon.

George Petrie

I SAT IN the car, staring out over the desert. I'd been there a long time now, on the side of Highway 50 a couple of miles east of the 361 junction. It was as far as I'd gotten after leaving the crossroads rest area. It was as far as I was going.

Over. Finished.

Beaten.

The dark-green van with the tinted windshield was long gone, miles and miles down 361 by now—the van that hadn't been driven by the gray-haired man from the Truckee motel, or by anybody else bent on stealing my stolen money, but by a fat young fellow traveling with his equally puddinglike wife and their two chubby daughters. Tourists who hadn't even glanced at me when they drove into the rest area, who didn't know or care that I existed, whose only interest was in food and toilet facilities. Long gone, but the fear hadn't gone with them. Nor had the core of paranoia. With sudden, sickening clarity I'd seen both for exactly what they were and would be if I continued on the course I'd set for myself—constant companions no matter where I went or what I did, partners in crime that would destroy me as surely as a fast-growing cancer.

It was stifling in the car. Almost December and the Nevada desert was still a furnace; I felt as though I were melting inside my clothes. Pretty soon I would have to start the engine, put on the air conditioner. But when I did that I'd have to start driving again, too, and I wasn't ready to drive yet. I sat and smoked another cigarette without inhaling and squinted out over the sun-blasted flats, the low, barren hills hazy and shimmering in the distance. Broken earth, clumps of sage and greasewood. Dry salt sink to the north, its floor as seamed and cracked as an old man's skin. Jagged splinters of rock along the bank of an empty wash, bleached white by the sun, like crushed and discarded bones. A wasteland.

As dead as all my big plans.

As barren as my future.

I couldn't go on, because I didn't have the guts to go on. A man like John Faith could steal $209,840 without a single qualm or backward glance, but George Petrie is too anxiety-riddled, too paranoid to be a successful thief. All I'd ever had was a meager supply of courage, and now the supply had been used up. From the first I'd built this mad scheme of mine on a foundation of lies, false bravado, self-deception. It was amazing I'd gotten this far before the flimsy foundation collapsed.

The only thing I could do now was to give it all up, slink back home to Pomo. Time enough left to do that and return the money to the bank vault before Fred and Arlene show up on Monday morning. Time enough to pick up where I'd left off, go begging to Charley Horne or Burt Seeley if I can't cover the $7,000 shortage any other way. Time enough to save my sorry ass, so I can start dying again, slowly, by inches.

The heat in the car was so intense now I was having trouble breathing. I threw the half-smoked cigarette out the window, rolled up the glass, started the engine, and put on the air conditioner. And then I made a careful turn across the empty highway and headed back the way I'd come.

Douglas Kent

THE ANCESTRAL KENT roscoe was a Smith & Wesson snub-nosed .38. After I lurched home from the *Advocate* offices, full of grief and Doc Beefeater's Magic Cure-all, bent and bowed under the weight of my bag of sticks, I rummaged in the closet and there it was, packed in an old shoe box. Carefully wrapped in chamois cloth (the old man's work, not mine), clean and well-oiled (not unlike its present owner), all six chambers bristling with shiny circles of oblivion. I carried it into the kitchen and laid it gently on the table. After which I poured another dose of salve and plunked myself down to contemplate the thing.

Pa Kent's piece, of course. If there is one thing Kent Junior has never been, it is a staunch supporter of the National Rifle Association. Wrote impassioned gun-control and anti-NRA articles, once upon a time. Thought about writing another when I first arrived in Pomo, but for a change prudency prevailed. There are gaggles of guns in Pomo County; half the adults and a third of the kids—or possibly, it's the other way around—have at least one tucked away within easy reach. If I had written the article for the *Advocate*, I would probably have been blown away at sunrise by an irate ninth-grader whose old man kept a collection of automatic weapons in the toolshed.

Still, even I had to admit that Pa Kent's rod had a certain deadly magnificence. Short and squat and ugly and cold, which, come to think of it, was an apt capsule description of the pater himself. He'd never fired it except on a pistol range, so far as I knew, but he'd always had it close at hand in case of burglars, bill collectors, and/or overly aggressive pink snakes or other figments of his pickled brain. It was one of the few, the very few, of his personal possessions that I'd appropriated after his fatal midnight plunge into the Monongahela. Wasn't sure why at the time, or why I continued to cart it with me on my various peripatetic wanderings—

Liar.

Bullshitter.

You know very well why you appropriated and kept it, Kent, my lad. Same reason you dragged it out of its nest this evening. Same reason Richard Cory kept a bang stick hidden away in his digs. Ah, Cory, that "gentleman from sole to crown, clean favored, and imperially slim," loved by one and all in his little New England town. Kent is a far seedier specimen, loved by no one, but underneath he and Mr. Cory are soul brothers.

> And Richard Cory, one calm summer night,
> Went home and put a bullet through his head.

Yes, indeedy, Edwin A. Robinson understood the private demons that lurk behind the public facade. Likely owned a few himself, being one of that breed held in even greater contempt than whores and newspaper hacks, poets. But failure wasn't one of them. Nor, I'll wager, was he plagued with unrequited love for a woman as stormy as the late Storm.

Storm, Storm. Gone and no longer blowing—metaphorically or otherwise. "Temporal skull fracture leading to subdural hematoma of mid brain." Ding dong, the wench is dead. "Death of brain due to necrosis or mass effect." Ding dong, the wench is dead, the wicked wench is dead.

And I wish, I wish, I wish Kent was, too.

And Douglas Kent, one dark Stormless night,
Went home and put a bullet through his head.

Or did he? Is he as willful as Richard Cory, as ready to plunge into the abyss? In the last analysis, are they soul brothers or simply two sides of the same tarnished coin?

I poured more salve.

The gun and I watched each other, like old enemies or new friends.

Lori Banner

"I TOLD YOU, Earle!" I screamed at him. "I told you there wasn't anybody but you, I never once slept with anybody else the whole time we've been married! I told you not to hit me anymore! I told you, I told you, how many times did I tell you? Why didn't you listen? Why didn't you believe me?"

I was shaking so hard I could barely stand up. I didn't sit in my chair, I fell into it. My mouth was bleeding where he'd punched me and opened up the cut he put there yesterday. Bleeding all over my sweater and jacket and dripping onto my pants. It hurt a lot and the blood tasted salty. My jaw hurt and my ear felt all swollen and my eye hurt, too. The eye was going to be black and yellow and purple, worse than the other times because it was already so puffy I couldn't see out of it. He always hit me in the face. Never cared how I looked the next day, that I had to go to work with my face all bruised and swollen, that I had to lie to people and see the pity in their faces and listen to Darlene and I don't know how many others tell me what an idiot I was for staying with a man who kept beating me up.

"You never cared, you son of a bitch! How I looked or what I had to put up with! 'Poor Lori, why does she let him get away with it,' why why why! That's what I had to listen to, that's what you made me put up with, you dirty son of a bitch bastard Earle, you."

I *am* an idiot. I must be. I quit loving you long ago, just like you quit loving me, and now I hate you the same way you hate me. Oh Jesus, I hate you so much, Earle. You know the one thing I regret most? That I didn't cheat on you not only once or twice but a hundred times, a thousand, that I didn't have men lined up around the block waiting to screw me the way Storm Carey did instead of hanging on to the stupid idea that a woman ought to be faithful to her husband, stick by him even if he beats the crap out of her for no damn reason. For better or worse, what a joke. My word was never good enough for you, oh no. You and your jealousy, you and your drinking, you and your hitting.

"You and your hitting, Earle. Didn't I tell you the hitting had to stop?"

He sat in his chair over there, staring at me.

"And then you had to go and follow me today. Why'd you do that, huh? Why couldn't you leave me alone today of all days, let me do something worthwhile for a change, let me care for somebody and have him treat me like a human being instead of a piece of ass and a punching bag? If I'd told you about John Faith, you'd have kept on hitting me anyway and then you'd have called the cops and turned him in and tried to get some kind of reward out of it. I know you, Earle, I know you like a book. I couldn't let you do it. John Faith's everything I wish to God you were and he's had a rough time of it and he deserves a break and I couldn't let you turn him in. Or keep on hitting me after I told you the hitting had to stop."

His third eye, the red one in the middle of his forehead, was staring at me, too. I didn't mind that eye. After all, I'd put it there.

"Well, how do *you* like it, huh? How do *you* like being the one who got hurt for a change?"

I wasn't shaking so much now. In fact, I was hardly shaking at all. I felt numb, numb all over. Just had to go and get your gun, didn't you, Earle? Just had to start waving it around and threaten to shoot me like a horse. Hit me and kept hitting me, made me all bloody, and then on top of that ranting about shooting me like a horse. A horse, for God's sake! Didn't expect me to knock it out of your hand, did you? Didn't expect to trip over your big feet so I got to it first. And then you had to laugh and call me a bitch and a mare in heat and say I wouldn't shoot *you* like a horse. Wrong, Earle, wrong again. Just never got tired of being wrong, did you? Ran at me, grabbed for the gun, and bang! Wrong Earle, dead Earle, three-eyed Earle. Just like that.

I was still holding the stupid gun in my hand. The three eyes, two blue and one red, watched me put it down on the end table.

"How do you like being dead, huh?"

He didn't like it, but I did. I liked it so much I laughed out loud. But my mouth hurt, so I stopped laughing and sat there trying to think what to do.

I ought to call the cops and tell them I'd shot Earle like a horse. But if I did that, then how would John Faith get away? But if I didn't call them, I'd have to stay here all night with Earle sitting dead in his chair, and I didn't think I could do that. I really didn't think I could do that.

I couldn't make up my mind. I was so tired and numb I couldn't even get up out of my chair and go pee, which I had to do very badly now. I just sat there. And looked at Earle's third eye and wondered how long it would be before it stopped dripping.

Richard Novak

THE DOORBELL JARRED me awake. I'd been half out on the couch, caught on the rim of sleep and cringing from a nightmare that I couldn't remember except for some of the things in it: blood, water, lightning, a huge phallus with an opening that kept winking like an obscene eye. I heaved to my feet, fuzzy-headed, sweaty and cold at the same time. Mack was there, up and alert; I almost tripped over him as I stumbled across to open the door.

"Audrey. What're you— Something happen?"

She shook her head. Her face seemed blurred, out of shape at the edges. Damn eyes wouldn't focus right.

"Then why'd you come?" I asked her.

"To see if you were home, feed Mack if not. The lights are on and I thought you . . . but you were asleep, weren't you?"

"On the couch."

She wanted to come in and I let her do it. She said as I shut the door, "Your face . . . is it any better?"

"Mostly numb now. Painkillers—codeine. Must be why I'm so groggy."

"You should be in bed."

"Didn't want to get undressed . . ."

"Dick, you're trembling."

"Cold in here. Forgot to turn the heat on, I guess."

"I'll do it."

She went away. When she came back I was leaning on the couch arm, massaging my eyes; they wouldn't clear and neither would my head. Mack was butted up against me. Audrey said something that didn't register, came over close on the other side. Warm fingers, soft and gentle, touched my cheek and made little scraping sounds on the beard stubble. I could smell her perfume, something like jasmine. Eva's favorite scent, jasmine. I pulled back from her.

"Dick, come and get into bed."

"No . . ."

"You'll be sick if you don't. You're chilled already."

No argument left in me; I was too groggy, too cold. I let her ease me to my feet, guide me into the bedroom on legs like heavy, dragging stumps. I couldn't seem to stand when she let go of me, and then I was lying sprawled on the bed. She didn't put the light on. In the dark I felt her hands on me again, taking off shoes, unbuttoning and unzipping clothing; I neither helped nor hindered her. Strong . . . she hauled everything off except my shorts, lifted and pushed to get the bedclothes around me.

I lay on my back, shivering, starting to drift. Weight on the bed then and Audrey was crawling in beside me, fitting her body along my right side. Naked, too, except for panties; I was aware of the hard points of her breasts pressing my arm and chest. *No*, I thought, and tried to roll away. The strong arms held me tight.

"Audrey, I can't . . ."

"I don't want you to. Just hold you, that's all. Make you warm, help you sleep."

". . . Too good . . ."

"What, Dick?"

"Too good for me."

"Sshh. Sleep."

I slept. Deeply this time, without any nightmare—suspension in a black void.

A long time later there was a ringing, distant, then louder, closer . . .

phone . . . and I struggled up out of the black, untangling myself from Audrey's embrace and the damp bedclothes. I reached out blindly, almost knocked the telephone off the nightstand. Eyelids came unstuck as I fumbled up the receiver; the numerals on the alarm clock swam into focus: 10:45. It didn't seem possible, but I'd been out more than five hours.

Verne Erickson's voice penetrated. ". . . something you'd better know about, Chief."

"Faith?"

"No. Another homicide, evidently unrelated."

"Homicide, you said?"

"Yeah. Shooting death, this time."

I was mostly alert now. Aware that the codeine had worn off and my nose was throbbing again, dully. Aware of Audrey sitting up behind me, her hand warm on my shoulder. I didn't look at her.

"Who? What happened?"

"Earle Banner finally got what was coming to him. His wife shot him with his own gun. Just now reported it."

"Just now? When'd it happen?"

"Around five," Verne said. "She's been sitting with the corpse ever since."

Audrey Sixkiller

AFTER DICK LEFT I sat propped up against his pillows, holding on to a last few minutes of the warmth and scent of his body. He'd said I was welcome to stay the night, but his heart wasn't in it. He'd avoided my eyes as he spoke. Plain enough that when he came back home—if he came home again tonight—he'd be relieved to find me gone.

I glanced down at my bare breasts. Brazen Audrey and her pair of meager offerings. Sad, rejected Audrey and her white-acting ways. William Sixkiller would hide his head in shame if he could see his little papoose tonight.

But that was foolish self-pity; I stopped indulging in it. Dick was the one who deserved compassion, not me. He'd looked so worn out when I'd arrived, I couldn't bring myself to confide my suspicions about Trisha Marx and John Faith; sleep was what he'd needed tonight, not guesswork and more upheaval. Upheaval had come anyway—another killing—but at least he'd had a few hours' rest first. And why should I feel rejected anyway? I hadn't really offered him my body; couldn't expect to be anything more to him right now than another burden, another source of worry.

I got up finally, straightened the bed, put my clothes on in the bathroom. The face in the mirror looked puffy and unappealing in its frame of tangled hair. Comb out the tangle? Why bother? And the puffy face could wait for a good washing until I was home. I made sure Mack had enough food and water, patted him, collected my purse, and went out to my car.

A mixture of heavy mist and light drizzle had laid a sheen of glistening wetness on the streets, blurred house lights and the car's headlamps. The low-hanging clouds were thick and restless; a soaking rain would fall before dawn. I drove slowly, with the radio on for comfort. And to keep from fretting about Dick, I let my thoughts center on Lori Banner.

I hardly knew her and I didn't know her husband at all, but even I had heard she was a battered wife. I hoped she'd shot him in self-defense and that she could prove it. Otherwise, she'd keep right on being a victim. That was one of the things that infuriated me about domestic violence, the no-win position the abused usually found herself in. I'd seen so much of it on the rancherias and at Indian Health in Santa Rosa. Spousal and child abuse, often alcohol-triggered, was among the worst of the many problems Native Americans had to struggle with on a daily basis. I'd never counseled violence as a way of ending violence; it was a poor choice of solution to any problem. Yet sometimes, in certain situations, people were pushed and prodded into corners where violence became the only possible alternative. I had learned that hard lesson myself the past couple of days. The Ruger automatic in my purse was bitter proof that I'd learned it well.

The drizzle had thickened by the time I turned into my driveway. It took four tries before the garage-door opener decided to cooperate; there was something wrong with the remote that a fresh battery hadn't fixed. The lightbulb on the inside frame had burned out again, too. I would have to make an appointment with the dealer south of town and then arrange to be here when a repairman came out. Maybe I could do it at the same time the glazier came to replace the broken bathroom window.

One or two more time-consumers to overload my already groaning week-day schedule.

I sighed and shut off the lights, leaving the garage door up for the moment. I'd close it with the push button next to the side door. When I latched the car door and the dome light winked off, I was in heavy darkness except for the misty gray square behind me. I made my way along the side of the car, feeling for the wall and the doorknob.

I smelled him before I heard him, a rank, sweetish odor like a sweating animal that had been sprinkled with something like Old Spice cologne. Foot scrape, grunting exhalation, and then his hands were on me. He dragged my body back tight against his, pinning my arms before I could get the gun out of my purse. Rough cloth chafed at my cheek and jaw: ski mask. His breath was hot and beer-sour; spittle sprayed my neck when he spoke.

"About time you decided to come home, bitch."

Same raspy voice as on the phone. For the first time I felt fear, a quick rush that drove away surprise and fired rage. I squirmed, couldn't get loose, and tried to kick back at him; but he had his legs spread and his body braced against the wall. He rasped something else that was lost in the rising pound of blood and adrenaline. I gave up trying to kick him and stomped down hard with the heel of my shoe, three times before I connected with an instep. He yelled and for an instant his grip loosened, just long enough for me to wrench free and twist sideways. I yanked my purse open, fumbled inside for the automatic—

One thick arm looped around my waist, jerked me back against the thrust of his hip; his other hand flailed, struck the purse, and tore it from my grasp. I heard it bang into the side of the car. Then his forearm was up and under my chin, snapping my head back, bruising my throat. The sudden pressure choked off breath. I ripped at the arm but couldn't break the hold. The darkness seemed to churn and bulge.

"Bitch!"

The pressure increased. And the darkness flowed behind my eyes, congealing—

"Bitch!"

—and I was caught in it and swept away . . .

Part IV

Sunday

Trisha Marx

I COULDN'T SLEEP.

I lay there in the dark, listening to the rain patter on the roof and whisper at the windows. The house was quiet otherwise. Too quiet. It was after twelve and Daddy still wasn't home and that meant he wouldn't be until morning. Playing poker at the Brush Creek casino like he did one or two weekend nights a month. Every time, he'd get into a tournament and be out all night—come home around eight or nine, bleary-eyed and grumpy unless he'd won for a change, and fall into bed and sleep most of the day. I didn't mind it when I was hanging with Anthony and Selena and Petey and the others, because then I could stay out all night myself. (That one Saturday I let Anthony stay over, sleep right here in my bed . . . we'd done the nasty three, no four times, bam bam bam bam, and he ran out of condoms after the second or third time. That must be the night he got me pregnant.) Tonight, though, I wished Daddy'd stayed home. Tonight I didn't like being alone.

Anthony . . . he was one of the reasons I couldn't sleep. Calling up, saying he had to see me. I hung up on him. Then, right after Daddy left, like Anthony'd been outside waiting and watching for him to go, there he was knocking on the door. As if I'd let him in. He only wanted to talk, he said. About our problem, he said. Problem! Like it was some dinky little hassle you could make go away by rapping about it. Like when we could just kiss and make up and everything'd be the way it was before. He stayed on the porch for about ten minutes, pleading and sweet-talking—"Trish, baby, you know how I feel about you, you got to know I love you"—before he finally gave up and went away.

I felt low after he was gone and I still feel low. Why'd he have to start in again with the love crap? He didn't love me, all he'd wanted was to fuck me. Why'd he have to come around and make things worse by pretending he really cared?

Then there was Ms. Sixkiller. She knew it was me broke into her house and used her boat, all right. Her coming over and talking to Daddy proved she did. When he told me about it I said it wasn't anything important and he didn't need to call her, I would; but I didn't. I'd have to talk to her pretty soon, though. I didn't think she'd call the cops until she talked to me first, and if I waited until tomorrow afternoon to see her, Lori would already have taken John away someplace safe. Then it wouldn't matter if the cops came and started ragging on me. I wouldn't tell them anything. They couldn't *prove* I'd been guilty of aiding and abetting a fugitive, could they?

The rain stopped and then started again. (Wow, that rain. If it'd been coming down like that this morning, the wind howling the way it was now, I'd never have been able to take Ms. Sixkiller's boat across to Nucooee Point and back. No way.) The house creaked, made groaning sounds like John's when I found him. I tried lying on my back, my stomach, one side and the other. I tried counting backward from one hundred. I tried a couple of other tricks. Nothing worked. I kept right on tossing and turning, wide awake.

I thought about John over there alone in the old lodge.

I thought about Lori with her banged-up face (that guy she was married to must be a real asshole) and how good she'd been to John and how I didn't really mind sharing him with her. I'd never tell on her no matter what.

I thought about Daddy and what he'd say when I told him I was pregnant.

I thought about the Bitch and how she'd probably laugh her dyed blond head off when she found out.

I thought about the baby growing down there inside me.

And it was funny because then, thinking about the kid, I started to feel sleepy and not quite so alone. Well, I wasn't alone, right? A baby was somebody else, even a half-formed baby. It was a *life*. First time I'd looked at it that way, and it was like a whole new perspective, not just on the kid but on me, too, as if maybe my life wasn't such total crap after all. John had said if you hurt, you cared, and he was right. I hurt every time I thought about the baby, so that must mean I cared about it. I mean, I'm not gung ho on being a mother and I'm not one of those antiabortion types; I believe a woman has a right to choose what she does with her own body. But now there was this thing growing in *my* body, a part of *me*, and the choice was *mine*, not somebody else's.

Just before I drifted off I knew I wasn't gonna go to a clinic. My choice, and it didn't matter what Daddy said or the Bitch said or Anthony said or anybody said. I was gonna have it and I was gonna keep it.

Audrey Sixkiller

CONSCIOUSNESS RETURNED SLOWLY, in a series of awarenesses. Of a sore throat and a swelling headache, first, as if my head had been pumped full of fluid. Then of motion under and around me. Then of suffocating darkness that stank of wool and dirt. Then that I was lying on my stomach on something hard but yielding . . . car seat . . . with my arms and hands drawn up behind me. I tugged and couldn't separate them. Taped together at the wrists, the tape pulling and tearing at my skin. Ankles bound, too. And another piece of tape tight across my mouth.

I'm not afraid. I won't panic.

Roughness along my cheek, and the wool-and-dirt smell. Filthy blanket. Thrown over the length of my body, covering my head, too. I managed to twist over onto my right side—movement that, even though I did it carefully, increased the pressure in my temples and behind my eyes.

Sounds: tires whispering on pavement; things whooshing past outside. From up front a faint gurgling, a satisfied, hissing breath, an explosive belch.

I snagged the blanket with the toe of my shoe, worked it down until I could ease my head free. Darkness thinned by the pale reflected glow of the dash lights. All I could see of the man driving was the shape of his skull above the seat back.

Other smells: beer, the sweetish animal stench from the garage—sweat and Old Spice. My stomach churned. I couldn't seem to swallow; I locked my jaws instead, shut my eyes, and lay very still. If I vomited with the tape sealing my mouth I would strangle.

The nausea passed. I squirmed onto one hip, swung my legs off the seat, and then lowered them to the floor—

"Hey! You stay down back there."

I froze. His voice . . . not as raspy as before. He wouldn't be wearing the ski mask while he drove.

"Give me any trouble, you'll wish you hadn't. Hear me? I'll use your own gun on that pretty face of yours. Yeah, that's right, I found it in your purse. Blow your fuckin' head off with it, maybe, like you tried to do to me the other night."

Familiar voice. Listen, put a name and a face to it . . .

"Won't be long now, bitch. We're almost there."

Almost where?

"Then I'll give it to you like you never had it before. My cock first and then your gun. How'd you like that, huh? Fucked with your own gun."

He laughed, and in the darkness his laughter was a Huk sound, a death sound.

But I was not afraid. I felt a cold fury, nothing more. No matter what he said, no matter what he did, I would not give him the satisfaction of making me afraid.

Richard Novak

LORI BANNER WAS in a bad way. Disoriented, face all bruised and swollen and caked with dried blood. She'd wet herself, too; the urine odor was strong in the cold room. And she kept saying things like "I put that third eye in his head" and "I fell asleep in my chair. Can you believe that? What kind of person kills her husband and then goes to sleep for hours in the same room?"

Seeing her, listening to her brought back the images of Storm last night; the hurt started all over again, inside and out. I turned the questioning over to Mary Jo Luchek, the first officer on the scene, and walked out into the cold, wet night to watch for the ambulance, Doc Johanssen, the civilian photographer Nichols.

A small clot of citizens had gathered in spite of the rain and the late hour; they seem always to sprout like toadstools at the scene of any violent occurrence. Here they were huddled under porch roofs and umbrellas and inside cars. A few were reporters, homegrown and leftovers from last night; they converged on me as soon as I appeared, hurling questions like stones ahead of them.

"Chief, is there any connection between this killing and Storm Carey's murder?" Dietrich, the kid who works for the *Advocate*.

"What kind of question is that? No, there's no connection."

"None with John Faith, either?"

"No. Domestic incident, that's all."

"What about Faith? Anything new on him?"

I didn't answer that. The ambulance from Pomo General was approaching now, no siren but its flasher lights staining the night. I chased Dietrich and the rest back out to the sidewalk, told Mary Jo's partner, Jack Turner, to keep them there. I spoke briefly to the attendants, showed them inside to where Mary Jo was talking to Lori Banner in the kitchen. Johannsen arrived a couple of minutes later and I took him in to where Earle Banner's corpse was sprawled in a beat-up recliner.

"Deceased several hours," he said when he'd had his preliminary look. "Advanced rigor and lividity."

"She didn't report it right away. His wife."

"Why not?"

"Said she fell asleep, slept for five or six hours. Possible?"

"Quite possible," Johanssen said. "Heavy, druglike sleep is not an uncommon reaction to severe stress. I remember one case during my residency—"

"Paramedics are with her now," I said, "but maybe you'd better have a look at her, too."

"Of course. You're not done with the deceased yet, I take it?"

"Not yet. Nichols still hasn't shown up."

He gave me a look as if it was my fault we had to make do with a not always reliable civilian photographer, and went off to the kitchen. I returned to the porch. A couple of minutes later Mary Jo came out and joined me.

"Hospital case?" I asked her.

"Afraid so. She's calm enough now; doesn't look like they'll need to medicate her here. If not . . . okay if I take her? She shouldn't have to ride in the ambulance."

"As long as Johanssen has no objections."

"Do I read her her rights?"

"Depends on the details of the shooting. She tell you?"

"Most of it. Banner'd been drinking all day, out and at home both. Trashed a bunch of her personal possessions, and when she got back from shopping he started smacking her around. Then he got his handgun and threatened to shoot her like a horse. Can you believe that? She managed to knock the weapon out of his hand, pick it up, and when he came after her again she popped him in self-defense. Happens like that sometimes, right? In the heat of the moment."

"Yeah," I said, "it happens like that. What started the abuse this time?"

"Same as usual. He accused her of being with another man."

"Was she?"

"No. She swears she was faithful. I believe her."

"About the shooting, too?"

"Absolutely," Mary Jo said. "Justifiable homicide, as far as I'm concerned. I'll write it up that way."

"Your call."

"Will you back me, Chief? With the D.A.? I mean, Earle Banner was a pig and everybody in town knows it. She shouldn't have to go to prison for shooting an animal that kept mauling her."

I was silent. I trusted Mary Jo's judgment; she may have been the youngest officer on the Pomo force, but she had a good head on her shoulders and a solid grasp of police work. The silence had nothing to do with her or Lori Banner. It had to do with Storm, and Faith, and suffering and retribution.

"It's not like she'll get away with anything," Mary Jo said. "She has to live with it the rest of her life. Punishment enough, isn't it?"

"For some people."

"For Lori Banner?"

I said, "For Lori Banner. No formal charges, Mary Jo. And don't worry, I'll back you all the way with Proctor."

Audrey Sixkiller

FOR WHAT SEEMED like a long time the car slithered along a mostly smooth, winding road, the tires hissing through rain glaze and puddles. No more laughter poured out of him, no more filthy threats; he seemed to be concentrating on his driving, on whatever thoughts crept and crawled through his sick mind. The windshield wipers clacking, the beat of the rain on the car's roof, the clogged, nasal rasp of my breathing were the only sounds.

I did not let myself think about anything except a brick wall. A very old wall, the adobe bricks rough and chipped in places, the mortar holding them together, thin but strong. Moss growing in patches, tangles of ivy at one end, and over it all, bright and warm, splashes of late-afternoon sunlight that gave the wall the appearance of glowing, as if with a pale inner fire. William Sixkiller's trick for inducing sleep or getting through any difficult static situation. Imagine something warm and pleasant. Focus on it, distinguish every detail, until it expands to fill your mind. I chose a wall, solid and unyielding, as a barrier against the forces of darkness massing on the other side.

Finally the car slowed and we turned off the smooth, paved road onto rough and muddy ground. The reflected shine of the headlights dimmed, but the dash lights remained on: driving now with just fog or parking lights. The car bounced, lurched, slid; something wet slapped against the passenger side, brushed along the window glass, and was gone. I watched the wall, the sunlight glowing on the waxy, stippled green of the ivy leaves. One of the tires thumped into a hole or deep rut with enough force to rock the car, nearly pitching me off the seat. He said, "Shit!" I continued to watch the bricks, the sunlight, the ivy.

The car stopped. All the lights went out briefly, then the dome light flashed on as he got out. Door slam. I expected him to open the rear door, drag me out or get in with me, but he had something else in mind. Footsteps squishing on grass or leaves, fading. Silence except for the rain.

I counted forty-seven ivy leaves, each a different shade or mixed shades of green. Then he was back; the rear door jerked open and he bent to fill the opening. Wearing the ski mask again, and that was good because if he was still hiding his face, it might mean he didn't intend to kill me after all. If he did let me live, it would be his second-biggest mistake. I knew who he was now. And knowing made it worse, too; he was a man capable of violent excesses, sexual and otherwise, fueled by power, alcohol, drugs, or a combination of all three. I mustn't let him know I knew his identity. Whatever he did to me, I must not let him know.

Hands on my body, and his voice raspy again when he said, "Here we go, bitch," and he dragged me out of the car. Threw the blanket over my head to blot out the sight of him and the dark, dripping night. Lifted me, slung my body over his shoulder. Car door slamming. Moving away from it. Shoes crunching and slithering; a lurch and another sharp epithet. Stopping again. Creaking sound . . . door on rusty hinges. The whisper of the rain diminishing, the thud of his footfalls on solid wood. Inside a building of some kind. He'd switched on a flashlight: I could see downward through an open fold in the blanket, make out the faint backsplash of the beam as it probed restlessly from side to side.

He carried me through a narrow opening like a doorway, scraping my arm and head against one side of it. Then he halted again, shifted my weight, set me down hard on my feet, and ripped off the blanket. Then he pushed me, hard, so that I toppled backward onto something springy that smelled of must and old leather. I bounced, slid off to the floor. Light danced through heavy darkness, shapes appearing and vanishing again with the suddenness of phantoms; then it steadied on my face, bright enough to cause me to squint and turn my head aside. He'd put the flashlight down on some kind of chair nearby, so he'd have both hands free.

The hands grabbed hold of me again, lifted me roughly off the floor onto the yielding surface, straightened my legs on it. Couch . . . leather webbed with cracks, stuffing like white blood leaking through holes and tears. Then he ripped the tape off my mouth, viciously enough to take skin with it. I didn't make a sound. Hurt me far worse than that and I still wouldn't even whimper.

"Okay, bitch," he said. He was breathing hard, but not from exertion. Excitement now—lust. His voice wheezed and quivered with it. "Now you get what you been begging for. All night long, just what you been begging for."

He'd been at the edge of the light; now he came into it, stood at a quarter turn so I could see what he was doing. Unbuckling his belt. Unzipping his fly. Lowering and stepping out of his pants, his underpants. He was already aroused.

"Some hunk of bone, huh?" He came forward a pace, his hand around his sex, stroking it, holding it high like a pagan offering. "Biggest bone you ever had in your mouth. Suck it dry, yeah, suck the bone dry as a bone."

No, I won't, I thought, I'll bite it off. But I knew I wouldn't. He'd kill me for sure if I hurt him that way, and I did not want to die like this, here, at his mercy. I closed my eyes—

"Look at me, bitch. We both gonna watch this."

—and I opened them again. He was advancing again, holding his sex, aiming it toward my mouth. I swallowed involuntarily. But only partway, because my throat was still sore, swollen as if with a blockage. If I couldn't swallow . . .

I'm not afraid, I won't be afraid.

The wall. Think of the wall, the bricks, the sunlight, the ivy, each leaf a different shade or mixed shades of green, glowing warm and bright and clean.

And he leaned close, almost touching my lips. The unwashed stench of him caused another upheaval in my belly.

And then—

Sudden sliding, scraping noise. A second light slashed on somewhere behind and to one side of me, this one even brighter, pinning the masked face with such dazzling brilliance that he threw up a startled arm and tried to turn away from it. In the next second something came hurtling through the crossing beams, a short, jagged-ended piece of wood, and exploded against the side of his head with a sound like a melon being split. He screamed, staggered, fell to one knee. A huge, dark shape rushed after him, swinging the length of wood, hitting him again as he groped for his pants. The next swing missed and that gave him time to tear the Ruger automatic out of his pants pocket, but not enough time to use it. The board swished down once more, thudding into the hand holding the gun, knocking the weapon loose and skittering it away across the floor.

He lurched to his feet, turning, still clutching his pants—no longer trying to fight, trying only to get away from the savage blows. His mask had been ripped loose along one side of his face; I had a clear look at the face, all bloody, the ear torn, one eye bulging as if it were about to burst from the socket. Then it was bare buttocks I saw, churning and pumping as he fled.

Confused scrambling after that, swirls and stabs of light. The two shapes coming together for a few seconds, creating a gigantic blob that filled the doorway across the room. Grunts, another thudding of wood against flesh and bone, another screech of pain. The shapes bursting apart, disappearing into the other room, the light forming wild, sweeping patterns and then something heavy hitting a wall or the floor. Running, banging sounds that soon faded into a thick, roaring silence.

I held my breath, waiting.

The flashlight beam steadied in the other room. Swung around and slid back into the one I was in. Man-shape behind it, heavy, uneven footfalls drawing closer. The beam shifted, picked me out, steadied on me but not directly in my eyes, allowing me to see him as he walked unsteadily into the stationary light from the other flash still propped on the nearby chair. Big, naked to the waist, a bandage obscuring part of his massive torso.

John Faith.

I was beyond shock or surprise. Not even capable yet of feeling relief. I lay there staring up at him.

"Son of a bitch got away," he said thickly. "Almost had him. Would've if I was in better shape."

I licked the inside of my dry mouth. Tried swallowing again, and this time I was able to do it. No crushed cartilage or damage to my trachea. Vocal chords?

"Pretty sure I've seen him somewhere before," John Faith said. "You get a look at his face? Know who he is?"

It took a few seconds and two tries before I was able to speak. My voice was stronger than I'd expected.

"I know him," I said. "His name is Munoz. Mateo Munoz."

Harry Richmond

THE RAIN WOKE me up. Not that I'd been in a deep sleep; I was too depressed to get a decent night's rest. Damn rain only made it worse.

I could've had another full house tonight if it hadn't been for the weather and the couldn't-care-less media. Just three cabins occupied on a Saturday night, and none by a newshound. Still a few of them around, but they were all over in the town proper—and they'd be gone, too, soon enough, if John Faith's body didn't turn up pretty quick. Well, good riddance. Liars, users, full of phony promises that got a man all stirred up and hopeful and then left him high and dry, with his expectations hanging out limp as a flasher's cock.

I rolled out of bed and put on my robe and went to the kitchen to find something to eat. Nothing much in the refrigerator appealed to me. Finally I dragged out a couple of powdered-sugar doughnuts I'd bought at Miller's, poured a glass of milk to wash them down with. Comfort food. That was what Dottie used to call milk and doughnuts. Cake and chocolate eclairs and butter toffee and hot fudge sundaes and every other calorie-rich thing you could think of, too. All that comfort food was what blew her up to two hundred and eighty-seven pounds, what killed her quick that hot July night ten years ago. Quick and comfortable.

Dottie. Wasn't often anymore that I thought about her, much less missed her, but tonight I wished she were sitting there across the table, helping me eat the powdered-sugar doughnuts. I'm not the kind of man who gets lonely; I like being by myself, doing for myself, not having to answer to anybody else. But sometimes, when I'm down like this, I crave other company besides my own. And I get mad as hell at Dottie for dying hog-fat the way she did, leaving me to run the Lakeside all by myself, put up with ten years' worth of hassles and frustrations and limp expectations and then for a reward be forced to sell out and go live with an ungrateful, man-crazy daughter and her rotten teenage kids for the rest of my life. She'd gone easy, easy and comfortable; she hadn't suffered. I was the one who'd suffered, who'd keep right on suffering. And when my time came I'd go hard, sure as God makes little green apples. Hard and uncomfortable.

I wedged half a doughnut into my mouth and the crumbs and sugar spilled down inside my pajama top and that made me so mad I smashed the plate against the wall and the glass of milk after it. Let fat-assed Maria clean up the mess tomorrow. Let it lie there until it rotted, for all I cared.

Those bastards. TV newswoman saying my interview was one of her best, promising it'd be shown today, and not even a whisper of my name much less the interview on the noon or seven o'clock or eleven o'clock news programs. Plenty of other Pomo residents and businesses getting attention, but not Harry Richmond and the Lakeside Resort. *Chronicle* reporter swearing he'd use my name and give the resort a plug in his story, and did he? Hell, no. Not a word. They wouldn't show the interview or mention me tomorrow or any other day, either. Not the way my luck was running.

All I'd asked for was one lousy little break, a few seconds in the spotlight, some free publicity. A small businessman fighting to survive, a hardworking, taxpaying citizen, is entitled to that much, isn't he? Why should others get some good out of what's happened in Pomo and not me?

It's not fair. It's just not fair!

Audrey Sixkiller

"DON'T BE AFRAID." John Faith had found the Ruger automatic and was tucking it into the waistband of his trousers. "Munoz won't be back and I won't hurt you."

"I'm not afraid."

He flicked the flash beam over my face. "No, you're not, are you? Of me or of him. He didn't do anything to you before he brought you here?"

"Rape me? No."

"Choked you, though . . . those marks on your throat. You breathe okay?"

"Yes. I'll be all right."

"Where'd he take you from?"

"My garage. Hiding inside when I came home." Some of the shock was wearing off; I felt relief now, a loosening of the tension in my body which created a tingling weakness in the joints. "My hands," I said. "They're numb."

"Roll over on your side so I can get at the tape."

When I'd done that he knelt and set the flashlight down. I could feel his fingers at my back, on my upper arms, but I was numb below the elbows.

He asked, "Why'd he bring you here?"

So no one could hear my screams. "I'm not sure where we are."

"Nucooee Point Lodge."

"Yes. Of course."

"He must've been here before. Seemed to know his way around."

"So do you," I said.

"Be glad I'm alive and I picked this place to hole up in."

"I am. If you hadn't been here . . ."

"Don't think about it."

"I can't think about anything else."

"Yeah. I wanted to jump him sooner, but I had to make sure I took him by surprise. I'm hurting and I wouldn't have done you or me any good if I'd lost the fight. But I'd feel better if he was lying on the floor right now with a broken head."

I said nothing.

"Bad choice of words," he said. "You probably won't believe it, but I didn't kill Storm Carey."

"All right."

"Gospel truth. Okay, your hands are free."

"I can't feel them."

"Here, I'll help you." He lifted one arm, laid it across my hip.

Turned me by the shoulders, gently, and propped me against the couch's side rest, then lifted the other arm onto my lap. Both hands felt like blobs of dead flesh. He took them in his big fingers and began to massage them. "Tell me when they start to tingle."

It took three or four minutes.

He kept it up for another minute or so after I told him, then let go and got slowly to his feet. Light from the flash caught his face and upper body; red smears stained the bandage on his chest.

"You're bleeding."

"Wounds tore open again during the fight."

"Bullet wounds?"

"Oh yeah. Good old Chief Novak. His aim was a little off."

"You broke his nose."

"Did I? Good."

"He believes you're guilty. Really believes it."

"Sure he does." John Faith switched off the other torch, sat wearily at the far end of the couch; the beam from his flash lay at an oblique angle between us. "Pomo's a hell of a deceptive place," he said then.

"Deceptive?"

"Looks nice and peaceful, but underneath it's a snake pit. I've been in wide-open boomtowns that weren't as hostile."

"It isn't that bad."

"Wasn't until I got here, you mean."

I didn't answer, and he misunderstood my silence.

"Yeah. Right," he said. "What the hell, you might as well blame me for what Munoz tried to do to you."

"I don't blame you. You're not one of his kind."

"What kind is that?"

"The ones who hate and fear women, who use sex as a weapon."

"That the only reason he went after you? Or was it something personal?"

"Well, I was responsible for him being expelled from school two years ago. Another teacher and I caught him using cocaine in an empty classroom. The other teacher wanted to let him off with a warning. I thought it was too serious for that."

"Two years is a long time to nurse a grudge."

"Not for a boy who suddenly decides he's a man."

"There was an attempted rape the other night," John Faith said.

"Novak questioned me about it. Guy wearing a ski mask, he said. Was that Munoz after you?"

"Yes. He tried to break into my house."

"Maybe you're not his first victim. Maybe he's the one . . ." He let the rest of the sentence trail off.

"The one who killed Storm Carey. Is that what you were going to say?"

He nodded. "Didn't look like she'd been raped, though. Was she?"

"No."

"But she could've fought him and he killed her before he had a chance to do anything else. He's the kind who'd panic in a situation like that. And then run in a hurry, like he did tonight."

"He'll keep on running," I said. "He must know we saw his face."

"He knows it, all right."

"Then we have to notify the authorities right away. Before he can get too far—"

"I let you go and you notify them, and then I give myself up. That's what you mean."

"It's the only way."

"For me to get off the hook? Uh-uh. If there was any proof Munoz killed the Carey woman, then, yeah, I'd take the chance. But there isn't any proof. Novak and the rest aren't looking any further than me."

"They can make him confess when they catch him—"

"If they catch him. If he's guilty. No guarantees any way you look at it. Besides, the law's already got me for assaulting a police officer and unlawful flight, among other things. I'd still go to prison."

"Extenuating circumstances. The charges would be dropped—"

"Would they? I doubt it. How're your hands?"

". . . My hands?"

"Feeling back in them yet?"

"Yes." Pins and needles now. "My ankles . . ."

"We'll leave them taped. Don't try to take it off."

"You're not letting me go?"

"Not tonight. Neither of us is going anywhere tonight."

"But Mateo Munoz . . ."

"Never mind him for now." John Faith stood again, grimacing. "I have to change these bandages. You stay put."

He walked away, his light picking out another abandoned couch at an angle across from the one I was on. Candles in tin holders sat on a pair of folding chairs at either end; he struck a match and lit one candle, then the other. He brought the second over and set it on the chair near me, positioning the chair so I would be visible in the flickering glow.

Several items were piled on the other couch: blankets, clothing, food, medical supplies. I watched him sit among them, wedge his torch between two cushions so its beam was fixed on his chest, and then peel off the bloody bandage and apply some sort of ointment to the wound. Now and then he glanced up to make sure I hadn't moved. When he was done taping a fresh bandage in place he repeated the process, with greater difficulty, with another wound in back, under his arm.

Sweat oiled his bare skin when he'd finished. He shut off the flashlight, I suppose to conserve its batteries; took a long drink of bottled water. For a time he sat limply, resting. Then he stood again, brought the bottle to me.

"Thirsty?"

I nodded.

"Use your hands all right now?"

"Yes."

He let me have the water. And another, smaller bottle: aspirin for my sore throat and the pulsing ache in my temples. Swallowing the water was painful enough; getting four aspirin down, one at a time, hurt even more. The skin was so tender around my Adam's apple it felt as if a layer of it had been scraped away.

When I could speak again I asked him, "How did you get here, John Faith?"

"Half the name's enough. Take your choice."

"How, John? All the way to Nucooee Point?"

"Same way I managed not to drown last night. Strong survival skills."

"You couldn't have made it here by yourself. Someone helped you. Brought you over in a boat."

"Wrong. I brought myself."

"Trisha Marx. In my boat."

"I don't know what you're talking about."

"The food and medical supplies—she got those for you, too."

"You think so? Is this Trisha a doctor or a nurse?"

"Of course not."

"You saw the bandages I had on before. Much more professional than the ones I put on myself, right?"

"Are you saying someone else besides Trisha helped you?"

"Someone else, period. Doctor, man you don't know."

"I don't believe that," I said. "There isn't a doctor in Pomo County who would give aid and comfort to a fugitive."

"Don't be too sure about that."

"Trisha can get in a lot of trouble, you must know that."

"Not if you don't start throwing her name around. Tell the cops about Munoz, tell them about me, tell them I had help if you want to, but don't mention Trisha Marx's name. Give the kid a break."

"How do you know she's a kid unless—"

"I met her last night, on the Bluffs. Gave her a ride home before I went out to Storm Carey's place. Her old man knows about it, among others." He paused. "You going to keep her out of it?"

"Yes. But you have to let me go."

"I will. Just not yet."

"When?"

"In the morning. Before noon, when I leave."

"Hours from now. We just sit here until then?"

"Sit, talk, sleep—whatever. You'll be comfortable enough."

"Is Trisha coming for you? With a car?"

"No. That's enough about her. My ride out of here has nothing to do with Trisha Marx, I swear that to you. All right?"

I believed him. He was too vehement, too fiercely protective of her. He'd let Trisha help him once, at considerable risk to both of them, because he'd had no other choice. But it hadn't set well with him. The second person . . . I didn't understand that, or have a clue as to who it might be. Not a doctor; that part I didn't believe.

He said, "You won't see who it is. And you won't see me leave."

"Tape my hands again? Blindfold me?"

"Tape your hands, but in front where you can get at them with your teeth. It'll take a while for you to get loose and flag down a car on the highway. By the time you make it to a phone I'll be long gone."

"Gone where? A man wanted for murder . . . there's no place that's safe."

"I know it. But it's better than rotting in jail." He laughed, a humorless bark. "Me and Richard Kimble."

"You'll never have a minute's peace. Have you thought about that?"

"I've thought about it."

"And it doesn't bother you?"

"More of the same, that's all. I'm used to it."

"Used to what?"

"Running," John Faith said. "I been doing it, one form or another, most of my life."

Anthony Munoz

FINGERS ON YOUR window in the middle of the night, man, it can't be nothing good. Rap, rap, rap, and I was off the bed and rubbing my eyes. But I couldn't see nothing at the window, just rain patterns on the glass and the black night beyond. I got hold of my aluminum Little League bat and drifted over there slow in the dark.

Rap, rap, rap. Then he must've seen my shape, because the fingers quit and he called out, "About time, Anthony. Open up, for Chrissake. Lemme in."

Mateo. What the hell, man?

I flipped the catch and hauled the window up. Rain and cold blew in. I backed off as Mateo climbed over the sill, laid the bat on the card table I use for a desk, and then flicked on the lamp there.

"Shut that freakin' light off!"

I snapped the room dark again, quick, but not before I got a straight-on look at him. It bugged my eyes. Clothes all wet and torn, whole left side of his face a piece of raw meat. Scraped, swelled up, bloody. And half his ear torn away, rest of it hanging there dripping red. And his eyes . . . wild, man, half bugfuck. Scared. That was the worst thing of all, the thing that chilled my guts. I'd never seen Mateo scared before. Never.

"Man, what *happened* to you?"

"No time for that. Listen, get your—"

"Fight, man? Some dudes jump you?"

"I said there ain't no time!" The scare was in his voice, too. It shook like an old woman's. "Get your shit together, make it fast. We got to *move*."

"Mateo, what're you talkin' about?"

"Clothes, cash, whatever else you need."

"Need for what?"

"Travelin', man. Don't be thick."

"Where to?"

"What'd we talk about this morning, huh? L.A."

"Now? Just pick up and split in the middle of—"

"Yeah, now, yeah. Haul ass."

"You in trouble, man?"

"Keep your voice down! Wake up the old man and old lady, for Chrissake?"

"You got to tell me what happened."

"I don't have to tell you squat. You comin' or not?"

"I don't know—"

"Don't know, don't know, that's all you know how to say."

"I'm just tryin' to find out—"

"You with me or what?"

"Always with you, man. But give me a clue what's goin' down here. Cops? Heat on you?"

"Yeah, all right, I'll be hot as hell pretty soon. The bitch saw my face, man. Her and the dude busted me up like this."

"What bitch? What dude? Jesus, Mateo, what'd you do?"

"*¡Cagon de mierdas!* Quit asking stupid questions!"

"Hey, man, don't dis me. You're the one—"

"I got no more time to waste with you, Anthony. Comin' or not? Yes or no, spit it out."

It was in me to say yes. He was my brother, man, I looked up to him all my life. But he done something real raw this time—the way he was beat up said so, the scare in his eyes said so, my chilled guts said so. Cops after him . . . I didn't want a piece of that. I'm no outlaw. I never saw nothing cool in being an outlaw.

"I'm no outlaw, man," I says.

"It ain't gonna be like that."

"Yeah it is. I wouldn't be no good at—"

"How much cash you holding?"

"What?"

"You heard me. How much you got stashed?"

"Not sure, man. Fifty, sixty bucks . . ."

"Give it to me. The whole wad and no more crap."

I went and got my stash from behind the loose board in my closet.

When I gave it to him, up close like that, I could smell him, and he stank. He stank of the fear that was crawling in him.

"Last chance, bro. You gonna go to L.A. with me or stay here and rot in this hole?"

I flashed on Trisha, the kid she had in the oven—my kid. My *brother*, man! Yeah, but he'd crossed the line, done something raw this time, turned outlaw, and I couldn't get past the stink of his fear. I couldn't get past it, man.

"I can't do it," I says. "You're my brother, I'd do anything for you, you know that, but this—"

"You ain't my brother. I ain't got a brother no more."

"Hey, Mateo—"

"Fuck you, Anthony," he says. "*Vaya a la chingada,*" and he went out fast through the window into the rain and dark.

But he left the stink of his fear behind. I couldn't chase it even with the window up and the cold wetness blowing in. It hung there, heavy, and I kept smelling it, and the more I smelled it, the sicker I felt. It wasn't like the stink of a brother, not anymore. It was like the stink of somebody I didn't even know.

Audrey Sixkiller

TIME PASSED IN a seemingly endless series of ticks and slow sweeps and frozen moments. For long periods it was as if I could hear the passage of each second—now like the faint pulsing of a clock just outside the range of hearing, now like the slow, steady beat of a heart. Then it would seem suddenly to stop. Then it would start again, lurch along, and then settle into the same methodical tempo as before.

William Sixkiller: "Patience is the great virtue of cats and Indians." Yes, but I had lost that virtue tonight. In its place was a restless need to be gone from this place, a frustrated sense of urgency even though Mateo Munoz was far away by now. Patience disappears from cats and Indians both when they are held against their wills.

Now and then John Faith would get up from the other couch and pace for a while, back and forth, back and forth. Once when he did that I complained that my legs were growing numb, and he did me the favor of unwinding the tape, rubbing circulation into the ankles, helping me stand and letting me walk awhile. I thought then of trying to run from him, hiding in the trees once I was outside, but it was a hollow scheme. Even if I could get my hands on one flashlight, he still had the other; and I didn't know the way out of the lodge and he must know it. I thought, too, of telling him I had to relieve myself and asking for privacy and taking advantage of that. But then I would not even have a chance at the flashlight and I couldn't hope to escape by blundering around in the dark. Besides, at some point I really would need to relieve myself and it would be an embarrassment to both of us if I forced him to stand watch over me when that time came.

When my ankles were taped again he returned to the other couch and I drew the wool blanket he'd given me to my chin. It was still raining steadily, the dampness intensifying the cold in there. For the third or fourth time, upstairs, there were faint chittering cries and leathery flutterings. Bats. They didn't like the wet weather any more than I did; it made hunting difficult for them.

Except for the rain and the night sounds, we sat in a monotony of silence. We had said all there was to say on the subjects of Mateo Munoz and Storm Carey and the fugitive status of John Faith, and there was little else to talk about. But when the silence began to drag intolerably—

"John, there's something I'd like to know."

". . . What's that?"

"Earlier you said you've been running most of your life. What did you mean?"

"Nothing. Another bad choice of words."

"They sounded true to me."

Silence.

"Has the law been after you before?"

"Once or twice. Minor violations, if it matters."

"Who else?"

Silence again.

"John? Please talk to me."

"People like you," he said.

"Like me? I don't understand."

"Ordinary people. Average."

"You think I'm average? A Native American woman?"

"You are as far as I'm concerned."

"I still don't understand," I said. "Why would you run from ordinary, average people?"

"I don't run from them. That's the wrong word, run—makes me sound like a coward. I don't back down from anybody. And I don't run unless I've got no other choice."

"Like last night."

"Like last night. I suppose Novak said I was running away when he showed up, but it wasn't because I'm guilty. I would've reported what I found. Anonymously, yeah, because I knew what'd happen if I called from the house and identified myself. Exactly what did happen—I got blamed."

"You only made things worse by assaulting him, trying to escape."

"Maybe. But I wasn't thinking too clearly at the time. You get pushed around enough, backed into enough corners, you figure your only chance is to push back."

"Has it really been that bad for you?"

"You wouldn't believe me if I told you how bad. Pomo's the worst by far, but there've been other times, other places . . ." He shook his head, as if shaking away memories. "The hell with it," he said.

"So that's why you shy away from people."

"Shy away? Let's say I'm better off with my own company."

"Isn't there anyone you're close to? Someone in your family—"

"I don't have a family."

"Friends?"

"No friends, either. And no woman, if that's your next question. I made the mistake of getting married once. I won't make it again."

"What happened? Or don't you want to talk about it?"

"No, I don't want to talk about it. Let's just say she decided big and ugly wasn't as exciting as she thought it'd be."

"You're not ugly, John."

"The hell I'm not. I look in the mirror, I see what everybody else sees. Big, ugly, mean-looking . . . dangerous. Face and body like mine, I must be some kind of monster."

"There's nothing that awful about the way you look."

"Nothing a team of plastic surgeons couldn't fix. Don't patronize me."

"I wasn't patronizing you, and I didn't say it to get on your good side. I mean it."

"Okay, you mean it. Some people don't judge a book by its cover. But ask most of your friends and neighbors what they think, what they thought the minute they laid eyes on me. Ask the guy who wrote the newspaper editorial, ask Novak, ask Trisha Marx's father."

"That's the poison talking," I said.

"The what?"

"Poison. Indians believe there's poison everywhere, in all things. Each person is born with some, and we can be infected with more, by others and by ourselves. Poison is the handmaiden of hate—my father said that. Together they can sour our hearts, eventually destroy us."

"I get the point, teacher. So there's poison in me, plenty of it. But I can't get rid of it without getting rid of myself. Simple fact is, I wouldn't be sitting here with a couple of holes in me and a murder charge hanging over my head if I looked like the frigging boy next door. And if you don't believe it it's because you don't live inside this body."

"No, but I live inside an Indian woman's body. I'm not a stranger to mindless prejudice."

A few seconds trickled away before he said, "I don't doubt it. So you ought to be able to understand how it is with me."

"Up to a point."

"What point? The amount of violence I've had to deal with? I'm a man, oversized and ugly, and that makes me a target."

"A small young woman isn't a target?"

"Sure she is. But her odds, your odds against it are a lot better than mine. You haven't had much violence in your life before tonight, I'll bet."

"Not directed at me, no. But that doesn't mean it won't happen again. Or that if it does, I'll survive it. There are as many men in this county who hate women and Indians as there are who hate big white strangers. The same men, many of them."

"Look, I don't want to argue with you. Maybe you're right, maybe we're more alike than I think and it's only the kind and amount of crap we have to deal with that makes us different."

"There's another difference, too. You keep dwelling on your crap, your poison. You let it rule your life."

"And you don't? No sourness or anger in your heart? Well, then, you're a better person than me. Or else you've got a thicker hide."

"I didn't say I have no bitterness or anger. I'm angry right now. My skin is thick enough, but I can still be poisoned."

"You don't show it."

"Indians learn to mask their emotions," I said. "And I channel mine into teaching, volunteer work."

"So you are a better person. Can't be easy to keep a mask on or to turn the other cheek in a place like Pomo."

"Easier than it would be if I drifted from place to place, always alone. I was born in Pomo, it's my home."

"Right," John Faith said. "And that's the biggest difference between you and me."

"What is?"

"I've never had a home."

That was all he would say; after the words were out he seemed to retreat inside himself again. It's the only place he feels comfortable and secure, I thought. Within his own skin.

I watched him for a time, sitting motionless and staring into the cold shadows beyond the candle glow. Swaddled in my thermal blanket, he seemed not nearly so large, but aged, shrunken somewhat, like an old man waiting quietly for his spirit to leave and enter the Abode of the Dead. But the illusion was false. I remembered him as he'd been earlier, when he'd finished changing his bandages: his bare torso sweat-oiled, the candlelight giving it a burnished look so that he resembled a life-size figure sculpted in bronze; shadows altering the rugged contours of his head and face without softening them. In that aspect, huge and dark and stoic, he might have been one of the People —a warrior marked by spear and arrow wounds after battle. One of the legendary chiefs, perhaps. Konocti, Kah-bel . . .

But that, too, was illusion. When he'd gotten up to bring the water bottle to me, he'd become again what he really was: another big, unfathomable white man. That was what I'd thought at the time, anyway. Now I wondered if there might not actually be something of the warrior in him, a man different from other men, strong, and big in ways other than size. I was not sure I liked him, or would care to know him well; but I did understand and feel compassion for him, and I sensed that he was an honest person, a good person, and most if not all of what he'd told me tonight was the truth. How can a wounded fugitive who risks his own safety to save a woman he barely knows from sexual assault be either a cold-blooded murderer or a threat to any community?

But the way I felt didn't change the fact that I was his prisoner and would remain his prisoner for several more hours. Nor did it help the time pass any more quickly. Nor did it prevent my body from protesting the treatment it had been subjected to tonight, or exhaustion from creeping through me until my limbs felt as heavy as pepperwood logs. My eyelids were heavy, too. Yet it seemed important to stay awake and alert; to give in to sleep was a kind of betrayal.

I dozed in spite of myself. And jerked awake.

What time was it? I fought the urge to look at my watch.

So cold in here. I snuggled down deeper under the blanket.

Had Mateo Munoz killed Storm? If John Faith was innocent, then Munoz must be guilty. Suppose he ran all the way into Mexico? He had family there. Could the authorities find him, bring him back . . . ?

Dozing again. Wake up! Stay awake.

But I was so tired . . .

Richard Novak

IT WAS NEARLY three before I went home again. Details to clear up, my recommendation on the shooting death of Earle Banner to bolster Mary Jo's report. Two cups of coffee and some pointless talk with Verne Erickson. And still no word on John Faith. It was the frustration of that, more than weariness and throbbing pain, that finally prodded me out of the station and back to the house.

Audrey wasn't there. Just Mack, and my bed neatly made. I was relieved at first, but when I popped another codeine capsule and crawled into the sack, it seemed cold and empty. Audrey's scent lingered, and I remembered the warmth of her nearly nude body pressed against mine. A feeling of loneliness and isolation welled up, the kind a castaway on a sand spit that was shrinking away around him might feel. Much as I didn't want to admit it, I needed someone now more than ever, someone who cared—I needed Audrey.

The painkiller knocked me out before too long and I slept another five hours and woke up just as tired, just as empty. Audrey was on my mind as I showered and shaved and dressed. Audrey and Storm, intertwined, like some sort of two-headed creature. I'd treated her shabbily, not only last night but for most of the time I'd known her. She cared so much; couldn't I care just a little?

I put the leash on Mack and took him for a short walk in the thin, cold rain. By the time I came back I'd built up a strong urge to see Audrey, apologize to her. Nothing more than that; I wouldn't tell her I needed her because I was afraid the need was surface, temporary, and I wouldn't hurt her with false hopes. Just let her know that she mattered to me, even if I hadn't shown it before.

I drove to her house. Her garage door was all the way up, her car slotted inside, but I didn't think anything of it until there was no answer to my doorbell ring. I went around back, knocked on the door there and called her name; still no answer. Why would she go away and leave the garage door wide open? And where would she go in weather like this without taking her car? Not off somewhere in her boat; I could see the Chris-Craft, tarp-covered, on the lift inside the dock shed.

An uneasy feeling began to work inside me. The attempted break-in Thursday night, the threatening phone call yesterday morning . . . somebody stalking her. The feeling worsened when I found the piece of cardboard taped over the broken bathroom window. What'd happened here? I punched out the cardboard, climbed through, and took a quick look through the house.

No sign of her. Except for her car in the garage, there was no indication she'd been here at all last night after leaving my place. The furnace was off; the interior was chill and damp.

I climbed back through the window and went into the garage. The car's hood was cold, too; it hadn't been driven in several hours. The sense of wrongness was so strong now it was like a squeezing pressure in my chest and groin. I opened the driver's door, checked the front seat, then the backseat. Nothing to find. I slammed the door, started to turn, and stepped on something. I looked down at the floor. Lipstick. I bent to pick it up, saw something else, and dropped to all fours to peer under the car.

Her purse was there, open, her wallet another of several items that had been spilled out of it. The one thing that wasn't there was the Ruger automatic she'd told me she was going to carry for protection.

Douglas Kent

I WOKE UP at dawn's early light, but there wasn't much of same, just gloom and rain, so I went back to sleep. I was awake again at nine, feeling fine, feeling fine. No hangover this a.m., whoop-de-doo. And some Good Samaritan of a sneak thief seemed to have made off with my heavy bag of sticks, whoop-de-dee. Walking unburdened, walking tall, I padded into the bathroom, shook some dew off the old lily, and had a squint at the Kent phiz in the mirror.

Amazing. I actually looked alive this morning. Doubly amazing, in fact, considering my morbid contemplations of last night. Eat your heart out, Richard Cory, you gentleman from sole to crown, you imperially slim rectal aperture. You may have put a bullet in your puddin' head one fine night, but I didn't and won't be a copycat. My demons are better than your demons, my demons can lick your demons any old day of the week.

Out to the kitchen. More rain and gloom at the windows, but 'twas of no import, for I was bright and sunny inside. Keep your sunny side up, eh, Kent? Oyez, oyez.

One glass, relatively clean, plucked from the cupboard. Splash in approximately two inches of ice-cold, delicious orange juice. Add approximately six inches of crystal-clear, delicious salve. Stir lightly with index finger. Over the lips and over the gums . . . ahh! Quaff again until glass is empty. Ahh! Repeat process, once immediately and then as often as needed.

Had I remembered to turn on my answering machine before doddering off to the sack? Wonder of wonders, I had. No messages, however. So. Nothing new on the fate of Faith or young Jaydee would've rung up as promised. Too bad, but that's the way the cookie crumbles. Heigh-ho! One thing at a time. All in due course, everything in its proper order. The Faith will be kept when the time comes to keep the Faith.

I chuckled. Kent really was in fine fettle this a.m.

"Yes you are, pal. In fine fettle, and for less we'll not settle."

I turned around. Pa Kent's .38 was sitting in the center of the table where I'd left him. Old enemies? Hell, no. New friends. Bosom buddies. My pal, Roscoe. I winked at him; he winked back.

"We had a gay old time last night, didn't we, pal?"

"Gay, of course, meaning lighthearted and carefree."

"Of course."

"Then we certainly did, pal."

"Shall we reopen lines of communication? Shall we talk of shoes and ships and sealing wax, of cabbages and kings? Shall we discuss the imminent collapse of Western civilization?"

"No," Roscoe said.

"Why not?"

"Guns can't talk."

"Damn right they can't," I said.

We both laughed until my sides hurt.

Oyez, I hadn't felt this cheerful since Pa Kent took his last late-night dive.

Harry Richmond

MY MOOD WASN'T any better in the morning. The media cheating me the way they had kept right on rankling. I managed to be civil to my few Saturday-night guests when they checked out, but Maria was late again because of church. Missed the early Mass or something, some damn excuse that I didn't pay attention to, and then instead of just skipping it altogether or putting her praying on hold until evening and coming to do her maid's work on time, she went to the nine o'clock Mass and didn't show up until quarter to eleven. I laid into her pretty good. More than I would have if I'd been in a better mood, probably, but those Indians have a way of setting me off. Say they're sorry but they don't mean it. Look at you with their big liquid eyes and you just know that behind them they're thinking about how much they'd like to cut your throat or lift your scalp. Savages, the lot of them, and no amount of education or religion or government handouts will ever civilize them.

Maria knew better than to argue with me. Just stood there and took what I dished out and then went and did her work and left again without saying a word. I walked around after she was gone and checked up on her, to make sure she hadn't sloughed off or done something else to get back at me, like stealing or damaging property, but there was none of that. And there better not ever be any of that if she wanted to keep her job and her fat ass out of jail.

Nothing much for me to do on a rainy Sunday except watch the morning NFL game on TV. In the middle of the first quarter Ella called. First time she'd bothered in a month. She'd been reading about the murder and everything, did I know any of the people involved? Gossip hound, like her mother. I cut her short on that subject, so then she started in with the kids' lives and her own. Jason said this, Kim did that, she'd heard this really funny story at the salon but it was kind of risqué so maybe she'd better not tell me over the phone, and all the while she was jabbering I could hear an unfamiliar male voice in the background, jabbering with my granddaughter. Somebody she'd just met, no doubt, and he'd spent the night like all the rest. My daughter, the slut. Try to raise your only kid right and this was what you got, a slut who was raising *her* daughter to be the same and her son to be a dope fiend. Jason had already been arrested once on a marijuana charge. I didn't even ask her about "the new man in my life," as she'd have put it; I said I got to go, the Packers were about to score another touchdown, and hung up on her.

The Packers scored, all right, and no sooner did they kick off to the Cowboys than I had another interruption. Chief Novak, to pester me again. I heard the bell go off on the front desk and thought it might be an early guest and went out to find him and his bruised and bandaged face. Nobody with him today. And looking about as hangdog as I felt. Tense, too, as though there'd been some new development that hadn't set well with him.

"What's up, Chief?"

"I'm looking for Audrey Sixkiller."

"That so?"

"Have you seen her last night or today?"

"Nope."

"Any idea where she might be?"

"Nope."

"Anyone mention her name to you recently?"

"Nope. You think we have mutual friends, Chief?"

"I don't think anything," he said. "I'm grabbing at straws. I've been trying to find her all morning, all over town."

"How come? She do something?"

"Personal matter."

"Uh-huh. Well, you know how Indians are."

". . . What's that supposed to mean?"

"Never around when you want 'em, always off doing what pleases them. They're not the same as us."

That touched off a scowl. He said snottily, "Don't like Indians much, do you, Harry? Or anybody with a different skin."

"You saying I'm a racist? Me?"

"Oh hell no, not you."

"Look here, you don't have any call to insult me just because you can't find your woman."

"She's not my woman."

"No? Somebody's woman, that's for sure."

He laid his hands on the counter and leaned toward me, so suddenly that I couldn't help stepping back. "Don't play games with me. You have something to say, spit it out."

I spit it out, all right. Might not have—might not've even thought of it—if I hadn't been in such a low-down mood and if he hadn't started throwing his weight around and accusing me of being a racist. As it was, I felt like sticking it to him a little. Sticking it to somebody the way it'd been stuck to me by the media. So I did. And I put a little twist on it, too, that hadn't even crossed my mind until that minute.

"You been over to Nucooee Point?" I asked him.

"Nucooee Point? No, why?"

"Might be where she's at. Her and her somebody."

"What the hell're you getting at?"

"She landed that boat of hers at the Point yesterday morning. I happened to see her, and that's sure enough where she went. Nothing down there but the old lodge and a lot of privacy. No reason for her to go there all by herself unless she was meeting somebody, now is there, Chief?"

Audrey Sixkiller

"IT'S NOON, JOHN," I said. "Whoever you're waiting for isn't coming."

"He's coming, all right."

"Then why hasn't he been here by now?"

No answer.

"Suppose he doesn't come. What then?"

No answer.

"You can't walk away from here, you know that. And the two of us can't stay here indefinitely. You know that, too."

"Okay, I know it."

"Let me go, and give yourself up, John."

"No."

"It's the only way you have a chance."

"It's the only way I don't have a chance."

"I'll testify for you. I'll tell them what you did for me last night—"

"That won't stop a jury from convicting me of murder."

"You won't be tried if Mateo Munoz is guilty. Please listen—"

"I'm through listening, Audrey. I don't want to hear any more. Either you shut up or I'll put tape over your mouth. I mean it. You want your mouth taped shut?"

I didn't; I shook my head.

"All right, then. Be quiet."

He was pacing again, as he'd done most of the morning. Earlier it had been for exercise and to work off nervous energy; he'd slept some, too, and he seemed stronger. Now the pacing was the result of tension and frustration. As I watched him I thought again of how warriorlike he was at times, even dressed in slacks and shirt and an old corduroy jacket that was too small across the shoulders and chest. The Ruger automatic inside his belt added a renegade touch. John Faith: warrior, renegade, misfit. A man apart, a man shunned.

Nearly five hours of exhausted sleep had renewed my strength as well. The headache and throat soreness were mostly gone; only a stiffness in my legs and lower back bothered me, discomfort that would've been worse if John Faith hadn't let me unbind my ankles and walk for a short time. He'd also given me milk, and bread and cheese to eat. Until these past few minutes, there had been little conversation between us. The night had invited as much intimacy as a man and a woman with too many fundamental differences and too few similarities could share. The pale morning light that seeped into the lodge caused us to pull away from each other. In a sense it was like a one-night stand between strangers: closeness and urgency in the dark, and in the morning, distance and embarrassment at having opened yourself up, even a little, to someone you didn't know.

"John," I said, "I'd like to walk again."

"No."

"My toes are starting to get numb."

"Tape's not that tight. Ankles or wrists."

He'd bound my hands more than an hour ago, in front of me as he'd promised. I lifted my arms; with my fingers splayed away from one another and the tape joining the wrists, my hands looked like an obscene caricature of the Christian symbol of prayer. I lowered my arms again, clasped my fingers between my drawn-up knees.

Something creaked and scraped in another part of the lodge, the dining room or beyond, at the side. John Faith heard it, too; he stood still with his head cocked, listening. The sounds weren't repeated. Rats, probably. They were everywhere in the old building, in the walls and under the floors; now and then you could hear them scurrying, gnawing. He'd been wise to put the food up next to him while he slept. The candlelight alone wouldn't have been enough to keep hungry rats away.

He said, "Going to take another quick look outside."

"He's not coming, John."

"Couple of minutes is all I'll be gone. Don't try taking that tape off your ankles."

"I won't."

He moved off through the archway, into the dining room. Enough daylight penetrated so he could make his way without using a flashlight. Only one candle still burned, the one on the chair near where I sat. Through its guttering flame I watched John Faith meld with the shadows beyond the archway. I leaned forward then, reached down to my ankles, but not to try picking at the tape. It would be foolish to disobey him at this point. All I did was rub the insteps in an effort to improve circulation—

A chain of noises jerked my head up. Thumps, scrapes, a sharp thud, and then a muffled, harsh voice that was not John Faith's—all from the far end of the dining room or in the room beyond. I sat up straight, staring in that direction. Silence again. Then footsteps. And then John Faith reappeared in a slow, stiff walk, his hands out away from his body at shoulder level. He wasn't alone; somebody moved close behind him, half hidden by his bulk and by shadows.

He was two or three paces into the lobby when I heard him grunt and saw him stagger forward, off balance—shoved hard in the back. The other man was still just a dark shape standing spread-legged, both arms extended in front, objects clutched in both hands, making them seem unnaturally elongated. In the next instant a flashlight beam stabbed out through the gloom, and in its back glow I saw the hard set of the man's face.

"Dick!"

He didn't answer or even glance my way. The light held steady on John Faith, who had caught his balance and was turning around, slowly, his hands still out away from his body.

"Go ahead, you son of a bitch," Dick yelled at him, "make a try for that gun in your belt. Give me an excuse."

The tone of his voice caused chills to run over me. Implacable, choked with rage. He'd meant what he said.

John Faith knew it too. He stood rigid.

"I ought to do it anyway. If you hurt her—"

"Dick, no! He didn't do anything to me. It was Mateo Munoz . . . he'd have raped and maybe killed me if . . . Dick, John Faith saved my life!"

Silence, clotted and electric. None of us moved; I was not even breathing. The stop-time seemed to drag on and on—

"All right, Faith," Dick said. Different tone, closer to his normal one. Controlled again. "You dodged a bullet this time. Literally."

I let out the air burning my lungs and sagged back against the cushions. As relieved as I was that Dick had found us, that there'd been no more violence and the long night was finally over, I felt sorry for John Faith. Very, very sorry for him.

Richard Novak

I ORDERED FAITH to take the gun out of his belt, left hand, thumb and forefinger, and set it on the floor—set it, not drop it—and then kick it over to me. He followed orders with such deliberate care, almost like a pantomime, that I wondered if he was mocking me. I couldn't be sure, so I let it go. I squatted to pick up his weapon, slip it into my jacket pocket—not taking the light off him for an eye flick. Then I told him to lie facedown, hands clasped behind him. And even then I wasn't taking any chances. I leaned over his body from behind and to one side, laid the muzzle of my service revolver against the back of his skull; held it there while I squatted again, lowered the light, unhooked the handcuffs from my belt, and snapped them around his wrists. He didn't move the entire time.

A quick frisk—no other weapon—and then I began to relax a little. I went to Audrey and shone the light on her. Bruise marks on her throat, but otherwise she seemed unharmed. She said as I started to strip the tape off her wrists, "How did you find us? How did you know to come here?"

"I didn't know. I'll explain later. You tell me about Mateo Munoz. And Faith, how he got all the way over here."

She told me. I had her repeat some of it so I could get all the facts straight in my mind. Mateo Munoz, for Christ's sake. Smart-ass trouble-maker with a record of minor offenses graduated to the big time now—kidnapping, assault, attempted forcible oral copulation. Made the mistake of bringing her here, where Faith happened to be hiding, and Faith had stepped in on her behalf. All right. Give him that much credit. And Faith had been brought here in Audrey's boat; his arrival was what Harry Richmond had witnessed yesterday morning. But it hadn't been Audrey driving the boat and she didn't know who'd helped him. The only thing Faith had told her was that a person he claimed was a doctor was supposed to come back today, before noon, to take him away, and hadn't shown.

I finished freeing Audrey's hands while she talked, began on her ankles. Every few seconds I shifted my gaze to Faith, but he still lay as I'd left him. Lucky to be alive in more ways than one; he was like a cat with extra lives. Lucky for both of us. In those first few seconds after I got the drop on him and prodded him into the lobby, when I'd seen Audrey bound the way she was, I'd come close to blowing him away. Very close. If she hadn't cried out as she had, I think I would have. It put a quivering in my belly remembering how close I'd come.

I unwound the last strips of tape, lifted Audrey to her feet, and helped her walk until she could do it without support. Then I left her and flashed my light around. On a second couch was a scattering of items that included medical supplies. Might be something there to iden-tify the accessory, I thought. But a quick inspection told me nothing, and there was no time and this wasn't the place for a thorough exami-nation. Sheriff's department could handle that; they had lab facilities and the township didn't. Nucooee Point was their jurisdiction, anyway.

Faith hadn't moved more than a few inches if he'd moved at all. I drew my revolver again, went over and told him to stand up. He didn't give me any trouble. The way he raised himself to his feet, the stain of fresh blood on his shirtfront, the bandages I'd felt when I frisked him confirmed that he was wounded and hurting. Medical attention for him first thing; from now on everything would be strictly by the book. I read him his rights and he responded with a grunt, nothing more. Grunts were all I got when I tried to question him, too. His face was tight-pulled and showed nothing of what was going on behind it. I had the feeling he'd put shackles on himself, his emotions, that were as binding as the handcuffs pinching his wrists.

Now we were ready to move out. I told Audrey to lead the way, let her reach the dining-room entrance before I motioned Faith to follow. And I followed him at a distance of several feet, with my weapon and flashlight on him the whole way. The outside door stood open, the way I'd left it, letting in wet, gray daylight. The open door was the second thing that had alerted me to the fact that the lodge was occupied; the first was the fresh tire marks in the muddy ground out front.

In the past few minutes the rain had slackened to a mistlike drizzle. The three of us slogged through wet grass and mud around front, out past the chain barrier to where I'd left the cruiser at the edge of the driveway. I unlocked the rear door, stood off a few paces while Faith folded himself inside, then threw the door shut and went around and flipped the dash toggle that locks the rear doors automatically.

Audrey was standing behind the cruiser. She beckoned to me, and when I joined her, curbing my impatience, she said, "I want to say something before we leave."

"Go ahead."

"All the hours I spent with him, we talked quite a bit. He swears he didn't kill Storm."

"Sure he does. Did you expect him to admit it?"

"I believe him, Dick."

"Why? Because he saved your life?"

"That's part of it."

"He also kept you there against your will."

"He thought it was his only chance. Self-preservation is so strong in him, it clouds his judgment in a crisis. That's why he hit you and ran Thursday night."

"He ran because he's innocent, not because he's guilty."

"Yes."

"I don't buy it," I said.

"Dick, it could've been Mateo Munoz who killed her. You can't deny the possibility."

"I don't deny it. If it was Munoz, we'll find it out once he's in custody. But first he's got to be found, and we're wasting time standing around here talking about it."

"I'm sorry," she said, "I just wanted you to know how I feel."

"Okay. Now I know."

Inside the cruiser I radioed in to Lou Files, who works the desk on Sundays. I gave him a fast rundown and then a series of instructions. Two officers to be dispatched immediately to meet us at Pomo General. Notify Leo Thayer and request deputies to stake out the lodge in case the accessory decided to show up after all, and to gather evidence for lab analysis. Notify Burt Seeley; he could take care of alerting the D.A. Pull the jacket on Mateo Munoz and notify the FBI office in Santa Rosa that he was wanted on a kidnapping charge, then put out a pick-up-and-hold order on him through the Justice Information System's computer hookup. Lou didn't waste time with questions; he said he'd handle it and signed off.

I cradled the handset. For a few seconds I sat motionless, feeling suddenly limp. Tension release. It happens like that sometimes, all at once.

Audrey touched my arm. "Are you all right, Dick?"

"Just getting a second wind."

I reached out to the ignition. She sat back, then turned her head to look at Faith through the steel mesh that bisects the interior. I found myself doing the same in the rearview mirror. He sat in the middle of the seat, ramrod straight; his face was still tight-pulled, expressionless. Pile of stone, I thought. All except for his eyes. They were the only things about him that seemed alive. And I didn't much like what I saw in them.

Not hate, not anger, not fear—nothing as simple as any of those emotions. They were the eyes of a hunted and trapped animal, the kind of animal that would do anything, even chew off its own leg, to be free again.

Jay Dietrich

THERE WEREN'T ANY other reporters at the police station when Chief Novak radioed in his bombshell. Nothing had happened on the Carey homicide in over thirty-six hours, and with there being no connection between it and the Banner shooting, the newspapers and TV stations had shifted their people elsewhere. The only reason I was at the station was my promise to Mr. Kent to stay on top of the situation. I'd finished my personal account of the Carey murder last night, and this morning I'd made a few improvements and then faxed hard copies to the Santa Rosa *Press-Democrat* and both the *Chronicle* and *Examiner* in San Francisco. So I was just hanging around, waiting for something to happen and watching the 49ers beat the Saints on Jake Maddow's portable TV. I went to school with Jake and we're pretty good friends, otherwise he wouldn't have let me watch the game with him while he was on station duty. The Chief didn't like his officers lazing around even when things were Sunday slow, but he hadn't been in all day and Jake didn't have any work to do, so he figured there was no harm in sneaking his portable in. He's a big 49ers fan, Jake is.

Anyhow, when Lou Files came hurrying in to tell Jake the news I was right there with my ears flapping. Jake rushed out on orders to meet the Chief and his prisoner at Pomo General, and Mr. Files went to do whatever else he'd been told to. I tried to pry more details out of him, but he wasn't talking. He said I should keep the news under my hat for the time being, but since I don't wear a hat and he didn't wait for an answer, I didn't feel honor-bound to obey him. News is news, after all. And the public has a right to know when something big breaks. Any good reporter knows that.

Besides, this story was all mine. My first exclusive. If the capture of John Faith and all the other sensational stuff that went with it didn't earn me a job on a bigger paper than the *Advocate*, I might as well give up on a career in journalism and join Pop in his printing business.

I drove straight home and made quick calls to the *Chronicle* and *Examiner* and *PD* and didn't tell any of the editors I talked to what'd happened until I had a promise from each to run a bylined story by me, either the one I'd already faxed or the next one I wrote on John Faith's capture. That's what Mr. Kent would've done. He always said to be aggressive, don't take any junk from anybody. Only, he used a stronger word than junk. He may have a drinking problem and be a curmudgeon and have a cynical outlook on things, but he knows the newspaper business backward and forward. He worked on a lot of sheets in his day, including some major ones like the Houston *Chronicle* and the Pasadena *Star*.

I owed him a lot, even if he did treat me like a dumb kid sometimes, so before I headed out again for the hospital, I took the time to ring him up and tell him the news. He didn't sound too happy about it, but that's

Mr. Kent for you. He never sounds happy about anything. He did say before we hung up that I could write all the news accounts and sidebars on the Carey homicide and Faith capture for the *Advocate,* so that'll be one more feather in my reporter's cap. I don't care what his problems are or what anybody says about him, underneath it all he's a great guy.

Douglas Kent

SO STORM'S MURDERER was still alive and kicking. John Faith, whose name suited him about as well as a virginal white gown would have suited his victim. The strange beast. The stranger in our midst. Bigfoot. The Incredible Hulk. Frankenstein unbound. The destroyer of beauty, the extinguisher of flames, the slayer of dreams. Alive, alive-o.

I built myself another vodka-with-a-hint-of-orange-juice and returned to the sofa in the parlor, on which I'd been sprawled before the call from Jaydee. Roscoe was on the coffee table, comfortably arranged on a copy of the current *Advocate* (whose cheap ink was doubtless staining his smooth walnut butt, no sexual connotation intended). As I stretched out again and lit an unfiltered wheezer, he studied me critically with his lone eye.

"You're glummer than before, pal," he said. "Bad news?"

"The worst. The son of a bitch is still alive."

"Which son of a bitch is that?"

"John Faith, naturally."

"How is that possible?"

"All Jaydee knows is that Chief Novak found him over at the Nucooee Point Lodge and arrested him."

"Look on the bright side," Roscoe said. "He'll probably get the death penalty."

"*Au contraire.* Prosecutors need to prove special circumstances to plunk a murderer in the hot squat nowadays."

" 'Hot squat' is slang for the electric chair," he pointed out reasonably. "California's preferred method of offing the offers is the gas chamber."

I didn't feel like being reasonable. "I don't feel like being reasonable," I said, blowing carcinogens in his eye, "so don't give me any bullshit semantic lectures."

"Bullshit *dialectical* lectures."

I sighed. "You're a gun, for Christ's sake. Guns aren't supposed to be the voice of reason."

"Well, excuse me. Where were we?"

"Special circumstances. Too hard to prove in a case like this. Crime of passion. Twenty years to life, that's all the cretinous bastard will get in a court of law."

"Sad but true. Ergo?"

"What the hell do you mean, ergo?"

"Sometimes a great notion, pal."

"Meaning what?"

"Meaning I have a great notion."

"Is that so? What sort of great notion?"

"A name just popped into my head. Or it would have if I had a head. A name out of the past. A flash of history, a name to reckon with."

"And this name is?"

"Lean over and I'll whisper it to you."

"Why can't you just say it out loud?"

"It's more dramatic if I whisper."

I leaned over. He whispered—dramatically.

Kent sat back in awe. "Brilliant. Absolutely brilliant."

"So you see what I'm aiming at."

"Oyez. You're right on target, pal."

"I knew you'd approve."

"Approve, yes. But there's many a slip between the notion and the execution. To coin a phrase."

"You're interested in theory only, then?"

"I didn't say that. I'm considering."

"Consider this: All your problems would be solved."

"Not necessarily."

"One, at least. Besides, it's your last chance for a taste of fame."

"The old blaze of glory, eh?"

"Well, more like a brief and tawdry spark."

"My, my. Such eloquence from a death stick."

"Guns don't kill people, people kill people."

"Fook you, pal."

"Fook *you*, pal."

I drank. He pouted.

Pretty soon he said persuasively, "It's the American way, after all."

"It is?"

"One hundred percent all-American. Think about it."

I thought about it. He was right, so right I imagined I could hear patriotic music playing: "The Star-Spangled Banner," "The Battle Hymn of the Republic." A tear formed in my eye.

"Are you with me, pal?"

"I'm with you, pal."

The nationalistic music was still playing in the cracked and dusty corners of the Kent brain. I felt a near desire to stand up and salute the flag, which would've been difficult since I didn't own a flag. I settled for hustling out to the kitchen and pouring Roscoe and me another drink to seal the bargain.

Brian Marx

THE PHONE RANG while I was in the kitchen making a ham sandwich. Wall unit was practically next to my ear and the sudden jangling set my nerves on edge. Damn all-night poker sessions were starting to wear on me. I'd quit at five A.M., earlier than usual, because I was having trouble concentrating. Just as well. I'd been into a bad run of cards and if I'd stuck around sure as hell I'd've ended up quitting losers. As it was, I'd won forty-eight bucks at stud and Texas Hold 'Em.

I answered the phone since I was standing right there, and for a change the call was for me. My mood had been pretty good; winning at poker always gives me a lift. But when I hung up five minutes later, I was shaking my head and feeling a sag. Man, oh man, nothing much happens in Pomo for years on end and then all of a sudden everything pops at once, like somebody'd opened up Pandora's box. I know about Pandora's box on account of that's the name Ed Simms gave his bar downtown and he'll explain the whole myth or legend or whatever it is to anybody who'll listen.

Trisha came into the kitchen as I was opening a beer to go with my sandwich. She said, "Who was that on the phone, Daddy?"

"Hank Maddow. He just talked to his son down at the police station."

"Did something happen?"

"Whole lot of somethings. A Pandora's boxful."

For starters I told her about Lori Banner blowing away that jerkoff husband of hers, no loss there. Her eyes got big as saucers.

She said, "Did the cops arrest her? Put her in jail?"

"No, they got her doped up in the hospital."

"Oh, God."

"That teacher of yours, Ms. Sixkiller, almost bought it last night, too. Kidnapped and nearly raped."

"What!"

I told her who'd done it and I didn't beat around the bush. A dose of hard-ass reality's good for a kid her age who's running a little wild. Sometimes it's the only way you can get through to them. "I told you those Munozes were a couple of punk losers. You need another reason to steer clear of Anthony, there it is."

"He's not like Mateo."

"How do you know he isn't? Maybe he just ain't shown his true colors yet."

"Ms. Sixkiller . . . is she all right?"

"Wasn't hurt bad. Lucky he took her where he did."

"Where'd he take her?"

"The old lodge on Nucooee Point. And who do you think was hiding out there, alive after all? John Faith. You'd think he'd be the last guy to play hero, but he stepped in and belted that Mateo punk and chased him off. Cost him, too. Faith."

Trisha's face was white now, white as milk. "Cost him?"

"Chief Novak showed at the lodge this morning, nobody knows why yet, and arrested Faith. Took him to—"

I broke off because she wasn't there anymore; she'd turned tail and run out. Ran upstairs. I followed her up there, and she'd locked herself in the bathroom. I could hear her throwing up and sobbing in there.

Kids. How she could get so worked up over a sleazeball like Mateo Munoz showing his true colors is beyond me.

Audrey Sixkiller

I WAS AT Pomo General about an hour, most of it spent waiting for Dick to drive me home. As soon as we arrived he and the two officers he'd asked for had taken John Faith upstairs to the security wing; I'd gone to the emergency room and submitted to an examination, even though it really wasn't necessary. My vital signs were normal and there was no cartilage or other damage to my throat.

Afterward, I sat in the waiting room and fidgeted. The young reporter from the *Advocate*, Jay Dietrich, found me there and wouldn't leave me alone until I'd reluctantly answered a few of his questions. Then Joan Garcia, who happened to be on duty in the security wing, came down briefly to see how I was doing. I asked her about John Faith's condition and she said it was stable; no apparent infection, but as a precaution an antibiotic called Cefotan was being administered by IV. She thought that if there were no complications, he would be released for transfer to the city jail later in the day.

Dick came down at last. The strain he'd been under was all too evident in the harsh fluorescent lighting—hunched shoulders, haggard and frayed appearance, pain etched again in his eyes. Now that John Faith was in custody, he had to stop driving himself so hard. If he didn't stop by himself, someone—Verne Erickson, Mayor Seeley, me—would have to take steps to force him for his own good.

Outside, as we crossed the parking lot, I asked him if John Faith had called a lawyer. He said, "No. Didn't ask for one. He's still not talking, not even to the doctors." The only other thing Dick would say about him was that, to prevent another escape attempt, he was handcuffed to his bed as well as under constant guard.

On the drive to my house Dick was mostly silent. When we arrived I expected a terse good-bye in the car, but he surprised me by walking me to the door. Then he really surprised me by gathering me close, whispering in my ear, "I'm glad you're safe, Audrey," and then kissing my mouth, hard.

It was freezing inside the house, but I was warm enough. Warmer than I'd been in a long time.

Richard Novak

SEELEY AND THAYER were waiting for me at the station. I ushered them into my office, and as soon as the door was shut the sheriff said heatedly, "What the hell's the idea, Novak?"

"The idea of what?"

"You know what. Nucooee Point Lodge is on county land. You had no right to make an arrest there without consulting me first."

"I didn't know Faith was hiding out at the lodge when I went there. I didn't even know Audrey would be there. All I had was a vague tip from Harry Richmond. Didn't Lou Files tell you all that?"

"He told me. But that doesn't change the fact that it was a breach of jurisdiction. You should've notified me before you went in, then waited for backup. You could've blown it, let Faith get away again."

"But I didn't."

"But you could have."

"Have it your way. Your people find anything incriminating among the stuff at the lodge?"

"No, and Faith's helper didn't show, either. If you'd waited and followed protocol—"

"The same thing would've happened. Why don't you admit the real point of this harangue, Leo?"

"Real point?"

"You're pissed because my hunch was right that Faith was still alive. And because you didn't get to arrest him yourself. No glory for Pomo County's esteemed sheriff."

"Bullshit! You listen here—"

Seeley said, "That's enough, both of you. Cool down. The arrest part of it's over and done with and there's no sense arguing about it. Faith's in custody, that's the important thing."

"Not to Leo, it isn't," I said.

Thayer took a step toward me. The mayor used his porcine bulk to block him off. "I said, cool down! No more infighting, and that goes double out in public. Media gets a whisper of dissension, they'll blow it all out of proportion. We've had enough negative PR as it is."

Negative PR. That was Seeley for you. Typical small-time political boss: He didn't give a damn about anything except the status quo and his and Pomo's image.

He said to me, "Dick, about this Mateo Munoz kid. I wish you'd talked to me before involving the FBI."

"Why? Notification is standard procedure in a kidnapping case where there's a possibility of interstate or international flight."

"Yes, but I don't like the idea of FBI agents poking around here. More fodder for the media."

That wasn't the only reason. He was afraid they might stumble on something by accident that he didn't want them to see—a little local dirty laundry, maybe. I had an urge to say that to him, put a crack or two in that smooth facade. I curbed it and said instead, "They'll only send one agent, if they send any. Low-priority case for them. If an agent does show, I'll see to it he stays out of our hair and in the background."

"You do that. One more thing about Munoz. Is there any chance he killed Storm Carey, not Faith? I mean, there are similarities between the Carey homicide and the Sixkiller kidnapping."

"A chance, sure. That's all it is."

"You're convinced Faith is guilty?"

"Until I see something definite to unconvince me."

"Good. Then maybe we can get most of this bad business finished with tonight. When are you transferring Faith from the hospital?"

"I'll have to talk to the doctor in charge before I know for sure. But the last estimate was a five o'clock release time."

"Perfect, if it holds," Seeley said. "When you bring him over, I want Leo in the car with you."

"Why?"

"A show of solidarity."

"For the media's benefit."

"For the benefit of every citizen of Pomo County."

"Whatever you say, Mayor. I don't want a lot of attention anyway for doing my job. Let Leo have the spotlight."

Thayer wasn't mollified. He'd been sulking behind one of his fifty-cent panatelas; he took it out of his mouth and aimed it in my direction. "Damnit," he said, "it isn't glory I care about. It's doing things by the book. Protocol, jurisdiction—"

"You've made your point," Seeley told him. "Dick won't step on your toes again. Will you, Dick?"

I shrugged. "No. It won't happen again."

"Now the two of you shake hands."

We shook hands like the good little flunkies we were.

Seeley said, "So it'll be the two of you who bring Faith over. That's settled. I'll make sure the media stays here with their cameras and microphones, everyone in one place. Once the prisoner's been booked and locked up, you'll both come out and join Joe Proctor and me and we'll answer questions. As many as we can for as long as it takes. Agreed?"

"If that's the way you want it," Thayer said.

"That's the way it's best. For everyone."

Except me, I thought. But I didn't say that, either.

They went away pretty soon and left me alone with my throbbing face and nose. One of the codeine capsules would probably make me fuzzy-headed, so I ate half a dozen aspirin instead. After a while I went out front for coffee and to ask Lou to order me a sandwich from Nelson's Diner; I hadn't eaten all day and the aspirin were like acid in my empty belly. Through the glass entrance doors I could see a white van angled to the curb in front, a man and a woman from it heading into the station, and two more men unloading camera equipment from the rear.

The vultures were already starting to circle.

George Petrie

IT WAS ALMOST six when I finally rolled into dark, rainy Pomo. I'd left Fallon late. Very little sleep last night, yet prying myself out of the motel bed had taken a tremendous effort of will. Delaying the inevitable. I'd driven at a constant fifty all the way; the last things I could afford now were an accident or the attention of the highway patrol. I'd avoided both. The interminable four-hundred-mile trip across Nevada, through the Sierras, across half a dozen California counties had been uneventful.

And now, here I was. Home. George Petrie, failed embezzler, slinking home in the dark. I was depressed and dog-tired, but some of yesterday's utter despair had left me. Maybe, after all, things aren't quite as hopeless as they seemed, sitting out there in the middle of nowhere. Maybe I can still salvage something out of the rest of my life, even if circumstances force me to spend my last twenty or thirty years in this backwater town. There have to be ways and means. I might not have the guts to pull off a really bold scheme, but I'm intelligent, shrewd enough; I ought to be able to come up with some way of lightening my load, some way to keep from dying by inches.

But first I've got to replace the $209,840 in the bank vault tomorrow morning. That's paramount. Then I have to cover the $7,000 shortage, even if it means going begging to Charley Horne. *Then* I can relax, retrench, make new plans. Maybe even convince Storm to give me another tumble in her bed. No more begging with her, though. No, by God. I'm not the same George Petrie who sat with her in the bank on Thursday, the one she accused of currying a pity fuck. You don't go through what I just had without learning a few things, changing, becoming more of a man. She'll see it in me once I'm back on my feet. I'll damn well make her see it.

Another thing I have to do, before very long, is dump Ramona. If I have to live with her, sleep with her, listen to her goddamn screeching and squawking for the duration, I might as well throw in the towel; I'd never get out of the trap. California's a no-fault state, so I don't need grounds to file for divorce. Just go ahead and do it. She'd demand support, but in turn I'd demand half of what her Indian Head Bay land brought when it finally sold. Even if I came out on the short end financially, I'd manage to recoup somehow; and in every other way I'd come out on the long end. I'd be able to breathe again.

She was home; the lights were on in the house. As soon as I pulled the Buick into the driveway and saw her waiting in the kitchen doorway, I felt another letdown. Her coming out to meet me, making a pass at kissing my cheek as if she were glad I was back, made it even worse. I pushed her away. "Don't, Ramona. I'm exhausted and I need a drink."

"The real-estate deal—?"

"Another dud. I don't want to talk about it."

"I'm sorry but my God what's happened around here while you were gone I can hardly believe it." All in one breath. "You must have heard about it in Santa Rosa?"

"I didn't hear anything."

"Oh, well, then you're in for—"

"Not now," I said, "for Christ's sake, not now."

I brushed past her, went through the kitchen and into the living room to the wet bar. Wonder of wonders, the screeching parrot didn't fly in after me. The first scotch went down quick and hot, like swallowing fire. I coughed and poured another and sank into my chair to drink it more slowly. The glass was half empty when I heard Ramona moving around in the kitchen, then bumping through the door into the living room.

"George."

The way she said my name made me look up. And all the skin on my back, my neck, my scalp seemed to curl upward. The glass fell out of my hand, splashing scotch over my lap; I barely noticed as I lurched to my feet.

"I opened the trunk of your car," she said in a voice I'd never heard her use before. "I thought I'd be nice and bring in your bag."

She was standing there with one of the new suitcases in her left hand. In her right were two of the banded packets of $100 bills.

Richard Novak

WHEN MY PAGER went off I was waiting with Thayer and Verne Erickson at the hospital, the sheriff standing off by himself and being pissed at me again because I'd asked Verne to ride with us on the transfer. Thayer and I were like gasoline and fire; Verne's presence would keep us from setting each other off. What we'd been waiting for the past fifteen minutes was for Faith to finish his phone call. He was inside the resident physician's office, visible to us through a glass partition, facing away and holding the receiver tight to his ear.

I left Verne to keep watch on him and called the station from the head nurse's desk. Della Feldman had relieved Lou Files. She said, "What's keeping you, Chief?"

"Faith. He demanded his one call as soon as Verne and I walked in. Changed his mind all of a sudden, Christ knows why. He's still not talking to us."

"Lawyer?"

"What else. One of the doctors gave him the name of a criminal attorney in Santa Rosa. He didn't want anybody from Pomo County."

"Can you hurry him up?"

"Why?"

"Big crowd outside already and getting bigger by the minute."

"How big?"

"Must be a couple of dozen reporters, photographers, camera people. You'd think you were bringing in the Unabomber's brother. Lot of citizens out there, too. Lining the street and congregating over in the park."

"Any trouble?"

"Not so far. But a lot of them are young and restless. I keep remembering how the crowds Friday night almost got out of hand."

"How many people so far? Rough estimate."

"Counting the media, over a hundred."

"You send anybody out to keep order?"

"Sherm and Jake. Nobody else here right now but me."

"Who's out on patrol?"

"Mary Jo and Jack."

"Call them in. If you need anybody else, go down the off-duty roster."

"Right."

"I'll have Thayer put some of his deputies on standby alert. And Della, make sure our people keep everything low-key, same as Friday night. The last thing we need is somebody provoking trouble."

Trisha Marx

I SNUCK OUT and walked down to Municipal Park because I had to see John one more time, even if it'd be from a distance and he'd be in handcuffs on his way to jail. I knew I'd cry when I saw him, and it was what I wanted—to feel even worse than I already did. Sometimes you just have to wallow in your own misery, you know?

I thought maybe Anthony'd be there, too. More reason to feel crappy, seeing him, even if I did feel kind of sorry for him. He must've been blown away to find out what a scumbag Mateo really was. Give him a little sympathy, show him I was a better person than he was. Show him I was more miserable than he was. I guess it's true what they say: Misery loves company.

But Anthony wasn't there. Home with his people, or else out somewhere getting high. That's always been his answer to anything wrong or lame—get high, feel good so you didn't have to think about feeling bad.

Some of the other kids were over by the bandstand, but I didn't see Selena so I didn't go over and hang with them. She was about the only one I could've stood to hang with tonight. I took a spot by myself under one of the trees near the street, where I could see the front of the police station. All the lights over there were blurry from the mist that was rising off the lake, blowing in in curls and long, ragged streamers. It made the people look sort of blurry, too, like will-o'-the-wisps. Newspaper and TV reporters waiting for John, not because they cared about him but because they thought he was a murderer and murderers are hot news. It was sick and freaky, in a way. If they knew he was innocent and a good person besides, they wouldn't want anything to do with him, he could drop dead in the street and they wouldn't even look at him twice. The guilty ones like Mateo, they'd fall all over themselves to get close and stick a microphone in his face and call him Mr. Munoz and feel sorry for him if he said he was a kidnapper and a rapist on account of he'd had a shitty childhood—

"Hello, Trisha."

Ms. Sixkiller. She'd come right up beside me and I hadn't even noticed her. Right away I was nervous and wary. But she didn't start in about John or her boat or anything; she just stood there hunched inside her coat, her arms folded and her breath making puffs in the cold night air.

I could've moved away and maybe she wouldn't've followed, but I didn't. Pretty soon I said, "I, um, heard about what happened last night. I'm real sorry it was you Mateo picked on."

"So am I. But it's over now."

"He's a pig. Anthony's not like him at all." Now, what did I want to defend Anthony for?

"I know he's not."

"We broke up. Anthony and me."

"Because of Mateo?"

"No, it was before that."

"Do you want to talk about it?"

"Um, no."

"All right. But we do need to talk about John Faith."

". . . Why would I want to talk about him?"

"He's why you're here, isn't he?"

"He's why everybody's here. You too, right?"

"Right. You know he saved me from being raped?"

I nodded. "So maybe you don't think he's the lowlife everybody else does."

"That's right, I don't."

"He didn't kill Mrs. Carey. I mean—"

"I know what you mean."

"Maybe Mateo did it. Did anybody think of that?"

"Yes. If he did, it'll come out when he's caught."

"If he's ever caught."

"He will be. Trisha, about John Faith."

"What about him?"

"I know you helped him. All you did and how you did it."

Oh, God. I didn't say anything.

"He tried to convince me otherwise, to protect you. He asked me not to give you away to the police."

Right. That was the way John was. "So?"

"So I'm not going to. I don't believe in making trouble for people I like. And I think I understand your reasons."

"Then you have to believe he's innocent, too."

"I do. I also believe it'll be proven eventually."

"Not soon enough to keep him out of jail."

"Life and justice aren't always fair, Trisha."

"Tell me about it. I figured that out a long time ago."

We stood there for a while. Then I said, "I owe you an apology, Ms. Sixkiller," and saying it was easier than I'd thought it would be. "About your bathroom window and your boat and everything. I feel . . . you know, wrong about messing with stuff the way I did."

"Can I count on you to use better judgment in the future?"

"Yeah. I won't do anything like that again."

"Then your apology is accepted."

"I'll pay for the window and fixing the damage—"

"I don't want your money," she said. "Tell you what I would like from you, though."

"What's that?"

"Three or four hours of your time next summer. You obviously know how to drive a powerboat, but you can use some lessons in how to dock one. Lessons in general boat safety, too."

I didn't laugh or smile and neither did she. We stood quiet again, and when the wind gusted and I shivered she put her arm around my shoulders and kind of hugged me. I didn't pull away. I guess maybe we both needed somebody to lean on, right then.

Zenna Wilson

WHEN HELEN CARTER and I arrived at Park Street, quite a crowd had already gathered. There must have been more than a hundred people standing and milling around. No wonder we hadn't been able to find a parking space any closer than three blocks away. I saw four television vans, and there were reflector lamps and handheld spotlights that turned the mist swirling in off the lake white and shiny, like crystallized smoke, and half a dozen men and women carrying portable microphones and those bulky cameras with lights jutting from their tops—Minicams, I think they're called. I recognized a roving reporter from Channel 5 in San Francisco, too. Everybody was talking in keyed-up voices, but other than that, the crowd was really very well behaved. I'd been concerned about that, the presence of rowdies looking to start trouble, and there *was* a noisy group of teenagers by the park bandstand, but uniformed policemen and sheriff's deputies, bless them, seemed to have everything under control.

Still, it was exciting. That was the word for it. You could actually feel the excitement in the air, like electricity. If it hadn't been the end of a terrible tragedy, I think I might even have been thrilled.

"I wouldn't have missed this for the world," I told Helen as we made our way to the parking lot on the near side of the station. She agreed. And if Howard doesn't like it, I thought but didn't say, well, that's just too bad. I'd asked him to come along, but he wouldn't even consider it. He'd been in such a strange and irksome mood lately—critical, even cruel at times. When I first heard that that evil man Faith was still alive and had been arrested, I took the news straight to Howard and he said nastily, "You must be really disappointed he's not burning in hell." I *was*, yes, as any good Christian would be to find out that one of Satan's own is still among us, but I didn't appreciate having it flung at me in a tone that made it sound like an accusation. Well, he could sit home and sulk or whatever. Helen was much more pleasant company. Much more agreeable, too. She's a member of my church and her worldview is a lot closer to mine than Howard's.

There was hardly room for one person, much less two, up close to where most of the media people were congregated. But we were determined and we made room. One of the men I accidentally jostled turned and gave me a piercing look. I was about to answer him in kind when I recognized him. Douglas Kent.

I altered my expression to a smile and said to him, "You remember me, don't you, Mr. Kent? Zenna Wilson."

He leaned closer, squinting. I drew back. His breath . . . well, he simply reeked of liquor. He wasn't very steady on his feet, either. Really quite intoxicated, to the point where he hadn't bothered to shave today, or, for that matter, to bathe. I find public drunkenness disgusting; uncleanliness, too. There is no excuse for either one. Even so, I decided that Christian charity was called for in Mr. Kent's case. Everyone knew the poor man had a drinking problem. And after all, he had written that inspiring editorial based on what I'd told him about the stranger in our midst.

"Ah, Mrs. Wilson," he said. "Of course I remember you."

"We've spoken several times, but only met in person two or—"

"In tongues, eh?"

"Excuse me?"

"Spoken in viper tongues."

"I'm sorry, I don't—"

"Not to worry, dear lady. What's your opinion of all this?"

"Well, it's very exciting, isn't it?"

"Exciting. Oh, yes. But it will be a good deal more exciting once the gladiators arrive."

"Do you really think so?"

"I know so. Absolutely positive of it. The Romans had the right idea, by cracky."

"Romans?"

"Death struggles on the floor of the coliseum. All thumbs down. Blood spilled while the hungry legions roar."

I glanced at Helen. She had no more idea of what he was talking about than I did.

Richard Novak

THE RIDE FROM Pomo General to the police station takes a little less than fifteen minutes. I talked Thayer into riding up front with Verne, and I sat in back with the prisoner. I kept watching Faith, but for his part, I wasn't even there. He sat with that ramrod posture, his big, shackled hands between his thighs, and stared straight ahead in stony silence. None of us had anything to say. The quiet in the cruiser had an odd, stagnant quality, like a pocket of dead air just before heat lightning.

When we neared the center of town the media lights were visible from a distance, a wash of brightness against the restless banks of tule fog. I could tell from the cars packing Main and the side streets that the waiting crowd had grown even larger. I tensed as Verne turned down Water Street, toward the municipal pier. The crowd seemed orderly enough, but that didn't mean it would stay that way.

"Look at that, will you," Verne said as we reached Park. "Must be a hundred and fifty people, maybe more."

Thayer muttered, "Damn three-ring circus," but he didn't sound worried or unhappy. If anything, he was eager. Anticipating the grinding cameras and exploding flashbulbs, probably.

Faith sat forward, his hands balling into fists. I sensed rather than saw the trapped-animal desperation in him again.

Verne made the swing onto Park. Heads and bodies had swiveled in our direction; arms lifted, fingers pointed. I could see mouths moving as though in an exaggerated pantomime.

"Pull up even with the entrance," I said to Verne. "You and I get out first and come around front and back. Leo, you stay inside until we're on your side."

"You don't have to tell me procedure, Novak."

"I'm not telling you anything. I'm reminding you."

"You're the one who needs reminders, not me."

"Don't start up again."

"It's not a dead issue," he said, "just remember that. I don't care what Seeley says."

We rolled past the gawking faces, into the outspill from all the lights. The glare seemed unnaturally bright. Half a dozen Minicams were on us like huge, hungry eyes. Thayer had his head turned toward the window glass, toward the cameras; I couldn't see his face, but I knew he was wearing his official expression, the one with flared nostrils and upward-jutting jaw.

The cruiser stopped. The door beside me clicked as Verne flipped the toggle to unlock.

We were almost there.

Douglas Kent

STANDING CLOSE TO the front of the gathered rabble, I patted Roscoe on his little hammer head.

"How you doing in there, pal?"

"Same as you're doing out there, pal."

"All set to lose the Faith?"

"Knock off the puns. We have serious business here."

"Very serious business here. Avenging Storm."

"Not a bad title for a book."

"I won't be around to write it."

"You never know. First-person account of a sodden newspaper hack who goes cunningly bonkers after the murder of his beloved town punchbag, anthropomorphizes his old man's—"

"Big word for a little gun."

"—I say, anthropomorphizes his old man's .38 to the point of holding interior philosophical discussions with it, and the two of them exact their vengeance in front of a couple of hundred eyewitnesses and an eager TV audience of many thousands. Socko stuff."

"Not really," Kent said. "All we're doing is following in giant footsteps—imitators, not innovators. Nobody'd publish it."

Voices rose around us in an excited roar. I looked and said, "Ah, the cop chariot enters the arena at last."

"Americans and Romans," Roscoe said pityingly, "you can't have your metaphors both ways. How many fuzz with Faith?"

"Three. And only one of you."

"I'll still get off first."

"You'd better. Look, they're climbing out."

"I can't look, I don't have eyes."

"Shut your muzzle."

"Then I can't get off at all."

"Here they come. Ready, pal?"

"Ready, pal."

"Heigh-ho, here we go."

Roscoe and me, and Jack Ruby makes three.

Jay Dietrich

I WAS INTENT on John Faith lifting his huge body from inside the police cruiser, Chief Novak on one side and Sergeant Erickson on the other and Sheriff Thayer standing off a couple of paces with his attention shifting between the prisoner and the TV cameras, when somebody bumped into me from behind, It was a hard, lurching bump, hard enough to nearly knock me down. I glared at the man who'd done it, who was now pushing past me.

Mr. Kent.

I hadn't even known he was here. Drunk as usual, that was obvious. How he could function with so much—

Hey, what was he doing? Staggering out onto the brightly lit sidewalk, making a beeline toward Faith and the officers. Pulling a shiny object out of his pocket—

Oh my God'

"He's got a gun!" I yelled it at the top of my voice. "Look out, he's got a gun!"

Richard Novak

IT ALL SEEMED TO happen at once, everything jumbled and compressed into one long, bulging moment.

I heard the warning yell, saw the man coming toward us, recognized him, saw the handgun he was bringing to bear, heard someone else shout and a woman scream and feet and bodies beginning to scramble out of harm's way—and on automatic reflex I threw a shoulder into Faith to take him from the line of fire, then lunged to meet Kent. I deflected his arm downward just as he squeezed off. The pistol made a flat crack that was lost in the bedlam around us, the bullet going harmlessly into the sidewalk, chipping pavement but not ricocheting. I battered Kent's wrist with my right hand, clawing for the weapon with my left. It came loose from his grasp, but I couldn't hold it; it fell with a clatter and by accident I kicked it with my shoe. Then I had both hands on his coat and I jerked him off his feet, flung him down hard. But I lost my balance as I did that, slipped, fell on top of him. A grunt, the whoosh of his breath, and he went limp under me.

All around us, then, there was a sudden rising hiss and babble—sharp intakes of air, little frightened cries, more shouts, another scream. I pushed up off Kent, swung around on one knee. And stayed there like that, motionless, going cold inside.

Faith had the gun.

And he was pointing it straight at me.

Verne Erickson

THERE WAS NOTHING I could do, any of us could do. Faith was on that pistol as soon as the Chief kicked it, quick as a cat on a piece of raw liver. I had my service revolver half drawn; so did Thayer, a few steps away on my left. But we both froze when we saw Faith come up with Kent's weapon and throw down on Novak. There might've been time to get off a shot at him before he could fire at the Chief, but training stopped me and the sheriff and any other officer close enough to think about trying it. People were milling around, pushing and shoving, but the immediate area was still crowded with those damn-fool TV cameramen and their whirring Minicams, photographers and their popping flashbulbs. You didn't dare risk a wild shot in confusion like this. It was six kinds of wonder that the round Kent had triggered hadn't ricocheted and taken some bystander's head off.

Faith kept us all in place with bellowed words like a series of thunderclaps. "Nobody move! Come at me, I'll shoot! Try to get behind me, I'll shoot!"

He was moving himself as he spoke, in a scrabbling crouch to get clear of the individuals clogging the station doors. When he had his back to bare wall he stopped and lowered himself to one knee. His eyes and the Chief's had been locked the entire time. There was maybe eight feet of wet pavement separating them.

Novak said loudly, "Do what he says. No sudden moves." If he was afraid, being under the gun like that, he didn't show it.

More flashbulbs exploded, the Minicams ground away. I could almost hear the reporters gleefully smacking their lips. I felt exposed and foolish and mad as hell—at myself and Thayer and Novak and Faith and most of all at that crazy drunken son of a bitch Kent lying there unconscious behind the Chief. What had possessed him? What in God's name did he think he was doing?

Faith said, "I didn't want it like this," still booming his words. "Let a lawyer handle it, get some more facts before bringing it out in the open. But that bastard trying to shoot me . . . that's the last straw. Now I want everybody to hear the truth, my lips to your ears, let the whole damn world know what this town's done to an innocent man."

Thayer found his voice. "This isn't buying you any sympathy, Faith. Surrender the gun before—"

"Shut up. I'll surrender it when I've had my say."

"Say it, then. Get it over with."

"Innocent man!" Faith thundered. "Innocent! I'm not a murderer, not some kind of monster. I didn't kill the Carey woman."

"Liar!" somebody in the crowd shouted back.

And somebody else: "You killed her, all right, you dirty—"

"No, by God, I didn't. But I know who did. You hear me out there, all you people? *I know who did!*"

Audrey Sixkiller

I STOOD AMONG a crush of others in the middle of the street, trying to see Dick and John Faith, listening to the words that were being flung against the night. But it was as if I were standing there alone, on a mist-shrouded plain, seeing and hearing everything from a great distance. I thought: Don't hurt him, please don't hurt him. At the same time I did not believe John Faith would shoot, knew that his cry of "Innocent man!" was the truth. The confusion spawned an intense, irrational desire to run away from here, away from the poison, very fast and very far, like the god Coyote rushing home to his sanctuary atop the *dano-batin*, the mountain big, that rises high above the south shore.

And when John Faith spoke again I almost did run—I took two faltering steps before the press of bodies stopped me. Then I stood tree-still with his words echoing in my ears, mixing with the frantic voices of the others to create a roaring, near and yet far off, like the mad gabbling of spooks and witches.

"*He* did it!" Pointing, accusing. "*He* murdered Storm Carey. Your fine, upstanding police chief, Richard Novak."

Richard Novak

VERNE ERICKSON ANSWERED before I could. He said angrily, "You're out of your mind, Faith. Nobody believes that. Nobody!"

"I'll prove it to you, all of you."

"You can't prove a lie—"

"The truth. Listen. I didn't know it was Novak that night. If I had ... the hell with that. This afternoon at the hospital, that's the first time I was able to do any clear thinking. That's when I put it together."

He wasn't talking to Verne, he was talking to me; his eyes never left mine. Hot with fury, those eyes, like red-rimmed crucibles filled with molten silver. But I wasn't afraid of him or his words or the gun in his hand. The one emotion I no longer felt was fear.

He said, "I passed a car that night, on the way to her house. Just turned out of her driveway. Dark, and I wasn't paying attention or I'd have noticed it was a police cruiser, Novak's cruiser. But he recognized my car, all right. And he saw me turn in. He waited long enough for me to find her body and then he came barreling back up there."

"You call that proof?" Thayer said. "Only your word you passed another car. Even if that much is true ... you can't swear it was Novak's cruiser."

"Then how'd he happen to show up just at the right time? Why'd he go there at all?"

I said, "To see her, talk to her. We were friends."

"Weren't there before me, Chief?"

"No."

"Had no idea she was dead before the two of us went inside?"

"No."

"Then how'd you know she was killed with a glass paperweight?"

I stared at him without answering.

"It was half under her body and covered with blood," he said. "I couldn't tell what it was and I looked closer than you did. You stood off fifteen or twenty feet and called it a glass paperweight."

"I don't remember saying that."

"Accused me of seeing red, picking up a glass paperweight and hitting her with it."

I shook my head.

"Your word against mine? Except I'm not the only one you said it to. When you radioed in you used the same words to whoever you talked to—"

"Me," Verne said. "I was on the other end."

"You remember him saying it? Skull crushed with a glass paper-weight?"

"I remember."

"All right," I said, "then I did say it. She kept it on an end table next to the couch. I must've seen it wasn't there—"

"And assumed it was what killed her? Hell of an assumption, Chief, for a man as upset as you were. Besides, the paperweight wasn't the only slip you made over the radio. Two blows, you said. Two." He asked Verne, "Remember that?"

"Yeah."

"How'd you know it was two, Chief, not one or three or six or a dozen? Her skull was caved in, blood everywhere, you're not a doctor and you didn't go near the body. No way you could know she was hit twice unless you did it yourself."

Verne's eyes were on me; everyone's eyes were on me. The combined intensity of their stares was like surgical lasers—cutting, probing, hurting.

"Answer him, Novak." Thayer's voice this time, hard and cold. "How'd you know?"

I told myself to stand up, get off my knees and stand up like a man. When I did that, Faith stood, too, in the same slow movements, so that we continued to face each other at eye level.

Thayer: "Answer the question."

Verne: "Say something, for God's sake."

Kent was the last straw, all right. It has to stop, right here and now.

I looked away from Faith for the first time. Didn't look at Verne or Thayer as I turned around, or at anyone else. I stared out beyond the light into the dark, above all, the laser eyes and all the faceless, buzzing bodies. Easier that way. It wasn't much different from addressing a roomful of strangers.

"Faith is right," I said, "everything he said is right. I did it. I killed her."

Epilogue

Leo Thayer

FOUR OF US were present in the interrogation room when Novak taped his confession. Me, Ben Seeley, Joe Proctor, and Verne Erickson because the mayor and city council made him acting Chief. We didn't have to prod Novak any, or even ask him more than half a dozen questions to clarify minor details. He just rolled it all off the top of his head in a flat, used-up voice—the tone most felons have when they know their ride's over and done with.

I read the transcript three times. The main part made me feel like puking every time.

She called me Thursday night, late. It was the first I'd heard from her since we broke off the affair six months ago. She practically begged me to come to her house. She was a little drunk but not that drunk. She said she needed me, really needed me. I didn't want to go because I was afraid of what might happen. I don't mean violence, I mean getting involved again. The affair hadn't been good for either of us, me particularly. She was the kind of woman who got under your skin like a tick and just kept burrowing. I spent six months trying to dig her out and I thought I had but I hadn't. I tried to say no to her that night and I couldn't. I went to her just like she asked me to.

We made love three times in three hours. For me, anyway, it was making love. But not a good kind, even then. I knew it but I wouldn't let myself accept the truth. She led me to believe . . . no, that's not right. I led myself to believe she felt the same way, that there was a bond or connection between us and we could rebuild what we'd had before. Except we hadn't had anything before, just sex, that's all. I don't know how I could have deluded myself like that. Ripe for it, I guess. Lonely, mixed up inside my head—midlife crisis or maybe just plain crisis. I don't know. I needed to believe, so I believed.

Friday night I drove back to her house, uninvited this time. Nine-thirty, quarter of ten, I don't remember the exact time I got there. She let me in, but she wasn't the same as the night before. In a strange mood even for her. No pretense of softness or sexiness. Bitchy, cutting, like she was spoiling for a fight. More than a fight . . . as though there was something in her that was pushing me to do to her what I ended up doing. I'm not trying to blame her when I say that. I'm through blaming anybody but myself. I'm only telling you the way it was.

She started yelling, provoking me right away. Saying I had a lot of nerve showing up unannounced and she was through with me, she didn't want me coming around bothering her anymore. I told her I loved her. She laughed at me. She said I was pathetic, a sorry excuse for a man in and out of bed. She got right up in my face and screamed at me—lousy lover, sorry excuse, get the hell out and leave her alone because a real man was coming over, a man who knew how to satisfy a woman. On and on like that, spitting it in my face. Provoking me until I couldn't take it anymore, couldn't think straight and started seeing red. I slapped her face, and she hit me back with her fist, screaming all the time. Tried to knee me, claw me. I slapped her again and she picked up the paperweight and swung it at my head, just missed me. I took it away from her and . . . that's all I remember. I don't remember hitting her with it. Only some part of me must have realized I'd done it twice or I wouldn't have said so to Faith and then to Verne on the radio. Next thing I do remember is seeing her on the couch with her skull crushed and blood all over her head and face. And I was standing over her with the bloody paperweight in my hand.

I panicked. At a time like that . . . everything's crazy, mixed up. You can't think at all. The only thing that seems to matter is getting away, saving yourself. You've heard all that before, same as I have, and it's true. You can't face what you've done, the instinct for self-preservation takes over, you panic and run.

I threw the paperweight down next to her body and ran outside and washed off her blood with the garden hose. There was some on my uniform sleeve, too, and I rubbed that out with water. Faith was too wound up to notice the sleeve was wet, or maybe it'd dried by then . . . doesn't matter. I drove away, fast. Just down the road from her driveway I passed Faith's beat-up Porsche. Only car like it in Pomo, and we'd had words earlier in the day. I guess that's why it registered, even in the state I was in. In the mirror I saw him turn into her driveway. I thought he was the man she'd been waiting for, the "real man" she'd thrown in my face. I still wasn't tracking too well. I drove on a little ways and then . . . I don't know, I turned around and went back there. I didn't think about what I was doing or why, I just did it. I had no intention at that point of trying to put the blame on Faith. That's the truth. If I had any intention at all, it was to cover myself by pretending to show up for the first time after the body was discovered.

But he came running out of the house just as I got there and things got all mixed up again. It was like I really was arriving for the first time and had caught him running out. Denial. Still wasn't able to face the fact that I'd killed her, that I was capable of such a thing. So I treated Faith the way I would've any other suspect in similar circumstances. And when I saw her lying dead inside . . . it was as though I was seeing her there for the first time and the pain I felt was the shock of discovery. As though somebody else had done it. Faith, because he was right there. I questioned him, accused him, started to arrest him. Didn't let myself think the whole time. Just doing my job, upholding the law, protecting the public interest. I know that sounds sick and crazy, but that's the way I was that night. Sick and crazy.

It just went on from there. Faith jumping me and breaking my nose, me shooting him before he went into the lake, the search for his body and all the rest . . . it made the fiction I'd built up more real. And the more things escalated, the easier it was to shift my guilt onto him, make him the scapegoat. If he was dead or in prison, there'd be an end to it, a closure, and then I could find a way to go on living with myself and do my job. But now . . . I know I couldn't have buried the truth, or even continued the pretense much longer. Too much kept happening, like there was an epidemic and I was the Typhoid Mary who'd started it all. I had that on my conscience too, along with Storm. I've been a cop too many years. A man like me can't keep on riding the tiger. Sooner or later I'd have been torn apart. Might've been too late for Faith by then, but I never much cared about him from the beginning. God help me, I never gave a damn about him, and I'm not sure I do even now. He was a stranger. He was just another stranger.

Well, maybe Novak never cared about John Faith, but everybody else sure seems to. That's one of the galling things about this whole lousy affair. They're whitewashing Faith. Seeley, Proctor, everybody else with any clout in Pomo County. Dropping all charges against him, including one of the worst felonies there is, for my money—assaulting a police officer. The official line is that he's suffered enough, that prosecuting him will keep the wounds open and delay a return to normalcy around here, but that's just bullshit. They're scared to death of a big lawsuit that might bankrupt the county; they made Faith sign a waiver against suing for damages as one of the conditions of the whitewash.

Another thing they're afraid of is more negative publicity. Faith's big show in front of the media and half the town, forcing Novak to admit guilt the way he did, made him a temporary two-bit hero and swung public sentiment over to his side. Prosecute him and there'd be another media circus throughout the trial, and if he was convicted, for a long time afterward, and that would have a negative effect on business throughout the county. Better to let the entire affair die a natural death, Seeley says; Faith goes away, the media has nothing to feed on, and pretty soon people start to forget it ever happened. He's got a point, I guess. But I still hate to see Faith get away with all he pulled here, all the felonies he committed. A man like that, a hard case, a damn stranger comes in and tears up Pomo County and then walks away scot-free. It just don't seem right.

That's one thing that frosts my nuts. The other is Novak. Proctor's going to prosecute him, all right, but it looks like he'll let Novak plead to Murder Two or maybe even voluntary manslaughter. Same bullshit about healing wounds and keeping Pomo out of the media spotlight, negative publicity harming family tourism, plus the county's just too poor to afford a high-profile or even a low-profile Murder One trial. Plus—and this is the one that really gets me— there's Novak's "spotless past record as a good, honest policeman," which Proctor claims is an argument on behalf of leniency.

Jesus Christ! Good, honest policeman, my ass. He kills a woman, tries to frame somebody else for the crime, starts a chain reaction that leaves everything in a shambles . . . a cop can't dirty his badge any worse than that, can he? I never liked Novak personally, and now I know why. The one thing I hate more than anything else is a cop who craps on his badge, and I think I saw something in Novak all along that told me he was that kind. I know what people say about me: I'm lazy, I'm a political flunky, I'm not the brightest or the hardest-working sheriff the county's ever had. Well, maybe there's some truth in all of that. But by God, there's one other thing I am and that's honest, an honest man who respects the law and does his level best to uphold it. I never took so much as a free cup of coffee in all the time I been in office. I never dirtied my badge in any way, and I never will.

If it was up to me, I'd stick Novak and every other dirty cop in a cell together and throw away the frigging key.

Harry Richmond

WELL, FAITH'S GONE. Left Pomo yesterday afternoon in that rattletrap Porsche of his, as soon as they released him from jail. Thrown out of town is more like it; rumor has it one of the conditions of his release was that he leave Pomo County straightaway and never set foot here again. He got off too easy, if you ask me. And I'll bet any man twenty dollars that Novak gets off almost as easy when his time comes. The muckety-mucks take care of their own around here, while the rest of us get the book thrown at us if we step out of line just once.

I don't mind saying it surprised me when I first heard about Novak's confession. He was the last one I figured could've killed that bitch Storm Carey. Just goes to show you, I guess. You think you know people and what they're capable of doing or not doing, and turns out you don't. Sometimes you can be so far off base with a person, like Novak for one—and like George Petrie, for another—you begin to wonder if maybe you're not as far off base with others. Not that man Faith, though. No sir, not him. I don't care what he did or didn't do in Pomo, or what anybody says about him, he's a bad one through and through. Look at all the damage he left behind. Like a hurricane or tornado that went slashing through. Like we all got hit by a devil wind.

Folks keep saying that with him gone, it's over and now we can get back to normal. I wish I could believe that, but I don't. All the publicity—and there was plenty of it for some people—will bring in curiosity seekers for a while, sure, but it'll keep away the family trade, the weekenders and vacationers the county economy depends on. Maybe most of the negative stuff will be forgotten by the time fishing season starts in April and it won't have any real effect on next summer's tourism, but I don't believe that, either. As sure as I'm sitting here, there'll be fewer fishermen and fewer overnight and short-term guests at Lakeside Resort next season. This part of Lake Pomo is never coming back to what it once was, and that's the plain hard truth. You look at it that way, you also see that what happened with Faith and Storm Carey and Novak and the rest wasn't much more than the beating of a dead horse.

Last night I took a closer look at my finances and prospects, and they're worse than I thought. And as if that wasn't enough to throw a man into a fit of depression, that thick-skulled Maria Lorenzo up and quit on me this morning. Came in and said her and her husband decided she couldn't work for me anymore, no other reason, and then she walked out again with her nose in the air like she'd been smelling turds. Goddamn Indians, they're all shiftless and worthless. Doesn't really matter much, her quitting, I suppose; sooner or later I'd've had to let her go, because I'll need even the little I was paying her for my own expenses. But now I'll have to start cleaning the cabins myself, unless I can find another Indian who'll work for less than minimum wage on a short-term basis, and the other downside is that I won't have that big fat ass of Maria's to watch anymore.

One more season. I figure that's as long as I can hang on, that's all the time I've got left on Lake Pomo. This time next year, if there's not some radical change—and I don't see how there can be—I'll have to put the resort up for sale and move to San Carlos and depend on Ella to support me and hope like hell she doesn't decide to marry some jerk who'll throw me out on my tail. Just the thought of it puts me in a funk.

Like they say nowadays, life sucks. Some people, and it don't matter how decent and hardworking they are, are just born to end up with the short end of the stick.

Lori Banner

BEFORE HE LEFT, John Faith came to see me at the Pomo County Domestic Abuse Center, where I'm staying now. He said how sorry he was about what'd happened to me and I said how sorry I was about what'd happened to him. He said he was glad the district attorney had decided not to press charges against me and I said I was glad the D.A. had decided to drop all the charges against him. It sounds funny and not very sincere when I put it like that, but it wasn't that way at all. We both meant every word we said. We wished each other well, and hugged each other, and then he was gone and I knew I'd never see him again, and it made me sad. But that's the way it has to be. I knew it, and so did John.

I wish I'd met him a long time ago. There might've been something between us, something good. I'm sorry I didn't and there wasn't and it can't ever be. Sorry about Earle, too—that I ever met him, and married him, and put up with his abuse, and killed him. But I can't keep on being sorry about everything, and I won't. I have to put the past behind me and start over fresh. That's what my counselor says. She says my life didn't end the night Earle's did. She says if I want it to be, my life is just beginning.

She's right. It won't be easy, but I've made up my mind and I'll stick to it. When I leave here I won't be going back to the Northlake Cafe and I won't be living in Pomo any longer. I'll be returning to school in Santa Rosa, reentering the training program. I'm finally going to do what I always wanted to do, and this time I won't let anything or anybody stop me.

I'm going to be a nurse.

Lori Banner, R.N. The best R.N. any hospital ever had.

Zenna Wilson

HOWARD LEFT ME.

Walked out, moved out, and he isn't coming back.

When I came home Sunday evening, bursting with news of Chief Novak's shocking confession, simply bursting with it, Howard was in our bedroom packing his suitcases. I said, "For heaven's sake, you're not going on another of your trips already, on a Sunday night?"

He looked me right in the eye. "No, Zenna," he said. "I'm leaving you."

"*Leaving* me?"

"I can't spend another night in this house with you, not even for Stephanie's sake. I'm moving out for good."

"Howard, have you taken leave of your senses?"

"Come to them, is more like it. I'll see a lawyer right away, have him start divorce proceedings. But you don't need to worry. You can have the house, as much support for Stephanie as I can afford . . . just about anything you want. All I want is out."

I must have gawked at him with my mouth open like a half-wit. I was utterly speechless.

He kept right on packing. And then, oh my Lord, then he said, "You might as well know the whole truth, Zenna. It's not just you, this empty marriage of ours . . . maybe I could've gone on, at least for a while, if that's all it was. But there's somebody else. I've been seeing someone else."

"Another woman!" I spat the words at him.

"Her name is Irene. She lives in Redding—"

"I don't want to hear about your dirty whore!"

"She's not a whore. She's a widow with two small children—"

I clapped my hands over my ears. "I don't want to hear it, I don't care who she is, oh my God, how can you do this to me? How can you do this to Stephanie, your own child?"

"I've already talked to Stephanie. I think she understands."

"Understands? She's nine years old! What did you tell her?"

"The truth."

"What truth? That you've been fornicating with a whore?"

"My reasons for leaving. All of them. She understands that most of the fault is mine, and she forgives me. Or will, in time."

"*Most* of the fault is yours?"

"That's right. Part of it is yours."

"How dare you! Mine?"

"I'm sorry, but that's also the truth. Believe it or not."

"You're the one who'll be sorry, Howard Wilson. You're the one who'll be sorry. Cheating, fornicating with God knows how many—"

"Only Irene. And we love each other."

"—and you have the gall to blame me . . ." I had to choke out the rest of the words. "Damn you, damn your lying, cheating soul to the fires of Hell!"

"Good-bye, Zenna," he said, and he was gone.

That was three days ago and I still don't understand how he could do such a terrible thing to his wife and daughter. To *me.* I've been a good wife, a good mother, I've made a strong Christian home, I never so much as looked at another man or lusted after one in my heart in sixteen years of marriage. Cooked his meals, washed his dirty clothes, cleaned his house, let him have my body whenever he wanted it even though I can no longer conceive. What more could a man ask of a woman, a marriage, a home? How could he do this to me after sixteen years? How could he humiliate me this way?

Well, he won't get away with it. I'll make him pay. As merciful God is my witness, when I get through with him he won't have a dime left to give to his Redding harlot and her two little bastards!

George Petrie

RAMONA MADE ME tell her everything. All of it, every detail. Then she made me write it all down and sign it and she took the papers and Christ knows what she did with them. And then she let me go ahead and put the money back in the vault. She'll help me raise the $7,000 to cover the shortage, too; she's already planning ways, in case the Indian Head Bay property doesn't sell in time. We're going to be much closer from now on, she said. A tight-knit unit, the way a husband and wife should be. Just Ramona and me. Together from now on.

So I'm out from under. Safe. I don't have to worry about a thing anymore. Ramona will take care of everything for the next ten or twenty or thirty years. I go to work, I come home, I eat and sleep, and if Ramona decides she wants me to, I'll even manage to perform stud service. But I'm not really here. I'm like one of the condemned convicts on death row, the ones who have no hope left—I'm already dead in my prison.

Dead man walking.

Anthony Munoz

I DON'T KNOW, man. They picked up Mateo in Southern Cal, all the way down near the border in some town called Chula Vista. He had a knife and he tried to rob this liquor store and the owner busted his arm with a bottle. They said he was trying to get money so he could cross over into Mexico. Where's the sense, man? He was always goin' on about how he'd never be caught dead in Mexico. L.A. was the place he wanted to be, he says, and he went right on through L.A. to this Chula Vista, heading straight for the border.

They're bringing him back to Pomo pretty soon. I ain't decided yet if I'll go see him or not. The old man says he won't, he washes his hands, and the old lady says she will, Mateo needs her as much as he needs God's forgiveness, but I haven't made up my mind yet. Sometimes I think I ought to, sometimes I think I'm better off if I wash my hands, too. Same as with Trisha and my kid. Sometimes I think I oughta go ahead and marry her—cool it with the drugs, get a job, maybe even finish school nights. And sometimes I think I'm better off the way I am, free and easy, get high and get laid whenever I want, go anywhere and don't answer to nobody.

I don't know, man. I just don't know.

One thing I do know. I don't want to end up like Mateo. Kidnapping, assault, attempted rape, attempted armed robbery . . . he's gonna be in prison a long time. He could've killed somebody, too. Maybe he would've, someday. If I'd gone with him like he wanted me to . . . man, I don't even want to think about it.

My big brother, Mateo. I always looked up to him. I always thought he was the coolest. But he's not, no way. *Es un don Mierda.* He's a real nobody, man. He's a real Mr. Shit.

Richard Novak

MY WORLD HAS shrunk to a six-by-eight rectangle, to steel bars and concrete walls, to a hard mattress and a sink and a toilet. I've exchanged police blue for inmate orange; I'm looking out through the bars instead of in; I've become what I always despised. And so I pace a lot. I lie staring at the ceiling or sit staring at the walls and bars. I think too much. I even pray a little. Eva would be proud of me if she knew. She always said it's never too late to reach out to God. Always said if you talk to Him, He'll listen and understand and forgive.

Maybe she was right. I hope He can forgive me, because I don't think I can ever forgive myself.

It's not Eva I think much about, or even God. Mostly it's Storm, and that crazy night, and what I did to her and to myself, all the things I threw away when I picked up that paperweight and brought it smashing down. Sometimes it seems it was someone else who committed that insane act—an impostor in Chief's clothing. How could I have done it? And why? Love, hate, jealousy, passion . . . none of it seems very real now. Or very important. It'd be easy to believe that it was outside forces driving me, fate lifting that paperweight and smashing it down to complete some cosmic purpose. But I don't buy that. It wasn't outside forces, it was converging forces inside me. My responsibility. My guilt. All mine to live with for the rest of my natural life.

So many regrets, so much thrown away. Because I think about Audrey, too, more and more often. All the good things she is and tried to offer me. I ask myself why I couldn't see her then as I see her now, why I couldn't feel for her then what I feel for her now. Storm is the easy answer, but there are no easy answers anymore. My responsibility. My guilt.

She's still there for me now; she comes to see me nearly every day. But I'd be a fool to expect her to be there when I get out of prison. My lawyer is confident he can plea-bargain the charges against me down to second-degree homicide, maybe even felony manslaughter. At the minimum that would mean a sentence of eleven years, with the possibility of parole in five to six. I can't ask Audrey to wait five or six years for a convicted felon. I won't ask her; I don't have any right to put that kind of burden on her. She has so much to give—let her give it to someone else, somebody better than me.

You're not given more than a couple of chances in this life. Screw them up, waste them, and that's all there is. You get what you deserve then. You get exactly what you deserve.

Douglas Kent

ONE OF THE croakers sidled into my white rubber room a little while ago. I opened one eye to a slit, and when I saw that he wasn't one of the shrinks with their idiotic questions ("Had any stimulating conversations with your bedpan today, Mr. Kent?") or a nurse with a needleful of temporary fixative for the shakes, shimmers, and other fun by-products of alcohol withdrawal (perfectly calm at the moment, Kent had no desire to have his ass punctured unnecessarily), I decided to wake up and be sociable for a change.

The croaker, however, didn't look particularly sociable. Very solemn, he was. Like a judge about to pass sentence on a miscreant. Which, as it developed, was precisely the case.

"I'm afraid I have unpleasant news for you, Mr. Kent," he said.

"Is that so?"

"There is no easy way to say this, so I'll be blunt. We have the final results of all your tests, and they're conclusive. You have cirrhosis of the liver."

"No surprise there, Doc."

"No, I suppose not."

"Prognosis? Terminal, eh?"

"Barring a regenerative miracle, yes."

Is that you I hear chuckling maniacally, Pa, you old fook? Well, clear a place for me in the hot coals and dish up a shot of sulfur and brimstone. When I get down there, we'll hoist one together and then go spit in Old Scratch's eye.

"How long do I have, Doc?"

"That depends."

"On where I end up and whether or not I have access to any more of the nectar what brung me here. Correct?"

"Essentially, yes."

"How long with the best of care and nary another drop of demon rum?"

"A year. Possibly eighteen months."

"And how long with continued pickling?"

"You'd be dead in three months. I'm sorry, Mr. Kent."

"Sorry? Sorry? Why, Doc, you couldn't have brought me a better gift if you were Santa Claus and this was Christmas morning."

Kent smiled. Kent winked. Kent could have kissed him.

Where there's a will, there's a way.

Trisha Marx

JUST WHEN I thought I'd never hear from John Faith again, the letter came. I knew it was from him even before I ripped open the envelope.

> Dear Trisha,
>
> I don't have many friends, so I'm not very good at saying good-bye. Maybe this isn't the best way to say it to you, but it's my way and I hope you won't mind.
>
> Thank you for being my friend when I needed a friend the most. I'll never forget you, Trisha.
>
> Good luck. And don't ever stop caring.
>
> > Your friend,
> > John

It made me bawl like a baby. Right away I took it upstairs and locked it in my treasure chest, where I keep all the stuff that means the most to me. I read it once more first. I'll never forget *you*, John, I thought. Don't you ever stop caring, either.

That night, when Daddy came home from work, I told him about the baby and that I wanted to have it and keep it. He was pretty upset at first, but he didn't have a hemorrhage like I'd thought he would. Actually, he was pretty cool about it. He asked if Anthony was gonna marry me, and I said I didn't know about that yet, which kind of surprised me because until that very minute I'd been so sure I wanted Anthony to stay out of my life for good, particularly after what that asshole brother of his tried to do to Ms. Sixkiller. Daddy said that, well, whatever happened I wouldn't have to raise the kid by myself—I could stay right here at home and he'd help me, if that was the way things worked out. Yeah, pretty cool. He stays out all night gambling too much and works too hard and sometimes I think he's like the Bitch and doesn't give a shit if I live or die, but I guess he really does love me after all.

One thing I didn't tell him about: the baby. I won't tell anyone until the time comes, not even Selena. It's my secret and I'm not gonna share this one.

If it's a boy he'll be named John, and if it's a girl she'll be called Faith.

Audrey Sixkiller

I'VE BEEN TO see Dick several times now at the county correctional facility. At first our meetings were awkward; he wouldn't look me in the eye and what little conversation we had was limited to neutral topics—my teaching and volunteer work, how Mack was adjusting to living with me. But at the end of each session he asked me to please come back, with a kind of desperation in his voice, and I couldn't have refused him even if I'd wanted to. He has no one else. In all of Pomo, in the entire time since his wife left him, he's had no one but me. And it wasn't until now, when it's too late, that he realized it.

There's a hard irony in that, and in the fact that our roles have been reversed. He needs me now, but I no longer need him. I still care about him, and part of me will always love him, yet the feelings are detached, heavy with sadness but without yearning. It's over. It would have been over even if there weren't bars and steel mesh separating us. Indians are as blind as whites sometimes, but when we do see, we see more clearly than anyone. And we know better than anyone how to make compromises and adjustments, how to live with loss, how to channel feelings and be satisfied with less than we hope for. There is no self-pity in that; it's a simple statement of fact. I would be all right. Continue to try to make life better for my people, and my own life would be better for the effort. Someday, perhaps, I'll meet someone new to need and love, and who will need and love me in return. I think if this happens he'll be red, or more red than white, but in any case it won't matter. What's important is that then the long nights won't be lonely anymore.

I told some of this to Dick the last time I saw him. He said he understood and I think he does. It was the first time we've been able to talk about what matters to both of us—a good omen for him, too. Jail has been difficult for him, and prison will be twice as bad, but he takes full responsibility for his actions; the bitterness he feels is mostly toward himself. He won't be the same man when he's free again, or necessarily a better man, but he will be a wiser one.

His one blind spot is John Faith's role in all that happened. He's said more than once, with anger in his voice, that if John Faith had not come to Pomo there wouldn't have been nearly as much trouble. Deep down he may even believe that if it weren't for John Faith, he wouldn't have killed Storm.

But he's wrong. What Dick doesn't understand is that John Faith is not guilty of anything other than poor judgment. He isn't a poison-maker; he's another victim, in a way the most tragic victim of all.

He can't help that he was born a catalyst. Or do anything about it other than destroy himself, and he isn't made that way. Hope hasn't died in him yet. Neither has a streak of idealism. That's why he keeps moving from place to place. It's what makes him both crave human contact and shy away from it. It's what makes him run.

John Faith is looking for a place where enough people can see past the outer man to the one who lives inside; a place where he'll be accepted for what he is, not what he appears to be. He's looking for what he's never had and wants more than anything else.

He's looking for a home.

And what he keeps finding, wherever he goes, is a wasteland of strangers.